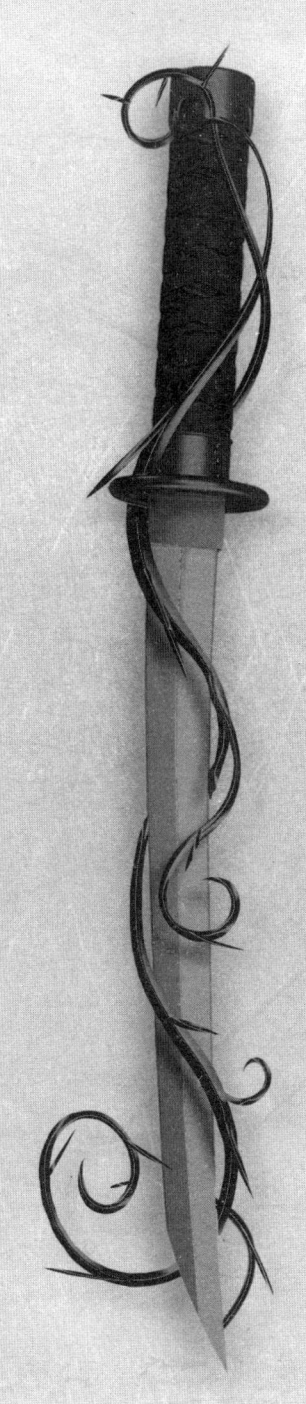

FIVE
BROKEN
BLADES

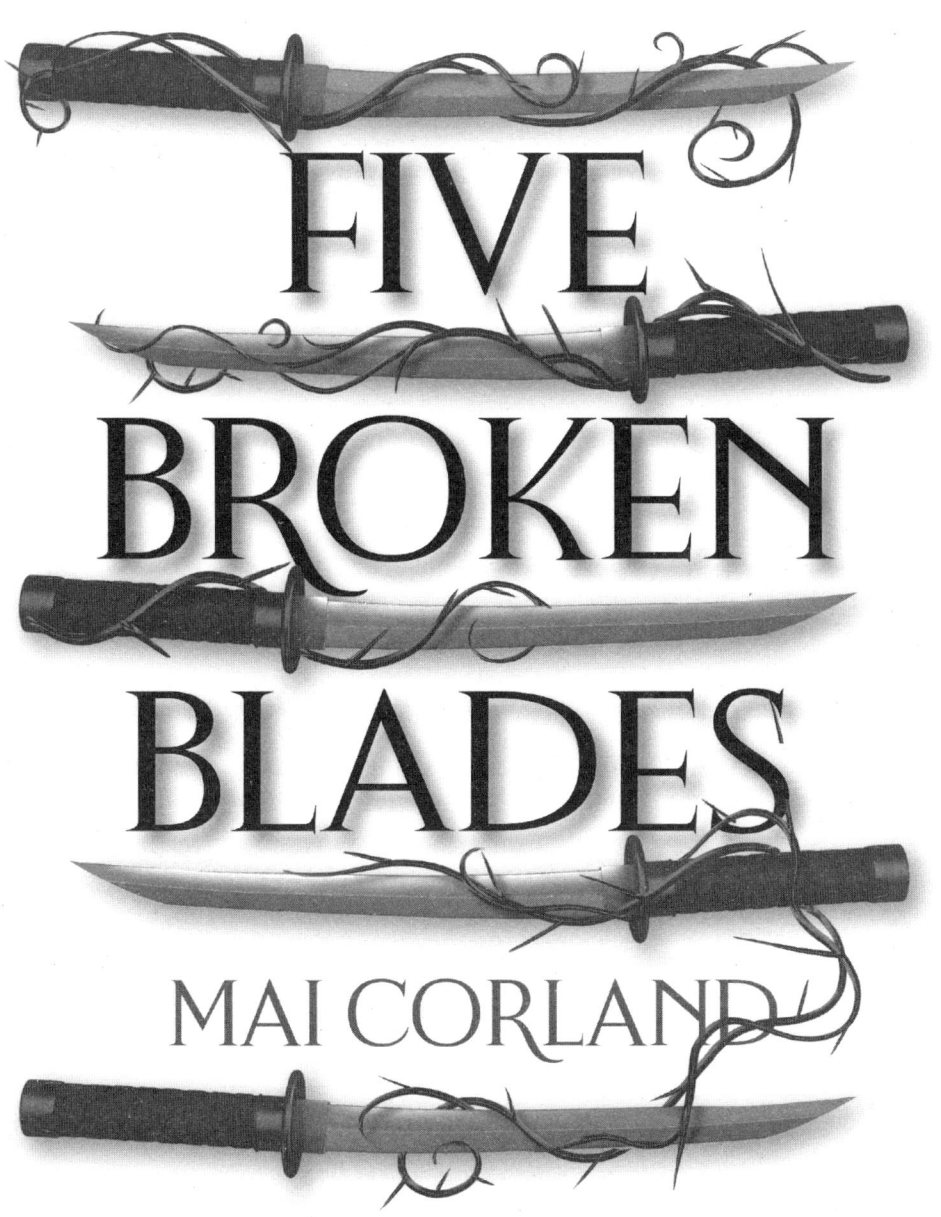

FIVE
BROKEN
BLADES

MAI CORLAND

ZAFFRE

First published in the United States by Red Tower Books
An imprint of Entangled Publishing LLC

First published in the UK in 2024 by
ZAFFRE
An imprint of Zaffre Publishing Group
A Bonnier Books UK company
4th Floor, Victoria House, Bloomsbury Square, London, WC1B 4DA
Owned by Bonnier Books
Sveavägen 56, Stockholm, Sweden

Edited by Liz Pelletier
Cover art and design by Elizabeth Turner Stokes
Interior map art by Elizabeth Turner Stokes
Deluxe Limited endpaper illustration by Juho Choi
Metal texture © Shutterstock/boonchai sakunchonruedee
Swords © Shutterstock/Anton Mykhailovskyi
Interior design by Jennifer Valero
Interior formatting by Britt Marczak

A CIP catalogue record for this book is available from the British Library.

Hardback ISBN: 978-1-80418-658-9
Trade paperback ISBN: 978-1-80418-659-6

Also available as an ebook

1 3 5 7 9 10 8 6 4 2

Typeset by IDSUK (Data Connection) Ltd
Printed and bound in Great Britain by Clays Ltd, Elcograf S.p.A.

Zaffre is an imprint of Zaffre Publishing Group
A Bonnier Books UK company
www.bonnierbooks.co.uk

*For my heart and my sunshine
and my man of steel*

Five Broken Blades is a dark adventure fantasy full of deadly liars, gray morals, and kingdom-destroying secrets. As such, the story includes elements that might not be suitable for all readers. Violence, blood, death (including the death of parents, children, incarcerated people, and animals), poisoning, substance abuse, alcohol, sexual activity, animal abuse, gender-based violence, sex work, suicidal ideation, and indentured servitude are depicted. Rape, assault, and graphic genocide are described. Readers who may be sensitive to these elements, please take note, and prepare to make a play for the crown...

AUTHOR'S NOTE

Korea has a rich mythology and vibrant culture all its own. And as a Korean American adoptee, I drew on my own personal story and experiences to fashion the world of *Five Broken Blades*. However, it is worth noting that this story is neither historical fiction nor fantasy based on the real world; it takes place in a unique setting that is inspired by my research of Korean myth, legend, and culture. Creative license has been taken throughout, but it is my hope that readers will leave the story with their lives enriched, as mine has been through the writing of this book.

—Mai

CHAPTER ONE

ROYO

CITY OF UMBRIA, YUSAN

Gold for blood—that's my advertisement and the words I live by.

The merchant slowly counts out gold mun, his gloved hands shaking as each coin lands in his palm. He's a little taller than me, but my shoulders are twice as wide.

"Hurry it up. I don't got all night," I say.

My deep voice startles him, and two bronze mun clatter onto the ground. He lets the coins roll away but pauses to consider chasing them down. Ten Hells. This is gonna take two lifetimes.

Finally, he slips the money into my hand, paying for the broken nose and leg. Then he darts away, fur-lined cape flapping in the night breeze. It's not a noble living, being muscle for hire, but the upper class ain't great neither.

I count my gold as I lumber between the soot-covered buildings. All there. I put the money in my coin purse and tuck it into my inner jacket pocket. Behind me, my latest victim whimpers in the darkness of the alley. If he keeps up that noise, the hael birds will peck him clean before morning. And the rich merchant prick didn't pay for a kill.

"Can you stop that racket?" I say.

The whimpering dies down.

"Thank you," I say. He's silent—shut up by my manners or his pain.

I think about going back to help. I always think about it. But it's none of my business. It's not my problem, what happens after my jobs are done. Or why the merchant wanted to send a message in the first place.

Those are roads that lead nowhere. And I've got somewhere to be.

I blow a warm breath in my gnarled hands. This fucking cold. Frost shines on the cobbled streets, and the runoff has already started to freeze. What trees there are in this cramped city are long bare. Winter comes quick in Umbria. But then, death always does.

I should probably buy some warm gloves, but my stomach tightens at the thought of parting with even one silver mun. Every coin counts, and I don't really need posh shit anyhow.

When I get to Inch Street, two well-dressed couples split around me. They're all fur muffs and expensive, feathered hats. Swells. They give me a wide berth, then scurry away like I'm contagious or something. I guess if my size don't intimidate people, the scar dividing my face does the trick. People stay away.

Good.

With a grunt, I shoulder open the heavy wooden door of Butcher & Ale. I've been in cleaner, nicer places with better grub, but those pubs don't fit me. The tavern is warm without being hot and noisy, without being loud, and that's all I need. Butcher & Ale is home. It's where I started doing business ten years ago. Right after I turned fifteen, I set up shop in the corner—forty pounds less muscle with no scar on my face. They know what I do here, but I keep the place safe, so they look the other way.

I sit on my usual stool at the end of the bar. Yuri sees me and pours me a pint. He could be forty; he could be sixty. Who knows with that bald head. But he's not the chatty type, and I like that.

He slides a beer across the worn wood. The glass is mostly clean. "Someone's been looking for you."

I raise my eyebrows and chug a gulp of ale. Somebody's always looking for me—to fight, to hurt, to kill. This ain't news. "Why should I care?"

Yuri puts the bar towel over his shoulder and leans forward. "It was a girl."

I stop drinking. My heart thuds and then lodges in my throat. I will it back down and play it cool. "What'd she look like?"

"Pretty," Yuri says. Not the most helpful description. I curl my hand into a fist and stare. His eyes widen, and he rubs his nose somebody else broke a while ago. Then he starts yammering. "About my height, big brown eyes, kinda short black hair. Around your age—like mid-twenties. Red velvet cloak."

I swallow, digesting his words. A tall, twenty-something girl asking about me is unusual. And I guess "pretty" makes a difference—can't remember the last time a pretty girl looked for me. Maybe she wants an old boyfriend taught a lesson or revenge on another girl. I don't hurt girls, though.

"She's staying at the Black Shoe Inn," Yuri adds.

The nicest joint in maybe all of Umbria. So she has money and she's not from here yet somehow knew to look for me. Here. This reeks of trouble.

"Not interested," I say.

Yuri shrugs. "Suit yourself."

He wanders down the bar to serve another customer. A guy looking old for his age sits on the stool four paces down from me. He only makes eye contact with Yuri, so he's also here to drink alone. Sometimes it feels less lonely to drown your sorrows in a shared barrel of ale. To vanish in the pub crowd. Even if you don't say a word to nobody. Most nights, that's me.

But I can't disappear tonight. I know in my guts it's going to be one of those times when I can't forget no matter how much I drink. So why give myself a headache that'll hit behind my eyes tomorrow?

I down my beer, leaving the dregs. I push back from the bar, the legs of the stool scraping the sticky floor. "I'm outta here."

Yuri's bushy eyebrows rise. It's like what he didn't get on his head went to his face instead. "Already?"

He's right to be surprised. I'm normally good for a few beers as I take up my corner and wait for my next job to come in. Trouble always has a way of finding me. Usually it's quick, but sometimes it takes four beers. Tonight, it's just the one.

"Headache." I tap my temple like he don't know where my head is. But it's a lie. And from his beady eyes going side to side, Yuri doesn't believe it for a second.

But he nods. "Night, Royo."

I take a step to leave, and something strange happens. An off feeling hits me, like a heart skipping a beat. Out of the corner of my eye, I swear there's a blur of red. I blink hard, look around, then glance into the bar mirror. Nothing. Just my scarred face and shorn head looking back at me. Nothing red in sight. I shake my head. I'm real off tonight. Best I leave now.

I trudge my way out of Butcher & Ale and back onto the frigid street. I'll need to repair the laces of my boots soon, probably patch the leather again—they still got some wear left.

I swear it got colder when I was inside. My exhale now makes little fogs in the air. I blow a hot breath into my hands again as I walk.

Five blocks in the wrong direction later, I pass the Black Shoe Inn. I can't help but slow down and stare at the lamps glowing in the windows. I wonder…then shake my head.

What am I doing? What am I even looking for?

I walk double time to get away. It's too suspicious. Too off. My instincts are always right, and the scars I bear are reminders of the times I've ignored my gut. The last time cost me everything. I'm not doing it again.

It's about a fifteen-minute walk along Avalon Road to my shack on the cheap end of town. The buildings get more run-down, smaller, as I leave the business district. Umbria's been going downhill since King Joon rose to power back when I was a kid. The whole country has.

The road bends, and then I have the river on my left. You'd think being near the water would be nice, but not in Umbria. The only waterway we got is the dirty Sol River. People empty chamber pots and dump trash right into the thing. And it's even colder, the bone-chilling kind, when you're close enough to hear the water lick the filthy shore.

I try to stay aware of my steps, my surroundings. There are too many dangers in Umbria from gangs, from men like me, from the hael birds, to be caught sleepwalking. But I'm off my game. Distracted.

I blame Yuri. He's a barkeep, not a messenger. He could've kept all that noise to himself.

But I'm not really mad at Yuri. Truth is, I'm thinking about *her*. When Yuri said it was a girl, I hoped. And hope is a jagged knife. Hope pieces together dreams out of broken glass only for reality to come and smash them all over again. Hope is the cruelest punishment of them all. Because without hope, I know: it's not her, you fool. It can't be. It can never be.

Because I killed her.

CHAPTER TWO

EUYN

CITY OF OUTTON, FALLOW

I'm being hunted.

I laugh quietly into my beard at this cruel twist of fate as I weave on light feet through the Outton marketplace. I was once a prized hunter—the best in Yusan, according to the king. And now here I am, in the badlands, in Fallow, and *I* am the prey.

I dart to the side, using timbers for cover to not give anyone a clean line of sight. I've spent the last three years trying to avoid someone collecting the twenty-thousand-gold-mun bounty on my head. At least this senseless warren called a market helps.

Outton market looks like it was hastily put together overnight, with timbers and whatever fabric they could salvage off a ship, and then the next morning they decided to leave it that way for a hundred years. I wonder if the markets in Yusan are the same— grimy and slapdash. I never stepped foot in one because we always had servants to shop for us. Servants to do anything we desired, actually. But that isn't the life I have anymore. It's just the one I can't forget.

I pass a stall of tanned hides being sold by a gruff-looking fellow behind the counter. He nods to me, and I nod back. I've seen him before, but I don't know his name. I haven't asked lest he ask for mine.

When it's clear I won't be purchasing anything today, he ignores me and continues scanning for light fingers, a blade in his hand. Without a king, justice is meted out individually in Fallow.

The feeling of being watched prickles my skin. I toss a quick glance over my left shoulder to see if I'm being followed. Nothing.

I continue past noisy chickens and aromatic spices. The scents of clove and cardamom are overwhelming as my boots shuffle along the dusty earth. I pretend to consider dried dates as I look over my right shoulder. Still nothing. Nothing but the ordinary scene. It's all tired women in rough spun dresses carrying wares on their heads and bearded men looking for goods or for a good fight. Children are rare here, and the ones I have seen are dirty little pickpockets.

But I'm not worried about my purse today. I'm worried about my neck.

My heart pounds in my chest, and my mouth is as dry as the earth around me. But it's not the sun. It's that I'm a target outside in broad daylight like this. I want to blend in with the peasantry, but I've yet to master that trick. I walk with a hood covering my black hair and dusty sand encrusting my tunic and trousers, just like everyone else, but there's something about me that refuses to be common.

Two women stare up as I pass. I turn to see if there's a threat, scanning the rooftops of the baked-clay buildings, but they were just looking at me. Because my features, my manners are too fine, my head too tall. Three years stuck in Fallow, and I still don't walk hunched over the way they do. My shoulders refuse to slump from burden. When I try to fake it, the pretty little innkeeper always squints and asks if I'm "deep in my cups"—their term for drunk.

I should've stayed at the inn until dusk, when I can blend better. I'm safe there—as safe as I can be. I've checked every corner, plotted every escape route. There's a rope ladder stashed in the drapes in case I need a fast exit out of my second-story room. It's hotter on the higher floor, but a ground-floor window might provide access to me while I sleep. Not that I sleep much. My eyes are ringed with proof of that. When I do pass out, it's with a poisoned dagger under my pillow and my crossbow hidden under the bed. There's a sword in the washroom. Loaded traps wait over the door and windows. I don't leave, especially during the day, if I can avoid it. But I couldn't ignore the red envelope at my door this morning.

Prince Euyn Hali Baejkin
The Stables, one bell
I have an offer for you

Prince Euyn. Prince. Euyn.

My eyes stuck on those words, and my stomach turned, spoiling my meager breakfast of cold sausage and stale biscuit. Someone knows who I am. And no one should know because Prince Euyn died from exposure three years ago. When powerful men try to kill you, it's best to let them think they succeeded. I go by the name of Donal now.

I crush the envelope in my pocket. I've been found. But by whom?

It's occurred to me more than once in the last six bells that this could be an ambush. I scan the crowd again, searching for the all blacks of royal assassins. Maybe it would be a gift from my dear big brother to finally put an end to this limbo. To kill me like a man. But the problem is, I want to live—or at least I refuse to die. And King Joon wouldn't directly order my execution—he didn't last time, relying on the elements to kill me instead.

So what is this?

Who sent this? I'm paranoid, but logically I know it's not

palace assassins—they don't send calling cards. They like to slit your throat before you can scream.

Madness. It's madness to follow this invitation. My body aches to turn around. To go back. But there's only one direction I can go for answers: forward.

My boots kick up dust as I leave the sprawling market. Dust gets in everything here. There's no point in trying to keep tidy. What I wouldn't give for the perfumed baths of Qali Palace; the spotless, cold marble corridors; or even the shade trees of the royal garden, where the servants spray a cooling mist in the summer and fan us with feathers. But I'm stuck with sun, dry serpents, and desert vultures circling overhead.

I check for tracks even though there are too many people going in and out of the market for them to be of much use. But our soldier boots leave distinct impressions, so I scan the road anyway.

The heat is oppressive as I cross to the stables, and I adjust my hood as I look back one more time. Nothing. Nothing but hazy air and commoners shopping. But nothing doesn't mean you're safe—it just means you haven't spotted the danger yet. I've hunted every creature in Yusan, and few saw me coming.

I'm almost inside the stables when I see it: another red envelope. And then I notice the hand holding it. And I know it's too late for me.

CHAPTER THREE

SORA
CITY OF GAIN, YUSAN

The meadow is beautiful this time of year. I run my delicate, bejeweled hand over the tall grass. The green grass is lovely and soft and yet, at the same time, hard and sharp. Like me.

I'm not entirely certain how the foraging lessons began. Or at least how they became a regular event. But every week, I meet five beggar children in the meadow outside of the great city walls. There are a surprising number of wild edibles and sweet berries between here and the tree line. I take the children under the trees on the hotter days to teach them about edible roots, but I don't dare go farther than that. I can't.

"Sora, what about this one?" Gli asks. She holds a spotted mushroom in her hand. Her little face with a cleft lip looks up at me, hopeful. Her thick curls are brushed back as best she can.

Gli is nine—the same age I was when I was taken. Well, not taken…sold.

My parents were paid a handsome price for their eldest daughter. My former parents. I, like these children, am an orphan. But unlike them, I'm not free.

I stare at the horizon. Sometimes I think about going past the tree line again, this time prepared for the Xingchi forest. I could run away from Gain and never return. Maybe I could make it all the way north to the safety of Khitan. But then I remember the collateral they have. The reason I can't leave.

"Sora?" Gli asks.

She's still staring up at me with her big brown eyes, waiting for an answer. I shake away my thoughts and return to the present.

"No, no, little dear," I say. I tuck my long black hair behind my ear as I lean forward to look at her mushroom. "You see these spots? Do you recall what those mean?"

I give her a moment to remember my lesson from last week.

Gli frowns, her chin dropping to her chest. "Poison."

"That's right," I say.

I stroke her cheek and raise her face. She has darker skin than my northern pallor. She's also near tears. Life has not been forgiving of her mistakes. But I can be.

"You remembered after forgetting, and that's just as valuable as knowing the first time," I say. "Perhaps more, because you will lock it into memory now." I pause and brush the mushroom from her hand. "We avoid the poisonous ones."

She smiles even though she was wrong, and I smile back. And then Tao, who is five and never seems to forage so much as hold my hand the entire time, pulls me away to chase a butterfly. I let him, raising the hem of my colorful dress. Childhood is short, and delights are scarce for the poor in Yusan. Even scarcer for assassins like me.

But the sun is shining on the meadow, and it's a temperate afternoon, and there are children giggling and butterflies floating on the gentle breeze. The air smells like earth and wildflowers, with a hint of the West Sea. The sunshine will soon be replaced by the heavy rains of the monsoon season. So I try to savor the sunny days. To remember.

I try to see that there is still goodness in this realm. That I am one of the lucky ones. I survived. *We* survived.

The children and I have barely finished foraging when I spot a figure at the edge of the meadow. A chill careens down my spine, and my shoulders push back. I'd know that black stallion and profile anywhere. It's the Count. And gods do I hate him. I have wished him dead well over a thousand times. But, sadly, the gods don't honor wishes from girls like me.

I suppose he's thought of as attractive, but money and status enhance people's opinion of powerful men. He is twenty-five years my senior with a heart as black as coal. I see him for who he is.

"Okay, children. Same time next week?" I ask.

"Yes, Miss Sora," they say in unison.

"Good." I smile, but my fingers are icy as I pat Gli's shoulder. "Now, best be on your way."

If the Count is in a foul mood, he can grab a child and slit their throat. I know he won't face any punishment for it. And I know this because I watched him do it years ago. I want to get the children away from him as quickly as possible. But these little ones have been raised by the streets. They understand the air shifting with danger and vanish in seconds.

I continue to smile at the empty field before walking toward the horse. It's a warhorse that would trample me as soon as look at me. Just like its rider. My smile disappears as I get closer.

The Count's brown eyes always scan me as one does offerings in a sugar house. As if he is figuring out where to consume me next. It's not desire, though—it's possession. Because he owns me, body and soul.

I give an almost imperceptible bow of my head. "My lord."

"You're looking well, Sora." He smiles, scanning my body again in case I happened to miss it the first time. "Although why you bother with those filthy brats, I'll never know."

I stare at him. He didn't ask a question, so I don't have to answer. And I'm not here for conversation.

The Count sighs and extends his gloved hand, giving me a calling card. There's a name scrawled on it. Just like that, I've been given another mark. Another person to kill. A soul to steal.

And I have no choice.

Murdering is the way I repay His Grace for all the gold mun given to my former parents. The money lavished on my education and training—the training I never asked for that has left innumerable scars, most invisible. Every kill goes to my purchase price and the steep interest that started twelve years ago when I was sold.

But I have to pay him back or my little sister, Daysum, will suffer unspeakable things. And she is the only family I have left. She is his "ward," which is a kinder word for prisoner. When I was sold, she was taken as collateral.

"When?" I ask.

"Tonight, Sora," the Count says. His tawny face takes on a cold look—his real expression that shows his naked cruelty. "His body should be cold by dawn. If it is, you may see your sister for one bell tomorrow."

He rides off and leaves me standing in the meadow alone. The threat is clear: fail, and you'll never see Daysum again.

CHAPTER FOUR

ROYO
CITY OF UMBRIA, YUSAN

I can't feel my fucking fingers by the time I get to my door. Other men—foolish, trusting men—walk with their hands in their pockets, but I can't afford to be foolish. I can't afford the time it would take to get my hands free or the blow I couldn't dodge just to keep my hands warm.

But I make it home. Home is a drafty shack close enough to the Sol to smell it, but the rent is one gold mun every two months, so I stay.

I check around the exterior for signs of a break-in. Windows are sealed shut. Faded clapboards are where they're supposed to be. Satisfied, I unlock the three dead bolts on the door, then push my way inside and light the oil lamps.

It's nearly as cold in the shack as it is outside. I don't leave the furnace on if I'm going to be out—it's a waste of money. But I kinda wish I had tonight. I need the comfort of a raging fire.

I stoke the embers back to life and warm my hands by the dimly lit coals. It takes a few minutes, but I finally thaw enough to start my routine.

There's not much in here—a table and two chairs, a big seat by the furnace, a bed, and a washroom. I get up off the seat, make sure the window drapes are totally closed, and move the bed to the side. Then I pry up the floor plank. Under that, there's the hideaway I dug out. And inside of the hideaway is my most valuable possession—sacks of gold mun.

I take out my coin purse. Fifteen gold coins. Five from the job tonight. Six from collecting this morning on yesterday's job. Four from a wager I won in the gaming district.

Fifteen gold pieces. It's a very good month's wage in Umbria, but I need more. I always need more.

I eye the sacks in the hideaway. Each contains five thousand gold mun. There are ten of them. It took ten years to get this much. A decade of threats, gambling, broken bones, near-death mishaps, and blood. So much blood. But it's almost worth it to see this gold crowding the small space. A warmth fills me. Pride. Safety. The things money buys. Then I remember—this is barely half of what I need.

I carefully lift the smallest sack. I add tonight's wages and count out the new amount—two hundred and five gold mun. I cradle it as I would a baby, hoping for it to grow fat and large like its siblings, and then I lovingly fold the fabric down and deposit it next to its brethren.

My nightly count done, I close up the hideaway and wash for bed. With the room put back to rights, I grab my empty coin purse. I'll need to figure out a way to fill it again tomorrow. More screams, more blood, more bets. Whatever gets me gold.

It isn't until I drop the coin purse into my jacket that I feel the card. I take it out of my interior pocket. It's white with gold edging, and the handwriting is fancy.

Royo

The Black Shoe Inn, tonight

I have a job for you

I turn the card over in my hands again and again. Where did this come from? When? I look around even though I know I'm alone. Still, I check, because it's impossible—no one gets the jump on me. But somehow, someone did.

Over and over, I search around my shack until I'm satisfied that no one else is in here. I still have my favorite blade in my hand, just in case. I do one more lap and catch my wild gaze in the washroom glass. My eyes are a cross between yellow and brown, but right now they look black. Black as the stubble of my hair.

I need to calm down and think it through. My door is locked; nothing was awry. The card didn't appear when I was counting my gold. It had to have been when I was out—walking home or in the pub. And then I remember that blur of red at Butcher & Ale, that off feeling. I wasn't seeing things. Someone picked my pocket.

No, not picked. They left the gold. Instead, they planted this card.

And there's only one person I know of staying at the Black Shoe Inn—the girl who was looking for me. I'd think it was a coincidence, but coincidences need luck and there's none of that in Umbria. At least not for me.

This is wrong. It's all fucking wrong.

I pace in my tiny house, crushing the card in my palm. The bare walls feel too small, and instead of freezing, it's scorching in here now. My face is flushed, my neck sweating. My heavy feet stomp across the worn wood floors.

How?

No one gets close enough to pick my pocket. I'm always alert. I have been since my face was sliced in half. So how did someone leave this without me knowing? Who? If it's the girl Yuri told me about, I got even more questions.

It doesn't matter, though. I should let it go. I should throw this card right in the fire. My gut is screaming that this note is nothing but trouble.

But I need to know how they did it. Because at five foot ten, two hundred and thirty solid pounds, I haven't been vulnerable in years. If someone could slip a note in my inside pocket, they could slip a blade into me. I need to know how. And most important: I need to know why.

I put my jacket back on and head out into the night.

CHAPTER FIVE

SORA
CITY OF USE, YUSAN

Looking back, I think it was my face that damned me.

I study it in the gilded mirror of the powder room. Straight nose, heart-shaped face, flawless skin, and violet eyes. The Count searched the whole realm for perfection, young girls who would turn into stunningly beautiful women. He had no use for the scarred like Gli or the sickly like Daysum. Sickly wouldn't survive the training. I barely did.

I make certain my bloodred lipstick is perfect, blotting the edge with a silk napkin. Of course, everything is satins and gilding in this villa. The place smells clean, like clove and sandalwood. The noble class always has fine private baths while commoners are resigned to dirty public bathhouses and the river. But not here. Not for them. And it *is* us versus them. They have freedom. We do not.

When I resent my victims, it makes this easier.

No, I'm lying to myself. Again.

I grip the marble counter. Nothing makes this easier. But it's this man or Daysum. And when I remember that simple fact, there's no choice to be made or mercy to be shown. I have to see this through.

I adjust the sparkling veil over my straight hair. It's silly to have a veil for modesty when my evening dress is nearly see-through, but I try not to think about my dress or anything else. I should be as thinking and feeling as a blade. Steel forged for one purpose—to end the lives of men. That's what I was taught. And that is the only way to survive nights like this.

My hands shake as I pull the edge of the veil over my shoulder. That's odd. My hands stopped trembling years ago after I completed my first few kills. I put my fingers out in front of me. They quiver so much that my rings blur. The jewels, of course, belong to the Count, but he wants me to wear them as a sign of his generosity. We both know he'd strip them off my dead body before I turned cold, but the jewelry adds to the appearance of the courtesan I'm supposed to be.

Exhaling, I close my eyes. When I open them again, my hands have stopped shaking and I'm ready to do what needs to be done.

I unlock the door.

He's waiting for me when I come out of the bath, sitting on the bed, perched like a hungry predator. The lamps are low, the door locked. Maricelus Silla is no longer interested in the pretense of wining and dining, I suppose.

He already has his shirt open, his chest and gut exposed. His pants are loose; his desire is clear.

I avert my gaze. "Thank you for entertaining me tonight, my lord."

"Come closer, Mila," he says.

It's the name I often give. The name of a courtesan traveling through the city on her way to Tamneki. Maricelus believes he happened to run into me while leaving a meeting of the lords.

Reluctantly, I nod and take small steps. I can't move much in this dress. And I suppose that's the point—a reminder from the Count that I can't flee. I take a second to wish him dead again, just in case the gods are listening this time.

Maricelus smiles and grabs me as soon as I'm within reach. I try not to shudder as he gropes me. My eyes close like it's pleasure, because acting is the only defense I have. I can't hide weapons in a dress this sheer. I have no strength. And Heavens know no one will help me if I scream. There is a guard outside of this chamber, but he exists to protect Maricelus. Not me. I have to let this noble take what he wants, as have the girls before me.

Dinner sours in my stomach. I want to retch. But I can't.

Gripping my exposed waist, he tosses me down. I land on the expensive feather bed, right where he wants me. The air leaves my painted lips. And then he climbs on top of me. My limbs go numb, tingling as fear creeps in, as it always does in these moments. Then his mouth is on mine. He tastes me like I'm a ripe fruit while he hikes up the hem of my dress.

I stay still and let him. Struggling only makes these men violent. They are used to the world bending to their desires. They will break you if you don't.

So I don't fight.

I let him kiss me. It doesn't matter that I don't kiss him back. It never matters to any of them. He removes his trousers, his tongue sloppy in my mouth as he hums with pleasure.

"I chose the sweetest nectar," he murmurs. Then his eyes widen. Fear streaks across his face as he is suddenly reminded even nobles are mortal.

Only sick sounds escape his lips because his tongue has already begun to swell. And then he's choking. He tries to scream as ungu poison courses through his bloodstream. I know the feeling. It seems like a million tiny hands strangling every one of your muscles. But his scream comes out a whimper. He's begging with his eyes, his voice whispering for help. But would he have had mercy on me if I'd begged? The flower he so readily plucked?

I look away. He's already dead to me.

He falls onto his back, gasping for air. Ungu causes a terribly painful death that's not very fast. I remember watching two girls die of it. How paralyzed they were. I remember the strangling sensation of the microdose, the locking up of my limbs, and the primal fear of helplessness, of being trapped inside a dying body. It's not my poison of choice, but the Count demanded I use it tonight. Ungu was written on the opposite side of the calling card.

I lean down and whisper Count Seok's name so Maricelus knows who he crossed. So he knows why he's dying. I view it as a kindness. To solve a final mystery for them.

The man shakes the bed as he writhes, but he can't get up. His limbs are going rigid. He won't be able to move at all soon, aside from blinking. And then the real pain will begin. I saw it flash in the eyes of the girls who died of ungu. Unspeakable agony. Their jaws contorting until they popped out of place.

As Maricelus stills, I stand and right my dress. It may take up to a bell for him to die. But he's past the point of an antidote being able to save him. I pull up the blankets, tuck him in, and extinguish the light.

Maricelus Silla is as good as dead. Kill number eighteen for the Count, complete. I will see Daysum tomorrow. We'll laugh and sew and wander the garden as if we're not both prisoners. As if we are the ladies of a grand villa.

I gently close the door and take my cloak from the hook on the wall where I deposited it.

"He is finished with me," I say.

The guard nods, his gaze freely roaming over my body as I don my cloak, pulling up the hood.

I walk out into the night. When I'm at the end of the road to the villa, I split the hem of my horrid dress and run to the horse I'd hidden earlier. They most likely won't find Maricelus until morning, but they could discover him at any point, and I've made the mistake of dawdling before. It took multiple bells to stitch myself back together and wash the blood off me.

I gallop out of Use and switch horses midway. With the fresh horse, I canter the rest of the coastal road to Gain.

Once I clear the high city walls, I feel a certain relief. I'm home, or at least under the protection of the Count. I live in a small cottage he owns in the quiet flower district. Lilies and peonies bloom up and down the street and in my window baskets. My door is a sunny teal color, the walls whitewashed.

I put my horse in the stable around back and get inside my cottage. As soon as my door is locked, I lean against it and exhale. I made it. The gods saw me through another night.

I light the oil lamp, as it's still dark for another couple of bells. Dot, my tabby cat, circles my ankles. I lean down and pet him. His soft fur and gentle mews remind me that I'm home. Dot doesn't care what I do at night, whose life I take. All he wants are scratches and the occasional mackerel. In exchange, he gives me a sense of calm and desperately needed companionship. I used to live with nineteen other girls. At first. Then they died, one by one, until only three of us were left. And then, at eighteen, I moved here.

With a long sigh, I hang my cloak, tear off the ruined dress and veil, and throw them into the fire. The embers catch the cloth, and the fabric is gone in a quick blaze.

I flop into bed, so exhausted I almost miss the calling card on my pillow.

See me when you return

Anger makes my hands curl into fists, and I curse to the Kingdom of Hells and back. What does he want from me now? It will be dawn soon. I think about tossing the card into the fire, claiming I missed it, but I don't have that option. The Count won't be ignored.

I dress in the casual trousers and rough spun shirt he hates and ride to his estate. Most noblemen can't afford to have villas inside the city walls, but the Count is the richest man in Gain. The rules never apply to him.

The shoes of my horse clomp along the cobblestone road that leads to the Count's villa. His estate is walled on a hill, sprawling despite the congestion of the city.

I've taken this road for three years, since I began murdering for him. Seok learned of poison maidens while traveling far outside of the realm and decided to create his own.

He called it a school for unwanted girls and hired Madame Iseul as headmistress, but it was the Count who was really in charge. The Count who'd purchased us with another set of children held as collateral. The Count who'd frowned at the ones who'd died horrifically, another investment lost, another girl unable to withstand the doses of ever-increasing exotic poisons. It was the Count who slit one girl's throat when she rebelled. The Count who was responsible for the death of my lover.

Madame Iseul simply stood by, wringing her hands as we were tortured and killed. I used to hate her for her silence and inaction. As I've gotten older, though, I realized she was just as much a pawn as I am.

When I think of Madame Iseul now, I remember that she was kind to us when she needn't have been. She held our hands as we writhed and suffered. She taught us well and gave us little treats out of her own pay to try to make our lives somewhat bearable. She taught us in the courtyard on sunny days.

As I attempt to cling to goodness, to kindness when I can, I realize she did the same. The world will grab and pull at your humanity, try to strip you bare, but ultimately you decide whether to hang on or let go.

I guide my horse up to the grand mahogany doors of the white stone villa. Next to the doors are two notches where guards wait with crossbows. Before I can ring the bell, Irad comes out in his pajamas, holding a lantern.

"Yes?" he says, irritated. His normally perfect gray hair sticks out in every direction, and his pajama shirt isn't buttoned properly. Irad is the Count's head of household and therefore thinks himself above me, although I'm not sure why. The Count could replace him tomorrow, whereas I'm nearly irreplaceable. Only three of us made it out of his school, and Hana was murdered in the first year. Sun-ye is the only other poison maiden left in all of Yusan.

"You tell me. I was summoned," I say, dismounting. I flash the calling card at him.

He nods, directs a page to take my horse, and brings me inside.

The Count is waiting for me in the study. He sits behind his vast, dark wood desk, wearing a robe over his silk pajamas. Expensive gas lamps illuminate his office like it's midday, and, as always, it smells like eucalyptus and leather in here. The Count looks perfectly put together for this ungodly time of day.

I stop in front of his desk and fold my arms.

"Sora," he says, glancing at me, then back to his work. He's always signing papers or examining books. Each line item no doubt represents a poor soul he owns. That's all we are—lines on a ledger.

"You already know it is done," I say. "Why am I here?"

"I will forgive your tongue as I am certain you are exhausted. Sit down."

He gestures to a chair, and I take it. I hit the cushioned seat with a loud exhale.

"My lord?" I say through gritted teeth.

He smiles, amused. He has a smooth brow and a nose that was sadly never broken. He steeples his fingers; rings of onyx, opal, and gold gleam in the light.

"So much hatred for the man who provides your bread. And the bread for your sister. Tell me, Sora. Do you wish to be free of me?"

I sigh inwardly. He's asked a question, so I must answer—even when it's rhetorical. Those are the rules. "You already know my response."

He smiles again. "I have a job for you."

I raise my eyebrows. I can't recall a time when he requested two deaths in close proximity. And never the next day. Normally, at least a month goes by before he slips me a new name.

"Another?" I ask.

He nods.

I wait, but he doesn't hand me a card. Uneasiness settles over me and makes me shiver. I'm glad my rough spun hides my goose bumps.

"Who is the mark?" I ask.

"King Joon."

I bark out a laugh, tossing my head back. But the Count is stone-faced. He can't be serious, but I don't know why he's joking about treason.

I smile. "You want me to *kill* the king of Yusan?"

"Yes."

I sit back and cross my legs. "You could be locked up just for this conversation, you know."

And I think about it. I think of going to the soldiers stationed on the walls of Gain and telling them about the Count's plot to end the king. I think about the joy I'd feel upon seeing Seok in chains, dragged away to be tortured and executed.

"Ah yes, but you know your and your sister's debts would go to Lord Sterling on my death or disappearance," he says. "Daysum is eighteen and handsome now. She'd make a fine addition to any of his pleasure houses."

I stand so fast the chair falls back. "Speak of it again, and you won't see another sunrise."

Lord Sterling is the count's brother and a truly disgusting man.

I stare Seok down, grabbing the side of his desk. It's a vow and a promise. The same way I promised myself I'd see him choke on poison before I meet the God of Hells.

The Count sits back in his leather chair, unintimidated. "You know, Sora, under different circumstances, I would've made you a countess. We are such similar creatures."

"Am I to lose my dinner now, too?" I ask. I know I'm toeing the line with how much back talk the Count will tolerate, but I must have bought some goodwill with killing Maricelus, not to mention that this plan is ludicrous. "The answer is no. I can't kill a god king. I have no idea why you're wasting my sleeping bells on this."

The Count shakes his head. "He's not a god. He's just a man."

I stare. Even that statement is blasphemy. All of Yusan believes that King Joon is a god king. His bloodline has ruled Yusan for a thousand years—we're approaching the millennial celebration soon. And I'm well aware that some men are untouchable. I'm staring at one now.

"If anyone can get to a man, it's you," the Count says, smirking.

"I'll have to pass on the attempted regicide," I say.

"Do this and all of your debt is cleared."

What? I blink at him, unable to get out a word. My pulse leaps, and I keep moving my head to the side. He's said something impossible. I must be misunderstanding—or I misheard, as my hearing is compromised on my left side.

"Figure out how to murder the king, and you and your sister are free," he says. "Your debts will be cleared from my books. You may take Daysum and pursue your own lives anywhere you please."

I shake my head over and over, my heart hammering in my chest so hard that I'm swaying. The ringing in my ear that comes and goes is absolutely chiming. It's…it's not possible. It's not possible to assassinate the king, and it's also not possible that the Count is offering me our freedom. He's never once mentioned the possibility. And for everything I hate about him, the Count is a man of his word. He never threatens or promises anything he doesn't intend to see through.

He means this deal. But why?

That would leave Sun-ye as his only poison maiden. At least a million gold mun spent on his poison academy for only one assassin? It doesn't make business sense, and he is, above all, a businessman.

I stand still, totally befuddled. He pulls out a sheet of paper from his desk and shows me the signed amendment to our indentures—upon the death of the king, Daysum and I owe nothing to the Count. Our servitudes end. It's been filed with the magistrate. Of course, the magistrate believed it was a way to mark the time, not a contract to kill royalty. All indentures are bound and taxed through King Joon.

I run my hand over the official seal of Yusan—the snake's scales are bumpy under my fingers. "What is in it for you?"

"Oh, Sora. You know better than to ask about your marks."

He rises, and his hand comes at me so swiftly, I don't have time to dodge it. The Count backhands me across the face. Off-balance, I fall onto the desk, my breath knocked out of my chest by the hardwood. My cheek stings and my eye bulges, but it won't leave a bruise. That's how the Count strikes—cold and calculated. Then he sits down like it never happened.

I stand straight and grip the desk, wishing it was his neck. If I had longer nails, I'd leave claw marks. I wait until I stop seeing stars, until the fear ebbs, and I breathe out my rush to return the favor. Anything I do that displeases the Count would only be taken out on Daysum. I know that all too well.

I lock gazes with him. "And if I die trying, what happens to Daysum?"

He shrugs. "Attempts are of no use to me. If you perish and Joon dies, she will be free. If he lives and you die, there would be no one to pay her debt. She'd have to pay it on her back, I suppose. One client at a time."

There is a letter opener on the Count's desk. I think about it. I think about stabbing him in the chest and pressing my lips to his. I didn't have the wherewithal to take off my poisoned lipstick yet, and there's enough poison left on my mouth to kill two men. Then Seok would feel a fraction of the pain I endured and I could only pray some of the heartache. But Daysum is safe under our agreement, and I've seen the way the Lord Sterling is hungry for us. I know he samples all of the girls first. He wouldn't dare touch me, as no one can be sure if my body itself is poison at this point. But he would happily taste Daysum twice. I can't allow that to happen. I won't.

"May you die slowly," I say, staring at the Count.

"Go get some rest. Daysum will expect you at three bells."

"As you command." I curtsy and turn to leave.

"Oh, one more thing," he says.

I pause, my shoulders tensing. There's more. Of course there's more.

"Tiyung will accompany you to Tamneki," he says. "You will depart the day after tomorrow."

I let my head fall back, eyes praying to the coffered ceiling. Tiyung is the Count's son. His only heir. As cruel as his father but useless, so possibly the worst person in the three realms. The *only* reason I say "possibly" is because I have not been to Khitan or the island nation of Wei.

"Wouldn't it be easier to just kill me?" I ask.

There's a shrug in the Count's voice as he replies, "It would, but you are my most prized possession. Tiyung will carry your indenture and burn it when you succeed. And then he will come back to Gain to release your sister."

In other words, I could murder his son and burn my indenture myself, but I'd have to forfeit Daysum's life. Never think about her being violated daily in the pleasure houses. Never worry about what becomes of her. And he knows I'd die first. The Count always makes sure I have something to gain and everything to lose.

"Succeed, Sora. All of Yusan, but particularly you and your sister, will benefit," he says.

As he's had the last word, he walks out of his office, leaving me to wonder how the lives of two girls equals the death of a god king in his ledgers.

CHAPTER SIX

EUYN
CITY OF OUTTON, FALLOW

"Your Royal Highness," Mikail says, bowing with a flourish in the squalid stables. The stench of horse manure nearly brings me to my knees as much as seeing him again.

He looks the same as three years ago—tall and muscular, with deep dimples. He has on tan riding pants and a blue shirt too fine for Fallow, not to mention the expensive, poisoned sword at his hip. Mikail sticks out like a waterfall in the desert, but fewer people stare at him because he's not trying to blend in. He never tries.

His face is clean-shaven, as it always was, his lips plump and skin a beautiful dark brown. His chestnut-brown hair is just long enough to not be military. His slightly wavy locks look perfectly tousled. In those ways, he's entirely the same.

But there is something sharper, different about him. A look in his teal eyes. A hollowness to his cheekbones and cut to his jaw. He seems more feral than before, and I wish I could say it made him less desirable.

I swallow, silently admitting it's the opposite.

"You're late," he adds, spinning the red envelope in his hand. "I thought I was going to have to leave a second note for you." He puts the card in his pocket.

I stop in the shadow of the stable, about six feet from him. As if the distance buys me any safety.

"I knew my brother would send an assassin," I say. "I'm flattered that he sent his best."

A man who could rip my heart out with a glance. It's as impressive as it is cruel—exactly the way Joon operates.

Mikail tsks at me. "Come now, Euyn. You know very well that I'd look awful in all black."

He smiles, and I remember that boyish grin. The one he first winked at me when we were invincible teens going through arms training. The one he gave me after our hands accidentally brushed during an orchestra performance in the royal orchard. The one as he laid back on my pillow, emptied and yet content, the same as I. The one he flashed at me right before my brother handed down a death sentence.

"Let's get this over with," I say.

I look around for soldiers closing in on me, but Mikail is alone. I'm briefly surprised, but then I remember that Mikail doesn't need backup. There isn't a more experienced killer in all of Yusan—or Khitan, for that matter. He's not truly an assassin, though—that's a rank far beneath him. He's the royal spymaster.

I wonder how he will kill me, what he'll use, and if he will do me the kindness of a quick and clean death. But instead, he just stares at me, amusement playing on his full mouth.

"I knew you'd make it," he says. "You're more of a survivor than you ever gave yourself credit for. The beard looks good on you."

Again that smile. Like this is a casual conversation and he's not standing in unclaimed, lawless Fallow talking to a dead man. And despite everything that's happened and everything I know, he still has an effect on me. Despite him being part of the reason I was buried alive in the desert, I want to go to him. But Mikail can always get to me. To all people. Anywhere. Espionage for the throne requires, at all times, a shocking amount of murder.

"You came all this way to compliment my face?" I ask, exasperated. I have spent six bells terrorized by his note. My heart is pounding against my ribs, and I may disgrace myself by fainting in this foul stable. Why is he tormenting me? Maybe Joon told him to prolong this.

"Is it too much to hope for a decent teahouse here?" Mikail asks, glancing around.

"What do you think?" I fold my arms, my body oozing sweat and frustration.

"I think you're still as prickly as you were before you left the palace," he replies.

"By 'left,' you mean before I was sentenced to death?"

He shrugs. "Same difference."

I draw a loud breath. We're in the shade, but it's still too hot for this conversation. Although I suppose it would be surreal anywhere. I've dreamed about seeing Mikail again so many times, but none of them went quite this way. I thought we'd run to each other and fervently kiss and embrace, tears cascading down his cheeks at finding me alive. Not talking horseshit in a stable when I'm pretty sure he's about to stab me.

"We could go to your room at the inn," he suggests. I raise my eyebrows. He either wants to talk privately or murder me discreetly. I'm not sure which, and to be honest, it could be both. But all things considered, I suppose it's better to die in an inn than a dusty old horse stable. So I nod in agreement.

We walk with him trailing me slightly, and suddenly Outton marketplace looks completely different than it did moments ago. The scents are sharper, the colors more vibrant. The air is hot but clean, and the chatter of shoppers sounds like music. But a dead man savors every last vision, every last breath. I already know this from when I was banished from Qali Palace.

With each step, I brace myself. I peer over my shoulder. I'm certain I am about to feel a poisoned blade run through my back, even though I know that's not Mikail's style. He'd stab anyone in the back without a second thought, of course, but he'd only kill publicly if he had no other option.

He always has options.

We get to the inn, and I pause right outside. My limbs refuse to cooperate as that same stubborn unwillingness to die kicks in. I try to think of a way out. There is a lobby downstairs—old couches by a fireplace that's purely decorative during the day and desperately needed in the cold desert nights. It's private enough for a conversation, and perhaps someone would intervene if he tried to slit my throat.

"Which room?" Mikail asks. Of course he already knows—he left the card outside my door at dawn. He's saying the lobby will not work.

But the odd thing is that I didn't recognize the handwriting on the card. And I'd know his scrawling hand anywhere. I used to wait by the window for messengers to bring his coded letters. Clutch them to my chest the way I couldn't do to him because he was somewhere in the country or in Khitan or Wei, spying for my brother. He's been a spy since he was sixteen, which is illegal, but what is legal for a spy, anyway?

Yet the card was written in cramped, small letters. So someone else wrote it for him, but who? Why?

Mikail waits for me, and, reluctantly, I go inside and take the creaky wooden stairs up to my room. My legs feel like heavy lumber, protesting this walk to the gallows. I try to quiet my nerves with the knowledge that if he wanted to kill me, he could've done it already. He must want something else or something in addition to the bounty on my head. I don't know what, but I doubt it's the loving pillow talk I've imagined.

It's only morbid curiosity that drives me forward. Well, that and the pride to die privately.

We get to my corner room, and I unlock the dead bolt.

He's too close to me, and it makes the hair stand on my neck. I can't figure out if I want him to move closer or farther away.

"Don't forget the trap above the door," he says.

I side-eye him, although I shouldn't. Mikail was the one who taught me these tricks. All the practical knowledge that's kept me alive these past years came from him. As a prince, I wasn't worried about setting traps for anything aside from prey.

I reach up and slide the spike. Otherwise, a mace would've come careening into our heads as soon as we stepped inside.

Mikail follows me into the small room, and I think about the last time we were alone together. The bittersweet final day of my life in the palace. Laughing with him as we drank sweet wine in my bedroom, tossing aside delicacies after a single bite, sweating in the silk sheets until we were both exhausted. That was right before the morning I was awoken by the king's guard and brought before the throne.

After that, I remember pacing in Idle Prison, the dungeon under Idle Lake, waiting for Mikail to save me or at least say a final goodbye. He never came. And then I was transported like an animal for multiple sunsaes until I got to Fallow. Three two-week intervals.

The guards had already dug the hole in the sand by the time they let me out.

Mikail closes and locks the door of my room, and we come to a stop too close together. I feel the heat radiating off his chest. His cologne fills my nose. Three years of unsatisfied desire suffuses me. I want to grab him and pull him close, if for no other reason than to hold him and make certain he's real. I've nearly driven myself mad with wanting him, with imagining him here. I've felt his featherlight yet firm touch on my thighs in my dreams. But I take a step back—because he shouldn't be here at all. And I hate my body for wanting him still.

"So you traveled to Fallow just for this reunion, did you?" I ask.

He smiles slowly as he relaxes into a patterned armchair. The two chairs and small table don't match. But Mikail crosses his long legs, comfortable like this is his office in the Hall of Spies. "I was waiting for the right opportunity."

There's something in the way he says it that makes the realization clear. The pit of my stomach turns. "How long have you known I survived?"

"About three years." He says it casually. As if it doesn't blow my imagined safety apart, as if the room isn't tilting beneath my feet.

He's known about me this entire time. That I made it out of the middle of the Amrock Desert through the providence of the gods. A sandstorm hit a bell after I was buried to my neck and left for dead. The winds shifted the dune so much it freed my body, and then I stumbled through the storm until I collapsed. Luckily, I made it right to the edge of an oasis. And there, I was saved by a nomad caravan that took me east to Outton. A full sunsae on their good charity.

My chest tightens, and a million questions rush through my head as the same amount of feelings pulse in my body. I'm impressed, outraged, and brokenhearted that he didn't care enough to contact me in the last three years—and hopeful because he's here now.

Suddenly, I think perhaps my name has been cleared. Maybe he's here to tell me that I am welcome back at the palace. Excitement and hope bubble inside me but then fall flat because he would've led with that. No, he's here for some other reason. I want to laugh. I want to scream. I want to kiss him once again. In short: I'm a mess.

"You're more of a Euyn than a Donal. Even with the beard," he adds, brushing dust off his pants leg.

Never mind. I hate him.

I stop cold at the use of my real name and swallow hard. "Does my brother know?"

He arches an eyebrow. "Do you think you'd be alive if he did?"

That's not an answer. Mikail is an expert at the nonanswer that sounds like honesty. But even though I haven't seen him in three years, I knew him for six before he perfected all these tools. Before he made honesty a weapon, like a poisoned sword to be used as sparingly as possible.

"Did you tell him?" I ask.

He smiles. "No."

I scan his face, and he lifts his eyebrows slightly. He's telling the truth.

Finally, I perch on a chair, mostly convinced he's not here to kill me. At least at the moment.

"Why are you here?" I ask. "And where does Joon think you are?"

"On a lead to locate the long-lost Amulet of the Dragon Lord," Mikail says with a wave of his hand. "As I said, I have a proposal for you. An offer."

I narrow my eyes at him. "Why the ruse? You could've shown your face and talked to me."

He draws a breath. "I needed to know you were desperate enough to consider my offer. Any offer."

I shift uncomfortably. "Consider what, exactly?"

He leans forward. "I need your help."

"With?"

"With murdering your brother."

Silence descends on the room like a blanket thrown in the air. It floats over us. Covers us. Smothers conversation. Mikail casually regards me, waiting for my response.

"You're not serious," I finally say.

"I am."

I laugh.

"It's possible," he says, his blue-green eyes intense. "No one knows your brother the way you and I do."

I stick out my hands, balancing impossible scales. "A few problems, off the top of my head…"

The first and foremost being that Joon is known as a god king for a reason. He's not divine, but he might as well be, since he has the crown of Yusan. The crown is a relic of the Dragon Lord, and it makes the wearer immortal.

Next is that sitting here, even talking about this, is plotting attempted regicide and fratricide, and those are both frowned upon by my brother. Either is punishable by lingchi—a public death by a hundred cuts.

Add in a bounty on me dead or alive; and that we are in Fallow, more than a month from the capital city of Tamneki; and finally that Joon lives in Qali Palace in the middle of Idle Lake. It's the most secure place in all of Yusan, maybe second to Idle Prison. Hard to say.

All of this is not a recipe for success, which I explain to Mikail.

I wait for Mikail to smile or crack a joke, but he stares at me, sitting forward. Gods on High. He really did come here for this— to plot to kill my brother.

"With Joon dead, you are the only heir to the throne of Yusan," he says. "You'd be king. Help me, and the crown is yours."

The crown. The throne. It's as tempting as it is impossible.

As the youngest son of the old king, I've never been expected to rule Yusan. Not really. But our middle brother, Prince Omin, died a while back, and Joon doesn't have any children, since Naerium died years ago, so Mikail is correct. I am the last heir.

But getting the crown is another matter.

The king of Yusan doesn't remove his crown, even to sleep. One of the old kings learned that the hard way, stabbed in his bed by his own son while on a war campaign in Khitan. Joon's crown only comes off for the briefest of moments when he bathes his head, though that is never predictable—and he is always alone at those times.

Moreover, why is Mikail proposing the king's murder? He's been loyal to my family for his entire life. More loyal to my brother than to me. After all, it was his agreeing with Joon that sealed my fate in the throne room.

"And what would you get?" I ask.

Mikail looks to the side, his eyes taking on a far-off look. "Something I've wanted."

I lean back. He doesn't want me to know, and no amount of begging, cajoling, or torture will get information out of Mikail if he has decided not to tell. They look for that trait in future spymasters; they found it in abundance in the boy beaten daily by his father, sometimes with reason, often without. I've asked him about his scars, and all he said was: "my family." I had to piece the rest together on my own.

"And to whom would I owe my throne?" I ask.

Mikail smiles slowly, the way he always does when I've said something clever. I pretend like it doesn't still affect me. That I don't love making him smile.

"The Queen of Khitan."

And that catches me off guard. It's been a while since I've heard from my sister.

CHAPTER SEVEN

AERI
CITY OF UMBRIA, YUSAN

It's very cold in Umbria. This city isn't much north of my town of Pyong, but somehow it's way colder. And I hate the cold.

Which is why I'm presently pacing by the fireplace in my room at the Black Shoe Inn. It's a roaring flame, but I just can't get warmth into my fingers and toes. I think about moving closer, but any closer and the sleeves of my dress will catch fire. And I like this dress. I love all my fancy dresses, but they're not heavy enough for Umbria—style over function and whatnot. Or maybe this blue dress is warm enough and I'm just nervous.

Yeah, I'm definitely nervous.

Where is he?

Maybe he didn't get the card. Maybe I should go out looking for him.

No. I need to be patient. Unfortunately, patience really isn't my thing. So, back to pacing.

It's nearly midnight when there's finally a knock on my door. Even though I've been expecting it for two bells, I jump. Which is silly. Get it together, Aeri. Of course Royo found the card I planted on him—that was the whole point of doing it.

I fix my hair in the mirror, wondering what he's going to be like. Then I pause a little, worried about talking to a strongman, but when I saw him earlier, he looked okay. And this is why I'm here—to talk to a killer.

A little giddy and a lot nervous, I throw open the door and frown. It's not him—it's a boy around the age of twelve.

"Yes?" I ask.

He cranes his neck to look up at me. "Oh, um, excuse me, miss. The innkeeper says there's a man here to see you. He's in the lobby."

"Thank you," I say.

The kid remains standing across from me. Right. He's looking for a tip. I mentally smack myself on the forehead for forgetting, then grab my velvet purse and give him a silver mun. It's too much of a tip, but I don't want to rummage around looking for bronze coins. Besides, what's the difference?

The boy's freckled face breaks into a wide grin, and then he takes off. He's already dust when it dawns on me that I should've told him to say I'll be right down. No. Not right down. Down in a moment. Yeah, that would've sounded better.

Oh well.

I take a deep breath and realize I'm slouching. Father *hates* when I slouch. I stand straight and push back my shoulders. That's better—tall and regal, dignified. Now I look like a lady. One with a tempting offer for a very dangerous man. And if he agrees, it can change my life. This job can fix everything, finally win Father's approval. No more stealing to scrape by. No more living a life alone. Never again having to freeze on the street.

Right. I can do this. Easy.

I bound down the stairs, but I stop short when I see him. I was sitting at an angle where I didn't get a great look at him in Butcher & Ale, but now I can stare at the very muscular man in the lobby. Royo's probably not traditionally attractive. Like if I closed my eyes and thought of a handsome man, it wouldn't be him. But he's much more attractive than I initially thought. His hair is just a little above shaved, his jaw hard, and his face scarred. He's a warrior minus the battlefield.

But he's something else, too.

Right now, Royo's jacket is over his arm, and he has a tiny figurine in his hand. Everything about him would make you think he'd smash that little ceramic bird. But he's holding it carefully, gently, with wonder in his eyes. Something about it is instantly endearing.

He's the one—the one I need.

I'm almost to the last step when he looks up at me. His eyes are slightly wide-set and the color of honey. They rapidly take in my blue dress, and I find myself holding my breath.

He doesn't smile.

I do. This moment is too tense. And my mother used to say a good smile can break through the ice of the North Sea.

"Hi, Royo," I say with a wave.

His brow furrows.

I clear my throat. Right. Too eager. Made it weird. "Thank you for meeting me."

Maybe I should've said, "Thank you for taking the time to meet with me." I don't know. I've never read a book on the etiquette of hiring muscle…or on trying to seem noble, or at the very least rich.

"How'd you get my name?" His voice has the rumbling of thunder, and I find myself following like lightning.

But the innkeeper sneezes and I'm reminded that this really isn't the time to be horny.

We both face him. The innkeeper is pretending not to watch us from behind the desk, but he's about eight feet away and there's literally no one else in the lobby. Of course he's paying attention. I need to be more careful.

"Huang, we'll take tea in the parlor, please," I say.

He nods and goes off to the kitchens as I wave Royo to the room on the other side of the fireplace. No one was in it when I scoped it out earlier, and I sigh in relief when it's still empty. You can't see more than the entrance from the lobby, so it's the perfect place to talk privately.

We sit at the small table in the back. We're both too tall for it. He's probably an inch or two taller than I am, but he's just so broad chested that he seems much bigger. I am a twig. He's an oak tree.

Our knees knock, and he reaches down and pats my leg. Then he yanks his hands back like I burned him or something. It's… sweet. He's gentle. I'd expected something else when I heard about him. A bad man. A brute. And he isn't one. I mean, yeah, he's a violent killer, but no one's perfect.

I cross my legs and stick them out to the side of the table. He glances at my thighs and then pretends he didn't, adjusting the jacket on the back of his chair. He's so interesting.

"There. That's better." I smile. "Sitting for tea like we're already friends. Yuri relayed my message, then?"

"Yeah, but I got your card."

Warmth flushes my cheeks. He's not exactly pleased that I got the drop on him, but I didn't know how else to get him to agree to meet me. I play with the hem of my dress. "I thought you might not come."

"Who are you?"

Duh. Right. Start with your name, Aeri.

"Oh, sorry. I'm Aeri. Aeri Soo."

I stick my hand out. He knits his black eyebrows and then eventually, reluctantly, meets my hand with his meaty palm. The second he touches me, a feeling rushes through me. Our hands fit together like a lock and key, but it's more than that. He feels like home.

Then I remember I should be shaking hands, so I rush to do it. I wind up waving his arm up and down.

"Oh. Too much. Sorry." I wrinkle my nose and then shove my hands under my thighs. Great. I made this weird.

He raises one eyebrow. I didn't mean for him to think I'm strange, but I guess when that's the truth there's not much you can do about it.

Royo folds his hands and leans forward like he wants to gain control of this meeting. Which is good. Someone should. Two of his fingers must've broken at some point and never been set. There's an old scar on his right hand—a deep wound and something that looks like a puncture mark. They are the hands of a fighter, a killer, the man I heard about.

"What happened there?" I ask, pointing to the largest scar.

"Life," he says.

My mouth drops open. "That's such an awesome answer."

He looks around like he's seeking help, then adjusts his body in the seat. "I should tell you up front that I won't take a job if it involves hurting a girl."

I blink. "A girl? Oh, no, that's not the job. I guess people do..." I trail off because I am well aware that people try to hurt girls. "Do people ask you to do that?"

He shrugs. "Sometimes."

"But you say no?"

He nods. Just so smooth. But he means it. I like that he draws a line. He has principles and sticks to them. Most people don't. Not when they conflict with desire.

The tea comes, and I smile at the innkeeper. He grins back, but then his smile fades when he looks at Royo. He doesn't like him here with me; Royo doesn't seem like a big fan of it, either. And that's no good. I need him. I need to win him over.

I'd smile at him again, but that just seems to upset him.

Once the innkeeper leaves, I pour tea for both of us. Scents of pineapple and green tea fill the air. I put an obscene amount of honey in mine.

"Well, no. I don't want to hurt a girl," I say. "I don't need you to hurt anyone, really."

Not necessarily, anyhow.

"Then I think you got the wrong guy." He sits back in his chair, not touching the tea. Closed off. Meeting over.

My stomach drops, and my palms itch. Without him, this whole thing gets a lot harder. And it's already not easy. I tap my fingers rapidly on the wood table.

"I need you to take me to Tamneki," I say. More like blurt out.

Tamneki is the capital city of Yusan, way south of here on the East Sea.

"I'm not a tour guide," he says with his jaw locked.

"I know you're not," I say. "But I need protection. There's a… job I have to do, and I need an escort getting there. I asked around when I came into Umbria, and I heard about you."

"Do you know how far Tamneki is from here?" he says. It's not really a question, but I figure I'll answer it.

"A week on the Sol with fair winds. Longer, otherwise. And then a sunsae east in a carriage." As simple as it is long and dangerous.

He seems ready to walk, but I'm encouraged by the fact that he's still in front of me. Something is keeping him in his seat. I just have to figure out what it is. What he needs.

I reach for my teacup. Mama used to say that having meals or even a beverage with someone encourages a sense of kinship. A bond. I sip the tea, and it immediately burns my tongue. I put it down, flapping my hands. Ugh.

"Too hot. Way too hot. I should've waited. I always do that." I smack my hand against the table. "My tongue is going to feel weird for a week."

He stares at me. "How old are you?"

"Twenty-four," I say.

I'm not sure why he's asking. Probably because I always seem younger. I guess having chin-length hair doesn't help, but I like it short. And age is just a number anyhow.

"So let me get this straight," Royo says, moving in his chair again. "You want me to travel for a sunsae and a half with you?"

I nod eagerly. "Yes. And keep me safe while I'm in Tamneki. So, figure a month total."

"And that's it?"

"Yes."

I grip the hem of my dress. Say yes. Say yes, Royo, so it's one less thing for me to worry about.

He narrows his eyes. "Why come to me when you just need a guard?"

Ugh, that's not a yes.

But he does have a point—there are guardsmiths all over Yusan. They're outfits who'll promise to protect your body, home, or business, and by that they mean they'll fall asleep in front or in back of your building. I've stolen from jewelers "protected" by guardsmiths. It's not enough. I need *real* protection.

"I'm not sure what dangers we'll face on the way, particularly in Tamneki. It's not safe for a girl to travel alone. And people say no one messes with you. I need that."

He rubs his temples. "Listen, lady, maybe you don't know how this works. But I'm muscle for hire. A strongman. You give me the name of someone you want hurt, and I hurt him. You pay me half up front and the other half once it's done. That's it. I'm not a guardsmith. I don't protect no one. I hurt them." He mimes snapping a bone in two. Danger flashes in his eyes. Is it wrong that it's kind of hot?

Never mind. Not the point.

We're silent for a full minute. I think about telling him about who I want to hurt, and then I think that's the last thing I should tell him. Finally, I settle on the truth.

"The king," I say.

He knits his eyebrows. "What?"

Right. He couldn't hear me because I was mumbling. Father hates mumbling more than he hates slouching. I stare Royo in the eyes and speak clearly. "I want to hurt the king."

"Why?"

"Because of something that happened long ago." I wave off the bitterness, the anger, because he doesn't need to know all that. "The long story short is that I lost everything because of King Joon, and I need to make it right."

"This is treason," Royo says, looking around. "Just this conversation could get us carted off to Idle Prison. It could mean lingchi. Do you know what that is?"

I shake my head.

"Lingchi is a hundred cuts of meat off your body in public, keeping you alive so you feel every last one, so hael birds can't finish you off—because that would be mercy. Everyone goes in thinking they won't beg for death. Every single one does. So, no, I can't help you."

He stands. This went...poorly. I'll have to find someone else, and it's already midnight. And I'm positive that it *has* to be him. Other guards or strongmen, even if they're capable, might betray me or try to take advantage of me. He's not like that at all. He's shy about even looking at my legs.

I pout. "I could pay."

"Not interested."

That's where I see an in: he's lying. There was a glint in his eye the second I said the word "pay." Money. Money, a lot of it, will seal this deal.

I reach into my velvet purse and plunk a diamond the size of a plum onto the table. I immediately second-guess parting with a gem worth so much—that was the biggest pain to steal—but Royo stops midway to his jacket. He freezes.

It was the right call.

"I need you to keep me safe," I say. "I can't worry about some lazy guardsmith or a strongman on the take who'll sell me out. If I pull off this job, my pay is…" I lower my voice and lean forward. "Half a million gold mun. So I tell you what: you get this, and I'll give you an extra fifty thousand bonus if I succeed. But even if I fail, this is yours at the end of the month."

Slowly, he lowers himself back into the seat. He stares at the gem without touching it. He keeps his distance like it may transform into a snake and bite him.

He swallows hard, unable to take his eyes off the gem. "What is that?"

What a question. "It's a diamond."

"I can see that, but…"

"It's worth fifty thousand gold mun," I say. "It's yours whether I succeed or not—if you agree to do whatever needs to be done, including murder, to keep me safe for a month."

It's a lot of money, way more than I should offer, but I stole it anyhow, so really, what's the difference?

"And I would *not* be helping you kill the king, right?" he asks quietly.

Gods, how to answer that? *Do* I answer that? I guess so. It'll look worse if I refuse, and I already told him about treason.

"Would it really matter?" I ask, hedging. When he doesn't blink, I add, "I have to remove the king's crown, that's all."

His eyes move around rapidly when he's confused, and I realize it looks like honey dripping fast.

"Why?" he asks. "To steal it?"

"No, because without his crown, King Joon will be mortal."

Royo's brow wrinkles. "Joon isn't a god?"

I can't help it—I scrunch my face. "No."

He purses his lips. "I mean…I never really believed all that about the king being a god on earth, because why would gods bother with Yusan? But I saw King Joon survive an assassination."

"You did?"

He nods. "When he visited Umbria years ago, I was in the crowd watching him speak. All of a sudden, there was a scream, and then it was chaos. A crossbow bolt hit his neck, and there was blood everywhere. He should've died, but he didn't. He walked off the balcony under his own power, and the assassin was subjected to lingchi. After that, I figured what they said in the temples was true—he can't die."

"No. Well, I mean, he can't, but it's because of the crown."

He shakes his head. "How does a piece of metal do that?"

Does he really want me to explain magic from the gods? Of all the things I thought would happen tonight, explaining god magic to a strongman wasn't one of them.

I shrug. "I dunno. Etherum."

He blinks hard. "Etherum? But there isn't any magic in Yusan."

That's what people believe, and outside of the relics of the Dragon Lord, there isn't. Everyone knows the Dragon Lord united Yusan and ruled for hundreds of years. But only those closest to the throne know that five relics were left behind—the crown being one of them. The legend is that the Dragon Lord gave his crown to the first Baejkin king, but his ring, scepter, sword, and amulet fell into the other realms as he ascended to the Heavens. I think it's just to explain why Yusan doesn't have them.

I shrug again, putting my palms up. "I don't know, Royo. The crown is etherum."

"How do you know that?"

"Because that's what the royal spymaster said."

He rubs his face.

Right. Maybe I shouldn't have mentioned Mikail this early, but he was the one who approached me with the job. And it's too hard to explain otherwise.

"All you have to do is protect me," I say. "I'll worry about the rest."

"How do I know that's real?" Royo asks, pointing to the stone.

I push the gem forward. "Take it and ask someone."

This should do it. He'll accept the job, and we can get started tomorrow.

His eyes move around. "How do you know I'm not just going to make off with it?"

"I'd find you and steal it back if you did."

I smile, but he looks like I struck him in the face. Did he not put together that I'm a thief? That's…odd. Doesn't matter. I don't need his brains.

"How do you think I got that card into your pocket?" I say, pointing to his chest. "Or the gem in the first place?" With that, I finish my tea and stand. "Can you let me know before noon tomorrow? I told Huang I'd check out then. If you don't want in, no hard feelings. But I'd rather you take the job. I like you."

I smile big, although Royo sits shaking his head. But he's going to take the job. I can feel it. It's why he didn't leave. He needs the money. I don't know why, and I guess it doesn't matter. But the more he thinks about it, the more he'll realize he'd be a fool to turn down this much money. And he's not a fool. I just need to disappear before he can tell me no.

Without another word, I walk out and leave the diamond on the table. I bite my lip as I take the stairs, hoping I'm right, because it'll be such a pain to hunt him down.

CHAPTER EIGHT

EUYN
CITY OF OUTTON, FALLOW

There is never an opportune time to arrive in Fallow—and it turns out there's never a good time to leave, either. During the day, the sun and oppressive heat can strike you down. At night, it becomes easy to fall into a dry serpent pit. Not to mention samroc mostly hunt in the dark.

Samroc are enormous black birds that developed a fondness for human flesh. As large as they are cunning, they can carry off a full-grown man with ease. The lucky victims are killed swiftly with a talon to the head. The unlucky ones are brought alive to mountain nests to be torn apart by young samroc just learning to kill. You can hear their piercing wails and pleas for death on still nights.

Before I was exiled, I'd thought samroc were just a myth, an exaggeration based on the carnivorous hael birds of Yusan. Hael also eat humans and watch us with ungodly hunger, but hael males grow to about two and a half feet tall, the females smaller. They can kill a man, but only if he's already on death's doorstep. The first time I saw a samroc, I nearly fainted from the size of the shadow it cast. It blotted out the sun.

Mikail decides we should leave Outton before dusk and hopefully reach Tile, a town straight east, before dark. The time before dusk is also known as the heat of the day. It has to be a hundred and ten degrees right now, but somehow Mikail doesn't look any worse for the wear as we ride. He seems unfazed as his horse carries half of everything I still own. Mine carries the other half.

I had to leave most of my possessions behind—the very first items I paid for through my own theft, skill, and work. I gave them to the pretty innkeeper for her kindness, and she was grateful. In a place like Fallow, everything can be sold second- or thirdhand. And the widow can use all the help she can get.

"You look lost in thought," Mikail says. "What's troubling you?"

He says it as if he's surprised that I have a lot on my mind.

"Oh, I don't know, perhaps the plot to kill my brother?" I say. "Going back to the country where there's a bounty on my head? Leaving the only safety I've known for the last three years for what seems to be a suicide mission? Small matters like that."

He arches an eyebrow. "What was the alternative? Stay in Outton and open a tea shop one day? Try to bed the innkeeper? You're a prince of Yusan—that is the only life for you. The only one worthy of you."

I try not to let my pulse race from his last sentence. I fail miserably.

But I can't focus too much on his words because there's something in the road up ahead. And in Fallow, by the time you can see trouble, it's too late to avoid it.

We go closer. An overturned cart lies in the center of the road. From the way it perfectly blocks the dirt path, it's no accident. My hackles rise. A chill careens down my spine, making the world around me sharper, time slower. I sniff the air as I used to on my hunts. I go still and listen for the slightest sounds.

I glance at Mikail and note that he's just as alert. I'm about to ask about the cart when six armed men appear in front of the barricade. Highway robbers or a gang—there are plenty of both in Fallow.

My shoulders droop. Of course we run into highwaymen just two bells outside of Outton.

Mikail tips his head, telling me to stay behind him as he continues toward them. From when we were teens, we could communicate without speaking. It's curious how we can pick up like nothing's changed.

He casually rides until he's just ten feet away. He proceeds as if he's oblivious to the danger. He is decidedly not.

"Let me guess: this is a robbery?" Mikail says, eyeing the scene. Two of the men look at each other, confused.

A man steps forward—probably the ringleader. "Put your hands up and give us your horses and weapons, and you may leave with your lives."

"I'm afraid I can't do that," Mikail says. "I do, however, have a counteroffer."

"What's that?" a second man asks.

"It's when the person rejects your original offer and has an alternative solution," Mikail explains patiently.

The second man blinks.

"Get them," the first man says. He doesn't take another breath before he's dead, a dagger lodged in his throat from Mikail. My hand is still in my saddlebag, trying to locate my crossbow, and Mikail has already killed his first man.

Gods on High, where is it?

The leader falls to the ground, and Mikail watches with all the dispassion of felling a tree. "I seriously suggest you allow us to—"

An arrow flies at him. Mikail parries it with his sword's scabbard, his reflexes, as always, unnaturally fast.

"Well, that was just rude," he says. "I was speaking."

The archer is dead now, too, a hilt sprouting out of his chest, also courtesy of Mikail. Two bodies, and I've just gotten my hand on my bow. I bring it up to my shoulder and turn the mechanism to pull the string. The four remaining men scramble to get their weapons ready, swords and knives in hand and maces swinging. Mikail sighs and draws his sword. The poison blade bursts into a flame the second it hits the air. The men freeze. They stare at the sword—moths to a fire.

"Gentlemen," Mikail says, his voice booming in the desert. "Run now or I promise on the God of Truth, I will skin every last one of you alive."

The men take off in four directions. I ride up to Mikail, and we watch them for a moment.

"Null," Mikail whispers.

My eyes widen, and my stomach turns. It means zero. Zero witnesses, zero survivors. With that one word, I know he's about to slaughter them all. Any safety from running was an illusion. I swallow hard and remember that Mikail isn't ruthless— he's realistic. We can't have the highwaymen telling people they saw a man with a flaming sword. Flaming swords are only bestowed by the king of Yusan. It would give away Mikail's presence and possibly mine, as there are only about a dozen in use.

But it still feels wrong. We're not in any danger now.

Mikail rides to the closest man, swings the sword, and decapitates him. One second he was alive, breathing, and now he is nothing more than a corpse. I look down as the severed head rolls a longer distance than expected. We both watch it, the eyes of the skull still open in the sand.

"Hmm. Curious," Mikail says. Then he spurs his horse to run down the next one.

The second man sprints in the direction of Outton. He's fast, but we are two bells outside the city by horse. I don't know where he thinks he's going.

There's no safety, no quarter. Mikail cuts him down with a slicing blow. He falls to the ground with a scream, likely dead already, but the poison from the sword will finish him off before he can bleed to death.

The third man went north. It's like they don't understand that there is nothing but desert yawning in front of them and one of the best killers in the world on their heels. Their fate was sealed the second they didn't let us pass. They should at least have the dignity to die well. But when it comes down to it, few men do.

Mikail stops his horse next to mine. I watch his chest rise and fall evenly. His keen eyes focus on the man flailing in the deepening sand. He wipes the blood off his blade and puts his sword into its scabbard. Then he extends his hand and I toss him the loaded crossbow.

It's a long distance, and he has to calculate the man's speed, but he shoots and drops the man to the ground with one bolt.

The aim was a little off—the man is not dead, but he's also going nowhere.

"You were always better with the bow," he says, frowning at himself.

Mikail hands me back the crossbow and pulls out his sword. It sparks to flame again, coated in oil anew.

One left.

Mikail smiles, bloodlust making him more attractive than ever. My heart speeds up as he spurs his horse and leaps the overturned wagon. Years ago, I thought I could watch him every day for the rest of my life and never tire of it. Unfortunately for me, I still feel the same. He's otherworldly when he's violent.

Transfixing. The God of War on earth. The most attractive being in the three realms.

Riding high on his horse, Mikail gallops until he reaches the last man. He swings his sword far back and then slices the man in half. Literally. A wail escapes the man's mouth, and then there's no sound because he's in shock. The lower half of his body has been completely detached.

Mikail stops and frowns as he shakes the blood off his sword. Then he dismounts and wipes the blade on the former man's shirt. I ride up to him.

"Foolish," he says, spitting on the ground. He returns his blade to the scabbard. I'm not sure if he's referring to himself or the highwaymen. "Shall we?"

He says it like he's inviting me to dance while he gestures to the body in pieces. His bloodlust got the better of him—only palace swords are sharp enough to cleave a man in two like this. We'll need to bury the evidence now.

Mikail takes the arms, I take the legs, and we drag the body off the road. It's not the first body I've moved, but it is the first pair of legs only.

Once the two pieces are in a shallow grave and Mikail has slit the throat of the man he shot with the crossbow, we continue down the road to Tile.

Mikail glows with sweat, with the effort he exerted, but it's more than that. He glows with the lives he took. Some part of him enjoys the slaughter. The same way crowds pack into the King's Arena to watch tuhko championships, knowing that the losing team will be ritually, horrifically sacrificed. On some level, people love watching others suffer and die. Mikail more than most. But it's understandable. A taste of death makes us savor our mortality.

"Do you ever think about all the people you've killed?" I ask.

"No. Do you?" He side-eyes me.

My breath catches, and I look away. He said it so casually, it caught me off guard, but I know exactly what he means. He's calling me a murderer. A mass murderer.

"You…you believe all of that?" I squeeze the leather reins in my hand.

He shrugs. "I have a funny way of believing things that are true."

There's not a shadow of a doubt in his mind that I deserved my punishment, my banishment, and these years of suffering because I killed those men. Because I am guilty. Because the king's charges were not a trumped-up accusation but real.

Because that's the truth.

It feels like a rock has wedged in my throat, blocking the excuses that rush through my brain. And Mikail won't want to hear them anyhow.

It's a while before I can speak again.

"You knew?" I ask.

He nods.

"I can explain," I say. "They…the thing is…we—"

He shakes his head. "Spare me the rationale in this heat, please, Euyn. I know who you are. I always have. And if you had to do it all over again, you would do the same thing—you just wouldn't let the last one escape."

I close my mouth, my teeth clicking together, because I know he's right. I've thought many times of how I should've just shot Chul in the head when I had the chance. How different my life would be if I hadn't been moved to mercy in that one moment. My family isn't known for their mercy—my brother has slaughtered tens of thousands of men, women, and children without losing a wink of sleep. And he's just one example of Baejkin ruthlessness. My sister is worse.

"Your energy would be better used looking for samroc," Mikail says.

After a few held breaths where words fail me, I tip my head and begin to scan the rapidly darkening sky. I suddenly realize that killing the highwaymen and burying the one added too much time to our trip. We won't make it to Tile before nightfall.

We'll be the ones hunted soon.

CHAPTER NINE

SORA
CITY OF GAIN, YUSAN

It's another beautiful, sunny afternoon when I arrive at the Count's villa, and now I'm happy to be here. I notice the grandeur of the sprawling estate. The way it soaks up the sun sitting on a terraced slope. Most houses are whitewashed in Gain, but his is white stone that shimmers. When the afternoon sun hits, it's glorious.

I like it all because I'm here to see my sister.

Irad looks extra pompous and put together as he escorts me to the terraced garden. He holds his chin so high, I'm surprised he doesn't trip. There are more blossoms in the Count's garden than in the entire flower district. The waterways babble, the trees are perfectly pruned, the flower petals delicate and silky. There's not a leaf on the stone paths or in the clear koi ponds.

I sit on a carved teak bench, waiting, and I close my eyes. I breathe in the gentle scent of orange and cherry trees and breathe out my crimes. I pretend I'm anywhere other than trapped in Gain, which is fortunately easy in a garden this tranquil. My soul will never be clean, but I'm nearly at peace when Daysum arrives.

"Sora!" She runs to me, hiking her skirts the same way she's done for a dozen years. She's not very fast, but she's only running a few feet.

I open my arms, and she hugs me. It feels like warmth, like spring, like contentment. Daysum feels like the piece of me that was ripped away when I was nine years old.

Often, I think back to that day. How I wasn't sure what was going on when Seok and four armed men showed up at our house. But I tried to hide sickly little Daysum behind me. Seok immediately understood what she meant to me—the bond we've always shared. I've wondered many times if she would be free had I not foolishly tried to protect her.

I've done the best I could to make up for that mistake every day since.

Daysum puts her head against my shoulder because, despite me being five foot six, I'm four inches taller than her. Because of her illnesses, Daysum never reached her full height, but I like that she's small. The same way I like the streaks of brown in her otherwise black hair. She does look older than the last time I saw her, though. Then again, everyone ages fast in Yusan.

Eventually, I let go. I cup her soft face in my hand, examining her. She looks far healthier than she used to; her cheeks are rosy. But her breathing is a little fast. I want to ask if she's okay, but Daysum hates when I pester her about her health.

"Don't you look beautiful," I say instead.

She rolls her eyes. "Like I'm anything compared to you." Then she smiles bright as the sun. "I'm thankful to the gods to see you again."

She sits beside me, holding my hands in hers. She knows to sit on my right because I have less hearing on my left—a result of being dosed with Erlingnow poison.

"How are your lessons going?" I ask.

Even though she is eighteen, legally an adult in Yusan, she missed months of instruction due to her sicknesses. The Count has pointed out several times that had she stayed with our parents,

Daysum would not have survived. And while I will never be grateful, I can admit that he is correct. Our parents, who sold us into slavery for gold, would not have been able to afford the medicine to save her. Or if they could've, they wouldn't have bought it. Obviously, I owe him for every apothecary trip, but that's the one part of my debt that I don't mind.

The odd thing is, I remember feeling taken care of by our parents. We were poor, like the rest of our village, but we were happy. I never doubted that we were loved…right up until I was sold and Daysum was taken. But I suppose that's the childhood I want to imagine, the lies I want to believe.

"The lessons are well enough," Daysum says. "Although I am not sure what to do once my schooling is complete."

I'm not sure, either. I didn't think we'd live this long. But fresh air, good meals, and quiet living have all helped Daysum survive. And sheer, stubborn will to see her again got me through poison school.

"I am sure you'll figure it out. You can do anything." I stroke her long hair away from her face. We both have thick hair, but Daysum is even paler than I am, with brown eyes, not violet. The contrast between her powder-white skin and ebony-and-brown hair makes her beautiful. Had she been healthier, I have no doubt that the Count would've selected her for poison training, too.

But when I move her hair, I see it. A long scar that reaches all the way up to her shoulder. Her white skin, once torn red. It's settled into a mottled brown. The wound that was entirely my fault because three years ago, she was whipped after I tried to escape.

Right after I killed my first mark, I couldn't stand it—the guilt, the thought of murdering for the Count until I die. Murdering men who did nothing to me, meant nothing to me, and pleaded with me to save them. I hadn't used enough poison the first time, and he lived long enough to fall to his knees, begging. It took three bells for him to die.

That morning, I ran and made it past the tree line—the boundary marker I'm not allowed to cross without the Count's permission. I made it far into Xingchi forest, but the Count's dogs hunted me down.

Once I was brought back to the villa, I expected to be beaten, but not a finger was laid on me. Instead, I was forced to watch as Daysum was whipped in front of the Count's entire household. She had three lashes before I fell at the Count's feet, kissed his boots, and swore I'd never try to run again. I also signed a debt for an additional fifty thousand gold mun—to repay His Grace for his efforts in hunting me.

Silently, I swore on every star in the sky that he would feel each lash ten times over. I have spent a sickening amount of time planning how I will kill him. How I will bring him right to the brink of death and revive him as many times as I can. Days. Weeks. Sunsaes. How he'll beg for the mercy of the finality of death, but I'll keep reviving him with antidotes until I hit nineteen times. One for each girl who died in his poison school; one for Hana, who was murdered as a poison maiden; and one for Daysum. And then I will whip Seok to death for *me*.

"Maybe it would be better for you if I were dead," Daysum says quietly. I must've been staring at her scar.

I vigorously shake my head. "No. Don't say that."

I stare her down despite the fact that I've had the same thought in some dark and desperate moments. Especially the day she cried out from the lash. But I'd never admit it to Daysum.

My sister smiles. "Because it's true? If I were dead, they wouldn't have anything to hang over you. You'd be free."

My hand curls into a fist. "Who told you that?"

"My brain."

I sigh. "It's true that if you were dead, they wouldn't have leverage."

Daysum nods and turns to the side, facing a small waterfall. Her shoulders droop ever so slightly, like peonies after a quick rain. I gently turn her chin back to me.

"But I would have nothing to live for, either," I continue. "You are everything that matters to me in this life and the next."

She smiles, although her eyes still look sad. I've kept as much from her as I could over the years. But I've visited her while sick from poisons and shaking from the aftereffects. I couldn't hide that something was done to me. And she knows that her life is contingent on me paying off our debts. She's never asked how I do it, but I have a feeling she suspects. I was always stronger and healthier, but Daysum was smarter.

This isn't our normal style of visit. Usually, we laugh and joke and try to forget. Our lives are heavy; our conversations don't need to be. But this may be my last visit with her—for better or worse. So there are things I need to tell her.

"I have been offered our freedom," I say.

She's silent as she tilts her head and blinks. Her long lashes flutter. "Who offered this?"

"The Count."

She gasps, then clutches my hands. "The Count? And you're sure he's serious?"

"He doesn't joke about business."

She sits back on the bench, stunned. She laughs and smiles, and I wish I could return her joy—even for a moment. Before I can say a word, though, she turns grave. Her life is cloistered, but she knows everything good comes with strings for girls like us.

"Sora...you have to do something impossible, don't you?" Her doe eyes scan me. She reads people better than anyone I've met.

I nod. While I try to keep things hidden from Daysum, I don't lie to her. Not directly.

"And if you fail, it will be taken out on me?" It's a question, but she knows the answer so she says it like a statement.

"He'll sell your debt to Lord Sterling if I fail." I leave out the part where failing means I'll be tortured in Idle Prison or mercifully dead. "Do you want me to try to get our freedom?"

She shudders even though she tries not to. Then she straightens her posture, with her shoulders back. She swallows hard and nods.

Brave girl. I'm so proud of the woman she's become.

"Do you want to tell me what it is?" she asks. "What you have to do?"

I shake my head.

"Okay," she says.

And just like that, she won't ask any more questions. My mysteries have never bothered her—or at least she doesn't let it show if they do.

"I'll be gone for a while," I say. "You probably won't see me for a month or two."

"Sora, I normally don't see you for months at a time." She smiles sadly.

She's right. I see her after I have completed a kill. Ever since I tried to run, Daysum has been kept somewhere outside of Gain and moved often so we can't flee together. I suspect she's currently in his country estate in a town called Pastor, but I can't be sure. The Count only brings her to his villa to meet with me. And this will be the last time.

I take a breath. "It could be longer than a month or two."

What I'm really trying to tell her is that I might not make it back. Even if I can get the king alone and poison him somehow, I'll be killed before I leave the palace. He's not like the trusting noblemen I've murdered. He's the most protected man in Yusan, not to mention a god. The more I think about it, the more impossible it is for me to make it out alive. I just have to hope and pray to the Kingdom of Hells that he will die as well. That somehow Daysum will be free.

Her chin shakes as she nods.

"Little one, I promise that we will spend every day together soon," I say. I haven't called her that in years, but the nickname flows from my lips. I squeeze her hands.

Tears prick my eyes because I don't know if it's true. I don't know if it's a promise I can keep, but I can try. I will always try to see her again.

"I believe you," she says. She stands, takes a deep breath, and smooths out her ruffled dress. "Come on. Let's walk and not talk about any of this. Instead, tell me about all the handsome men you've met recently."

I laugh, and it's genuine. "Dot is very handsome."

"Dot… He's a cat, Sora." She frowns. "Come on. There must be someone of interest. The best-looking man in my life is Irad. You know that's not okay."

I smile and shake my head. "Definitely not. Sadly, I have no handsome suitors to report."

She arches an eyebrow, skeptical. But it's true. I have no interest in romance. Not since the Count killed my lover. Loving is just another thing that Seok can hold over me. It is a liability at its core.

We walk quietly for a while, just enjoying the nearness of each other. I still think she's breathing harder than she should, but she's in layers of heavy skirts, as is the current fashion, despite the heat of Gain.

"All right, then. What would you do if you were the queen of Yusan?" she asks.

We used to play this game all the time—imagine what we'd do if we were royal. The typical daydream of poor children throughout the realm.

"I'd free every indenture, then take us somewhere safe—just you and me," I say. "We'd have paid servants to feed us cherry-blossom ice and fan us with peacock feathers in the hot summer months. In the winter, we'd be wrapped in furs, sipping chocolate."

"After you kill the king," she says.

I trip forward slightly and catch myself. My heart pounds in my body-hugging dress. "Pardon?"

"You'd have to kill the king to free every indenture at once. In the end, they're all bound and taxed through the Baejkins."

It takes me a second to recover, and that's a second too long. Daysum's eyes narrow just a little.

"Well then, I suppose I'd make sure he died of natural causes." I smile. "Or however god kings die."

"Like the queen of Khitan?" she asks.

I turn my head and stare at Daysum.

"I overheard the Countess talking to the Count. The king of Khitan is dead, and the queen is ruling as regent for their young son. They say the king died of natural causes, but there are whispers that she killed him and wears the ring."

I smile. My little sister must've been listening at the walls. The Count would never discuss this kind of thing in front of her. But maybe the Countess is less careful. I rarely see her, and I doubt the married couple even likes each other. She stays away from Gain and travels with Daysum. My sister has said the Countess is firm but kind—I'm grateful for that.

"I didn't know you went in for royal gossip, Day," I tease.

"I keep my ears open." She shrugs with a half smile.

Then she stops and faces me, and I can see she wants to ask. She's heard enough of their whispers to have pieced together some or all of what I do. And this may be her last chance to ask—how, why, whom. Whatever is on her mind. I steel my spine and resolve that I'll answer anything.

Daysum looks away, and when she meets my eyes again, the question is gone. "I love you, Sora. No matter what. Through this life and the next."

My shoulders relax. "And I, you."

Irad appears on the expansive stone patio of the villa, scanning the garden for us. Somehow the bell is already up. I want to take her arm and run. I always want to. But this time, my muscles spasm, aching to run away.

"I will…" I begin, suddenly panicked. My heart wants to escape my chest. My knees knock. I don't know how to say goodbye to her. Not now. I didn't when she was six and was pulled from my arms. I just screamed her name until I had no voice left. But it's twelve years later. I am an adult. I should know what to say, how to tell her goodbye. Yet I don't.

"I will see you soon," she says.

It's what I always say to her. I exhale. She's so grown up. So steady and brave.

I try to shake off the dread pooling in my stomach as we embrace. But then she kisses my cheek and whispers something in my left ear. I think I hear her. I think she says, "Sora, I think it's time." But that doesn't match her expression. I want to ask, but guards have come to get her. She just smiles and waves goodbye.

I keep thinking about what she could mean by "it's time." Maybe it's because our bell was up, but we knew that already. Irad approaches, and I stop wondering. I put on my haughtiest face as I walk past, but I get a sinking feeling that I missed something vital.

CHAPTER TEN

EUYN

OUTSKIRTS OF TILE, FALLOW

There are too many ways to die.

That becomes evident as darkness descends on the road to Tile. It's past dusk and solidly night as we travel. We're going as fast as these miserable horse/camel half-breeds can take us, but it's not fast enough. They're not palace halibred stallions. They're not even the horses we rode out of Outton. They're hamels—what we could exchange our horses for with a wandering caravan. I'm quite certain we were cheated. Our horses were too exhausted to continue because of the heat, so we had little choice. I assume the nomads only had these beasts because no one else wanted them.

Mikail and I don't speak. We don't dare light a lantern. Tile is illuminated in the distance, so at least we know we're going in the right direction, and the moon and stars help light the path. But it's too dangerous to not be under cover this late, this far from a city center.

Every muscle in my body is tense as I try to scan the dark sky. Spotting a black bird in a dark-blue night isn't easy. I flinch at every noise, my pulse pounding in my neck. But despite feeling like I want to jump out of my skin, we're making progress—one miserable stride at a time. The lights grow closer until there's about a mile left.

We might just make it.

The moment I have the thought, a loud caw rings out somewhere south of us, sending my stomach into flips.

Samroc.

I shudder, my shoulders wobbling, and exchange glances with Mikail. He's silent—which means it's dire. I was right to panic.

I can't tell how close the samroc is, but with a thirty-foot wingspan, they can travel a mile with ease. Because of their size, someone long ago tried to domesticate them. The man thought that if he could ride a samroc, if he had a flying vessel, he'd be invincible. Legend has it he is the reason the birds developed their taste for human flesh. They devoured him and then came for the rest of his family. It's likely an exaggeration—the part about his family. The rest, I believe.

"Dismount," Mikail whispers.

"It'll be faster on a hamel," I say.

"Faster for a samroc to pluck you into the air, you mean?"

"No, I mean we could make it to Tile…"

Mikail sighs. "Do you want to continue to whisper, or would you like to help me save us?"

Samroc are rumored to have excellent hearing. If I weren't absolutely terrified right now, they'd be a great challenge to hunt. Something worthy of my skill.

As far as I'm aware, no one has been able to bring one down. Their feathers are longer than a man and rumored to be impervious to a weapon. They almost sound like pigars, who have hides so thick, arrows from a safe distance glance off them. They can be speared, though you have to risk your own body to do it. I assume samroc are the same, as nothing is truly impervious, but I've never wanted to find out.

I have my crossbow ready. A weapon may provide a false sense of security with an animal this large, but I was also the best shot in Yusan once upon a time. I know how to kill man and beast.

A caw rings out again. This time, it sounds more like a war cry. Mikail and I both turn to the noise. It's still to the southeast but much closer to where we stand.

Because it's coming for us.

I quickly dismount and run, holding the reins of this frustratingly slow beast. Mikail runs next to me.

My arms and legs pump, my stride so wide my lungs burn, but we'll never make it to the city. Not if a samroc is closing in already. Not dragging these hamels.

Gods on High, how are we faster than them?

We apparently come to the same realization and let go of the reins at the same time. Then we run on our own. We're only a few yards away from the beasts when an earsplitting screech rattles my skull. The desperate sound of my hamel disturbs the night, making my spine go rigid. The scream of braying and the smell of blood fill the air. Lots of it, hot against the cooling desert atmosphere. I hazard a glance back as I sprint.

It's a terrible scene. The samroc has grabbed hold of my mount, but it can't lift a full-grown hamel, so the animal fights for its life, its flesh tearing as it tries to get away. Bile rises in my throat. I turn and focus on the gates of Tile.

Mikail pulls me by the arm and starts running north off the road. I protest. There's nothing north. I want to at least try to make it to Tile, *try* to escape with our lives. Samroc stay away from city centers. And maybe there will be help farther down the road.

"Will you stop fighting me while I'm trying to save your ass?" he snaps. "There's a tunnel up ahead."

I squint, scanning the rocky outcrops. Then I spot the opening. It's so far away that I can barely see it. It's still a distance from us, but it's one hell of a lot closer than Tile.

We run like mad through the sand. I can only hope the bird is satisfied with the hamel. I still hear the beast braying—quieter, though, as it's being eaten alive. On top of that is the content cooing of the samroc digesting its meal.

It's the worst sound I've heard in my life. If I were a lesser man, I would've soiled myself.

The sand is loose and deep, flying in every direction. What I wouldn't give for hard-packed earth or even spongy grass. But we get closer. I can fully make out the tunnel opening now. It's maybe forty feet away.

Suddenly, the air changes. Wings descend on us with a whoosh of animal stink. A second samroc. Hells. I thought they were solo creatures. I was told they hunted alone.

Mikail lets out a cry, the sound sending razor-sharp blades along my veins. He falls forward, trying to get out of the way as a samroc grabs at him.

Gods on High, the smell. They have the worst odor of bird and blood. Like airborne death. And now one almost has ahold of Mikail. He's rolled away, but the bird has landed.

I lift my crossbow and steady myself. I pull the mechanism, take aim at the beast's heart, and I fire. I expect it to drop, to cry out.

Nothing.

My bolt bounces off the bird's chest. It did absolutely nothing.

I stare with my mouth open. The drunken tales I heard in the pubs of Outton were real—the feathers make a samroc impervious to weapons. But that's not possible. I'm fifteen feet away. My bolt should've gone right through.

Now I have the attention of the samroc as Mikail lays on the ground. He's moaning, hurt, but I blow out a relieved breath. He's still alive. At least for now. I want him to crawl away. I will him to move, to get to the entrance of the tunnel, but I don't know if he can make it on his own. Either way, I can try to distract the samroc and buy him time.

I back up another step and reload. Then I bring the bow to my shoulder again. I exhale, and then I shoot. This time, I hit the bird's neck. It's a clean shot that would've felled nearly any creature. But it still does nothing.

Disbelief and shock hit me in waves. I'm so close, yet the bolt falls harmlessly to the ground. The bird takes one step toward me. I lean back, but I don't run. I can't. I want its attention, even though I'm feeling very mortal at the moment.

But then Mikail moans and the bird cocks its head. The iridescent feathers on its neck shine in the moonlight, marking the plumage of a samroc mother. The male is fine with gorging himself on the beast I left behind, but she'll take Mikail back to her nest. Alive.

No.

My blood races through my veins like fire. I look around wildly for another weapon. A distraction. Anything.

Me. There's only me.

"Hey! Hey, you bastard!" I yell, wave my arms, jump up and down, even shoot the bird again. I aim at the folded wing, hoping the feathers are thinner at the joints. Again, nothing.

Mikail starts to crawl away. He's made it about six feet, but the bird takes a single step and closes the distance. Her beak opens.

No.

Desperate, I reload again even though my bolts won't do a thing. Despair fills me, the pit of my stomach turning with uselessness. I'm useless. The bird is armed to the teeth…well, to the beak. There's nowhere I can even affect her. I've tried every weak spot I can see. But wait—the eyes. Eyes are never armored. But I need to hit black eyes against black feathers at night, far above me. It's an impossible shot.

I wipe sweat from my brow with the back of my hand and take a steadying breath. I exhale. It's just me and my bow and my heartbeat. The gentle wind. The clear sky. And a monster. No, a target. I search for the moon's reflection in the samroc's eye. The second I locate it, I take aim and fire.

An earth-shattering sound follows. The cry reverberates through me, shaking my very bones. It's so loud, I drop to the ground and put my hands over my ears. The pain from the scream is incredible, intolerable. Finally, it ends, but my ears ring.

I look up. I did it! Hit the samroc right in the eye. The old thrill of the hunt runs through me. Victory. Success. But it's quickly replaced by dread—because the samroc is still very much alive. The bolt, even in the eye, didn't kill her. She's just pissed off. And I now have her *and* her mate's attention.

Gods on High.

I toss the crossbow and get to my feet. I scramble, sand flying all over. Mikail. I have to reach him. Each gut-wrenching foot feels like a mile, feels like it takes a year. Finally, I get to him and lift Mikail onto my back. He's really, really heavy. He's four inches taller and he has far more muscle than I do.

Still, I run with him on my back to the tunnel opening. It's so very far away. But I will my legs to move, to pump. Twenty feet to the opening. Ten feet. Five. The smells of the bird and death nip at my heels. But we're almost there.

Three.

Without any grace or valor, I toss Mikail in and then try to dive into the tunnel after him. The bird grabs the back of my shirt with her beak. The heat from her mouth and the stench are unbearable. She has me. Then I feel Mikail's arms around me. He pulls me to him, and my shirt rips. I'm free.

We roll, a mass of limbs, down the sloping entrance and come to a stop at a wall. The samroc tries to stick her head in, but she's too big. She can't reach us.

Frustrated, the bird screams, shaking the entire tunnel. We both cover our ears, but it's almost no use. The booming sound is only amplified by hollow space. My palms do nothing against the pain.

Finally, the noise ends and the bird blocks the stars with her remaining good eye, staring in at us. It's a terrible sight that sends shivers along my skin. I have an eerie feeling she will remember me. That the legend I heard of the birds tracking down the man's entire family were true.

CHAPTER ELEVEN

MIKAIL
THE TUNNELS, FALLOW

You know, all things considered, I don't think I'm a fan of samroc.

I'm on my side in the sandy cave, bleeding and broken. Euyn's body is next to mine, and he's breathing hard.

Euyn saved me. He risked his own life to distract the samroc so I could try to escape, and then he carried me when I couldn't walk.

Never underestimate a person's ability to surprise you.

I can say with absolute certainty that the prince I knew never would've given his life for mine. But Euyn offered it to the gods tonight. And here we are.

I'm not sure how many times I'm going to cheat death. I hope it's more times than I have already, but I must be at seven or eight at this point. Eventually Lord Yama, the King of Hells, will win. But not tonight.

"Mikail, Mikail, are you okay?" Euyn asks. His voice has a desperation, an urgency I've never heard before. Being banished to Fallow and almost getting killed several times has truly changed him.

Who knew that's all it would take?

"I'm dandy," I say. My voice sounds hoarse. It has to be the desert dust or the near-death experience. Okay, maybe it's both.

I can almost feel his frown. Euyn doesn't like me making light of this. But we were almost bird food, and now I'm bleeding to death in a dark tunnel that, for all we know, is an animal's den. It's nothing to laugh about, which is exactly why you need to.

"How are you really?" he asks.

"Extremely worried that these claw marks may lessen my overall beauty," I say.

I move to get to my feet, and *stars* that's not a great feeling.

"Wait, don't stand," he says.

He's right to worry. I'm woozy and in so much pain that I don't feel it. My back is soaked to the point that it feels like rain is falling, but I know it's not. It's just my own warm blood. So that's rather disconcerting. But I've been through worse and survived it. I'll make it through this, too.

I draw my sword. It feels heavy as all Ten Hells, but the blade flames reliably and illuminates the space. There is a whole cavern here. Something, or someone, made this. Makes sense with those beasts hunting from the air. But I hope there's nothing else down here. I'm not in the mood to fight even a tiny moon owl right now.

I shiver. Being pursued for meat was…not pleasant.

Luckily, Euyn is in better shape than I am. He scrambles to the torch on the wall and uses my sword to light it before the flame goes out. The poisoned oil in the scabbard makes the sword flame for about sixty seconds before it extinguishes itself—the scabbard is the trick to the whole thing, unlike the real Flaming Sword of the Dragon Lord.

I'm glad to not have to hold the weight of the blade, since my arm has started to shake. It's a good sign, though, that I can move my limbs at all.

Now that the cavern is lit, I can look around. Even as lawless as Fallow is, people have left torches and jugs of water in the tunnel so that strangers may live. It's a thankless kindness. And, therefore, the best kind.

I'm staring at the water pots when I fall to my knees. Too much blood lost. The cavern is spinning like a top.

"Mikail!" Euyn cries.

I watch from the floor as he rifles through my cross-body bag and finds my apothecary kit. Every soldier has one. Laoli for pain, tourniquets, bandages, a vile of spirits to disinfect wounds, and most importantly at the moment, needle and thread to stitch together torn-up skin. I'm kidding, of course. Laoli is most important.

Euyn gives me the drug pouch. It's a serious painkiller derived from the charm plant that only grows on Gaya. My hands shake, I'm so eager for the relief of the drug. I normally stay away from the stuff, but this is not the moment for principles. There are very few moments when principles come in handy, really.

After I suck on the powder, I try to relax. I crush the velvet pouch in my hand.

"That's better," I say.

Euyn waits a few minutes for it to kick in, pacing in a very worried fashion. He's frightened for me, but he also startles and flinches at every little noise. I see his neurotic paranoia survived banishment. Now that I've gotten a better look at it, the cavern is nearly sealed. Anything small enough to go through the holes isn't big enough to be a threat, and anything trying to squeeze through would be at our mercy. We're fine here.

Probably.

"Are you ready?" he asks.

"As I'll ever be," I say.

"No, I mean has it kicked in?" Euyn examines me even though he's no healer.

"Null," I say. In this case, it means I feel no pain. It isn't true, of course. I have an ungodly tolerance to laoli, but Euyn believes me. He tends to believe my lies.

The prince tears off my shirt and then pours most of a water jug over my wounds to clean them out. To say it's unpleasant is putting it mildly. My fingers grip the dirt, leaving claw marks like an animal fighting for its life. But the laoli in my system *does* begin to take the edge off. I would just require a lot more than one pouch for the relief I really need.

The charm plant is such a blessing and a curse. The power to relieve pain is undoubtedly a gift from the gods, but it ultimately doomed my homeland. Because of the charm plant, Gaya was colonized. And because charm refuses to grow outside of Gaya, Yusan will never let the island go. And because of *that*, there's poverty and violence all through Gaya and beyond.

But the plant's pollen just causes a mild high. It was distilling and fermenting that created laoli—the pain-relieving, addictive drug. Production of laoli fills the royal coffers, so they have no interest in keeping it in check. In fact, King Joon encourages it. Laoli is in soldiers' kits for a reason.

Of course, Euyn doesn't know that I'm Gayan. Or that his brother slaughtered my family when he put down the island's rebellion nineteen years ago. He thinks I'm from Yusan, just like him. No one knows who I really am because I've lied my entire life—to Euyn most of all. At times I wonder if he'd love me the same if he knew the truth, but there are questions best left unasked.

Euyn gets to work pouring alcohol on my wounds, lighting the needle on fire to keep it clean, and then he stitches and mends all the damage from the samroc.

"Am I still as handsome as a demon?" I say to break up the silence.

"More," he says. Then he clears his throat and gets back to stitching.

Ah, so he still hasn't forgiven me.

Euyn's problem isn't that he doesn't trust me. Quite frankly, he shouldn't. His issue is that he resents me because he is a dreamy romantic at heart. The handsome, youngest son of the old king, Euyn was coddled and spoiled. He expected love to be like storybooks, like the royal plays.

Although I doubt he'd admit it, Euyn expected me to storm Idle Prison—the political dungeon under a monster-filled lake, literally the most secure place in all of Yusan—and rescue him. And when I didn't, it meant that I didn't love him.

I'm just not sure what good he expected to come out of both of us being dead. Sometimes revenge is a long game and, as much as you want a small win now, the larger victory needs time to manifest.

I am a man of few virtues, but patience is one of them.

Soon, Euyn is done and I'm good as new. That's a lie, of course. I'm wrapped in bandages with dozens of stitches, but I don't think I'll bleed out. With the laoli making me comfortable, I'll call it a win.

I used to run through the charm fields as a kid, which built up tolerance to the pollen, but I haven't had any in so long that it does actually work. Laoli will drive you mad after enough use, but I'm not worried about that. I doubt I'll live long enough for it to matter.

"Is it worth going out and checking for our things?" Euyn asks. He looks to the tunnel opening.

I wait for him to laugh, but it appears he's serious. That's curious. The youngest prince of Yusan would never have cared about some weapons, a frying pan, and old clothing, but Euyn does now. Deeply. I have to say, I like this new version better than the old. Even if he's being completely unreasonable at the moment.

"You want to go another round with a samroc?" I ask. He shivers, eyes wild. "Wait until daybreak."

"What do we do until then?" he asks.

"Play tuhko," I say. He cocks his head. Apparently Euyn still struggles with a sense of humor when he's stressed. "Sleep, Euyn. We sleep."

"You sleep," he says. "I… I'll keep watch."

Somewhere during his banishment, Euyn learned how to truly care for another person. He continues to surprise me. It's one of the things I love about him.

Of course, the last thing I wanted to do was love him. And as attracted as I was to him, he was such a brat in the palace. I never thought I was in any danger of falling for him. But love has a funny way of sneaking up on you. It went from a purely physical attraction to him worming his way into my heart. I loved studying him and yet not being able to predict his reaction. When he'd surprise me by being thoughtful or kind or sensitive, I'd fall for him a bit. The next thing I knew, I loved him. It didn't even bother me that he was also a cruel man, because in the end, aren't we all?

He sits near me with his legs out. "Put your head on my lap."

I arch an eyebrow. "I've heard that one before."

He rolls his eyes. "It will be more comfortable for you. You shouldn't sleep with your ear to the dirt."

With his help, I put my head on his legs. He's right—it's more comfortable.

I'm on my stomach, but I look up at him. "I missed you, you know."

He side-eyes me but can't resist running his hand through my hair. "Get some rest."

Euyn quickly removes his hand like he can't afford to get closer to me. He thinks I'm the villain of our story. That I'll betray him simply because I have before. Because I lie as easily as I breathe. And that all seems like terribly unfair character assassination to me.

Accurate as it may be.

But between Euyn and the laoli in my system, I fall asleep, bandaged and surviving the night. For now, we've saved each other. Tomorrow, we may stab each other in the back.

Hard to say.

CHAPTER TWELVE

ROYO
CITY OF UMBRIA, YUSAN

The diamond Aeri left on the table checked out.

I couldn't get to sleep last night, so right at dawn I brought it to a reliable guy in the gem district. He assured me it was worth fifty thousand mun. And then he offered me forty. Prick. I reluctantly gave it back to Aeri when I met her at the Black Shoe Inn a bell ago. Turns out it ain't easy to hand off a fortune. But I believed her when she said she'd steal it back. And maybe I was curious about her.

When I said yes to taking her to Tamneki, Aeri ran into my arms, her willowy body clinging to mine like a vine against a brick wall. It felt... Doesn't matter. I pushed her away, because who does that? But she still jumped up and down. Happy. Smiling. Bubbly. There's something wrong with her. No one is bubbly in Umbria.

"It's so good that you're early," she said. "I have some *things* I could use your help with."

I put my hand by my blade, ready, but then I saw she had five trunks waiting in the lobby. Five. Each the size of a man. And she needed my help carrying them.

I'm underpaid for this job.

But here we are, in a carriage on the way to Succession Point.

That's the port where the fancy riverboats load. The port's not far—it's on the southernmost end of Umbria, maybe a fifteen- or twenty-minute walk—but we didn't have the option to walk because of all of Aeri's shit.

It's not often I'm in a carriage, especially not a private one. The velvet seats are pretty plush, although they're a little springy.

Occasionally, a merchant wants to meet in a coach so he doesn't have the risk of being seen with me, but it's rare. I've never been in one just for the hells of it. Then again, nothing that's happened since meeting Aeri has been normal.

My jobs usually come from cloaked men constantly looking over their shoulders, not girls in slinky blue dresses inviting me to tea at midnight.

And I guess it's worth it to say that she *is* pretty. Along with being super strange and way too friendly. I'm looking around the coach when I accidentally make eye contact with her.

"Do you have any pets?" she asks.

What? "Why?"

She shrugs. "For companionship, I guess. I don't know." She taps a finger to her lips. Her mouth is small, with a big, pillowy lower lip. Her eyes tip up at the corners. They're beautiful. Not that it matters. It's just that Yuri was right about her.

"Mice, if it's a cat?" she adds. "Or guarding, if it's a dog, maybe?"

"No, why are you asking?" I cross my arms over my chest and lean back.

"Oh, I was just wondering." She folds her hands on her lap, but she can't sit still, so she runs her palms along her cream-colored dress. I try not to watch her hands, but I fail. Like yesterday, the dress is form-fitting. It's short and shows off her legs again, but it has a high neck. I guess that's the fashion where she's from. I don't hate it.

"I don't have a pet," I say. More like grunt.

"I don't have one, either." She stares dreamily out the window. "But I'd have one if I could. Probably two dogs and a cat. Maybe two cats, like in addition to the dogs. If I had a permanent home, you know? Maybe once this job is done."

We're traveling alone in this coach, so now seems as good a time as any to ask.

I sit forward, resting my elbows on my knees. "So let me get this straight. The plan is for you to cross Idle Lake uninvited, which would mean swimming for it and somehow surviving the iku in the water, then getting past the thousand guards of Qali Palace, finding the king, taking his crown off...and *walking out?*"

I resolved not to care as I counted my gold a second time last night. Unable to sleep, I counted all of it. More than fifty thousand pieces. But as I counted, I forced myself not to care about her or whatever job she has to do. I won't. I get my fifty thousand either way, and that is exactly what I need. But she offered to give me twice that if she succeeds, and the shot at a hundred thousand makes me need to know my odds. A hundred thousand would clear my debts *and* change my fate.

Aeri shakes her head. "No, no, the palace won't work."

"Then where?" I ask.

After the assassination attempt in Umbria, the king stopped leaving the palace. I guess even if the crown does make him immortal, he still feels pain. Not dying is a hell of a difference from being a god. So he mostly stays in Qali Palace, where he's impossible to get to. It's good she's not thinking about going there. But if not the palace, then where?

Aeri shrugs. "I'm not sure."

I rake my fingers down my face.

"I *will* know," she rushes on. "I just don't know *yet*. When we meet the spymaster, he'll tell us."

"We're meeting the royal spymaster?" My eyebrows rise so fast, it hurts my eyes. This is new information.

She blinks at me. "Yes. This is his plan. I'm just one girl—I can't kill a king."

I try to come up with something to say back, but it's the smartest thing she's said so far. Still, it feels dangerous to have other people know what we're up to, especially a trusted spy for the throne. What if this is a trap?

"Are there other people in on this?" I ask.

"I dunno," she says with a shrug.

Once again, she's back to sounding like a street girl. I noticed it last night—how she flipped between seeming like a shy lady and sounding like a cocky street thief and back again. Something about her is wrong, but for a hundred thousand I can overlook a lot.

"Seems like it'll take more than just two people to kill a king," she adds. "But you'll have to ask him."

"What if the spymaster betrays you?" I ask.

She tilts her head. "That's what you're here for."

A guttural sound escapes my throat, and I ball my hands into fists. Murdering the royal spymaster, which is near impossible, would mean a life hunted, on the run. But I guess that's why she's paying so much. Still, I don't like being blindsided.

I shake my head. "You didn't think to ask any questions after being offered half a million mun for one job?"

She meets my stare dead-on. "How many questions did *you* ask?"

I shut my mouth. I can't say nothing to that. A creeping sensation goes up my back. A hint of respect. I'm almost impressed by her boldness—that she's not afraid of me. That she caught me not asking enough questions. But before I can say anything, the carriage stops. We've made it the short ride to Succession Point.

"I've always wanted to ride on a riverboat! This will be fun," she says.

She winks at me, and I stare while my jaw drops open.

I just... What?

Aeri hops down from the carriage, ignoring the driver who offered his hand. He gives me a confused look. I shut my mouth and shrug as I step out of the carriage, too. I'm getting paid a fortune to protect her. A stolen fortune, but whatever. And I...I want to follow her. Just to figure her out. Nothing else.

Aeri effortlessly weaves through the crowd, so it's hard to stay on her tail. She weaves in and out of people like she's made of water. I try to mirror her footsteps, but I bump into people every three feet, even knock a couple down. They're annoyed, but when they look up at me, they murmur apologies and hurry away.

I find a porter and direct him to take the trunks to our room... because apparently *we* have a room. She's already told me that I need to sleep in the same space as her because it's when she's most vulnerable. She's not wrong—but sleeping in the same room is something I've never done with a woman. Ever.

And I'll have to do it for a week. That's how long it'll take to travel the Sol to Rahway—longer if we hit weather. The river takes us west of where we need to go, but it's faster than by land.

"Hi! I'm Aeri. What's your name?" she asks as we cross the plank onto the ship.

The ticket guy furrows his brow at her, then looks her up and down. He opens his mouth to say something, but then he notices me and shuts his trap. Good. He takes her tickets, then waves over another man. An old guy in a porter jacket bows to us and escorts us to a room above deck.

He unlocks the door, and I can't help it. I gawk—at the room. The suite is bigger than my house and swank, with a damask couch, a bed, a desk, a dining table, and a washroom. There are paintings on the walls, and the guy says he'll be our servant for the trip. Aeri gives him a couple of silver mun for doing nothing, and he leaves with way too many bows.

Aeri flops back onto the bed. "This is more like it!"

I don't look at her on the bed…much. I study the room and check the doors. It's good there's a couch I can sleep on. I press on the cushions. It'll work, and it's a lot better than the floor.

There's a small, private balcony off the room. I step outside and survey the boat and people getting on board. There are only eight rooms like this on the ship, plus the captain's quarters. Everybody else will sleep in hammocks and bunks below deck. This room had to have cost a hundred gold mun. Maybe more.

The girl is pretty careless about money, but if she can steal fifty-thousand-mun diamonds, I guess she can spring for a nice room. Still, I can't figure it out. Why does the royal spymaster need her? Yeah, she's a better pickpocket than I've seen, but it don't add up.

I shouldn't have agreed to this whole thing so easily. But it was the money. Just the money. It wasn't her smile or her saying she liked me or nothing. I'd take a job from the King of Hells himself for a hundred thousand.

I grip the railing and sigh at myself. A part of me says to run. To not leave Umbria. Tamneki is too dangerous a place to not know what you're in for, and I can't trust this girl.

But when I come back to town I'll have fifty thousand gold pieces to add to the fifty thousand I cashed in for gold bars. They're in the bag on my back. One hundred thousand guaranteed in less than ten years is a miracle for a guy like me, and just enough—if I can give it to Savio in time.

All too soon, the ropes are untied and the bridge is pulled up. We push away from the dock, and the crewmen run around unfurling enormous white sails. The fabric billows as they catch wind and we're dragged out of the port. Then we drift away on the muddy brown water.

As the city fades in the distance, I get a feeling this is the last time I'll ever see Umbria. I shake it off and go inside.

CHAPTER THIRTEEN

SORA
CITY OF GAIN, YUSAN

What does one wear to kill an immortal king?

I stand before my wardrobe, tapping a finger to my chin. Then I pack my trunk full of my best dresses and veils, marveling at the assemblage of silk, satin, and tulle, and last, I carefully fold in my fastest-acting poisons. Sweet poison for desserts and wine, tasteless and odorless poison for food, and then my best poisoned lipsticks. I pick the most toxic and exotic ones, ones that don't have a known antidote, but I have to assume they have antidotes to all poisons somewhere in the palace. I'll have to get the king alone, preferably outside of Qali, in order to have even a glimmer of a chance of making it out alive.

The trunk is still open, but I sit on the bed and put my head in my hands. This is hopeless. I just have to be willing to accept that I won't survive. I won't see Daysum again. But Daysum will be free. I just wish I could figure out what she whispered before she left.

Dot jumps up in my lap. He nuzzles my face as I kiss and hold him. I've hired Gli to look after him while I'm gone. It'll give her some mun, and Dot will have company. I hope that she'll continue to care for him after I die, but nothing is promised in this world.

I lock the poisons that won't be needed into a chest and put it on top of my wardrobe in case Gli is the curious type. I worry for a second about leaving so much poison here, but I'm sure the Count will clear out the cottage once I leave. After all, everything belongs to him.

There is a knock on my door at exactly noon. Tiyung. I make a face at Dot and snuggle him goodbye. I know he'll be okay—he's a survivor. I'm not sure about me.

I open the door, and there stands the Count's only son. He's six feet tall with black hair and the same nose and arrogant air as the Count. But he has blue eyes like his mother, lighter brown skin than the Count, and a softer face. He's a year older than me at twenty-two, and his handsomeness masks his cruelty.

"Have your man take my trunk," I say.

"Hello to you, too, Sora," Tiyung says.

I take a steadying breath. I really could kill him without violating my agreement with the Count, but I'm sure Seok would come up with a fitting punishment for destroying his empire.

In Yusan, only sons can inherit land and title. Should a noble die without issue, everything goes back to the king's treasury. Madame Iseul taught us that—how we were lucky to be purchased from our families because we would've been worthless as peasant girls.

She told us a lot of pretty lies.

"Are we leaving today, or are you just going to continue to stare at me?" I raise one brow, hand on my hip.

He shakes off his stupor. "Right. This way."

His footman opens the door to the coach and then goes to retrieve my trunk. I take one last look at the cottage that's been my sanctuary for the past three years. As close to a home as I've had as an adult. Then I wave to Madame Balam, my neighbor, who stares from her window. My nosy neighbors believe I am the Count's whore. They're not far off.

Tiyung offers his hand to help me into the varnished midnight-blue coach. I ignore it. I don't want to touch him. Ever. I climb in and sit facing forward, making Tiyung travel backward. But as I sit down, I realize we're not alone, and I startle. There's a man passed out in front of me, and it reeks of alcohol and perfume in here.

Tiyung gets in facing me and follows my line of sight.

"Long night in the pleasure district," he says, gesturing to the man.

I curl my lip. I can't contain my disgust at noblemen's sons who use indentures for their own pleasure. They have everything, but they need to take bits and pieces from people who can't say no. Boys and girls like Daysum who could be sold to pleasure houses.

But then I remember it'll never be Daysum. Not if I have any say in it.

"I was visiting with my uncle this morning, and I found Duri in a chaise, passed out drunk," Tiyung says. "I'm just seeing him home safely."

"Yes, it would be so unfortunate if someone took advantage of another vulnerable human being."

"Like poisoning an unsuspecting man, I know," he says.

I stare at him and then look out the window. It really is a shame that I can't kill him.

We ride out of Gain and then up to a villa. It's not nearly as grand as the Count's estate, but it's clearly noble. The carriage stops under the portico of the house. Tiyung kicks his friend awake. He uses so much force I wince, certain it'll bruise.

"Get up. You're home," he says.

Duri slowly comes to, blinking, then stares at me like he's been given a fantastic gift.

"Hello there, doll," he says, sitting up. His brown hair is sloppy, and his bloodshot eyes look me up and down.

"She belongs to my father," Tiyung says. "And we need to be on our way."

Duri rubs his red eyes. His white shirt is half untucked, pale against his dark-brown skin. I assume he had a jacket, but it's been lost.

"Huh?" he says.

"Get out," Tiyung says. He stares coldly, and I cringe. He looks just like the Count.

Duri puts his hands up. "Thanks for the ride."

"Conduct yourself with more honor," Tiyung says. "You don't want it getting back to Lord Kang."

I assume that's his father because the threat is so clear. Duri sobers and bows his head. "Tiyung-si."

The "si" is added to noble names as a show of respect. It's almost never deserved.

Duri stumbles out of the carriage, and we take off.

"A lord," Tiyung mutters.

"Nice friend you have there," I say.

"He's not my friend. He's just another nobleman."

Tiyung takes his jacket off and rests it on the now-empty seat. I'm surprised by how much his body has changed. Every male in Yusan has to serve in the military for two years. Tiyung only recently returned, and he's much more of a man than the boy who left. Like the Count, I'm sure many people find Tiyung attractive, but I know the worm he really is.

"If he's not your friend, then why care about him being drunk in your uncle's pleasure house?" I ask.

"Because now he'll be in my debt for my discreetly bringing him home. I don't have real friends, Sora. Friendship requires trust."

"I had real friends once," I say. In my northern village, then in the poison school. "Your father did away with them."

Tiyung leans forward, resting his elbows on his legs. "I'm not sure why you think it's different for me. Being home is a reminder."

An intensity flashes in his blue eyes, and then it's gone, replaced by his normal indolent expression. There was something about the way he said it, though—something that makes me understand him. Then I realize I'm looking too far into him. I should stop expecting hidden depth out of a puddle.

"We should avoid Use on the way to Tamneki," I say, staring out the window.

"Why?"

I gesture with my hands out. Of course Tiyung knows I'm a poison maiden. He knows I'm owned by his father, as is Daysum, and that I kill for the Count. But he doesn't know the details. And he doesn't care to know.

"Business in Use?" he asks.

I stare at him.

"Doesn't matter," he says, waving his hand. "We're not going east. We're going north."

Gain and Tamneki are both situated on the curving coastline of Yusan. Gain is on the West Sea, Tamneki is a bit north on the East, and Leep is a straight shot between them.

"Leep, then?" I ask.

"Rahway."

I tilt my head, wondering if I heard him correctly. He couldn't have said Rahway.

"Rahway?" I repeat.

He nods.

Both Rahway and Leep are north of Gain, but Rahway lies a sunsae west of Tamneki. I have no idea why we're going there. It makes no sense.

"Father directed us to go there and await further instructions," he says.

Of course he did. I shift in my seat. I don't like it. I don't like the plans being switched up without anyone telling me. I already have to figure out how to kill a god king. I don't need more riddles.

"Why?" I ask.

"Sora, you of all people know my father doesn't share his motivations. We are expected to follow and obey."

"You act like you don't have a choice," I say.

"I have less than you think." He smiles at me, and something in his face makes me believe him. The pain in his eyes, I suppose.

Conversation drops when I remember I shouldn't empathize with Tiyung. I hate that he pretends to be charming or friendly or tries to relate to me in any form. I hate that I come close to falling for it because he has nice shoulders and a square jaw. Or maybe because I want a friend so badly.

But he can never be a friend. I lost everything because the Count wanted to increase Tiyung's wealth, his inheritance. And it was Tiyung who grabbed my arm and dragged me back through the Xingchi forest as I begged to be let go. As I told him how his father had purchased twenty girls, twenty, and poisoned them and sold off their brothers or sisters to the brothels when they died. How I was one of the few survivors. I hate how unmoved he was. How he said nothing, forever pushing forward until we returned to Gain.

Still, I know that we each have to obey orders. I could forgive him for all of that, for just doing his father's bidding. It's what Tiyung did when we got to the Count's villa that will forever make me hate him.

He was the one who whipped Daysum. The one who said, "Is that all?" when the Count told him to stop.

And then I resolve: once Daysum is free, I *will* kill Tiyung and send his head in a basket to the Count.

CHAPTER FOURTEEN

EUYN

TOWN OF TILE, FALLOW

It's well into the afternoon when I wake up at the Boat Inn in Tile. I slept dreamlessly, so exhausted that I dropped into the bed and passed out immediately. But I suspect I'll have nightmares about the samroc for years—assuming I live for years. It doesn't seem like I'll have to worry about a long life at the rate we're going.

The room is nautical-themed. I suppose the innkeeper is unbothered by the fact that we couldn't be farther from water. I glance over, expecting to see Mikail passed out on the other bed, but it's empty, the bed made. Startled, I sit up and look around.

Where is Mikail? Did something happen to him? Was he taken? Or worse, did he leave me again?

My heart pounds, but I exhale when I find him sitting on the couch by the table. He smiles when our eyes meet, and suddenly I remember how the samroc grabbed at him. I didn't have time to process it all as it was happening, but I could've lost him forever. And while I wasn't sure how I'd ever see him again, a part of me always knew I would. Knew our story wasn't finished yet. But a beast in the night almost ended it. If he hadn't had his soldiers' kit, if his reflexes weren't unnatural, if I weren't such a good shot, if I'd been a step slower, a little weaker, he could've bled out or been carried off. And then what would this life mean?

Nothing. It would mean nothing without him.

Gods on High, I still love him. As much as I ever did. Maybe a little more. I groan to myself. Only I, the greatest hunter in Yusan, would fall permanently in love with the man who can never be captured, who can never really belong to anyone.

What a fate.

"Good day, sunshine," he says. "I found some lunch, some fresh bandages, and best of all: more laoli." He shakes two velvet drug pouches in the air.

Laoli is extremely addictive. I asked Joon about why it was in our soldiers' kits when I was fifteen, and all he said was: "Go hunt your game, Euyn—leave the country to me." And then I overheard him say to our sister that I would be dangerous if I ever had a thought in my head aside from whom to bed next. She laughed like it was a fantastic joke. Hypocrites.

I should say my half brother and half sister. My mother was the king's second wife—the one he married after the death of the Great Queen. It is why I am twenty years younger than Joon. And why Joon and Quilimar have never respected me.

The king already had an heir in Joon and a spare in Omin before I came along. I was just excess, and my siblings made me painfully aware of it.

After that… I don't know. If I was only going to be seen as a lazy playboy prince, then why strive to be anything else? Why care about anything?

Then along came Mikail.

"Careful with that," I say, eyeing the drug pouch.

"With lunch? I happen to be a lunch expert," Mikail says. He smiles, but it's not totally genuine. He must be in a terrible amount of pain. I stitched him as cleanly as possible, but I'm not a professional healer and I was working by torchlight.

"But technically, it *is* dinnertime," he adds.

I look at the clock. Gods on High, it's five bells.

I kept watch all night, nearly waking Mikail a couple of times after I heard sounds echo in the tunnels connected to the cavern. But although I waited with my breath held and his sword gripped in my hand, no one approached, so I let him sleep.

At dawn, I was able to track down his hamel. It had somehow come out of the samroc attack unscathed. I wanted to kiss it as I grabbed ahold of its reins. All of Mikail's things and half of mine were salvaged, plus I found my crossbow buried in the sand. But all that was left of the other hamel was a carcass. It was being picked apart by desert vultures when I left the tunnel. I chased them away, looking like a madman yelling at birds. But everything I had in my saddlebags was too blood-soaked to be usable. I had to leave it behind.

Mikail woke when I came back into the tunnel, but he was in so much pain that he could barely move.

"The hangover is worse," he said through gritted teeth.

My chest twisted in sympathy, and then I leaned down to help him.

With a great amount of effort, I was able to move him out of the tunnel, but getting him onto the half-breed was another matter. Eventually, I slung him over the saddle and walked the beast to Tile. The first stop was an apothecary to get him more laoli. I couldn't stand seeing him in pain, but the drug worked. Apparently, he went and picked up more while I was asleep. Two more. I'd worry about his usage, but Mikail would never let a substance get the better of him.

I sit down and realize I'm famished. We haven't eaten since before we left Outton. Mikail eats with the same ravenous hunger I remember. But now it feels like we're racing to clear the table.

"Did you actually just finish that custard bun, the salt potatoes, *and* the ostrich steak?" he asks.

I smile sheepishly. "I was hungry."

Food was one of the many things I took for granted in the palace. And whatever Mikail found for lunch is far better than the travelers' inn I called home for the last three years.

He studies me and then nods. "I like that."

We're sitting so close that our legs touch. I'm in an undershirt and rough spun pants. He's in a loose shirt and trousers. This is the kind of life I imagined for us while I was in Outton—minus the attack from samroc who'd tried to eat us. I'd daydreamed so often about a casual existence with Mikail. I thought we'd stand a chance at being happy. As it stands... I don't know.

I think about him drugged and bloody, telling me he missed me. It sends aftershocks across my chest that gather in the pit of my stomach. And then I want him all over again. Even after all this time. Even though he agreed I should die.

Wow, I need better standards for the men I fall in love with.

Mikail claps his hands clean after wiping his mouth. "So do you want to get the crumbs off the plate first and then hear the bad news, or are you ready now?"

I look down. I have completely cleared my plate.

"I'll refrain from licking it," I say.

He raises an eyebrow. "Don't ever let me stop you from using your tongue."

I choke on my water as heat rushes to my face.

He raises both brows. "You know, you're awfully prudish for a man who bedded half the palace."

He's exaggerating. Slightly.

"Don't you have some bad news you need to tell me?" I ask. I wish I hadn't just thought of the many times I've used my tongue on him.

He smirks, pushes aside some dishes, and unfurls a map. It's a miniature of one that hangs in the palace library. No doubt he secretly made a copy. Mikail is a talented artist. I admire his hand while listening.

"We're at least another two days out from the border, but we need to pick a location to sneak across," he says. "That will determine our trajectory, since, as you've seen, we have limited bird-free travel time. The only part of the border that's not regularly patrolled is the Tangun Mountains."

"Okay, so we'll go through there. There has to be a pass," I say.

"There is, but we can't be sure there aren't samroc nests in the mountains."

I pinch the bridge of my nose and try not to shudder. I never want to smell those beasts or hear those cries again. "So we'll cross during the daytime."

Mikail grimaces. "The shortest mountain pass will take fifteen bells by donkey. Longer on foot."

"And stallion?"

He shakes his head. "The ground is too rocky for stallions."

I know what he's getting at, but I don't want to acknowledge the truth. I stare at the table, wishing there were more warm custard buns. "And how many bells of daylight are there?"

"Twelve. There are twelve, Euyn."

I close my eyes slowly, remembering the samroc I hit. The way she looked at us in the tunnel. They'll come for us. I can feel it.

I rub my beard. "Is there any good news?"

"Yes. There is a Fallow city called Lark right at the foot of the Tangun Mountains, so we can leave for the pass right at dawn on the day we pick to cross. That would put us in danger for less than three bells. And after we're in Yusan, we'll head to Rahway to meet a girl who can help with our little endeavor."

I wrinkle my nose. "A girl?"

"Yes, the gods make those, too."

"Wouldn't a man…"

He raises his eyebrows. "I see you inherited your brother's disdain for the female sex. Surprising, given how many shared your bed."

I purse my lips. I suppose he's right. Joon doesn't think much of girls. He even sold Quilimar to broker peace with the king of Khitan five years ago. She wasn't pleased, but she had no choice. Women cannot inherit in Yusan. Once our father died, she was at Joon's mercy. And he's not known for mercy.

"This girl has skills I've never seen," Mikail says.

That does give me pause. Mikail has seen everything. But still, it doesn't seem like we'll need a girl's help in killing my brother. What could she possibly have to offer?

"I don't know…" I murmur.

"You don't have to trust me in matters of the heart," he says. "But do respect my ability to scheme." He stands up carefully, grimacing.

I reach for him, and my hand encircles his wrist. I hate seeing him in pain. I'd battle the God of Health to end it. Mikail glances down at my fingers. It had felt so natural to touch him that I didn't think twice. I drop my hand.

"Now, if you'll do me the favor of changing my dressing and applying the salve to my wounds, I'm going to drug myself into tomorrow morning," he says.

I nod.

He removes his shirt, and I try not to stare. But his muscles and lines down his stomach are worthy of my attention. Even bandaged, he's still unreasonably attractive. I remember tasting the salt of his skin, every second of exploring each other's bodies until we learned the expert touches that made the other shake with pleasure. How eager we were. How innocent. And then how experienced we became. How there was never anyone I wanted in my bed more than Mikail.

He reaches down and slowly runs his thumb over my bottom lip. It sends sparks right to the base of my spine.

"You look hungry, Euyn," he says. "Should I seek out more food first? Or perhaps you'd like something else?"

I sigh and get up to find the salve.

Of all the men I could've loved, the gods cursed me with this one.

CHAPTER FIFTEEN

ROYO
THE SOL RIVER, YUSAN

I have a headache, and she's sitting across from me.

Aeri ordered room service for a late lunch. Fine steaks, crisp bok choy, a half chicken, and salt potatoes from the Tangun Mountains arrived on silver-coated platters. I'm in a swank room and there's a pretty girl across from me, but she won't stop talking. I would never push her overboard (despite maybe thinking about the splash she'd make), but I can't say I'd dive in after her if she fell, neither.

All right, I would. But for the mun. Only for the mun.

We've been on this boat since yesterday afternoon, and she got bored by about nine bells last night. I have not known peace since. She is the most insistent, irritating person I've ever met. We've taken more strolls than I can count along the deck, and she's read a book and insisted I read some passages, but mostly she's amused herself by talking.

"So, I don't know, I kind of think Gayan chocolate is better than water ice," she says. "Although in the summer nothing beats water ice, no matter how pricey. So maybe it depends on the seasons."

I didn't ask. Really. Didn't ask a single question.

I grunt and chew my steak. We eat in silence for a blessed minute. She's in another high-necked dress. This one is yellow with puffy sleeves, but it fully shows off her long legs. Not that I'm looking.

"Anyhow, who is Lora?" she asks.

The name pierces the quiet. I drop my steak knife, and it clatters onto my plate. I reach for my beer because my throat is suddenly parched. Aeri eyes me with keen interest. Like she finally hit pay dirt.

"What?" I say after I can swallow. I feel too hot and too cold at the same time, like when I've had a fever. But I must've been hearing things. I couldn't have heard her right. "What did you say?"

"Lora—who is she?" Aeri asks.

"Where did you hear that name?" I flinch every time she says it. I hate hearing the name come out of her mouth. Of anyone's mouth, really.

She frowns. "You really shouldn't answer a question with a question. It makes people think you have something to hide."

My hand curls around the smooth handle of the steak knife before I can think about it. "I'll ask you once more nicely: Where did you hear that name?"

She raises her eyebrows, fear streaking across her face. I realize I've caused it, and I drop the blade.

"You said it," she says.

Never.

I shake my head, my heart pounding in my shirt. "I didn't."

"Yes, you did. A lot. In your sleep last night. You said, 'Lora, I'm so sorry.' That seemed important, so I asked." She shrugs, but she still eyes the knife. Wary.

I push back from the table and take a step away. Her brown eyes question me.

"I'm taking a walk," I say.

She glances at all the food. "But we just— Okay, I can take a walk."

"Alone." My hands lock in empty fists. I'm barely holding it together, and if I snap, this all goes wrong. She'll fire me, and then I won't have the money to free Hwan. And then he'll die.

She frowns. "You said you wouldn't leave me."

Fuck.

"I'll be on the balcony, then."

I race to the glass door, then slam it shut behind me. My hands shake, and I pace like a caged animal. I feel like I'm going to burst from my skin.

The balcony is only ten or so feet long, so I do about fifty laps of it, breathing hard. But at least it's cold, and the shock of fresh air feels good. We're far enough from Umbria that the Sol actually looks clean. Nothing about Umbria is clean.

Except Lora. Lora was.

I can't believe I said her name, but there's no other way Aeri could know about her. There are people in Umbria who might have mentioned a girl named Allora, but only I called her Lora.

And I killed her.

I whip around at the sound of the balcony door sliding. Aeri stands in the opening. "Royo, I'm sorry. I didn't mean to upset you. Really, I didn't."

I want to stay angry, but something twists inside my chest at hearing her tone. Guilt, maybe. I dunno. She didn't know the spot she was poking at was a raw wound. How could she have?

"I just need time," I say.

"Okay." She ventures out onto the balcony, giving me as much space as possible. She leans against the railing, too. I wait, shoulders up to my ears, because I think if she says the name again, I'll dive right off this boat.

Instead, she's silent. Totally quiet for more than a minute for the first time. And the silence stretches for long enough that I can just think again.

How could I have said Lora's name? It's been eight years since I've said it, yet not a day has passed without me thinking about her. My first love. My only love.

Eventually, it's so quiet that I glance over to where Aeri was standing. Maybe she went back inside and I didn't notice. But no, she's still there, just looking out onto the water.

"Is it your mother?" she whispers. She looks at me from the corners of her eyes. "I can't… I don't really talk about my mother much."

She holds her chin high, but there's real heartbreak there, and something else that's real familiar: guilt. Something in her tone and expression makes me think Aeri does understand the feeling of losing someone and being the one to blame.

"No, my mother died ten years ago," I say.

I leave out the part that she died in Tamneki and that my father had fucked off when I was a baby, so it left me fending for myself from when I was fifteen. I used my talent for violence to earn a roof over my head and food on my plate. But Aeri doesn't need to know all that, and I'm not big on sob stories no how.

It's quiet again—just the murmur of the passengers and crew far from us and the rushing sound of the breeze. Aeri's gotta be cold in that dress, but she stands still on the balcony. Because… she cares. She knows something is wrong with me, and she cares enough to want me to be okay. My chest feels warm for a second, and then I shake it off. She shouldn't care. Look what happened to the last girl who cared about me. Murdered as I walked away. I didn't put the knife in her, but they were after me and I might as well have been the one swinging the blade, since I didn't do shit to stop it.

"She was...a friend," I say.

Aeri's eyes dart toward me. "I see."

She doesn't at all buy that Lora was a friend, but she's nice enough to not say I'm full of shit. But I don't want to tell her what Lora was to me. I don't want anyone else to have any part of us.

"I knew her a while ago," I say.

What I don't say is that one day, when I was sixteen, I saw a girl being picked on by some rich little prick. There are guys who think they can take whatever they want because they're bigger, stronger, more powerful. I fucking hate them—square up with someone your own size. Someone who can do real damage.

But this rat fuck had Lora cornered and was groping her as she tried to push him away. The fear and pain in her eyes called to me like a siren. I grabbed the guy and broke his hand—and Lora looked at me like I was her hero. And I guess for that second, I was.

That shoulda been it. But she kept meeting me in secret, and every time, I was convinced she'd come to her senses and want nothing to do with me. She was a rich merchant girl. I was a street thug. We didn't belong together. But I savored every second. Every kiss. Every quick fuck when she was home by herself. I knew it couldn't last, but I fell in love anyhow.

I was a fool.

"Why are you sorry, though?" Aeri asks, pulling me back into the present.

My pulse pounds in my throat. Why am I sorry?

I'm sorry Lora ever met me. I'm sorry she fell for me, too. I'm sorry I met her father. I'm sorry Hwan treated me like I was worth something. I'm sorry he became like a father to me, a role model as a self-made man. He owned a tea shop and a sugar house, but it was the two gambling houses that made him rich.

I'm sorry I turned down Hwan's guardsmithing offer. I'm sorry I took the wrong strongman job and killed a gang member. I'm sorry they didn't just take me out like men.

"She died because...of me," I say. Somehow, I manage to get the words out. They feel grainy and rough, but there's something clean about having said it out loud.

Aeri's eyes widen. "You mean you...killed her?"

I shake my head. "No. Two gang goons followed me to her house. They were after me, but I left right...right as she was being killed."

Aeri turns a shade paler as she tries not to judge me.

She should judge me, though. I judge me.

We were mid-fuck that night when we heard someone at the front door. We thought it was her dad, home early. And I climbed out her bedroom window.

It was the last time I ever saw her.

"What do you mean, you left right as she was being killed?" Aeri whispers. She's moved a foot closer to me.

"I'd been...at her house, and I left. I was a block away, maybe two, when there was this scream." I pause and swallow hard. I still hear it in my nightmares—that loud, high-pitched wail of real pain. It was all wrong. I stopped in my tracks that night and listened, but no sound had followed it. It got to the point where I wasn't even sure I'd heard it. "I didn't think it was her because I'd just seen her, so I kept walking."

It was Umbria. Bad shit happened. Girls screamed. And I thought Lora was safe at home with her dad. Still, a few steps later, something made my feet turn toward her house. Something in my brain said to go back. But I shook it off and kept walking. Why the fuck did I keep walking? The saddest part was I had nowhere to be.

If I could change one and only one thing about my entire life, it would be to go back. To run back to her house. To save her.

It wasn't until the next day that I found out she'd been murdered in her bed. Stabbed thirty times. And Hwan had been arrested for it. He'd been found covered in her blood, a blade in his hand. He claimed someone had broken in and he found her and the knife, but no one believed him.

From the second I heard, I knew Hwan hadn't done it. Not only would he never have laid a finger on Lora, but he didn't get home until nine bells. We'd heard the door at eight.

"But…Royo, you didn't know," Aeri says gently, even though her eyes are glassy. Not sure if it's sympathy or fear.

My throat feels like a vise is clamped down on it. I clear it. "I should've known."

I knew I was to blame, but I didn't know how much until later. Hwan was already serving life in Salt Prison when two guys jumped me in an alleyway. I'd been so broken about Lora, about Hwan, that I got caught wandering the streets. In a way, I wanted death because I wanted to see Lora again. They sliced my face in half and stuck a knife in my hand, and I was ready to go to the Ten Hells. But then they said Lora's name. They joked about how she'd called out for me as they stabbed her again and again. How they'd followed me to her house that night. How they'd wanted to kill me but, when they couldn't find me, settled for the fun of killing her.

Something in me snapped. I grabbed their necks and bashed their heads together. While they were passed out, I gagged them— like they'd done to Lora. Then I killed them both slowly, cutting body parts off while they were still alive, showing them pieces of themselves. I left them torn apart as a treat for the hael. In the morning, I sent their rotting hearts to the gang leaders. After that, I was left alone. Either because I was too willing to die or too willing to murder. Or they feared the grisly scene I left behind. I really never gave a fuck.

I wish I could say it made the guilt easier. It didn't.

"I... I'm just... I'm trying to make it right," I say.

I stop yammering, and regret hits. Why did I say all of this? I shouldn't have said nothing. But...she asked. And she seemed to get it. But who'd want someone like me to guard them now? I brace myself, waiting for her to say she doesn't want me. That I should take a hike. I brace for everything I've done to fail because I couldn't stop spilling my guts.

Aeri nods, eyes still glued to the water. "I get it. There are mistakes that can't be unmade, but you try your best to make things right."

I'm so fucking shocked, I'm silent. She... Not only did she not fire me, but she gets me.

And I *am* trying my best to make things right. I spent a while just trying to drown myself slowly in ale, but then I found Savio—a guard willing to help Hwan escape in exchange for an absolute fortune. But getting the hundred grand gave me a purpose again. Because it's a chance—a way to make things right. As right as I can.

But I don't have much time. King Joon ordered all old convicts in all prisons to be hanged. Savio said he'd put Hwan to the back of the line but that it would only buy him two months max.

Two months. That's all the time I've got before Hwan goes to the gallows. Before everything I've been working for turns to dust. But two months is enough if everything goes to plan.

The problem is, Aeri is nothing according to plan.

I stare over at her—she's snuck another foot closer, and now she's leaning with her arm almost touching mine. I really shouldn't have said nothing. But...the truth is, my chest feels lighter for the first time in eight years. Like just telling someone made the guilt less. And yeah, that she somehow understood. She's...different.

"Do you want to tell me about your mother?" I ask.

"I..." she begins. But then she stares, eyes narrowed, at the horizon.

I turn and scan the water. And then I see it: a flicker in the distance. A fire ship.

A fire ship can only mean one thing. We're about to be attacked by pirates.

So much for everything going to fucking plan.

CHAPTER SIXTEEN

SORA
THE NORTHERN ROAD, YUSAN

I try to sleep in the carriage, but it's nearly impossible. The problems are that I had a full night's sleep, it's been too long since we've eaten, and my mind is constantly trying to puzzle out how to kill an immortal king. In short: I'm awake, hungry, and doomed.

"Did your father tell you why we're going to Tamneki?" I ask.

Tiyung startles. He was wide awake, but I suppose he didn't expect me to speak to him. I haven't for about seven bells. His long lashes sweep his eyes as he blinks.

"No," he says, his voice low and gravelly. "I suppose he wants me to be able to deny any knowledge of his plans."

"But you figured it out," I say.

He draws a breath. That's a yes.

"I know that I'm supposed to burn your indenture upon the death of the king," he says. "I assume he's not speculating on when that will be."

"Yes, upon King Joon's death, I will have my freedom and my sister's—and all I have to do is kill a god," I say and shift my weight on the uncomfortable seat.

Tiyung is silent for a few seconds. "I doubt he's a god."

I arch an eyebrow. The nobility may think he's just a man, but commoners know he's a god king. "It's been a while since I've been in the Divine Temple of Kings, but I'm fairly certain that's blasphemy."

Tiyung shrugs a wide shoulder. "Gods don't cower. If he were a god, he'd freely leave Qali Palace. He doesn't. Not since the Count of Umbria tried to have him killed."

My eyebrows shoot up. "The northern count tried to kill the king?"

There are four counts—northern, southern, western, and eastern—who rule the four regions out of Umbria, Gain, Rahway, and Tamneki, respectively. The four largest cities in Yusan. The capitals of four old nations before we became one Yusan fifteen hundred years ago when the Dragon Lord united the country.

The most powerful *men* in the country are the four counts. Above them is the king, a god. So it's important that a count wanted the king dead. And now the southern count, Seok, is making an attempt.

Tiyung nods, tapping his fingers absently against his knee. "Around eleven years ago. Of course, Count Bay Chin didn't shoot the crossbow—someone else did—but nothing happens in Umbria without the count's say-so."

"Like in Gain."

"Exactly."

"But the attempt failed," I murmur.

"They weren't you," Tiyung says. "You are special. My father favors you for a reason."

I bark out a laugh. "Some favor."

Tiyung looks away. I never thought he was particularly intelligent, but I didn't think he was this dense. I am the Count's slave—that is not favor.

It's getting dark, and I stretch in the seat. Tiyung eyes my body, although he tries not to. I catch him and raise an eyebrow.

"We'll stop soon and spend the night at Lord Shan's," Tiyung says to the window. "The lord is traveling, so we will have the manor to ourselves."

I nod, relieved. I don't have the patience that rich men require tonight. But if I don't have to deal with a lord, villas are always better than inns.

We pull off the Northern Road and take the trampled dirt path to Lord Shan's estate. It's not as grand as the Count's villa, but it sprawls in the open country. We pull up to the door, and the lord's head of household rushes out to greet us.

"Tiyung-si," the man says with a deep bow. "We are honored to host you tonight. I am Hada, the head of household."

"Thank you, Hada," Tiyung says.

Again, Tiyung holds his hand out to help me down from the carriage, and again I refuse it.

"My lady," Hada says with a second bow. He's around fifty-five and wears a wig that's styled high and somehow stays in place as he bows to me. I smile. Irad could learn from his manners.

We're escorted inside. There is a giant crystal chandelier in the entryway, shiny tile floors with wood inlay all around, and yet it's still nothing compared to the Count's estate.

"Please have the kitchen prepare supper for us as soon as possible," Tiyung says.

"Of course. Right away." Hada gestures to a young servant with a thick black braid who runs in the direction of the kitchen.

"You're going to risk dining with me?" I whisper to Tiyung.

"I'll be fine—you wouldn't waste good poison on me," he deadpans.

The timing is so perfect, I can't help but laugh. Tiyung smiles, thrilled with himself, and I instantly regret my sense of humor.

Hada looks at us, confused.

"This way, my lady," Hada says. He shows me to a sumptuous bedroom filled with red silks.

I'm almost inside when I look back over my shoulder. Tiyung is staring at me. I've seen that look before. He had the exact same expression as a boy when I was first purchased by the Count. It's not a smile. It's not a blank stare. I couldn't figure it out then. I still can't now. And in the end, it doesn't matter.

I close the door and relax on the feather bed. I stretch and stare at the posts of the bed, the soft satins and silks and expensive woods. Before I was bought by the Count, Daysum and I slept on woven floor mats, as most poor children do. We'd hold each other at night, huddling together for warmth.

There's none of that here.

But I will say, these villas are far more enjoyable when I'm not trying to murder the inhabitant. I wash in the powder room, and my trunk is waiting for me when I get out. I've been in a travel dress all day and decide to change for dinner. I perfume my hair and powder my body, my movements precise and deliberate. When I get dressed up, it always feels like donning armor, invisible though it may be.

Not long after I have on a golden spun dress, the young servant from earlier comes to my door, her head bowed.

"My lady," she says, lifting her chin. Then she gapes at me. Most people do.

I follow her to the dining room, her braid straight and unmoving between her shoulder blades. Eight dishes are already laid out on the polished wood table, and there are spaces for more food to come. My nails dig into the flesh of my palm. Eight. And children like Gli are foraging for scraps in the meadow.

Tiyung enters the room, wearing a crisp white button-down shirt and blue trousers. His top button is undone, and his sapphire eyes shine. It's a shame that such good looks are wasted on him.

His eyes drink me in, but he speaks to the servant girl.

"Please tell the kitchen this is plenty," he says.

The young girl nods and takes off.

That was strange. Nothing is ever enough for the nobility. They grind down their servants to impress one another. But Tiyung gestures for me to sit, then rests his hands on the back of a chair.

I'm about to sit in that seat when Hada scurries into the dining room with a deep bow. "Is there trouble with the meal?"

"Not at all," Tiyung says. "But this is all we'll need. We appreciate the generosity of Lord Shan. I will write to my father about this fantastic welcome."

Hada looks stunned. "But, but, my lord, the kitchen is preparing six main dishes. Delicacies. They will be delicious, I assure you."

"I have no doubt, and I appreciate that. But please see that the servants are fed instead. We have traveled all day and will sup lightly. I should've informed you of that when we arrived."

I continue to stare at him, and so does Hada. Eventually, Hada bows again and leaves the room.

"I assume you can be content with this paltry spread," Tiyung says. He's still holding the chair.

"Yes. I'll manage," I say as I settle into it.

"You look stunning." His voice rumbles in my good ear before he pushes in my chair. A chill runs across my back. I shake it off.

"This isn't a date," I say.

Tiyung sits to my right at the head of the table, his gaze holding mine. "Given how your dates end, I'll consider myself lucky."

I suppress a smile.

The servant girl appears again and pours generous wine goblets for each of us. No doubt it is the best bottle Lord Shan had in his cellar.

"Thank you. That will be all," Tiyung says to her. The girl gives the same confused look as Hada, smoothing a hand down her thick braid before catching herself. She clasps her hands and disappears faster.

"To your health, Sora," Tiyung says, lifting his glass.

"To a fitting end to our business." I lift my glass, but I don't drink from it. I don't drink alcohol. I see no reason to poison myself when I don't have to.

As I put the red wine down, it sloshes, bleeding down the stem. I once again imagine Tiyung's severed head in a basket in his father's office. Seok's screams echoing throughout the grand villa. All of that torture and murder and betrayal for nothing. When a nobleman dies without a son, everything he owned goes to the king. Although with King Joon dead and his brothers already deceased, I'm not sure who that would be. Maybe that's the point. Maybe the Count wants the throne. I don't care who rules Yusan, so long as Daysum and I are free, but I'd rather it not be Seok.

But I can't control any of that, so instead, I eat.

The kimchi pancake bursts with flavor. There's buttered crab, egg soup, spicy pork, rice cakes, glassy japchae, seared steak, and fried tofu. Plus, there's a mound of fluffy white rice and a basket of crisp bitter greens.

I help myself to small portions of everything and then realize that Tiyung is watching me, his plate empty.

"I'm not about to serve you," I say.

That should be my role without a servant here. Even if we were equal in status, women are expected to serve the men and then eat whatever is unwanted.

"I wasn't expecting you to," he says. "I want you to take what you desire first."

I glance over at him. "Why?"

"Because I think we have things backward in Yusan. I think ladies should be served first."

"How progressive," I say, rolling my eyes.

But...it is. I've never heard a man talk like this. Then again, the nobles I've met have been too busy trying to tear off my dress to converse much.

We help ourselves. It's odd, but I get used to it.

"Where will you go after you succeed?" he asks.

"Somewhere far from you." I give him my most dazzling smile as I spoon some of the buttery crab into the bitter greens.

"I'm not your enemy, Sora," he says.

I rest the bite of crab on the plate. "Ah, yes. I forgot we're old friends."

"I have known you for a dozen years, and I...I'd like us to be friends—or if not friends, then allies..." His blue eyes sear into me. I don't understand why he's putting on this act, but I wish he wouldn't.

We aren't friends. We aren't allies. We never will be.

I wipe my mouth with a napkin. "Allow me to eat in peace."

"Very well, Sora." He swallows some wine and cuts into the steak.

We continue in silence, the only sounds the occasional scrape of a utensil against a plate, until we're both full. But there's still more than half of the food remaining. It's pure waste—it always is with the nobles.

Tiyung has stared at me over his wine goblet half a dozen times. But I don't want to see the conflicted stare on his face. I don't care what else he has to say. I will never forgive him for whipping Daysum. I will never forget. I will kill him when the time comes.

I get up from the table without another word.

CHAPTER SEVENTEEN

ROYO
THE SOL RIVER, YUSAN

Pirates. Fucking pirates.

I lean forward on the railing to see better, but there's no doubt a fire ship is heading straight for us.

The Count of Umbria and the Count of Rahway can't decide whose job it is to protect the Sol, so with the two of them doing fuck all, a gang took over. They call themselves pirates, but they're not the pirates who roam the East Sea. Those are men without a country. This gang is Yusanian—and they prey on other Yusanians.

I've heard about fire ships before—boats with some kind of coating that lets them flame without burning. I don't get how, but it don't matter—those flames mean death. And this riverboat is a big, plump target. We can't outrun them, there's no king's guard, and there's too much money on board.

At first, the pirates just took mun and cargo, but with no one cracking down, they started looking for young boys and girls to sell—the exact thing I was hired to prevent.

Ten Hells. I need to get Aeri off the riverboat. Now.

Leaving her on the balcony, I race back into the room, looking around for what we could use to lower ourselves into the water. There's not much. We'll have to jump.

"We need to get off this ship," I say.

Aeri's followed me into the cabin. Her mouth falls open. "What?"

"There are pirates coming. We need to get off this ship. Now."

She blinks like she doesn't understand. Frustration builds in my chest. We don't got time to be thick.

"Um, okay, just let me get my things, I guess."

Her things? What things?

She goes over to her trunks and begins to pull at a handle. It goes nowhere.

Ten Hells, she means *all* her things.

"And we'll what? Float five trunks down the river?" I shake my head. "Leave the shit. Where's the diamond?"

"I have it, but…" She chews her lip, not moving.

Lord Yama, we do not have time for this. I can't seem to get through to her, and I can't lose her. I can't go back to Umbria empty-handed. I need to get Aeri to safety. Now.

"Okay then, let's go," I say. I gesture with my arm to the glass door.

"But my trunks…"

I have no idea what's inside. So far all I've seen are books, teas, and an unreasonable amount of clothes. Nothing important. Definitely nothing worth dying over.

I can feel my face turning red and that vein on my temple popping. The one that makes people back away. Maybe the cold, hard truth will get through to her. "When the pirates get here, they'll take everything and *everyone* valuable. Do you want to be sold with your trunks?"

Her eyes widen, and she gets paler than I am. "No."

"Good. Then grab what you absolutely can't do without and let's fucking *go*."

I sling my bag over my shoulder and tie it tight to me. It has daggers, knives, brass knuckles, a medical kit, some clothes, and, of course, the gold bars. She grabs a velvet bag out of one of her trunks, and then I practically drag her onto the balcony. She'd started considering dresses. Dresses!

We go out the sliding glass door to the balcony. The conversation we just had about the past feels like a lifetime ago because all that matters is surviving the next few minutes.

"Can you swim?" I ask.

Her eyes dart to the side. Great, that's reassuring. I'll probably have to swim through the frigid river for both of us.

A cold breeze blows, making her shiver. It's warmer here than Umbria, but that ain't saying much. Water this cold can kill, especially since her legs are bare and she's so slight.

"I swear to the gods, I'd better get that bonus when you finish your job, Aeri." I climb on top of the waist-high railing.

She nods but doesn't move.

"Do we have to get in the water?" she asks. Then she tries to climb up after me, but she has trouble with her shoes on the smooth wood. I grab a hold of her wrist and yank her up with enough force to pull, but not hurt her. She's just scared. I know that. But it would be nice if she could make this a little easier.

I gesture with my hand out. "You got a better way of getting off a boat?"

She looks around. "There are lifeboats right below us. Surely one of those…"

"Do you have to argue with me when I'm trying to save you? We'll be spotted in a rowboat, and they'll run us down or light us on fire. Let's go. Now. I'll jump in and then you—"

But I'm cut off by an arrow hitting the deck of the riverboat. The metal connects to the wood with a thud. And then twenty, thirty more rain down, whistling through the air.

I look to the source. The fire ship is a hundred yards away—less, more like fifty—and coming in fast. Pirates continue to fire longbows from their deck. The flames of the ship burn bright on the gray late afternoon. There have to be fifty pirates on board, screaming with their weapons raised.

Fuck.

People on the riverboat are scrambling. A few are bleeding, and a bunch are shouting. But Aeri just covers her head, shaking.

Suddenly, the arrows stop. There's a second of relief before grappling hooks land on the prow. We're about to be boarded.

"Fuck, we're outta time," I say, running a hand over my head. "Because *you* had to argue with me."

I have no idea what to do now. Aside from yell at her, apparently. Aeri is exactly the kind of girl they'll take to sell to a brothel in another city. And then I get nothing. No diamond, no bonus, and without the money to pay off Savio, Hwan will die.

No. I have to figure out a way out for us. I can't fail. I won't. Not when I actually have a way to fix everything. Not after all I did for eight years to get here.

But nothing comes to mind except my hands. They're already balled into fists, ready for blood. I guess I'll have to fight our way out or die trying. Maybe I'll see Lora again after all.

"Let's jump," Aeri says.

I run my hand down my face. Now? Now Little Miss Late Decision finally agrees?

"We can't. They'll see us," I say. "They'll chase us down."

Some people have already tried to jump. Arrows met them in the water.

"We have to try," she says.

Just as I'm looking overboard, weighing our chances, the door to our room splinters apart, kicked in by pirates. They must've boarded from the other side of the ship, but, of course, they're checking the swank rooms first.

I get down off the railing, leaving Aeri perched up there.

"Stay behind me," I say. "And if anything happens, you don't help. You got me? You dive off this boat and take your chances. Don't look back. Understand?"

"What are you going to do?" she asks, her voice wobbling.

"I'm gonna kill a bunch of pirates."

I stand on the balcony, blocking her from view, and get two blades out—the one strapped to my chest and the one hidden under my pants leg. The rest are unreachable in the closed bag on my back. Three pirates are ransacking the room. It's chaos on this ship. But they're so busy going through the trunks that they haven't spotted us yet. I wait. Once they see me, they'll have to come through the sliding door one at a time. Then numbers won't mean nothing.

The second I think it, the pirates see me through the glass. One is a gangly fucker a head taller than I am. The next has an average build. The last is pretty short.

They move together toward the door but then stop, realizing somebody's got to be the first through. Come and get me. The shortest one slides it open. Before he takes a full step onto the balcony, I stab him right through the neck with my dagger. No hesitation, always a kill shot.

He falls to his knees, grasping at the blade. If he pulls it out, he's dead. If he leaves it in, he'll die slower. If it don't matter to him, I'd rather get my blade back, since the next pirate is already through the door. Aeri gasps, but I got this. I swing around and stab pirate number two in the gut, then I kick him, sending him barreling into the taller one. They're just getting rebalanced when I rush them. The railing is low, and they fall overboard before I can kill them.

Unfortunately, they both scream as they splash into the Sol.

Motherfuckers.

It attracts attention, and attention is the last thing we want. But Aeri is still okay on her perch when two more pirates rush into the room.

I need another weapon. I look around and then rip my dagger from the throat of the first pirate. Blood rushes out.

"Royo!" Aeri yells. "Go left."

I move just in time to dodge a crossbow bolt. Stupid. He should've shot through the glass from farther away. I spin and kick the archer's leg out from under him. Then I grab his arm and break it, twisting the crossbow free.

With the bow nicely reloaded for me, I shoot the other pirate, who's nearly made it to Aeri. But I'm a shit shot. I hit him in the dick, and I'm kind of sorry about it. He howls and grabs his crotch. Ten Hells. I rush to him and slit his throat. But now the archer is howling.

Noisy fucking pirates. Every one of them is going to be in this room soon with this racket. I bend down and twist the neck of the archer to put him out of his misery. With one snap, he falls limp onto the deck.

Three dead, one as good as dead, one flailing in the Sol.

I'm breathing heavily as I check on Aeri. She's staring at me with her mouth open, but then she watches something in the distance.

"We need to go," she says.

I hear it—footsteps of a bunch of men coming. She must see them from higher up on the railing.

"It's no use," I say.

"We have to try," she says.

I shake my head. "They'll see us."

"Gods, Royo! Now who's being the pain?"

She takes my hand and grabs on tight. Just as I focus on the shock of her touch, she suddenly dives backward. I mean, she basically does a backflip while gripping my arm. It causes both of us to fall overboard.

I brace to hit the river—to feel the stabbing pain of cold water. But the next thing I know, I'm in a boat.

What the fuck?

I blink. What just happened? I'm on my back, staring up at the early-evening sky, so it's the same time of day—around six bells. I'm dreaming. I gotta be. I gotta be floating face down in the river with an arrow through my neck or something. But no. Neck is fine, and there's no blood. Well, there's blood on my hand, but that's from before. I'm definitely not in the cold water of the Sol. I should be, but I'm not.

I struggle to sit up, my head and back in screaming pain. I give up and lie still. It feels like my head is about to split in two, like I hit something so hard, I blacked out. Maybe that's it. Maybe the pirates got to me, knocked me out. That would make sense. But the last thing I remember was Aeri doing a fucking backflip and pulling me overboard.

No! Aeri! Where the hells is she? Did I lose her? Did she drown? Do the pirates have her?

Frantic, I sit up, despite my head feeling like it's in pieces. My heart thunders in my chest like fists on a door. I'll get her back if I have to take on the pirate ship all by myself. But no. Wait. There she is, across from me. We're in a lifeboat, and she's calmly rowing it. Like we're a couple taking an afternoon paddle on the Sol.

What? This can't be. I'm seeing things. Or we died. Yeah, that makes the most sense. We died and I'm stuck in one of the hells with her.

Figures.

But why does the Kingdom of Hells smell like the fucking Sol?

"What the fuck?" I ask.

Aeri stops rowing. Sweat glistens on her brow and she looks exhausted, but she smiles. "Oh, good, you're finally up. Here, you row."

She tosses an oar handle at me. I grab it, but I can't make sense of it.

Okay, okay, I passed out when we dove off the riverboat, hit something on the way down, and somehow she got us onto a lifeboat. That makes sense.

Except it don't.

I stare at the oar in my hand. This noodle-armed girl can't move me—especially not to pull my deadweight aboard a boat. I'm not even sure how she yanked us overboard, except I was off-balance and the railing was pretty low. But, no. I'm totally dry. I pat my shirt and pants. Bone dry. Even my underpants. And her yellow dress doesn't look wet, either. Not that I'm looking. Well, I am. But just for water damage.

Still, she catches me.

"Row the boat, Royo. We're not out of danger yet," she says.

She's eyeing something behind me. Her brown eyes go wide, fear flashing in them.

I turn. Two ships are on fire—the fire ship and the riverboat. I don't know who or what was taken. I don't know how we got away. And I don't have time to stare. All that matters is that we stay away from them.

I take the second oar and the seat from her. Ignoring my headache, I row hard. My arm muscles pump, my chest strains, and my shoulders rotate as I put all my power into sending us down the river. I'm so focused on getting us to safety that we're another mile away before I can form the question.

"How the fuck are we alive?" I ask.

"I saved us. You're welcome," she says. "Keep rowing."

And I do. Because any second, the pirates are bound to notice we got away.

CHAPTER EIGHTEEN

MIKAIL
CITY OF LARK, FALLOW

I have to say I'm not really looking forward to today's little adventure. Turns out almost being eaten by a giant bird while traveling cools one's wanderlust.

My back aches. It stings and throbs like it's tearing anew every time I move. I want laoli and to not be leaving a safe city with the prospect of being exposed at night. But I suppose I have a long list of wishes. Laoli, sadly, is at the top right now.

I'd much rather stay in Lark, blissed out on the drug, than almost anything. It sounds so remarkably pleasant—just spend the day in a pretty drug haze where there's no pain or violence. Maybe lure Euyn back into bed with me (even though he seems to be trying his best to be a killjoy and keep himself out of my sheets). Along with reducing pain, laoli heightens pleasure. A full day in bed with him sounds like reaching the Heavens. But he's kept his distance ever since I found him in Outton. No matter—the drug is temptation enough to want to stay. It's almost as important as revenge.

Stars, what am I thinking? Nothing is more important.

I rub my clammy face. I'm cold sweating even though it's not yet dawn. This is withdrawal. I didn't think it would be this bad after so few doses. But it feels like my lungs are trying to reach through my chest to go get the laoli. And as my body grasps for the drug, it claws my mind instead.

I try to force myself to stop craving the poison, resolve that I won't take it again. But it's not as easy as saying "no more." And Euyn is testing my rather limited patience.

"Just pick an ass," I say.

He stops evaluating the donkeys to eye me. I don't normally take a sharp tone with him. But I am in bad shape. My hands shake and then tremble, and I'd like to get a move on. I hide it from him as much as I can, though.

"Please continue to haggle and delay us further. I'm sure the samroc will appreciate it." I smile, even though it's hard to.

Euyn blanches and finally agrees on his donkey. Then we start the long trip into the pass. It's not comfortable, riding through a mostly narrow pass with walls of mountains on both sides. Nowhere to run, nowhere to hide. Higher ground everywhere but where we are right now. But I have my sword, and Euyn picked up an arsenal of crossbow bolts in Lark. Between the two of us, we have enough weapons and an impressive body count. I've killed dozens of people for the crown. He was known as the Butcher of Westward Forest.

It's odd that Euyn really believed that I, the royal spymaster, didn't know what he was up to. It had all started as a joke. A noble said something along the lines of: "You can track beasts, but what about something as cunning as a man?" And the challenge came out of that. Of course, Euyn didn't kill the nobleman—he hunted him in the woods for a bell and won the pride bet by shooting the hat off the lord. But something about it was too novel for Euyn. He liked it too much.

Life in the palace meant Euyn getting anything and anyone he wanted at all times without the responsibility of ruling or the yoke of authority. That has to fundamentally change a person. I tell myself that had he been born under different stars, Euyn would've been a good person. Sometimes I wonder, but mostly I believe that the palace can corrupt anyone and anything.

He scans the mountain slopes, constantly alert.

"Are you looking for people or samroc?" I ask.

"Both," he says.

"Why did you let the last one go?" I ask.

He tilts his head at me. "The samroc?"

"Chul," I say.

Euyn pales, gripping his saddle. I suppose I should've prefaced that question, but I don't have the grace at the moment. I keep my hands busy with the reins to stop them from ripping open the laoli pouch I know is in my shirt pocket. But I've been through worse. I will make it through this.

I force myself to calmly wait for Euyn's response.

Euyn swallows hard, the ball in his throat bobbing. I simply remain quiet. Silence is a fantastic tool for getting to the truth, especially when you're patient.

"I… They were prisoners, Mikail. Sentenced to life in the dark of Idle Prison or awaiting execution or death by lingchi. All of them were guilty."

"As were you," I say.

He draws in a sharp breath.

"Most of the people in Idle Prison are political enemies of Joon," I say. "You know this. They're locked away on treason or conspiracy charges, not usually the murder of thirteen men."

That is how many Euyn hunted, according to the prison guards who were tortured and promised death for their confessions. Frankly, I think the number is a little low. I believe they were still concerned about what Euyn might do to their families if they told the truth. It was likely more than twenty. I checked the rolls.

"I gave them a fair chance at freedom," he says. "It was legal."

I roll my eyes. Yusanians and their contracts. They believe contracts for all things are legitimate so long as the form is correct. Slavery is illegal simply because there's no compensation in exchange for the labor and no end to the term; otherwise, they'd be as fine with it as Wei. It's a strange thing—how paper contracts keep our country from complete moral collapse.

"Your brother didn't sign those contracts," I say. "Only he could give the prisoners their freedom."

Euyn freezes and then exhales. "I didn't believe any could survive the bell."

"Oh, good. We have arrived back at my original question. Why did you let Chul live?"

"I missed." His eyes dart to the side.

I tsk. "You really should be a better liar by now, Euyn. It's embarrassing."

He sighs at me.

"You don't miss," I say. "You didn't miss at night with monstrous birds about to eat us. You're not missing a casual shot in Westward." Westward Forest lies between the palace and Tamneki. It's a royal hunting ground that Euyn knows like the back of his hand.

After a full minute of silence, Euyn tries to speak. He fails a couple of times.

"He... I don't know," he says.

"Masterful reason, sire."

He stares at me, unamused. "He was only in Idle Prison because he killed a magistrate who'd arranged for his daughters to be taken. To be sold to the pleasure houses years ago."

I scrunch my nose. I'm not one for pleasure houses. I don't understand how people satisfy themselves on unwilling and typically drugged boys and girls. But it's so unlike Euyn to care. What isn't he telling me?

"Since when have you been concerned with the fate of young peasant girls?" I ask.

Nobles can't be sold as indentures, so they had to have been commoners.

"I wasn't, really," Euyn admits. "It was that…Chul wasn't sorry for what he did—only that he got caught. His only regret was that he couldn't keep looking for his children. I admired the dedication, I suppose. The way nothing would stop him. Plus, he'd lasted nearly the entire bell—far longer than anyone else had. When I finally hunted him down and asked if he had last words, he said: 'Yes, tell my girls I died trying to find them.' And he just stared at me, ready. I just… I couldn't take the shot."

Now, I'm silent. None of it sounds like Euyn—not the Euyn I knew, anyhow, the beautiful, careless boy. But he's also the worst liar in the three realms. And I've always liked that about him—naturally terrible at lying, so he never learned how. He's telling the truth right now. This is really what happened and why he didn't kill Chul. Because he respected him as a father.

As much as it surprises me, I suppose it shouldn't.

Euyn didn't know his father. The old king died when he was four years old. That's the one thing he wanted in life that he didn't get: a father.

I've long suspected that Joon had something to do with the death of King Theum, but it's nothing I can prove. My suspicion comes from the fact that Baejkin kings easily live a hundred years with the crown, and their father died at age sixty. Joon ascended to the throne at age twenty-five. The earliest in centuries.

It's said that King Theum had a heart attack and died while washing himself. I find that timing amazingly convenient. But my issue is killing the current king, not solving the murder of the old one. Gaya was just as colonized under Theum as they are under Joon. But it was the change in power and new taxes of Joon that made the island revolt. And it was Joon who ordered no prisoners. No survivors as he put down the rebellion. Everyone was slaughtered. I wasn't supposed to live, but a soldier betrayed orders. He couldn't find it in his heart to kill me. Instead, he smuggled me across the Strait of Teeth from Gaya to Yusan and raised me as his own.

He is my father.

There are so many other ways my life could've gone. I could've died in Gaya or been bought as an indentured servant. I could've had an abusive man take advantage of me, murder me, because in the end I was never supposed to be here. But my father adopted me, made me his son. He was kind. He loved me when he needn't have. And for that I'm forever grateful.

Yet when I'm asked about the scars on my body, I imply it was him. I say *my family*, because it immediately gets people to stop asking. It's not an honorable thing to do, to sully his good name, but my father doesn't care. He says he deserves it for what he did in Gaya. I don't ask, and he's never told me what he means. We comfortably exist in the space of unsaid regret.

At least now I can say my scars are from a samroc—silver linings and all.

As we get farther into the pass, it becomes less and less possible to turn around. But I suppose turning around was never an option.

From when I was first approached with this plan to kill Joon, I was set on a path. I survived the Charm Revolt for a reason: to put an end to Joon's life and Yusan's rule over Gaya. I have to see this through and hope Euyn and I both survive.

But if only one of us can make it, it has to be Euyn. Without him, there's no one to put on the throne. The country would be thrown into chaos, and the nobles would war to take the crown. Or Wei would come in and slaughter everyone again. I've already seen the cost of war. It's too great a price borne by the people who benefit the least.

Thus, I'll do whatever I need to in order to protect Euyn. Even if it costs my life.

But that determination might be put to the test sooner rather than later. It's not dark yet, but a shriek echoes along the canyon walls in the distance. I grab my sword.

CHAPTER NINETEEN

AERI

THE SOL RIVER, YUSAN

I lost every single dress I own, all my makeup, and all my books. I'm in a rowboat. It's freezing cold, and it's getting dark fast. I've gotta say, this is less than ideal.

But I have my freedom, my incredibly brave protector, and diamonds in my bag. All in all, not the worst—even if I did also lose my favorite pair of shoes. Damn. I'm never going to find another pair of heels like that. But I should be thankful. Other people on board weren't as lucky.

It was luck, really, that I was able to get us into the rowboat. A few feet more and we would've fallen into the river. Maybe we'd have survived, maybe we wouldn't have. But that's what life is. A little off, a little too slow or fast, a little too early or late, and everything would be different. Life is timing, and timing is luck.

Royo has rowed for miles. It's incredible—watching his broad shoulders work. He doesn't get tired, even steadily propelling this boat five times faster than I did using all my strength. He's so casually strong. And the way he took on the pirates, the way he killed to protect me, was…something.

I cross my legs. It isn't wet-undergarments time. And I probably shouldn't be turned on by unflinching murder. But "shouldn't" is meaningless. It's not the same as "won't."

"There's an isle up ahead," Royo says. "We can stop there overnight."

I turn and scan the horizon, excited for a safe haven. But I don't see an isle. What is he talking about? I search again. There's no isle, unless by "isle" he means a pile of rocks that barely clears the water level. That can't be what he means.

That's definitely what he means.

"Let's go ashore," I say, pointing to the riverbank. Surely there must be inns or something nearby.

He shakes his head. "The isle is safest."

"It's a pile of rocks."

"It's a sandbar."

"You're being super generous. It's not much bigger than this rowboat." I gesture with my arms out.

He frowns. Which, yes, is his normal expression, so he frowns *deeper*. "By all means, continue to argue with me. Worked out great last time."

We've bickered a bunch, but this time his heart isn't in it. His head must be aching, even though I asked him like a dozen times if he was okay and he said yes. He hit it hard on the bench when we fell into the boat. He probably just needs to rest.

"But shouldn't we go ashore?" My tone is nicer, my voice rising at the end like a question. Mama told me men like when you suggest instead of demand. That's the ego game I have to play sometimes.

"There are no major ports between Umbria and Rahway," he says. "No stops for the riverboats, and hiring a small boat would take forever."

I mean, he's right, but that's not the only way to get to Rahway. "Couldn't we find horses and take the Northern Road?"

He shakes his head and winces, his jaw clenching. I reach out to touch his temples. Royo stares at me like a wild animal, his eyes both daring me and warning me. I drop my arm. He exhales, looking relieved. We got closer on the balcony, I thought, but that seems like months ago now.

"The river is still the fastest," he says. "The Northern Road swings way west, and getting to shore ain't cake. Look at the embankments."

The river is at its lowest point of the year with monsoon season a month away. Once the rains hit, the river will be ten feet higher, so the embankments are steep. It's almost a ravine. Still…

"Rowing can't be faster," I say.

"It's not. But if we stay on the water, another riverboat will leave from Umbria tomorrow, and they'll recognize one of their own boats and maybe rescue us. Taking the Northern Road will add nearly a sunsae to the trip."

In other words: our choices are shit. I can't afford to spend an extra sunsae getting to Rahway. The spymaster won't wait that long. He'll figure me dead or captured and move on. And then I'll have nothing. I'll have to go to Father empty-handed…if he'll see me at all. Since I was disowned, I haven't exactly been re-owned. And he's all I have.

"Okay," I say.

"What?" Royo blinks hard at me.

"I said okay. We'll try the isle. If nothing comes to get us tomorrow, we go ashore. Deal?"

He skews his face but eventually nods. "Deal."

A few minutes later, we row up to the "isle." I'd like to note how very generous the term is for what I'm looking at. Slick black boulders surround a patch of sand and gravel. This isle is probably twenty feet long and maybe ten feet wide. In a month, once the rains come, this will be far underwater. But we're still in the dry season, so there's…this.

There's no firewood. I thought maybe there'd be some

driftwood or at least enough sticks to start a modest fire, but there's nothing. Nothing to keep us warm tonight. I'm going to freeze to death here. I've already lost feeling in my legs. Then I remember: I have a cloak in my bag.

"We can use this to keep us warm." I pull out the cloak with a smile.

Royo knits his eyebrows at me. I didn't expect him to faint with gratitude, but some kind of reaction would be nice.

"Us?" he says.

How many people are on this isle, Royo?

He puts his hands in his pockets. "You cover up. I'll be fine."

Of course he's going to tough it out. But without a fire or some source of heat, I can't get through the night. I've been freezing before, not knowing what to do, curled around myself for warmth and barely surviving. I'm not doing it again.

"I need your body heat," I say. "Or we need to get off this rock."

"I'm not cuddling with you." He folds his arms across his chest. He sounds really outraged about it for a guy who was recently staring at my thighs.

"Oh, okay, I'll just freeze to death instead. Good plan."

"It's not cold enough for you to die."

"No, I'll get hypothermia and then a fever. I'm very fun when I'm feverish. Super chatty."

He balls his hands into fists at his sides and lets out something that's a cross between the most aggrieved sigh in the three realms and a groan. Then he walks away from me and sits on one of the boulders.

Maybe I played this wrong.

The wind howls over us, and there's no shelter. No choice but to just be chilled to the bone. I put the cloak on—it's a little better, but I know it's not enough. I have to figure out how to get him to lie next to me when he seems like he'd rather be in Khitan right now.

I really don't have any ideas. But being quiet got him talking on the balcony, so maybe it'll help now.

"Royo?" I say. Okay. I'm not good at being quiet.

"I need a second."

I've never saved someone's life before, but I thought it came with a little bit of gratitude. Like a smidgen. I guess not. Then again, he saved my life, too. A bunch of times already—if we're counting each pirate. And he's been through a lot. I'm certain that Lora was not his "friend" but a girl he loved. It was scrawled in the pain on his face. There isn't anyone who'd react that viscerally to my name. But one day maybe there will be. If I do this job. If I can even make it to this job.

I sit on the sand, then let my head fall back and look at the darkening sky. Dusk is so beautiful, even though it's the death of the day. It's so cold on the sand that I think maybe it's wet, but I keep my palm down and it's dry. If it were damp, the ground would leach all the heat out of me, even with my fur-lined cloak. I clap my hands free of the grains. It's still not great, but what choice do I have?

I'm frowning at the sky when I feel him near me.

"Okay," he says.

I blink up at him. "You mean it? You'll sleep next to me?"

Another record-breaking sigh greets me. But there's something else in his face. He's faking it. Well, I mean, he finds me weird and exhausting, but he's not as put out as he seems.

What an interesting man.

"Yeah," he grumbles. "We'll sleep back-to-back."

"Well, that's boring."

He stares at me and then starts to walk away. "I'm going to sleep on that rock."

Now it's my turn to sigh. "Fine, Royo. Back-to-back it is. I'm just saying there are better options."

We both lie down on the sand. It's actually not that uncomfortable, but it's really, really cold. Royo spreads the cloak over us. But it's not enough. Definitely not for the two of us, especially considering my bare legs. Our backs are pressed against each other, but my chest is so cold. I should've worn a long dress, maybe trousers, but I really hadn't anticipated freezing to death today.

The sun goes down, and then we're both shivering.

Minutes later, my shivers turn into shudders. I can't stop. I don't have a body that retains heat. Really—I'm built like a malnourished, hairless cat. My limbs quake, trying to stay alive. Royo is doing a bit better, quietly shivering.

"I hate this cold," I say.

"Me too," he mutters.

"One day, I'll live in Tamneki, where it's always warm," I declare.

"Save your breath," he says.

I close my mouth and then realize that talking doesn't affect how cold I am—he just wants me to be quiet.

Jerk.

A few minutes more and I'm violently shaking. My teeth chatter in my skull. I can't control these muscle contractions. It has to be annoying him, but I'm not doing it on purpose. It's painful.

He sighs and then suddenly flops over, his chest to my back.

I'm so shocked, I actually go still.

"Come here." His voice rumbles in my ear.

I turn over so I'm facing him. He wraps his arms around me so I'm pressed up against him. I hug him like a pillow and shake into him, but there's so much more warmth coming from his chest.

I soak it all in. He wraps the edges of the cloak tight around us, and it's almost comfortable.

Except for that he very obviously doesn't want me this close. He moves away when I rub my thighs on his, but my legs are really fucking cold, Royo.

He cranes his head away from me, and I wonder how long he can stay like that. I tuck my face into his neck, since he doesn't want to look in my eyes. My nose has to be freezing against his warm skin, but he sighs and puts his head against mine. He nuzzles me slightly, holding me near.

What a strange one.

But we're warm enough to survive this way. Together.

I've never had this before—a man I want wrapped around me or someone to save me. And yeah, it's his job, and we're just trying to survive and make our fortunes, but he's still here with me. And that's new. I've always had to save myself.

I let myself enjoy his nearness, the heat thrown off his chest. He smells like leather and pine but mixed with something sweet. It's such a good contrast. I breathe it in until I'm nearly asleep in his arms. But as I drift off, I wonder if he'll be back to gruff and untouchable tomorrow.

CHAPTER TWENTY

EUYN

TANGUN MOUNTAIN PASS, YUSAN

Eleven bells into our trip, we clear the marker dividing Fallow from Yusan. We are home. Maybe. If we make it. Well, I suppose I'm home either way.

Other than the occasional shriek in the distance, we've thankfully not encountered a single samroc. But arriving on a donkey and sneaking across the border at nearly dusk wasn't exactly the exalted return I had in mind. Of course, I was never supposed to return—that's the point of death by exile. I suppose I am fortunate to be alive at all. And now that the day is fading, I feel quite certain the God of Fortune is about to turn his back on me.

I glance at Mikail, but he's been in a foul mood all day. He won't admit it, but I think it's the laoli. Mikail is strong, stronger than anyone I've ever met, but laoli doesn't care how strong you are.

It would be easier to leave him alone if his beauty weren't as sharp as a knife. If I didn't remember him moaning into my neck, my skin still damp with his sweat instead of my own.

"You're staring, Euyn," he says.

I purse my lips. His damn peripheral vision.

I clear my throat. "What is the plan?"

"Once we come out of the pass, we can stop for the night in Gorya," he says. "Then we'll take a fleet carriage to Rahway."

Gorya is a small town on the Yusanian side of the Tangun Mountains, probably three bells east of the pass on donkeys.

"Isn't Swift closer?" I ask. It's a larger city right at the foothills.

"Too many soldiers," he says. "There's a garrison there. You'll have to stay out of sight as much as possible now that we're in Yusan. Your hair and beard hide you some, but anyone looking for you will know you."

I nod. I do know there are people searching for me. Or at least there were. I had to kill two men the first year I was in Fallow. After they were dead, I rifled through their belongings. I stole what I could and learned of the bounty on my head from a crumpled wanted poster. The throne had posted illustrated drawings of me with the words "dead or alive." But I've changed enough to not be as easily recognizable—I thought.

Mikail is probably right, though. He had no issue finding me, and soldiers know me. I'd completed my two years in the king's guard not long before I was banished. It was more of a ceremonial position, traveling the country to meet the military on behalf of the crown, but I enjoyed it. I drank with soldiers from Gain to Umbria, and they loved me.

However, in order for our plan to matter, we have to survive the next four bells. I've never heard of samroc being spotted in Yusan, but I'm certain those creatures don't respect our man-made borders. And I'm sure the ones who attacked us have been combing the desert searching for us ever since. I feel it in my bones.

I don't say this to Mikail. He'd just tell me I'm being paranoid. But being paranoid doesn't mean I'm wrong.

I look up at the sky even though it's likely too early for them to hunt. Any time a shadow passed overhead today, I tensed. So yes, I did, in fact, worry over every cloud.

All I want to do is get out of this pass. I'd rather deal with the bounty than be eaten. It's a horrific feeling—being hunted.

Maybe I shouldn't have hunted those men in the woods.

The thought shakes me. I hadn't stopped to consider it before now. We kill for sport all the time in Yusan. I didn't see how what I was doing was fundamentally different from tuhko.

Every four years, at the Royal Tuhko Championship, two hundred and fifty thousand spectators watch as the winning team is bathed in riches and all ten players of the losing team, along with their coach, are slaughtered in ritual sacrifice to the gods. The players know the stakes, and yet they agree to compete—even some low nobles' sons—for a chance at glory. And for their share of the four-million-gold-mun prize. The danger is part of what makes half a million eyes unable to turn away. Every kick, every pass is crucial. Every point can literally mean life or death. It is why people pack the largest arena in the three realms and why occasionally the judges are torn limb from limb by the crowd or the players. The intensity heightens the enjoyment.

It wasn't any different for me, hunting convicted criminals.

But now, instead of believing I shouldn't have spared Chul, I think perhaps I shouldn't have hunted anyone at all. I still know I was wrongly banished, though. What I did was no worse than anything Joon has done. My brother just knelt to the lords.

And Mikail agreed.

"You're deep in thought, Euyn. I can almost hear your brain grinding," Mikail says.

"Why did you agree?" I ask.

He glances over, his face illuminated in the last of the sun's rays.

This was not how I meant to begin this conversation. This is not the time nor the place for it, but the words have been spoken. No sense in pretending otherwise.

"I'm surprised you didn't ask me before we left Outton," he says with a smile. "You still believe that I betrayed you in the throne room by agreeing with Joon. You believe that had I aligned myself with you, you would've been allowed to stay in Yusan."

Well...yes.

He draws a sharp breath as he stares up at the colorful sky. He's biting his tongue like it's a steak. "Euyn, I am begging you to have more than a child's understanding of politics or your brother's motivations at the age of twenty-three."

Okay, of all of his possible responses, I didn't think he'd insult me.

"I am not a child," I say.

"Then stop thinking like one."

"I'm not."

Another sigh. "So you believe that your god king brother would've changed his mind due to the opinion of your commoner lover?"

I glance to the side. I will admit: put that way, it doesn't seem as likely.

"Or do you believe your fate was sealed when Chul ran to the king and, in front of the entire Council of the Lords, told them how you were hunting convicts of Idle Prison, killing them in the forest for your own amusement—in violation of, let's say, a half dozen Yusanian laws? In addition to it just not sounding all that great?"

I'm silent. I had no idea that the Council of the Lords had convened. Twice a year, all four counts, along with high nobles from the major cities throughout Yusan, meet with the king to discuss issues of the realm. They all stay in Qali Palace for a week. It's always a tense time, as many of them have tried and failed to kill one another. It was just my luck that the Council of the Lords was in session, I suppose.

Mikail shakes his head. "Even your brother's hands were tied."

I think of the scene, of Chul bursting into the throne room, leaves and dirt still clinging to him, with the story of being hunted on his lips. How the lords would've feigned outrage and demanded my head, as if they don't murder and scheme constantly.

Still, even if Joon had to take action against me, it was Mikail smiling and agreeing that sealed my fate.

"You could've—" I begin.

He arches an eyebrow. "Stood up and been banished with you? It's a lovely scene that you've imagined—us holding hands with our chins high, facing your brother as one, but that's the stuff of a royal play. If Joon could've proven that I knew of your activities and failed to relay the information, I would've been a traitor. I would've been executed on the spot, or put into Idle Prison, or sliced apart in lingchi. Hard to say. But I would *not* have been banished with you. Death by exile was invented by your brother to keep him from directly ordering your execution."

I...I hadn't thought of that. I wipe my brow. Somehow, I'd never really considered what would've happened to Mikail. He's always been so close to me that I thought of us as the same. But he's right—he is a commoner while I am a prince. Or at least I was. Hard to say what I am now. And over the last three years, I've seen how little power commoners have. How little choice.

The remaining arguments die on my tongue.

"By agreeing with Joon, I proved my loyalty to him," Mikail says. "That way I could rescue you. While I will admit it is not a romantic fantasy, it was the way to actually save you."

"You call this saving me?" I say, gesturing around.

Mikail throws an arm up. "You think you just happened to land at the edge of an oasis? And that a caravan happened to show you mercy and bring you a sunsae east, all the way to Outton, for free? Stars!" Mikail's annoyed voice echoes through the pass, so he lowers his volume. "You are thicker than mud, Euyn."

I blink hard. The oasis. The sandstorm. But I got myself to the oasis on my own two feet. No…I woke up there. There is no way for him to know where I came to or that there even was a wandering caravan, except… He was there. It was Mikail who'd risked a sandstorm to pull me to the edge of the oasis, and *he'd* arranged for me to be brought to Outton, the closest major city to the border. Where I could blend in. He paid for me to be saved. This whole time, I believed it was divine providence and random generosity, but it had actually been Mikail. His love for me. His loyalty to me.

We ride without speaking, just the sound of the donkeys moving over the rocky ground.

I'm a fool.

For as much as I believed Mikail had abandoned me, had even come here to kill me, he's the only reason I am still alive.

"Mikail…" All my regret is somehow squeezed into those two syllables.

He shakes his head. "It's okay, Euyn. You weren't supposed to know. It was safer that way."

He doesn't seem upset, but I am. I'm devastated that I doubted him. I should've been smart enough to figure it out. He was always there for me—since we were boys. He wouldn't have betrayed me. But I'd been so desperate, so broken-hearted in Idle Prison, that I allowed myself to think the worst.

"I'm sorry nonetheless," I say.

Mikail glances over, then nods. "I am sorry, too. I wish I could've come up with an opportunity sooner."

We continue in silence. I scan the mountains again, but they are mostly covered in darkness.

"Joon didn't have much of a choice, either." It's a question and a statement.

"That is correct."

"Then why kill him?"

He stares straight ahead. "Your brother is not a fair king. I hope you will be."

"But he…"

"Euyn, if you are looking for someone to blame and you're done with me and your brother, might I suggest the Butcher of Westward Forest?"

My heart sinks and my stomach turns at my old nickname. I didn't actually butcher anyone, but the first few prisoners were so disoriented by the daylight that it was just a slaughter. They were dead within two minutes. And Mikail knew. He knew what the prison guards had nicknamed me. Yet he still loved me. Despite me trying to hide it from him. And he still thinks, in spite of all I did, that I will be a better king than Joon.

I have so many more questions and things I want to say, but the sun sinks below the horizon. Mikail and I exchange glances. No more talking until we clear the pass.

I keep my crossbow loaded on my lap, bolt aimed away from Mikail. He has his hand resting near the hilt of his sword.

We continue through the pass. The donkeys know the route, even in the dark. We traded our one surviving hamel for the asses, but it's a little comforting that they must have taken this pass many times and survived.

So maybe there aren't samroc nests here. Maybe we'll make it out of Fallow mostly in one piece.

I cling to that thought as we travel a bell into the night.

Then a cry echoes in the darkness. And this time, it's close by.

CHAPTER TWENTY-ONE

TIYUNG

THE NORTHERN ROAD, YUSAN

I've been traveling for the last three days with Sora. Beautiful, deadly, loving, hateful Sora. At times, she looks at me and my heart fills, but then it's clear she's plotting my death in those violet eyes, so it's less than desirable.

"What are you trying to accomplish?" she asks.

I shift at the sound of her voice. It's the sound of wished-for rain on a scorching day. The clear, soul-rising ring of temple bells. The divine music of the gods. And ordinarily, she'd rather kiss a toad than talk to me.

"Pardon?" I say.

"What are you trying to accomplish by feeding servants and giving money to beggar children?" she asks.

Frankly, I'd forgotten about the second part. We had an uncomfortably quiet and yet delicious lunch at a tavern, and there were beggar children outside on our way back to the carriage. There's desperate poverty throughout Yusan, and it hits children the worst. My father says that many of those children have lazy, able-bodied parents at home. That they are acting like orphans to get free mun. But even if that's the case, I'd rather give mun to a hundred actors than walk past a child in real need.

It's one of many areas where I don't see eye to eye with my father. Where he says I have the softness of my mother. At this point in my life, I don't mind that. It is better than the alternative.

I shrug. "Why do I need to accomplish anything?"

She narrows her eyes at me.

"Ah, I see," I say, crossing my arms as I lean back. "You think this is all for show. And you're wondering why I'm putting on a performance."

"Well…yes. You gave the children silver mun. That money will keep them fed for days. Your father would've run them down."

She's not wrong.

"I am not my father."

She scoffs. "You certainly used to be."

As usual, Sora is right. I haven't always been a good person—especially not to her. For too long, I was striving to be like my father, to impress him or at the very least to earn his approval. I didn't want him to think me soft. I cringe remembering how I used to go to his poison school in my hat and jewels and demand they serve me tea and biscuits. Especially Sora.

But if I had shown interest—or worse, kindness—I could have made life harder for her. My father loves only one thing more than power—teaching his son to be ruthless. So I was always the tyrant they both expected. But at least I got to see her, however briefly.

Still, trying to act like my father would make me sick to my stomach—witnessing how the girls would all be so pale and weak and shaking. Sora handled it better than any of the rest of them, and I was always secretly proud of that. As I got older, I would agree to go with my father to the hidden school because I wanted to make sure she was alive. Too many girls died.

One time, we arrived just as the emaciated body of a girl was being burned on a funeral pyre. She'd died so horrifically, they couldn't shut her jaw. She had long black hair, and I was terrified it was Sora, but then I saw her standing among the survivors. I wanted to cry, to scream and throw up in relief, but I was a teenager. I forced a fake yawn because my father was watching. Seok is always watching.

Once the girl's soul was freed, the ashes were buried like the rest. Not even released to the wind, as is custom—not these girls. These were victims to be forgotten about. But I remember them.

"You are correct," I say. "Although, I suppose not about everything." I don't bother to elaborate, to explain, to plead forgiveness. Sora wants many things—my father's death, mostly—but one thing she'll never want is me. She'll have no interest in my confession of love.

Her eyes take on an intense look when she's puzzling something out. She's clever and more capable than she gives herself credit for.

"What does that even mean—'I suppose not about everything'?" Her hand slaps the carriage cushion in frustration. "Why can't you just speak plainly?"

I lean forward. She doesn't flinch. Ever. I love that about her. I love everything about her. I think about telling her. It sits on the tip of my tongue—how I've loved her since the very first time I saw her. When she was nine and I was ten. But this isn't the time. Maybe I will before this is all over. But not today.

"It means I am bored with this conversation, Sora," I say with a yawn. I lean back and rest my head against the carriage seat.

Sora stares out the window at the passing scenery but says nothing. More silence. Just the sound of the horses clomping on the road and the wheels spinning. She may not speak to me again until we reach Rahway. But I tell myself it's for the best—or at the very least it's deserved.

"Does your father want the throne?" she asks seconds later.

I'm not sure if I'm more surprised by her speaking to me or her question.

"I assume he does," I say. "Or at least a greater share of power."

"Why? Why isn't having all of Gain and being the southern count enough? A quarter of the country is under his control, and he is answerable only to the king. And yet he's risking treason to get more."

I draw a breath. It's the very thing I've wondered about my own father many times, even though in my heart, I know the answer.

"There are some men who only know hunger," I say. "If they drank the East and West Sea, they'd want the ice of the North. You know this. You've seen it."

She frowns. "But I don't understand it."

"Because you're not empty inside," I say. She blinks at the comment. I suppose it's something of a compliment, but really, it's just a fact. "You're also not a powerful man."

"Sometimes I feel like I've been emptied, like there's nothing more of the girl I used to be." She speaks in a low voice, really more to herself than to me. But her confessing anything makes my heart swell. Still, I maintain my distant air.

I shake my head. "You have Daysum. You are still you."

Her face falls. Just a touch. What was that? Before I can figure it out, her expression changes.

"One day, you will be as powerful as your father," she says. "Maybe more so."

I nod. "I'll try not to let it change me, but I'm certain it will. I have to imagine my father began life as a good man."

She arches an eyebrow. "I've seen no evidence of that."

"Nor have I. But it's what my mother told me—that he was a good man long ago."

Sora taps her finger to her chin. I am certain she can't imagine my father as a good man. I don't blame her. But my mother maintains that Seok was a sweet young lord. That he was thoughtful and loved her with his whole heart. And my mother doesn't lie.

"What happened to him?" Sora asks.

"Power corrupts everyone," I say. "The more you have, the faster the slide. I want to help you, Sora. So let me, while I can still be the man I want to be. We don't have to be friends," I urge her again, "but we can be allies."

She tries to speak a few times, but then she sighs and gives me a single nod. It's more of an agreement than I thought I'd have from her. She must be desperate, but I believe she'll accept my help, which is good. She'll need it.

My father has ordered me to kill her once the king is dead.

CHAPTER TWENTY-TWO

EUYN

TANGUN MOUNTAIN PASS, YUSAN

I shiver from my neck to my lower back at the sound of the cry and clutch my bow. It wasn't a full-grown samroc—they're far louder—but we could be near a nest. Their babies must be as big as a man, and they could sound human. The thought makes my blood run cold.

"What *was* that?" I whisper. I load my bow and train it on the sound. But Mikail is already headed toward the noise.

"It's a child, Euyn," he says.

I exhale at the false alarm, then bring my donkey over to Mikail. There, huddled on the ground with his knees to his chest, is a small boy. Maybe seven or eight years old in an ill-fitting tunic. I relax, but then my hackles rise. This feels wrong. A young boy has no business being in this pass alone at night. Not when we're three bells from the nearest town; not when there are so many dangers.

I scan for lanterns, for a sign of an impending attack, but there's nothing. The night air is still. But this scene isn't right.

"Leave him, Mikail," I say.

Mikail shoots me a look so harsh in the moonlight that I recoil. "I am not going to leave a boy here by himself."

"It has to be a trap," I say. "What is a child doing here?"

"Why don't we fucking ask him?" Mikail whispers sharply. He faces the boy. "What is your name?" he asks, gentler.

"Kito, sir," he says.

"Kito, where are your parents?"

He doesn't say anything, but his eyes volley to the left. The whites of his eyes shine, and I ride forward, crossbow at my shoulder, but then I put it down.

It stinks of death, and for good reason. Even the mule has been slaughtered, blood pooled all around its neck. The blood has congealed some and attracted a swarm of desert flies. The wagon is tipped over on its side. This was not samroc but people who attacked. I don't risk lighting a lantern, but I look closely.

The man I assume was Kito's father is dead with his throat slit. I walk the area, but all I find is a dead mule and a dead man. Belongings are scattered on the ground. I look closer. There's a dress, a ball, and a doll. Then I find another body—the mother. Her face is frozen in agony, her skirts raised, and her legs spread. No dignity, even in death.

I ride back.

Mikail turns and searches my face. I shake my head. No other survivors.

"Armed men attacked your family?" Mikail asks.

The boy nods.

"Were they Yusanian or Fallow?" I ask.

He starts to cry. "I don't know. I hid. I shouldn't have run and hid, but I did. And now…"

"You were smart," Mikail says. It's a sweeter tone than I've ever heard him use. Mikail has always had a soft spot for children, but I have no idea why he's taken to this boy so quickly.

Kito shakes his head. "They took my sister and brother. They… attacked…her. I should've helped. I shouldn't have just covered my ears—"

"There was nothing you could've done against armed men except be taken, too," Mikail says. "Do you know which way they went?"

The boy shakes his head. "I don't."

"What town are you from?" I ask. It's not light enough to fully make out his features, but something about this is making the hairs on my arms rise.

"Gale, sir," he says. Gale is ten bells southeast of Swift.

"Why were you going to Fallow?" I ask.

The wagon was facing into the pass, not out. And even having seen the bodies and the blood, it feels wrong, almost staged. This child shouldn't be here. Men capable of killing two adults and taking two children to sell wouldn't have been careless enough to let this one go. The children are the point—they fetch the highest price.

"Papa said for a better life," Kito says.

I exchange glances with Mikail. How would Fallow be better? His family must've operated in something illegal—that would at least explain traveling into the pass after dark.

"We are going to Yusan," Mikail says. "We can take you back with us."

The boy slowly nods.

"Mikail…" I say. "No."

"He comes with us, or you go alone," Mikail says. It's so final that it feels like a slap in the face. He'd rather help this child he has no attachment to than see me to safety? The man he loves? Not to mention that it feels like something is crawling across my back. Something bad is coming. We need to leave. Now.

"We can take him as far as Swift, I suppose, but—" I begin.

Mikail stares daggers at me and then looks at the child. "We'll bring you back to Gale. You have to have other family there, correct?"

The boy nods.

"Come with us, son. We'll get you home."

Suddenly, the boy hesitates. He looks around wildly. I begin to look around, too, wondering what the child is searching for. His eyes are wrong. Why doesn't Mikail see this?

He is the only one staring forward.

"But I..." the boy says.

"Your family isn't coming back," Mikail says. He speaks gently but firmly. "But the men who did this may. They may realize they let you escape. So we have to leave here. There aren't words now and there may not ever be words for what happened tonight. But you were spared. It is your job to carry them in your heart and to do what you can to earn your salvation. But there is nothing you can do for them and no way you could've stopped this. I wish we could've been here sooner, but I'm glad we're here now to help."

I stop wanting to flee as I digest what Mikail is saying. It's strange. I get the feeling he's said all of this before. But when and why? It doesn't make sense, but I truly don't know what he's done in spying for my brother. I know he's taken lives and lied and seduced, but I haven't asked questions.

Maybe I should've.

The boy sniffles but stands.

"Now, make your peace and then come with us," he says. "Don't look as we pass. There is nothing for you to see."

Mikail puts the boy on his donkey and walks holding the reins. I ride next to him.

We're almost past the carnage when the boy whispers, "Run."

CHAPTER TWENTY-THREE

ROYO
THE SOL RIVER, YUSAN

It makes no fucking sense. None of it.

I've tried to let it go. But I've thought about what happened with the fire ship since I woke up. Well, just about. I came to at dawn with Aeri wrapped around me. Somehow, this waif of a girl helped keep me warm through the night. She smelled like flowers, like spring, somehow, even on a sandbar in the middle of a river. No one in Umbria smells like flowers. I laid there breathing it in—not because I like her or nothing. It's just different.

And she was so pretty in sleep. She seems younger than twenty-four, especially when she's asleep. Then I realized I was staring at her and I looked away. The rowboat caught my eye.

I was so worried about getting away from the fire ship, finding safety, and then surviving the night that I hadn't really thought about how we fell off the balcony into a rowboat.

But as I stared at it, I knew there was no explanation. The lifeboat was too far away from where we fell for us to land in it. But somehow we did. Even more surprising, though, is that somehow we got away.

Just then, Aeri woke up, chipper with a bright smile. And it shocked me because who wakes up happy? The girl is just unnatural.

"Good morning, Royo," she said.

I got to my feet and busied myself preparing to get off the isle. Which wasn't a real thing, but it got me away from her.

For ten minutes.

For the next five bells, though, she followed me around, listing out all the food she wanted to eat. My empty stomach rumbled and twisted, and I once again dreamed of the splash she'd make if she *happened* to fall into the river. But it was less satisfying than before. Probably because we saved each other from the pirates and then the cold.

I was about ready to snap regardless when a speck appeared on the horizon. Just a dot. But Aeri shut her mouth as we both watched it. Hope stirred in my chest. Just a little at the beginning. I told myself to brush it aside, to not be fooled, that hope picks you up to watch you fall, that it probably wasn't a riverboat. But then it got closer. It was.

"Do you think they'll rescue us?" she asked.

"They can't reach us here—it's too shallow. We need to row out to them."

I wasn't sure if they'd help, really, but we had to try. We hopped into the lifeboat, and I rowed closer as she shouted for them to stop.

Crewmen saw us—saw her, really—and pulled us up.

Once we were on board, Aeri's fine but ruined clothes and her manners got us another plush room on the ship. So we are back in comfortable quarters and a day behind schedule. But as I stand on the balcony of our new room, it just don't make any sense. I don't get how we got away from the pirates. Yeah, it was chaos. Yeah, they were ransacking the ship. But how did they let an entire rowboat escape? We should've been dead or captured.

Maybe the gods are on our side.

I grimace. That doesn't seem real likely. I've never known them to give a shit about me and my plans. But that's what Aeri said as she told our tale to the captain and crew. How I spotted the fire ship on the horizon and how arrows came down like hail and I fought them like a hero, then how we narrowly escaped, falling into the lifeboat. I blacked out, which explains my headache and back bruises, and she cut the lines.

It makes sense, I guess, but also it don't. Why didn't they set our boat on fire or shoot arrows at us? What's more is, Aeri is a storyteller. Which means she's a liar. But I also can't figure out why she'd lie. There was nothing in it for her to lie about rowing us to safety, and there's gotta be a reason to lie. Few people do it for the hells of it. So back around I go.

I give up. What's important is that we made it. It don't matter how—survival ain't got nothing to do with glory. I walk back inside.

"Royo." Aeri smiles as I shut the sliding door. She's talked a lot less since we got on board, so maybe the gods do like me.

I lock the door, which is pointless because if someone wanted to break in from outside, it would be pirates and the lock wouldn't help. But I do it anyhow.

Then I notice Aeri's in a bathrobe. She washed her dress as best she could, and it's drying outside.

"I can't wait until we reach Rahway. Ugh." She flops back on the bed, then sits up, leaning on her elbows. Her robe falls open slightly, revealing the top curve of her breast and a necklace. I don't think about what else is underneath.

I look around for something else to stare at.

She's still talking at the ceiling, though. "I'll have a trunk of new dresses made. Maybe two trunks. And I'm sure they'll have a beauty house. It's just so hard to replace a makeup collection, but I have to look the part, you know?"

I don't. Sometimes it's like she's speaking gibberish or Weian. She pauses and eyes me just as I was looking at the neckline of her robe again. I look away.

"I can have them make you a couple of suits, too," she says.

I glance at my shirt and pants. "Why would I need a suit?"

"For when we meet the spymaster? Because people treat you better when you dress nicely? Because I'm paying? I don't know, Royo." She shrugs. "But I think they make men look sharp."

"They make men look like marks."

She tilts her head. "Don't you want nice things?"

"We're not all rich merchant daughters or noble girls or whatever you are," I say. "Some of us make do."

"I'm not noble, Royo," she says. "Or a merchant. My mother was a courtesan."

I raise my eyebrows. Courtesans are like professional girlfriends. They're attractive, smart girls who attach themselves to nobles in hopes of being shown favor and in hopes they can produce sons who will inherit. It's weird to me, the whole heir thing, but I don't judge. Not the girls, anyhow. They're selling the use of their bodies the same way I sell my services, but I don't have to let nobles slobber all over me. And why guys would go for that, I don't know.

But this is what she'd started to tell me before we saw the fire ship. I sit down on the couch across from her.

"Oh," I say.

"Yes, 'oh.'" Aeri mimics my deep tone. "Because I was born a girl, I got nothing. And my mother died last year without a mun to her name."

Her tone is suddenly acid. She's as bitter as any drunk I've met in Umbria who felt cheated out of a chance at a good life.

"I'm sorry," I say.

Aeri nods. "I know you are, Royo. Are you still close with your father?"

"He was never in the picture." I don't want to tell her all this personal stuff, but I also can't seem to stop. It's like she's got a spell on me.

"I understand," Aeri says.

She meets my gaze, and there's something there. Something I believe. Same as when she talked about mistakes not being able to be undone. Her father must not have been around neither. She gets it. I want to move closer to her, but then I remember it doesn't matter. She's a job. Only a job.

"Once I remove the crown, everything will be set right." She folds her hands on her lap, prim as ever. "For both of us, I mean."

Her eyes are bright and clear as she looks at me. She's beautiful, really. Not what you'd imagine when you think *beautiful woman*, but the more I look at her, the prettier she is. But I don't know what she means by "everything will be set right," and I remind myself that I can't trust her. I gotta stop spilling my guts every time she asks a question, because I can't afford to trust nobody. Especially not her. I need to draw the line. It's gotten blurry over the last day.

"Aeri," I say.

"Yes?"

I stare her dead in the face. "Double-cross me, and I swear it'll be the last thing you ever do."

She smiles, amused. "You don't have to worry about that, Royo."

"Why not?"

"Because you don't have anything I want." She holds my gaze for a second and then gets up off the bed. "Let's go for a stroll. We could use some air. It's so much nicer down here than in Umbria!"

With that, she leaves the room. In her robe. I look around for answers, and my eyes land on her velvet purse. The one thing she took from the other boat, and it's big enough to hold a fur-lined cloak. I wonder what else is in it and if it'll explain her at all, but I just said she's only a job. And I don't have the time to snoop with Aeri waiting for me outside. At least not right now.

But I'll figure her out. I swear it.

CHAPTER TWENTY-FOUR

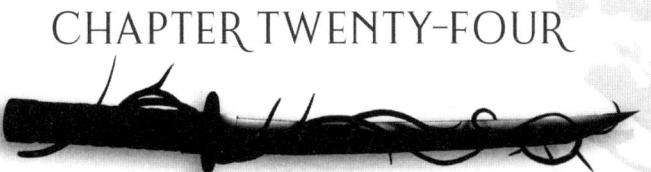

EUYN

TANGUN MOUNTAIN PASS, YUSAN

Gods on High, I hate being right.

Men leap at us from behind the wagon and down the pass. Four of them, maybe more. We're surrounded. This was a trap, the kid bait. And I knew it the whole time! The boy delayed and distracted us long enough for these ruffians to close in. They might've done the same to the couple in the wagon—a young child crying at just the right moment so they stop. And their pity cost them their lives. And Mikail's almost cost us ours.

But the kid tipped us off, and it was enough time for me to dismount and get the crossbow to my shoulder. Energy flows through me, but everything quiets. It's always the same feeling during a hunt, whether it's man or beast.

I fire, reload, fire, reload, and fire again. Three bolts in less than a minute—the fastest reload time of any archer—but the men evade two of my shots. Only one of them hits home, which tells me that these are experienced fighters. I look over, expecting a flaming sword, but Mikail is standing stock-still next to his donkey. I have never once seen Mikail freeze in fear. That's not what this is, but he's a statue as four men come at us.

"A little help, Mikail!" I yell. I dodge a sword attack, rolling out of the way. I balance back on my feet, but I won't be able to evade them for long. Not four of them.

Mikail shakes off his stupor and lifts his sword. It flames in the night, and two of the men stop. Everyone knows what that sword is and that a flaming blade means death. Mikail pushes the donkey and kid out of the way and then runs his sword through the closest man. The man falls with a piercing wail.

And then it's a battle. It's three on two in deadly combat. Two attack Mikail at once. One comes after me. I recognize these moves—they were trained in the Yusanian military. They aren't the inexperienced highwaymen we ran into on the way to Tile. They know how to attack and evade. And they probably know who we are.

I fire my bow again and hit the man in the shoulder, but he's still coming at me. No time for another bolt. Panicked, I grab the sword from the back of my donkey. I turn just as a blade comes down, heading straight for my spine. Steel strikes steel so hard that it sends sparks flying into the night. The pain of the blow reverberates through me. I parried the sword—barely. But the force he used makes me fall to the rocky ground. My left hand stings as I cut it. Despite all my tutors, I've never been very good with the sword. I'm too lanky and not fast enough.

I try to get to my feet, but the man kicks my blade out of my hand. Disarmed, with my wrist smarting, I raise my arm to shield my face, even though I know it won't save me.

Gods on High, I'm going to die on the ground of this pass.

The man's sword rises in the air. A killing blow. No chance at redemption. At the throne. At a life with Mikail. The life I should've had flashes before my eyes, and I accept that I won't live any of it. That all I'll get is the chance to die honorably. To not cower or beg. I make peace with it.

But then the man freezes. A blade suddenly pokes out of his chest and then rips through his abdomen. Mikail has run his sword through the man's back.

I'm so shocked, I stay on the ground, staring up at him.

"Stick to the crossbow," he says. He spins his sword, ready for the next attack, protecting me as I scramble to my feet.

Two on two. Mikail holds his sword and lets the other man attack first. My arms tutor used to say that sword fighting is like a dance. And that's what it resembles. Steel clangs as they move back and forth. One leading, one responding. The man actually hits Mikail's blade several times. Then Mikail skirts to the side and raises his sword. It slices the man's neck apart with a glancing blow. He's not even trying—not really. Something else is bothering him.

Then there's the last man. The one dodging my crossbow bolts. But the man is so busy fending off my attacks that he doesn't see Mikail coming with his sword raised.

"Da!" the kid screams.

Kito jumps in front of his father and takes Mikail's sword right through his chest.

Gods on High.

It feels like everything moves in slow motion. Clouds that had blocked the bright moon part. The scene is clear. Kito has Mikail's sword sticking out of his chest, just below his collarbone. Mikail immediately releases the jade-and-gold-encrusted hilt—something he's never done. The sword was too hard earned, too precious to let go of. But his face is frozen in horror. The kid's face is frozen in shock.

As Mikail stills, the man rushes forward. Instead of attacking, he pulls the sword from the kid's chest. Then, with it still in hand, he takes off. Just yanks the blade out of the child's body without a second look. A prayer. A word. Nothing for the boy who just saved his life.

The boy falls face-first to the ground with a sickening thud. His father runs like a coward in the night, eager to keep his new prize. Because the blade was worth more to him than his own son.

I shoot my crossbow, but I'm so shocked by his barbarism that my aim is off. Plus my hands are both aching, and one is slick with blood. Still, I hit him in the back of the thigh instead of the chest. It's enough, since Mikail sprints after him as the man hobbles.

With one jump, Mikail tackles him to the ground and then sits on his chest.

"You want my sword so badly, have it," Mikail says. He's already ripped it from the man's grasp, and he pierces the man's arm with it.

The still night is filled with screaming and the sounds of killing. I grimace. It is different—what I do versus Mikail. I kill with a crossbow. There's something detached, clean, and quick about pulling a trigger and shooting a man at a distance. Right now, Mikail is getting soaked to his shoulders with blood, but he doesn't care. He's furious. He's not allowing this man a fast or quiet death. I'm pretty sure he just castrated him as he shouted something about the woman in the wagon. It's just hard to tell over all that bleating.

Mikail has been called many things—a bastard, a demon, the King of Hells. Nothing I've ever listened to, of course. But then he gets like this, and I see it. There is a seething rage, an underbelly to all his charisma that can't be just from his father punishing him. There was something in the way he trusted this child, how he didn't see or feel that it was a trap, that doesn't make sense. Mikail is many things, but he's never naive. Something is off about all of this. But unless he wants to, Mikail will never tell me. It's the aspect of his personality that I admire and hate the most.

"You set up your own son," Mikail says. "Your soul will never be redeemed."

I think that's what he's saying. I look up at the sky. I suppose there aren't samroc nests nearby, because if there were, this man's screams would've drawn twenty of them. But I would wager on a demon Mikail versus twenty samroc right now.

Now, certain the birds are far from here, I light a lantern and scan to make sure there aren't any other men hiding or lying in wait. It's an ugly scene of murder and dying. The rocky ground has been painted red.

I check Kito. I hope he isn't hearing his father moan like a pleasure-house whore, but as I suspected, he's dead. He must've died seconds after the blade was removed.

I rub my face. How many lives are we going to take? How much blood will my crown cost? And will I ever be good enough to warrant the price?

CHAPTER TWENTY-FIVE

SORA

CITY OF RAHWAY, YUSAN

We enter the outskirts of Rahway, and I've never seen a city like it.

I've traveled outside of Gain to kill men for the Count, but that was only around the southern region. I've never been this far northwest before. The village where I was purchased was in the northeast.

It's different here.

Rahway rises out of nothing. The horizon was empty, and then all of a sudden there was a sandstone metropolis, like a mirage. The air is temperate but much drier than Gain. I suppose the sun-hardened rock is what's allowed them to build tall spires and towers. Like Gain, the city of Rahway is walled, but Rahway has a bridge that needs to be crossed to enter the city proper.

Where Gain is colorful, Rahway is all tans, beiges, and browns. The splashes of green are palm and date trees. There are fields of spiky orange plants as we approach. I believe those make alcohol, but I'm not sure.

I stare out the carriage windows as we roll over the high, arching bridge. Below the bridge is an enormous port. I catch Tiyung looking at me. I sit back.

"Don't stop on my account," he says.

"You're staring."

"I'm sorry. I…I just like seeing wonder on your face." He looks out the other window. It's nice even though I don't want it to be.

I have thought about his words, his offer of help, his shows of generosity, for days as we've traveled. I've decided that he's sincere. Maybe he simply wants to be thought of as a good person or he pities me. But he seems to genuinely want to help. I still don't know if I can trust him. I don't put anything past his father, and I've seen the sway the man holds over Tiyung. But for now, I suppose there can be a truce of sorts. For now, I could use an ally, especially if it saves Daysum's life.

I've been trying to figure out what she said to me and why she'd whisper on my left side, where she knows I'd have difficulty hearing her, but I still don't have an answer. *Sora, I think it's time.* It's time for what?

If only I knew where the Count was keeping her. I could write and ask.

"We'll meet the Count of Rahway tonight," Tiyung says.

"You're kidding," I say, smoothing the rich brocade dress against my thighs.

Tiyung shakes his head, watching the movement of the fabric. "He is the one who has instructions for who we need to meet and where."

"Both counts are in on this?" I ask.

"I assume all counts are."

I knit my eyebrows so hard my eyes hurt. How could all four counts agree on anything? Especially high treason. Moreover, how could all four believe that I am the solution when I don't even know how to do it? It doesn't make any sense. There have to be important facts being kept from me. These men would not bet their lives on a long shot. But maybe there will be answers tonight. I have to hope.

We ride into the city. The Temple of the Sun God sits in the center and towers over the landscape, just as the Temple of the God of the West Sea does in Gain. The buildings are a little more colorful than they appeared from far away, though not by much. But the stone and stucco add a nice uniformity.

About halfway into the city, we stop at a fine inn that reaches into the sky. It's called the Troubadour, and it'll be our home while we're in Rahway.

We get out of the carriage and stretch. People, of course, stare. They believe they're seeing an excessively handsome young couple. Or a young noble and his courtesan. Their fashion is different here. The men wear longer, lighter tunics. The women's dresses wrap.

It's just dawned on me that it's strange that we're staying at an inn at all. High nobles stay at each other's villas, as we did when we stopped at Lord Shan's.

"Why aren't we staying at the count's estate?" I ask.

"So that he can deny having anything to do with my father's plan if we fail," Tiyung says.

He says it so matter-of-factly that I do a double take as I process it. Tiyung gestures for me to go ahead.

"We won't fail," he says. "But they always hedge their bets."

We walk into the inn. The lobby is all pink marble and carved stone. It's just shy of tacky. The innkeeper comes racing at us and greets us with a deep bow. "Tiyung-si. My lady. I am Sanu, the owner and proprietor here. If you would do me the honor, I'll show you to your rooms."

Tiyung tips his head in acknowledgment. "Please."

The short man escorts us up several flights of stone stairs. He might be smaller than Daysum.

"But we're still having dinner with him tonight?" I whisper.

Tiyung nods. "He naturally would dine with the southern count's son. It would be strange if he didn't."

I rub my forehead. How does all of this scheming never get tiring to any of them? How are they never content with all of the riches they have? All of the people under their thumbs, from assassins like me to innkeepers like Sanu?

"Here we are," Sanu says, a little winded as he opens the door. It was a long climb, although he's likely not much older than we are. "Our finest suite. I daresay the finest in all of Rahway. It spans this entire floor, as you can see, and boasts two private bathing rooms and two in-room servants. They will be here for you if you need anything, day or night."

The suite is absolutely enormous, with a sunken living room by a large fireplace and long balconies outside. The space is four times larger than my cottage. Maybe more.

"Thank you," Tiyung says. He attempts to give Sanu mun.

Sanu backs up, waving his hands. "No, no, just let me know if there's anything at all you need or want, Tiyung-si. The count has personally asked me to ensure that there is no desire unmet."

"Thank you," Tiyung says.

Sanu bows with a flourish. He must practice it in front of a mirror.

I glance at Tiyung. He's so used to being treated this way that he doesn't even notice the great effort Sanu is making.

"Draw baths," Tiyung says to the servants. "The lady will take the room next to mine. Have her trunk brought in, but don't open it unless she instructs you to."

I shudder at the cold tone. He sounds like his father, and I wonder if he can hear it as well. But the servants scurry to do his bidding. So he has changed, but only with those he chooses.

Had I been born less beautiful, I'd have a position like a room servant, solidly beneath the notice of nobles. Both are humiliating, but I would've preferred servitude.

Tiyung takes off his travel jacket and tosses it onto the nearest chair. There was an envelope waiting for him.

He smiles at the envelope, then looks at me. "Make yourself at home, Sora. We'll leave at seven bells."

A little under two bells from now.

"What will you be doing?" I ask.

"Reading some correspondence, sending a message to my father, and then enjoying a hot bath." He gestures to the seal around his neck. The nobility coat their paper envelopes in a fine layer of fast-drying clay and roll their seals over it to prevent anyone from secretly reading their words.

The envelope in his hand is sealed.

I want to ask who it is from because that is not Seok's mark, but for all I know it's just the Count of Rahway writing about dinner. Somehow I doubt it, though. Tiyung is visibly excited to open the letter. I want to know, but it's not my place, so I start toward my bath.

Two bells is just enough time for me to prepare to meet the western count. Although if he's anything like Seok, a lifetime wouldn't prepare me.

CHAPTER TWENTY-SIX

EUYN

THE EASTERN ROAD, YUSAN

Mikail is hiding something from me. Well, I suppose he's always hiding things, but this time it's troubling me. Whoever said there's no love without trust was deep in their cups. Of course there can be love without trust. Harmony without trust, however, is a different story.

He's not covered in blood as we ride to Rahway, so I suppose that's an improvement. We had to throw out his shirt and trousers when we got to Gorya. They were irredeemably soaked in blood and guts—some of it his. One of his wounds had reopened because of his exertion in the mountain pass. It wasn't until he took his shirt off that I realized it—he'd said nothing about the pain. I quickly sewed him back together, hopefully doing a better job this time.

While I was working on him, I tried to ask him about the boy, Kito, and he just said, "No, Euyn." And that was it. No.

Sometimes I wonder which of us is royalty and which is the spy.

But I suppose I'm holding more secrets from him than he can ever keep from me. The largest one, I don't even dare think about. As if remembering it will scream my shame for all to hear.

We're taking a fleet carriage—a team of eight horses specially bred for speed and endurance will get us to Rahway in half the time it would usually take. They cost a handsome amount and aren't widely available, but Mikail brought a deep purse.

Which means that Quilimar is being generous. Not a trait she's known for. I don't even know how she's managing in a country that lets women have rights.

This mission continues to have more questions than answers. Starting with why my sister, who could never be bothered with me in the palace, wants me to have the crown. Why not take it for herself? It would be war, of course, but that's nothing new for Yusan and Khitan. I try to puzzle it out, but I'm not built for riddles.

"Euyn, my dear, you are squinting," Mikail says.

"Why does Quilimar want me to be king?" I ask.

Mikail raises his eyebrows.

"That's what I was trying to figure out," I add, adjusting on the divan. This coach could fit a dozen people, so there is plenty of room here for just him and me.

"I see," Mikail says. "Well, she's not a fan of Joon, and you're the only other option outside of a costly war."

All of that is true, especially her hatred of Joon. I remember the scene she made when Joon put his seal on her sale to the king of Khitan.

Khitan invaded five years ago, and Quilimar was sold as a peace offering. It was called a wedding. In exchange for her hand, the king pulled back his women-led troops and stopped raiding our northeastern towns. Marriage to Quilimar was likely what he'd wanted in the first place. Although why he'd want to live with her is beyond me.

Their marriage was supposed to broker everlasting peace between us and our neighbor. I believe this is the seventh "everlasting" peace between Yusan and Khitan. We're too different to ever truly be at peace. Unless Wei is involved. Then we're the oldest and best of friends.

"But the king of Khitan…" I begin.

"Is dead."

I stare. "I beg your pardon?"

The king of Khitan isn't immortal like my brother, but he's nearly as hard to kill. The Ring of Khitan is also a relic of the Dragon Lord. Its power is alchemy. It is the reason why the barren land of Khitan is even a country—otherwise, it would be like Fallow. The king of Khitan can fill his treasury with gold at a touch of his hand, which is a boon, as mercenary troops happen to love gold.

But the ring can also provide protection. An assassin once got all the way to the throne, and the king turned him into solid gold with a touch. An alive human being one moment; a gold statue the next. He was sent back to Wei as both a payoff and a warning not to cross into Khitan again.

"He is dead," Mikail says. "Quilimar is making her moves."

My sister has always been ambitious. Had she been born a boy, it is said that our father might've passed over Joon and Omin and given her the crown. She was, undeniably, his favorite. But girls cannot inherit under our laws. They can't in Wei, either. Only Khitan allows that nonsense.

I have no idea how my sister killed her husband, but I do believe she's capable of murder.

"She's ruling as regent for their son, and reports are that she's wearing the ring, which no regent has done before," Mikail says.

He shoots me a look, and I know what that means. He either doubts the child will live or doubts he'll ever see the throne. I wouldn't put either past Quilimar.

"I still don't understand. Why Yusan?"

"She wants Joon dead—I believe the entire court heard her scream that before the wedding."

"I know, but…"

"Quilimar likely believes she can control you," Mikail says with a sigh. "That you will be a weaker king, able to be bought off by Khitan gold."

I let the sting of that insult settle in my bones. The man I was before I was banished would've been a weak king—there's no sense in denying that. I would've been tempted by envoys carrying riches. I would've probably spent it expanding the palace and lavishing gifts on Mikail and myself. But I am different now. And maybe it is good to be underestimated.

But it doesn't feel that way. Growing up without a father, all I had wanted was the love of my siblings—or if not love, at least respect. It doesn't appear I achieved either. And if your family doesn't love you, how can you ever really have a place in this world?

Mikail's teal eyes scan my face. "She doesn't know you. None of your siblings ever really knew you."

He is right. No one, royal or otherwise, took the time to know me. Except for Mikail. No one ever accepted me, all of me, until him. None of them gave me a home.

Beautiful, deadly, secretive Mikail. At times, I want to tear him apart to get to the bottom of him. To really know him in order to possess him. But it wouldn't work—he'd take his secrets to the grave, and I'd never hurt him. Because I love him. I've loved him. I will always love him.

He glances at me, long lashes and sharp cheekbones. I reach forward, giving him time to back away, before I cup his face in my hand. He doesn't move. His cheek is so smooth, his skin soft. And those lips. Those lips I haven't been able to forget. Not for a second of the last three years.

I'm staring at his mouth, and then his lips are on mine. They're so plump and firm. My hands grip his hair, his face. His do the same as his tongue circles mine. Then it's a race. It's always been frenzied with us. But this is something else. I'm biting his lips to make sure he's real, sinking my fingers into his skin. I'm inhaling his cologne like it's my drug. I'm making sure that this whole thing isn't another fever dream. And he's handling me the same way.

He's real. He's really here with me.

And it's like no time has passed at all. Like the throne room never happened, because I have him. But the difference is that I want him more than I ever have. More than I even thought was possible. It feels like I'll wither and die if I don't have him right this second.

This kiss. This kiss is worth going through the hells for. It is worth starving to be nourished like this. His hands run down my shirt. He still hums the same when he kisses me. He still tastes the same. Every part of me responds to him in a way I never have with anyone else. I've had countless lovers, but with Mikail I always want more. All I ever want is more.

Soon, I'm kissing down his chest and unbuttoning his trousers. It's been too long. Way too long. I need to taste him. To possess him as much as I ever can.

"I love you, Mikail."

I whisper it into his skin as I get on my knees in front of him. I won't be content until I have all of him. So I will never be content.

CHAPTER TWENTY-SEVEN

ROYO
CITY OF RAHWAY, YUSAN

I really don't like having some guy's hands near my crotch. But I have to hold still. I'm being fitted for new suits because Aeri insisted. And the tailor is on his knee and has to measure something called an inseam. I'm tense as I wait, holding my breath. This is real uncomfortable.

We barely docked in Rahway before she was dragging me to the finest dress house in town. I've murdered and mutilated, and she's swiftly becoming the worst job I've ever had.

The more days I spend with Aeri, the more and less I mean that.

The night we were rescued, I had a hard time falling asleep on the couch. I should've passed right out because I was bodily exhausted. My head was aching, and I had an impressive bruise from falling onto my gold. But instead of sleeping, I lay there wondering what was wrong with me. Finally, I admitted that it was because I wanted to feel Aeri's light breathing on my neck. The little rise and fall of her chest under my arm. I forced myself to cut it out, to stay on my couch, to go the fuck to sleep. Some people call wanting something you can't have "aspiring." I call it setting yourself up for disappointment.

The next night, it got easier. And now I don't even think about it. Much.

Right now, she's sitting in an armchair, sipping tea, and picking fabrics. Her long legs are crossed in front of her. She wants three suits made for me. The fuck I'm supposed to do with three suits, I don't know. But she ordered no fewer than a dozen dresses for herself. So I guess three suits is nothing in her mind.

"You'll be able to have the first of these ready by tomorrow morning, correct?" she asks.

"Yes, my lady," the tailor says. He's a nice enough old guy. He stands and puts his tape measure over his narrow shoulder. I'm done, I guess. I step off the raised platform.

"Great!" Aeri claps her hands and stands.

She makes sure to grab her velvet bag off the chair. I eye it, still wondering what's inside, as I sling my heavy bag over my shoulder. Yeah, we still have our stuff. We didn't even check into our inn yet, but Aeri is happy. She has a new dress she bought off the shop mannequin. It's a little baggy on her even though it wraps, but she couldn't stand wearing the old one for a second more.

I have to carry out her dirty laundry and a bag full of undergarments she purchased. She insisted on buying me some new ones, too. I don't get who's gonna see my underwear, but it was easier to take it than to argue with her again. We had about twenty little arguments on the ship, and I'm tired. She could exhaust a fleet horse.

We leave the posh dress shop, and the sun is overwhelming. Where Umbria is all gray stone and sharp pitched roofs, this place is light creams and tans. The warm sun makes the walls glitter. I hold my hand above my eyes to shield them. I didn't know buildings could glimmer.

"Where are we staying?" I ask.

"The Troubadour Inn," she says.

"Where's that?"

"I dunno." She looks around and then grabs a random man's sleeve as he walks by us. "Excuse me. Where can I find the Troubadour?"

He's as surprised as I am, but he's nice enough. He points to the right. "It's about four blocks that way. Good day, my lady."

"What luck!" She smiles, delighted.

We had to take a carriage here because Aeri insisted it was too far to walk from the port, but I guess four blocks is close enough for her. She skips down the sidewalk in her new dress with her mysterious velvet bag while I follow. And I would normally be annoyed, but it's nice here. It's twenty-five degrees warmer than Umbria, which feels balmy. And yeah, there's something about her happiness that's okay, too. Or at least I've gotten used to it.

The tower rings out eleven bells. We'll be here all day and into tomorrow. Since we made it to Rahway, it's now just a matter of hiring a coach for the Eastern Road to Tamneki.

"All of those suits and dresses will be ready by tomorrow?" I ask.

Aeri tilts her head. "No, just two. I paid extra to have those and your suit ready quickly."

Just two? "What about the rest? We're leaving tomorrow, aren't we?"

She shakes her head. "I think we'll be here a few days."

"What?" I stop in the middle of the road.

She pauses on the sidewalk. "When we meet with the spymaster, we'll plan out the timing of Tamneki, but I think we'll be here a couple of days or so. If the clothes aren't ready when we need to leave, I'll have them couriered to the capital. No big deal."

It's a very big deal. I remain standing in the middle of the road, gesturing with my arms out, until carriage drivers shout for me to get the hells out of the way.

Aeri squints at me. "Why do you look so annoyed? You didn't even *want* the suits."

I throw my hands up. "Because it's another delay!"

"So?"

"So it'll take even more time!"

"And? You promised me a month."

"Yeah. The thirty days started the day we left Umbria." I point in the general direction of the city, frustration making me fling out my arm. Apparently, I do have the energy to fight with her again.

She stares at me. "And?"

"And we were delayed a day on the Sol, and now you're talking two or three days here."

"Yeah, and that's still less than a month, even with it taking more than a sunsae to get to Tamneki, so again: What is your problem?"

She faces off with me. With her new shoes on, we're the same height. She stares me dead in the eyes, not the bubbly lady or the cocky little thief but something else. Something made of flint and teeth. A tiger staring down a lion, waiting for the other to turn or attack. But she's not a tiger. I could break her in two without even trying, yet she doesn't back down or shy away. And that takes guts. Or a real high level of madness. Maybe both. But a feeling flushes through my chest—admiration. She's worthy of some respect. And I haven't thought that about very many people.

"You're w-wasting time," I sputter.

She shrugs. "It's my time to waste."

Then she turns and walks into the Troubadour Inn.

After a second, I follow with her underwear, because I am definitely not favored by the gods.

CHAPTER TWENTY-EIGHT

SORA
CITY OF RAHWAY, YUSAN

The villa of the Count of Rahway sits on a hill next to the Sol. It is the only place I have seen that can rival the Count of Gain's. Their estates are equally grand, which makes sense, but they're completely different styles. This one is three stories of sandstone, with a high turret serving as the villa's own lookout tower. And I once again wonder if I will ever truly understand men. Why would someone risk all of this under thumb to open their hand for more?

We're in the tower now as the count continues a lengthy tour of his estate. We've seen his armory, spotless stables, extensive library, and massive ballroom. Rune is a tall man with short, dark-brown hair and dark-brown skin. He wears the longer jacket favored here. It's cream-colored and embellished with gold thread. He also has a thick noble collar made of solid gold and diamonds, and his white shirt is lined in gold thread. He seems ageless like the Count, but he's somewhere between forty and fifty. My estimate changes depending on the angle and his expression.

The room in the turret is beautifully decorated with inlaid lapis and carved rare wood. Its open archways allow a breeze to blow through. I run my hand over the mosaic tile that reaches high up the wall.

The count offered me his arm when the tour began, and I walk holding it as he points out his favorite pieces and vistas. Tiyung looks vaguely dissatisfied but says nothing.

Tiyung wears a blue jacket. Only counts are allowed to wear this shade of blue made from boiling thousands of beetles alive. He wears a collar of sapphires, each the size of a kiwi, and a puffy black hat. All in all, he looks ridiculous, but there's something endearing about the fact that he doesn't carry himself with enough ego to pull it off.

"You can see all the way out to the Tangun Mountains on clear days," Rune says, pointing to the west.

Dusk is a spectacular sunset of pinks and purples, and with the scent of cactus blossoms on the breeze, I can almost forget that I am a prisoner in enemy territory.

"It's beautiful," I say.

"The view is nothing compared to you," the count murmurs. "I have heard rumors of your splendor, and it is nice when stories don't exaggerate."

I have on an emerald-green dress that hugs my body, and gold earrings dangle from my lobes. I have on my normal amount of jewels and bangles, but the green brings out the purple of my eyes.

"Your Grace is too kind," I say.

"No, I'm simply honest," he says.

Somehow, I doubt it. These men can all seem charming…at first. And when the masks are lowered, they are more hideous than any creature in the three realms.

We finish the tour in a dining hall. The ceiling vaults overhead, and the table is long enough to seat forty, but places are set for five.

Two other guests will be joining us. I glance at Tiyung. He eyes the plates as well.

"I am expecting two other honored guests tonight," the count says, looking at each of us. "Please have a seat while we wait. Sora, sit to my right, dear."

I don't like it because my nerve-damaged ear will be to the count, but I lower myself into the high-backed chair. I have the sinking feeling that we've walked into a gilded trap, so my hearing will be the least of our worries. Tiyung takes the place to my right. The count, of course, sits at the head of the table.

"I was unaware anyone else would be joining us, Rune," Tiyung says. His tone is cool, but I can tell he is being truthful. And nobility hate surprises.

"As was I, until recently," the count says. His face betrays no emotion, but it feels like he doesn't care for Tiyung. "They have had a harrowing journey and are washing up now before supper." Then he turns his attention to me. "My dear, can I offer you a drink? Wine? Or we have a full selection of coju."

"Water is fine for me, thank you."

The count gestures to a servant who has already started to move toward the water pitcher.

"I'll have a twenty-year coju. Tiyung, will that suit you?" the count asks.

Tiyung nods from down the table.

Rune leans toward me again. "Coju is made from the spiny plants you see on the way into Rahway. Those lands are all mine, and distilling coju is my pet project. The liquor is smooth, especially aged over twenty years."

I nod, used to faking rapture with men's interests. "How are plants made into liquor?"

"By roasting the hearts and fermenting them. I can take you on a tour of my distillery, if it interests you."

It doesn't. "That sounds fascinating."

He smiles at me like he knows I'm lying.

"Ah! Here are our most honored guests," he says.

Two men stop under the enormous doorway.

The count and Tiyung both stand and bow. And a count and a count's son bowing to someone can only mean one thing: royalty.

CHAPTER TWENTY-NINE

EUYN

CITY OF RAHWAY, YUSAN

I feel like a new man, bathed and groomed and wearing finely tailored clothes. Plus, I'm seated across from a stunningly beautiful woman. Rune and the southern count's son bowed to me as I entered the room. It is my old life, rejuvenated. Mikail sits to my left, handsome as ever. But who is the woman in front of me? She is more striking than courtesans in Qali, and that's no small feat.

"Sora—is that correct?" I ask.

She nods.

"That is an unusual name."

She smiles. "It was Athora, Your Highness, but my sister couldn't pronounce my name properly when she was young, and after I became part of the southern count's household, I went by Sora."

I nearly choke on my wine.

"Are you all right, Your Highness?" the count asks. His eyes aren't exactly brown. They're so light that they're nearly yellow, which reminds me of a snake.

I raise my hand for a moment to regather myself. Rune looks at my wine goblet and then suspiciously at the servant.

"I am fine," I say, clearing my throat. But I am not. It's not possible that she is the girl I'm imagining. It's completely impossible. I turn my attention back to Sora. "Athora is also a unique name. And your sister—did she also have an unusual, perhaps hard-to-pronounce name?"

Sora smiles again. "No. Her name is Daysum."

I force myself to breathe normally. I was lied to years ago. But I can't think about it at the moment. That's a score to settle later, and we're here to discuss the future. Mikail glances over at me. Of course he knows me well enough to recognize that I am bothered. But we will speak in private.

"I gather, Your Highness, that you are wondering about the stunning creature before you and what she has to do with our plans," the count says.

I nod.

"A demonstration, then," he says with a smile. "Excuse me, my dear."

He takes her water glass. She eyes him, confused. Rune whistles, and a large mutt is brought into the room. He has to be a hundred pounds. He's sniffing around and breathing oddly.

The whole table watches, curious. The count carefully puts Sora's glass on the floor. The dog eagerly laps up the water.

Seconds later, the dog chokes, and then he begins convulsing. Sora's eyes widen as she stands, gripping the table. Tiyung stands beside her, his mouth open. Within twenty seconds, the dog is a corpse. Dead on the ground with his tongue black.

Sora's pale skin has turned even whiter. Her painted lips part. "What did you do?"

"Tabernacle poison," Rune says. He gestures to the former dog, and servants take the body out of the room.

Sora is barely breathing, horror written on her face. But I'm too confused to be horrified. She'd been sipping out of that water glass right before the count took it from her. If it had tabernacle poison in it, she should be dead.

The count gestures to Sora. "You are looking at the most powerful poison maiden in Yusan."

Mikail goes rigid as he eyes her. His face washes with a certain look. And I know that expression—a formidable opponent. Mikail respects her. But he also pities her. You only become a sharpened blade by having the soft parts of you stripped away. He knows that better than anyone.

"Please sit, Sora, Tiyung," the count says. "That concludes the demonstration."

"That was not necessary, Your Grace." She speaks sweetly from her chair, but her voice wobbles. And it's not nerves—she is seething. The set of her shoulders and hands gives it away. Her nails dig into her palms to keep herself from reaching for his neck.

"My apologies, my dear. Bring her fresh water, please." He gestures to a servant, but I am certain that this girl is not going to eat or drink anything else here.

"There was tabernacle poison in her goblet?" I ask. "How is she…well…not dying?"

Tabernacle is one of the deadliest poisons in Yusan. It's colorless and nearly tasteless, and even just a drop can kill a grown man. And yet I saw her drink water out of that glass several times. I would think it was a trick, but whatever was left in her goblet was enough to kill the large dog.

Rune smiles, all white teeth. "Incredible, isn't it? Sora ingested, by my estimate, a hundred different poisons in Seok's poison school. She is one of the few who survived the training. And she is now immune to all of them."

"A poison…school?" I say. I glance at Mikail.

The count nods. "Highly trained, highly skilled female assassins, at a hidden school outside of Gain. Illegal, of course."

I wonder if this is the girl to whom Mikail was referring—with skills he'd never seen before. But they don't seem to know each other. And he's just as surprised by her as I am. There's always something that flashes in his eyes when he learns new information. He relishes secrets like someone eating a treat from a sugar house.

"Tiyung, how many girls did your father kill to get one Sora? Twenty?" Rune sips his coju and waits with amusement playing on his face.

"Seventeen," Tiyung says, swallowing hard. He isn't amused at all.

The count delights in making this man squirm. "Ah, yes, seventeen. Of the strongest, healthiest, most beautiful girls in the country, put through nearly ten years of poison dosing. All of that suffering and death to create a girl who can kill with a kiss. And yet even knowing that her body itself is poison at this point, it is difficult to stop the attraction."

"Why stop yourself?" Sora smiles as if it's a joke, but her eyes are all defiance. She'd kill both men at this table. Maybe Mikail and me, too, if she could. And she certainly can. I wonder what holds her back.

"Believe me when I say you need me, my dear," Rune says. He turns to Mikail and me. "We give you a girl who can kill without weapons. Who can pass any screening by palace guards. It took ten years, twenty girls, and a million gold mun to cultivate her, and she is at your disposal for our great work. I hope this demonstrates the level of commitment of myself and the southern count to your glorious rule, Your Highness. Get her alone with Joon, and he will be a dead man."

"It is indeed impressive," I say. "We thank you."

He nods.

"And the northern count?" Mikail asks.

The count can't hide his disdain, although I'm not sure he's trying. "Bay Chin remains unaffiliated, still in fear of being watched by Joon. And I am not sure we need a fool who believed a bolt would kill a god king."

Joon, of course, knew the Count of Umbria had tried to kill him, but he could not, even under torture, get the assassin to confess that Bay Chin had ordered it. So Joon placed sanctions on the city and left Bay Chin alone.

"And Dal?" I ask.

"As you know, the southern and eastern counts do not speak, but he's no fan of Joon. He supports our plan. You will meet him in Tamneki."

The northern and eastern counts have been aligned for centuries. The alliance of the western and southern counts is fairly new, likely to combat the powerful northeast rather than out of any affinity for each other. All of these men hate one another. It's what keeps them from overthrowing Joon.

"Of course, there's still the matter of removing the crown," the count says.

I eye Mikail, and he nods.

"We have procured someone with the skill necessary," he says. It is as vague as an answer can be. But the count seems satisfied.

He smiles. "Very well."

"The crown?" Sora asks. Her stare volleys around the table. "Forgive me for interrupting, my lords. But I don't understand."

"The crown will obviously need to be removed before you can poison him," Mikail says, waving his hand.

Her eyes move around. She doesn't know. She doesn't know that it's the crown that makes Joon immortal.

No one told her.

The count looks at Sora, his snake eyes rolling from side to side. "Seok sent you here thinking you have to kill a god?"

She doesn't react aside from a nod as dinner is brought out

by a dozen servants. The smells of roast meat and fragrant spices fill the room.

Rune's laughter rings out around us, delight scrolling across his face as he sips his coju. "Oh, Tiyung, your father is an abnormally cruel man."

Tiyung turns burgundy.

There is the normal amount of politics going on at the table. But the girl seems lost, and Tiyung doesn't seem to be doing much better.

Everyone is silent until Sora pushes back from the table. "Excuse me, my lords. I need some air."

Tiyung rises.

"Alone," she says. Her tone is final as she hurries out of the room.

CHAPTER THIRTY

SORA
CITY OF RAHWAY, YUSAN

I walk until I'm outside, my heels clicking on the fine flooring. I don't know what to do with myself. With this rage. The best I can do is go outside for fresh air.

I exit through a door and find myself on an enormous stone patio overlooking the river. I go right to the edge and hold the railing. My hands are shaking, tremoring from anger, from humiliation, from despair. There's nothing to do with this feeling other than to hold on and dig my fingers into the stone. The river seems to be a good twenty feet down. Maybe more. It rushes to its end point in Lake Garda, south of the city. And Garda feeds the rest of the country.

I watch the water. There have been many times over the years when I thought about taking my own life. I've considered it down to the details of how I'd do it and how easy it would be. But I've never tried. Not because I fear the Kingdom of Hells, but because of what would become of Daysum. But I just figured out what she told me. What she said in the count's garden.

"Don't jump," a voice says.

I whip around and find Rune by the patio doors. He's alone. I'm glad Tiyung isn't with him. Truce or not, I'm capable of doing real damage right now.

But the western count is no better. He killed a dog for no reason. The dog had done nothing wrong. It died merely for spectacle. That is how these men are.

"You think me reprehensible," the count says. "Over a mutt." He shakes his head and comes a step closer. "Would it help you to know that the dog was just bitten by a rabid fox this morning and would've suffered a far worse death?"

"You're lying."

He purses his lips. "I have no reason to betray your trust over a dog, Sora. And no reason to kill a good guard dog. I don't lie for the hells of it."

I'm not sure if he's being truthful or not as he walks to the railing. He keeps his distance, and we both watch the Sol rushing, ever flowing to its end. The river is so rapid here that the water is white.

I should've tasted something off with the water, and I did, but I thought it was just that the desert water was different. Tabernacle has nearly no taste. Nearly. Consume enough and you can tell the difference.

"You poisoned my water," I say.

He nods. "I did. My apologies for keeping you in the dark, but I had to see for myself and for our royal guest if you were everything Seok said you were. You didn't disappoint. And there was no harm done."

"How very fortunate for me," I say.

Rune chuckles and leans against the railing, facing me. "Seok never broke your spirit. How interesting."

"Not for lack of trying," I say.

He stares at me. "I would've succeeded. You would've been as docile as a lamb by my side."

I arch an eyebrow. "I think I'd prove more formidable than you imagine."

"I would've relished that." Rune grins, and I see it. He loves pain—inflicting it. He would've loved every second of my poisoning. Where Seok never made me go to his bed, this count would've. He would've figured out how to break every piece of me.

He returns to facing the river. "It's probably why he wants you dead."

"Why who wants me dead?"

He smiles. "The Count of Gain. Why else do you think Tiyung was sent with you?"

"To burn my indenture," I respond, but I realize I'm simply parroting what I was told.

The western count shakes his head. "I'm fairly certain you'd be capable of destroying your indenture yourself. And it's not about you running, because you wouldn't. Not with what Seok's brother would do to your sister. So tell me why else Tiyung would be here."

I…can't. A chill runs over my whole body, and my hands tremor again. Rune is correct. I could've burned my own indenture, and Seok is well aware I wouldn't run. But Tiyung…

I dig my nails into my palms. I was a fool. His showing me how he'd changed—it was just so I wouldn't suspect him. His saying he wanted to help. It was just so that I wouldn't think about his real reason for escorting me to Tamneki.

Rune studies me. I'm certain he knows where my logic is leading me, and he's in ecstasy. He loves my anguish. He loves that I was desperate enough to trust my enemy.

"Why tell me?" I ask. "You're in league with Seok."

"Because I disagree with destroying you. You are a gorgeous woman with an incredibly useful skill. It would be a sin to waste a million-mun investment. And I abhor waste." He picks an imaginary speck of dust off his jacket.

I laugh. "You'd rather keep me as a slave."

He shrugs. "I'd rather keep you alive. Terms can be negotiated. Especially as we form a new realm. But you are an illegal assassin, my dear. You are lying to yourself if you think this ends with your total freedom."

"Then why shouldn't I end it now?" I point to the river.

"Because your sister can be free," he says.

I close my eyes slowly. Can she, though? It really is a liability—to love deeply. And that's what I was just thinking before he interrupted me—I finally figured out what she said in the garden. It wasn't "Sora, I think it's time." It was "Sora, I think I'm dying."

I draw in a jagged breath. It can't be right. It just can't. Either I misheard her or she doesn't know. She can't know for sure. But the look on her face matches what she said. And that's why she whispered it in my left ear. She wanted to tell me without me realizing it. What now? Where does that leave me? How does someone go on when they know their heart may be dying?

"Sora," Rune says. I open my eyes. "At the end of this, there will only be one man standing. I intend for it to be me."

More politics. Of course. Because they love no one and nothing more than power.

"I think you'll understand my disinclination to dine with you tonight," I say. I put my arm behind my back to hide that it's shaking uncontrollably. I need to get out of here, and soon.

"Nothing else is poisoned, Sora. There'd be no point to it. Unlike Seok, I am not cruel for the sake of it. You are free to go, but I'd think you would want to stay and get to know our royal guests."

"Why?"

"Because Euyn will be the king, and you could become a legitimized assassin or a spymaster like his lover, answerable only to the throne. It is a good future for you. The best you can hope for."

Fury builds so quickly in my heart, I don't have time to tamp it down. "You're all assuming I can survive killing a god king!" I yell. My bangles clang on the stone as I strike my hand against it. It is so ridiculous. All of it.

Rune isn't the least bit fazed.

"The king is not a god, Sora," he says. "That is what we were just talking about—what Seok didn't tell you. The crown of Yusan is one of the five relics of the Dragon Lord. The crown protects the wearer through etherum. Joon can still age and feel pain, of course, but he cannot die so long as it rests on his head. It is why man-made weapons are ineffective against Baejkin rulers. And why past assassination attempts have failed. Kings rule until they are tired of life or someone is clever enough to remove their crown. It is why we'll need to take it. The spymaster has found someone who can do it. The second it is removed, Joon will be mortal. And that is when you'll strike."

Rune offers me his arm. I hesitate before taking it. I get my tremors under control and force all thoughts out of my mind, because I can't show what I'm really thinking or that I'm thinking anything at all. It's too dangerous. Instead of shaking with anger, I'm now trembling with excitement, but he'll mistake it for nerves.

"Why are you helping me?" I ask.

"Isn't it obvious?" He stares at me, and there's sincerity in his gaze.

I look to the side quickly and then shake my head. "No."

He swallows, and his expression changes. "I hate Seok, and I want you to be indebted to me."

It wasn't what he was going to say. My mind floods with what else he could mean. But it doesn't matter.

We take a few steps toward the doors.

"Play the game, Sora," Rune says. "And lock your lips with Tiyung if it comes down to it."

My stomach drops, as does my jaw. Just the other day, I'd thought about sending Tiyung's decapitated head in a basket to the Count. But something about the western count suggesting his death isn't right, either. Still, I allow Rune to escort me back into the villa, because he said something that could change my stars.

I walk in and pretend everything is okay. I sit and smile and eat dinner as if I'm hungry. As if nothing is different.

As if I didn't just hear that the crown of Yusan, the gold band of the king, makes the wearer immortal. As if Daysum hadn't whispered in my bad ear that she thinks she's dying. As if I wasn't just handed a way to save her life, if I can just figure out how to steal it.

CHAPTER THIRTY-ONE

MIKAIL

CITY OF RAHWAY, YUSAN

Well, that was an interesting dinner.

I've heard of poison maidens in the outer lands but never here in Yusan. The southern count must've gone to great lengths (and a stunning array of money and murder) to keep an entire poison school hidden from the crown. And I can see why.

A woman like Sora is as deadly as they come because she'll never be suspected.

This country doesn't think much of girls to begin with—no one would believe a pretty woman like her could murder. And even after her work is done, she can remain anonymous, as so many poisons leave no trace. She can seduce the way I can, but with the benefit of all her murders appearing like her victims died from natural causes. I'm not sure how many men she's killed for Seok. Dozens, probably. I'd put the number higher, but she is still so young. Barely twenty-one, if I had to guess.

Not that I'm ancient at twenty-four. It just feels that way.

It is all falling into place. We have a girl who can get a deadly weapon past the guards and another one who can steal the crown, but the issue is still how to get to the king. Sora and Aeri could pass as courtesans, but sneaking Euyn into the palace is impossible. Every guard knows him. Few are more loyal to him than Joon.

The tales of his banishment spread far and wide and got worse with every retelling.

Nearly as bad as the truth.

I've pulled him into the wardrobe with me in my bedroom. I'm quite certain there are many ears attempting to eavesdrop. Villas like this tend to have hollow walls specifically for spying on guests. But I checked the wardrobe, and it seems solid. Plus, the fabric provides natural soundproofing.

"I've given this some thought, and as much as I'd hoped to do this privately, we have to strike at the millennial celebration," I say.

"The millennial celebration?" Euyn asks. "As in the one in fifteen days in Tamneki?"

"One and the same."

It's nearly pitch-black in the wardrobe, but I can see him stroke his beard. "Why?"

"He'll be out of the palace, Euyn. You know what the palace at Qali is like. There will be four of us to get in and out—you being the hardest. Even if I could sneak you in, the girls will not know the layout. And chances are that someone will give you away for the bounty or to curry favor. Plus, there is no exit strategy to make it out alive if things go wrong. We have to strike outside of Qali. And Joon will only leave for the celebration."

Euyn is silent. He's overthinking something, but I'm not sure what.

"I just... I saw what she can do, but I still..." he begins. "I don't know if we need to rely on girls."

I can't control my heavy sigh. Of course gender is the hang-up. The Baejkins lack many things—empathy, an ounce of conscience among them, human decency, mercy—but sexism, they have to spare.

"Euyn, what is the alternative? You try to pry the crown off Joon's head while I run my sword through him in the throne room? I'm fairly certain the palace guards will notice that."

He is quiet for a few seconds. Stars. That was likely his thought. I pinch the skin between my eyes.

"What is the plan?" he asks.

"We'll strike at the millennial celebration. The details will depend on what conditions Aeri needs."

"Who is Aeri?" he asks.

The last and most important piece of the plan. All of this falls apart if she can't take the crown off Joon. But there's no need to tell Euyn that. He'd just panic.

"She is the thief," I say.

"Is she the daughter of a lord? A count?"

"No, she is the commoner with skills I have never seen before."

Euyn pauses. "Our plan to take the throne in a sunsae depends on a street girl?"

Ah, yes—worse than relying on someone female is depending on a commoner. Like with Sora, Euyn will need a full demonstration of Aeri's abilities to even begin to believe in her. He wouldn't need it from a nobleman. But that is how the Baejkins think. They're as narrow as they are exhausting.

"Meet with her and then tell me if you think she can pull it off," I say. "If you are not impressed, I will come up with a new plan."

He sighs. "When?"

"In the morning. We'll have to leave by tomorrow evening to get to Tamneki before the celebration."

It's not the timing I'd hoped for, but almost dying a variety of ways trying to get him out of Fallow didn't give us the opportunity to linger in Rahway and casually meet with Aeri.

"Mikail…"

"Trust me enough to keep an open mind," I say and reach out to stroke his face. His beard and hair are now trimmed, so instead of looking wild, he's dignified. I like both. "Believe I'll do what's best for you."

"All right," he says.

I find his mouth in the darkness. I've been thinking about it since he surprised me on the road to Rahway. Reconnecting with him turned the long carriage ride into an orgy of pleasure. After the first couple of frenzied orgasms, we took our time. In many ways, he's like laoli—the ecstasy, the pain relief, the madness. Although the drug is easier to quit.

But there's no reason to deny myself when it comes to Euyn. Not when I likely won't live past the millennial celebration.

I haven't told Euyn everything because he'd balk. But I have my own reasons for killing Joon and my own plans for the crown. For now, there's nothing more to be done than to grab every last bit of pleasure I can. I'll remember every moment in the Kingdom of Hells. I hope.

His lips trace down my neck, and I get hard almost instantly when he reaches into my trousers. It's always like this when it comes to Euyn. He's put his mouth on me for nearly a decade, but I never get tired of seeing a prince of Yusan on his knees. And he never tires of the transgression of being the lover of a commoner. Of letting me use his body however I please. I would send him coded letters with how I intended to use him when I saw him next. And he'd always be ready. But I can't see him in this damn wardrobe.

I grab him, open the wardrobe, and then I toss Euyn onto the bed. He needs a distraction, and so do I. Euyn lands with a bounce and takes off his clothes, eager as any courtesan for me. I disrobe, too. Maybe he feels it—that we probably won't both survive—or maybe it's just desire. In the end, it doesn't matter.

"I'm sure the count's servants are watching," I whisper in his ear. "Let's give them a show."

He grins like a demon, and then I sink onto the bed over him.

CHAPTER THIRTY-TWO

AERI
CITY OF RAHWAY, YUSAN

We're in the amusement district of Rahway, but Royo is anything but amused. There are jugglers, acrobats, fire-eaters, games, tons of food stalls, and more. I just pet a tiger! But it's like he doesn't even notice all the different-colored floating lanterns rising into the air around us.

I'm drinking spiced wine and it's getting me drunk kind of fast, so I'm also eating a sweet rice cake. Royo didn't want either.

"Are you ready to go yet?" he asks as we pass a contortionist. The soles of the guy's feet are over his head, and Royo is yawning.

It's like he's desperate to sit in our room and do nothing. We're not supposed to meet with Mikail until tomorrow, so we have time to kill. What better way than at a night carnival? I thought, anyhow.

Okay, to be fair, I knew Royo wouldn't want to come here. But I saw the lanterns rising from the window of our suite and asked him to go for a long walk with me. I thought maybe once we were here, he'd enjoy himself.

No.

"You know, you're really not very fun," I say.

"You're not paying me to be fun," he says.

"How much extra does that cost?"

He glares at me and then goes back to continually scanning around us, like one of the jugglers might pull a knife.

"These night markets and carnivals are always full of pickpockets and fights," he says. "At least in Umbria. Tourists are nothing but marks."

"I *am* the pickpocket, though."

I press my shoulder into him, and he looks affronted. Right. He doesn't like that I planted the calling card on him. He really needs to get over that.

"Can't you ever be serious?" he grumbles.

I roll my eyes. "Because you're so happy being serious all the time? It's a *night carnival*, Royo, not a pirate ship on the Sol."

He clams up and somehow looks more miserable. I didn't think that was possible. I guess we're just going to pretend like that whole thing didn't happen—sharing secrets on the balcony and saving each other's lives on the Sol. Two steps forward, ten steps back.

"All right," I say, giving up. I toss the dregs of my wine and blow out a breath. It's a gorgeous, starry night, but he's nothing but grumpy stewing. "We can go."

I frown, but I'm resigned. If he's truly determined not to have a good time, I don't want to keep him here with me. I don't want to make him miserable. I'd just hoped he'd change his mind.

Royo looks at me, then exhales. He lets his shoulders drop slightly. "We can stay for a little bit longer."

I stand on my toes, joy coursing through me. "Really?"

I smile, and there's just a hint of softness in his eyes. Then he nods and it's back to constant vigilance. But that's still a win in my book.

We pass a series of stalls selling wares—trinkets, things like that—and then there's another row of games. Royo stops for a moment. The stall he's looking at has tuhko hoops set up—if you make a perfect shot, you win a prize. Even professional tuhko players usually have to get right to the goal to score, but in this game you have to throw through it from a distance. A vertical hoop.

"Come on and try your luck like the pros!" the man yells from inside the stall. He tosses a ball up and catches it, trying to drum up business after the last guy walked away empty-handed. "Who's next? Who could be a star at the Millennial Championship?"

"Do you want to play?" I ask Royo.

"No," he says, although he's still looking.

Good gods, it must be exhausting to never say what you feel.

"Sure. You don't seem interested," I say.

He frowns. "These games are all rigged."

Everyone knows that.

"Of course they are," I say. He looks over at me. "The trick is figuring out how they're rigged and playing that angle."

He shakes his head. "That's not possible."

Ugh, Royo. Always so concerned with what's possible that he misses what's in front of his face.

The game seller realizes he has potential new victims as he sets his sights on us and calls out, "Come and try your luck. Win a prize for the lady, big guy."

"He doesn't think he can win," I shout back.

Royo turns nearly crimson. "Aeri, I swear…"

"If you can't make it, you can't make it." I shrug. "But don't blame the game."

That earns me another glare. Royo trudges up to the stall. He reaches into his coin purse, then slaps down five bronze mun. He grabs three winter melon–sized balls from the game seller and shoots them slowly, reevaluating his angle each time. He's a very good shot—excellent, really—but as the balls ricochet off the hoop, I see what's wrong. The goal that's supposed to be stable tips down the second it's struck. Not a lot—just enough to make the ball ricochet instead of going through.

"See," Royo says with his teeth gritted. "I told you no one can win."

"Oh, no. Better luck next time," the greasy game seller says. He's about my height, with the face of a rat.

"Go again," I say. I toss down a silver mun, and it's gone before I can blink. The man moves nearly as fast as I can. Nearly. Change soon replaces the mun.

I lean in and whisper in Royo's ear. "Send the shots quickly— one right after another, the second and third aimed a hair lower than the hoop."

"What? Why?"

"Because it'll work."

He shakes his head. "No, it won't."

Of course he doesn't believe me.

"Or you can just try it on the off chance it will, Royo."

He huffs but grabs the tuhko balls and sends them in rapid succession. The first hits the hoop. The second misses, but the last goes in.

Victory lights up inside of me as Royo raises his arms and punches the air. Then he remembers he's Royo—the man who hates everything and can never be happy because he made mistakes in the past. But I saw it—his pride. His boyishness returning for a second.

He's so unexpected.

The game seller reluctantly hands me a stuffed animal from the prize shelf. It's a colorful little dragon—mostly red, with wings of blue, a yellow belly, and dashes of green. I hug it to my chest, thrilled as we walk away.

Royo doesn't acknowledge I was right, and it's bothering me. I really hope he's not one of those men who think they get through life solely powered by their own brilliance.

"I'm going to call him Royo," I say. "He's my angry little dragon." I hold the toy by Royo's face and roar.

Royo blinks at me and then sighs. "Fine, you were right. Can we go now?"

"Yes, we can go," I say. "We make a good team, you know."

I'm teasing him, of course, but as we leave the amusement district, it strikes me how true it is. We're different as can be, but it works. It makes us stronger. Like how iron and fire make steel.

I've never had someone make me stronger. Father loves me and wants me to be better, but I'm not sure that's the same. Once I prove myself to him by doing this job and setting us up for life, I'll have a home and a family again, but...he hasn't ever worried about keeping me safe the way Royo does. He and I went to a messenger house earlier, and I didn't even mention the pirates as I wrote to my father. I said to myself that it was because I didn't want to worry him, but in the back of my mind I suppose I wasn't sure that he'd care.

Maybe one day I can have both—someone who makes me better and stronger. For now, Royo and I walk back in the direction of the Troubadour. It's not long before we're lost, despite Royo not acknowledging it at all. He marches forward like he knows where everything is, but it's not hard to lose your way in a city where all the buildings look alike.

"I don't think we passed this on the way here," I say, eyeing a statue of the old Baejkin king—King Theum. There aren't many statues of King Joon—he's not particularly popular with the nobles or the people.

I glance back, and the lanterns from the carnival still rise from the northeast. We come to an intersection and pause. We need to go left to get back.

"It should be another few blocks to the right," Royo says, glancing at the buildings around us.

"No, it's left."

Royo sighs. "We should've stayed at the inn."

"Maybe, but we're kind of past that, aren't we?"

I look down the paved street. There are two men straight ahead of us. "There are guys over there. I could ask them."

He narrows his eyes at the figures in the distance. Then he looks at me, eyes now wide. "Are you out of your mind?"

"Royo, not everyone is bad."

"Not everyone is good."

We face off with each other. Of course, since we can't agree, we're both going nowhere now.

"I know it's not to the right," I say. "And you think it's not to the left, so let's ask and…"

"Get you killed? No, thank you."

I swear, he's a mule in men's clothing.

I go to move by him and get three steps before he grabs my arm. I yelp in surprise, clutching the little dragon. Royo looks furious, but then he's staring down the road. I follow his line of vision. The men down the street took notice at the exact wrong time—currently, there's a big, gruff man grabbing my arm as I just screamed.

"Stop, in the name of the king!" they say.

"You're fucking kidding me," Royo groans, muttering under his breath. "King's guard."

"Run," I whisper.

He stares at me. "What?"

"Run."

"Aeri, you have the worst ideas."

But we need to go. I don't want to get arrested with all of the stolen jewels on me, and I'm sure nothing good will happen to Royo, either. Being a strongman isn't exactly legal.

"I mean… I have some things I don't want them to find, and I assume you do, too," I say. He glances to the side in confirmation. "Run."

With a nod, we turn and run the other way. Royo takes my hand so we don't get separated as the king's guard sprints after us.

Our feet pound the pavement and my heart pummels my chest as we go block after block, turning, trying to lose them. But they're gaining on us. Royo suddenly stops and pulls me by the waist down a narrow, dark alley. The king's guard comes flying down the street a second later. I'm holding my breath, hoping they won't find us, swaying to the pounding of my heart. Because if we get arrested, we'll never meet the spymaster in time.

They continue past the alley. But we're not in the clear yet.

"You're the worst," Royo whispers.

"Yeah, I know," I say.

We both listen for the soldiers' boots, but in the quiet I notice how very close we are. How we're chest to chest and I'm pressed up against him in the dark. Heat radiates off his body like it did on the isle in the Sol, and he still has my waist in his hands. Royo can snap a man's neck, but he's holding me the same as that little ceramic bird figurine in Umbria.

Now I'm not moving or speaking for a different reason.

We're both breathing hard, face-to-face. He stares at my lips, and his eyes skim down my body. I lean in closer, just a little. He looks at my mouth again and bites his lip. My breath catches. Then he looks away and clears his throat.

"I, um, I think we've lost them," he says.

He drops his hands from my waist, and he moves as far from me as he can. I try not to be disappointed. Deep down, I know it's for the best. He's too busy running from the past to love in the present. I know that feeling better than anyone else.

I clutch dragon Royo to my shoulder.

We wait another minute, and then Royo nods and I peek out of the alley. No king's guard—we're in the clear. I'm looking around when I see that there, a block away, is the Troubadour Inn. Royo steps out of the alley, wiping sweat from his brow. He also adjusts his trousers. We exchange glances, and I arch an eyebrow.

He ignores me and pretends to be very busy walking to the entrance.

I look up at the towering inn. Tomorrow, we'll meet the spymaster and whomever else is in on this scheme. Just one more sunrise and this whole plan will begin.

As I step inside, I know it's just as well that Royo keeps his distance. I should, too. Because until I complete this job, I can't afford to trust him...or anyone else.

CHAPTER THIRTY-THREE

ROYO
CITY OF RAHWAY, YUSAN

There is, apparently, yet another Aeri. Aeri on edge and stressed out makes regular Aeri look tolerable. It's like finding out there's an Eleventh Hell.

The tailor got sick overnight or something, and my suit wasn't ready when we got to the shop yesterday morning. Not a big deal…I thought.

Nope. I was wrong.

Aeri got so red, she was nearly purple as she stomped her foot and demanded they finish it right that second. I felt bad for everyone at the store—most of all, me. She's not a spoiled brat. Not exactly. But her throwing a fit was a new side of her. She seems to have a lot of them.

One can escape pirates, one runs from the king's guard, one likes tea and books, one likes to steal gems. One can outsmart a game stall while the other loses her shit at a dress house. And I haven't known her that long.

Turns out we had plenty of time, though. Whoever the royal spymaster is, he didn't get here yesterday as planned. And he's not on time this morning, either. Aeri is in her new dress, pacing the room. It wraps around her lanky body in just the right way. But it's hard to notice because my eyes are bleary. It's not even ten bells and we've been up for four. She's done enough laps that I'm surprised she hasn't worn a path in the wood floors. I've tried to ignore her, but she's also been talking the entire time.

"Where could he be? Did he go to the wrong inn? No, there isn't more than one Troubadour Inn. Is he not coming? Did he find someone else? No, no one else can do this. Does he think this is a trap? No, he believes in me. Maybe he's in trouble. Maybe he needs help. Maybe he's been apprehended. But by who? And what happens then?"

None of these questions are for me, by the way.

She's about to do another lap when a red card is pushed under the door. We both stare at the crimson splash on the floor.

Aeri races to the card and grabs at it, so eager that she sends it flying. Finally, she gets the paper. She reads it, flips it over, and reads it again. She doesn't say a word.

Sure, now she's quiet.

"What's it say?" I ask.

She takes a deep breath. "We need to go upstairs."

I glance around. They were supposed to be coming here. I got no idea who "they" are, since all she said was the royal spymaster. But she said not to worry about it when I asked who else. Which ain't comforting.

"What if it's a trap?" I ask.

She shrugs. "They could've been thinking that about our room."

I run my hands down my face. "I don't like this, Aeri."

"I'm not paying you to like it," she snaps.

Who is she today? Last night, I'd really started to... Doesn't matter. I'm not going to be talked to like this. Not for fifty thousand. Not for a hundred. I set my shoulders and face her. "Excuse me?"

"You're paid to keep me safe," she says, correcting her tone.

"All right. I don't think it's safe."

"We're going."

"Of course we are." I grab a dagger and shove it into my belt. The brass knuckles are already in my pocket. I will say this about the suit: it conceals weapons nice. I already put two throwing knives in the inside breast pocket of the jacket. I have another blade under the pants leg. And what the hells, I grab another knife, just for fun. I tuck it into my waistband.

We make our way up to the top floor and stop at the double doors. I check around. There's only one room on this entire floor.

Aeri knocks. A man around our age answers. He's tall and noble. I'm sure of it. You can tell just from their features and air of uselessness.

"Hi. I'm Aeri," she says in her normal too-cheerful tone.

The guy blinks at her, confused.

"Who is this?" he asks, gesturing to me.

"Royo. He's my guardsmith."

Fuck my life.

The guy looks behind him for approval and then opens the door. "I am Tiyung."

I don't know if that's supposed to mean something to me or what. I nod and then pass him. For some reason, no one searches me for weapons.

Smug satisfaction washes over me—fools.

We walk into a suite that's the size of Butcher & Ale. Bigger. There's a total of four people inside. The guy at the door. A stunning woman on the couch by the fireplace who smiles when we come in. And two other men sitting across from her who catch my eye. They are both young and good-looking, and neither stands.

Aeri drops into a clumsy curtsy. "Your Highness."

Highness? I stare at her and then at the man with the beard. It's not King Joon. I've seen him before—he's a lot older than these two. But the lighter-skinned man looks kinda familiar, and then I realize why: I've seen his face on wanted posters.

He's the prince of Yusan. The one who butchered a bunch of people. Who's supposed to be dead. The man next to him has to be the royal spymaster. What in the Ten Hells is a dead prince doing at this inn?

Blood drains from my face, and I want to grab Aeri and get out of here. She and I are in way over our heads. But instead, I bow quickly.

"Prince Euyn, this is Aeri Soo," the guy next to him says. "And I'm sorry, who are you?"

He looks directly at me, teal eyes questioning my very existence.

"I'm Royo," I say.

"He's my guardsmith, Mikail," Aeri says, chipper as ever. As if we're not talking to two mass murderers. Men who could kill the likes of us where we stand and walk out of here smiling.

Mikail nods. "This is Sora, and that is her guardsmith, Tiyung."

The woman smiles slowly. Obviously there's an inside joke here I'm missing.

"More like my jailor," she says. "But I *am* Sora."

Aeri waves. "Aeri."

Sora blinks but does a small wave back.

"Well, I'd love for us all to get to know one another better, but I'm afraid we're a bit short on time," Mikail says. "Euyn and I were almost eaten, and we got shot at and trapped on our way here." He pauses at the stunned expressions of everybody in the room. "We can regale you all with our tales of heroics later, but since we were a bit delayed, we'll need to get right to it. Aeri, I need you to demonstrate your skills for the prince, if you please."

I stare at her. Everyone does.

She shrugs. "Sure."

"Do you need anything from us for a demonstration?" he asks.

Her eyes circle around. "Um…a hat?"

"Tiyung has a very stylish one," Mikail says.

The man who answered the door glares at him but leaves the room and comes back with a black cap in his hands. I've seen one of those before, but only on one man.

"You're a count?" I ask.

"I'm the southern count's son," Tiyung says.

What the fuck. So it's not just a dead prince and a royal spymaster—a count is in on this, too. Chills spread across my chest. This is too much, too big. Aeri is too naive, too pure for all of this. And with this much power involved, I'm not sure if I can keep her safe anymore.

I stare at her, waiting for a sign she wants to leave. Ready to fight our way out of here to protect her. But she's just looking at the hat. Smiling. I stand down…a little.

"How perfect!" she says.

The other people in the room exchange confused glances.

"I mean the fit will be similar to a crown," she says, shyer. "Would you put this on, Your Highness?"

He nods, and Tiyung hands him the cap. It doesn't look ridiculous on Prince Euyn despite it being a generally ridiculous hat.

"Okay, now we'll need a bit of distraction," she says. "Royo, can you juggle?"

All eyes turn to me. I ask again: How did my life come to this? "No."

"Sing? Dance? Something. I need a distraction."

"Are you kidding me?"

"It's for the demonstration. Please, Royo," Aeri pleads. She looks at me with her big brown eyes.

I hiss out a breath. One hundred thousand gold mun. This is for one hundred thousand gold mun.

"Fine, I can juggle," I mutter.

"You didn't need to lie the first time," she says, tilting her head at me.

Hwan. Hwan's life, his freedom, righting the wrong I did by walking away that night. That's what this is for. That's why I don't turn around and run out the door with Aeri over my shoulder like a sack of flour.

I sigh and grab pomegranates off the counter.

"Sora, sit next to Euyn, if you please," Mikail says. "Tiyung, I suppose you can play at being the prince over there."

Everyone moves around, and I have no idea what's happening aside from the fact that I now need to juggle like a jester for these incredibly powerful people.

"Okay, whenever you're ready, Royo," Aeri says.

Fuck my entire life.

I start juggling, throwing one pomegranate up and then another until I'm alternating three of them in my hands. A long time ago, a traveling magician showed me how to juggle. I always liked it. But I haven't had a reason to juggle as muscle for hire. I guess as a stupid guardsmith, I do.

Aeri starts at the end of the couch. A blur of pomegranates later, the hat is off Euyn's head and onto Tiyung. And she's standing next to him in the kitchen.

"Simple," she says.

I was watching her, and I didn't see it. How? How did she grab the hat? How did she move so quickly?

Ten Hells. What the fuck?

CHAPTER THIRTY-FOUR

EUYN

CITY OF RAHWAY, YUSAN

Gods on High, Mikail's plan could actually work.

I just had the hat on my head a second ago. I know with absolute certainty I did. And now I see it on Tiyung. Not only that—I didn't feel it being removed.

I never saw her coming.

Admittedly, I was focused on a rather large man with a giant scar on his face trying to juggle and hating every second of it, but even knowing she was about to remove my hat, I didn't know it was missing until it was too late. With Sora so close, she could've easily kissed me before I realized the crown was gone.

This could work.

It could actually work.

I sit back, stunned. All of us are shocked. Even Mikail. He was correct: this girl has skills I've never seen before. A million scenarios of the future hit me all at once as ruling Yusan becomes a real possibility.

But there is one significant issue with his plan. While some people know about the power of the Dragon Lord's relics, only royalty know about the curses. The four other relics exact terrible prices for their use. It's why Khitan, for example, can't just become a country of solid gold. The ring causes enormous pain with its use, and the alchemy works by pulling iron out of the wearer's body. The more it's used, the greater the pain and the closer to death the person becomes. For the crown, it's a little different because, unlike the other relics, it doesn't change anything at the whim of the user. It simply protects.

When the Dragon Lord left for the Heavens and gave his crown to the first Baejkin king, it was sealed with their mingled blood, creating the center ruby. Therefore, it is said that the crown can only be worn by the bloodline. And that is the reason we've only had Baejkin rulers for a thousand years.

Of course, this is a foundation myth to solidify the rule of my forbearers and control any attempts at rebellion, but I also happen to believe it's true. Around a hundred years ago, there was an attempted coup. The general of the palace guards decided to usurp the throne. With a blade to the prince's throat, he forced the king to give up his crown. But once he crowned himself, the general's body disintegrated to ash—everything but his head. The king stooped down and simply took the crown off the traitor's head; the coup ended as quickly as it had begun. All the palace guards who'd rebelled knelt at the king's feet and were later subjected to lingchi. Order was restored. Yusan lived happily ever after.

I would think it was all a legend, a story that conveniently took place outside of recent memory, to reinforce the divine right of the Baejkins. Except there was an aftermath of the coup. The king was so outraged at being betrayed by his own guard that the ten traitors' heads were placed on pikes, including the general's—the greatest dishonor. Their bodies were not properly burned so that the traitors' souls could never find rest, even in the next life. And their skulls stared at me with empty eyes inside of Idle Prison.

Aeri may not even be able to handle the crown. I am not sure, since no one outside of the Baejkin bloodline has attempted to touch it during my lifetime. But we can have her wear gloves, as the curse is likely based on touch. However, because she is not trying to crown herself, she will probably be okay. That's just a minor issue.

I take a deep breath, watching the others talk excitedly around me.

No, the major issue is the fact that I am not Baejkin.

CHAPTER THIRTY-FIVE

SORA

THE EASTERN ROAD, YUSAN

After the demonstration of Aeri's ability, we sat around the fireplace and began to formulate a plot to kill the king. Mikail said that King Joon will attend the millennial celebration in Tamneki in just a sunsae. A full day of events has been scheduled in the capital to celebrate one thousand years of Baejkin rule, culminating with a special game of tuhko in the King's Arena—the Millennial Championship. And that is where we will strike, in front of two hundred and fifty thousand people.

It's...bold. I'll give them that.

I suppose it makes a certain amount of sense. Aeri said she needs a distraction, and what better distraction is there than the deadly sport? And Mikail pointed out that the arena is the easiest place to access the king. With so many people there, any attack will cause chaos, and we can disappear into the crowd if it goes wrong.

He mentioned everything going wrong a worrisome amount of times.

But I suppose with the stakes this high, we have to be prepared.

When I have poisoned men for the Count, I have plotted multiple escape routes and scouted locations beforehand. Especially after the night one of the nobleman's guards realized my mark was dead. For whatever reason, the guard checked the noble's bedroom and then came rushing at me before I got out of the house. I had to kill him and another guard with a blade I'd hidden in my cloak. And I nearly died because I'm not a professional swordsman. One of their blades just barely missed my neck, and another cut my side.

We had some combat training in poison school, but not as much as lifetime soldiers. But the guardsmiths were also not well trained, and one had been half asleep. I hated killing them—poor men just trying to earn some mun, who were unlucky enough to be there that night. It took multiple bells to wash the blood off me and sew myself back together. The Count was so furious that it had looked like a planned murder that he wouldn't let me see Daysum for three months.

I never was that sloppy again. Until perhaps now. I don't know these people, but I have to depend on them in order to have a chance at pulling this off.

I glance at Prince Euyn still seated next to me. He's speaking in hushed tones with Mikail and so engrossed in the spymaster's every move, an assassin would have an easy time killing him. I wonder briefly how long he will sit on the throne if Mikail isn't by his side.

Tiyung and Royo are debating the merits of brass knuckles versus "honest" fighting. I can't say that either would choose fair combat if given the choice. But I don't know Royo yet. I just know that he doesn't seem quite like a guardsmith.

And Aeri is…confusing. Her shiny black hair is kept shorter than is fashionable, but her dress is expensive and on trend. She talks constantly as though we are all trusted companions but casts a nervous glance at the others when she thinks no one is watching. I can't decide if Aeri is hiding something or is just painfully aware that she can't trust anyone here.

I take a deep breath and try to calm the sense of dread pooling in my stomach. Either way, good or bad, *this* is the group that will decide Daysum's fate. And mine.

I need to figure them all out if I can hope to save her. And we don't have much time.

With all of us agreed, we pack our things and get into a fleet carriage. The trip to Tamneki usually takes a sunsae, but this carriage will get us there in less than ten days.

Just ten days to figure everyone out and a sunsae before we try to dethrone a king.

There are three divans in this coach, and Euyn and Mikail sit together, as do Aeri and Royo, which leaves me next to Tiyung.

I'd far rather sit next to Mikail. He's charismatic, and I feel a certain kinship with him that I can't explain. I'd like to figure it out, though.

And I like Aeri's guardsmith, even though Royo doesn't say much.

Maybe it's just that I don't want to be next to the man sent here to murder me after I kill the god king.

"How will I get near enough to the king in the arena?" I ask.

"Dal, the eastern count, will bring you to the game to show you off as his newest courtesan," Mikail says. "The king and the Count of Tamneki have a long-standing, bitter rivalry. Joon will want to steal you simply because you belong to the count, but he'll be swayed by your beauty, I'm sure."

He makes it sound so effortless. So easy. And he's so casual about three of the four counts now committed to this treasonous plan.

"All right," I say. "Once I see the crown removed, I kiss him?"

Mikail nods.

It's…impossibly simple. How can that be all there is to it? But my real question is: How will I be able to take the crown before Aeri places it on Euyn's head?

After seeing how fast she moves, I'll need to convince her to give the crown to me. I've thought about it, and there's no way I can steal it from her. In order to convince her, I have to figure out what she wants. Why she's agreeing to this mission. And then maybe I can bribe or barter with her. My only skills are seducing and killing, but people do tend to need those.

I catch her eye, and she smiles like she's thrilled to be here. I smile back. Then her focus shifts to Tiyung.

"I'm sorry, who are you again?" she says to the Count's son.

"I'm Tiyung," he says. "But you may call me Ty."

"No, I got your name, but how are you involved in everything?"

Everyone in the carriage is quiet. I look over at him. He adjusts his jacket even though it's warm in here. He must be ruffled by not being important.

"I'm…not, really," he says.

"Then why are you here?" she asks. The question sounds innocent, but it's also pointed. She doesn't trust him. She's sharper, less trusting than she seems.

"My father has committed Sora to this mission. I am here to burn her indenture once the king is dead."

"Inden… You own her?" Aeri's brows come together, and she looks horrified.

Tiyung shifts on the seat. "No, not at all."

"Not at all?" I say, glancing in his direction. He flushes.

They're the first words I've said to him since dinner with the western count. Tiyung has tried a dozen times to start a conversation and has asked what is wrong, but there's no point in explaining it. I have no interest in hearing his lies or excuses. He said he wanted to help me, and I feel excessively foolish for not understanding that helping me die is still helping me in his mind.

"My father holds her contract," he says. "And the contract for her sister." He's regathered himself and sits straighter.

"Your father holds the contracts?" Euyn asks. I hadn't thought he was listening. "Seok purchased Sora and Daysum?"

Tiyung nods with an indifferent look on his face. "Yes, when they were children."

The carriage is silent. Tiyung holds his chin high, but he is not used to anyone questioning the Count's ownership of me. Indentures are legal—it's just business in their minds.

"So, she has no choice to be here?" Aeri asks.

"No, she does…" he begins at the same time I answer.

"I didn't have a choice. Not really. I could do this and get my freedom and my sister's, or I could remain a slave for the Count. If I didn't take this job, I could never earn our freedom—the interest in the contracts is too high to ever repay. If I fail or run, my sister's debt gets sold to Tiyung's uncle, who owns the largest pleasure houses in Gain. He is here to ensure I do my job."

Tiyung looks to the side as everyone stares at him.

"So, you're doing this for your family?" Aeri says to me. "I understand that."

"Is that why you're here?" I ask, sitting forward a bit.

She wavers, head moving slightly. "Money and family, yes. It's similar, I suppose. But I'm also settling an old score with the king."

A spark of hope lights up inside me. She relates to me, to what I said. If I can just build on this connection, build a friendship, maybe she'll understand why I need the crown. Maybe she'll help me. Maybe together we can betray everyone else here.

CHAPTER THIRTY-SIX

ROYO
THE EASTERN ROAD, YUSAN

I dunno what I've gotten myself into. Ty's family owns Sora. Aeri has a score to settle with King Joon, and yeah, she said that when she hired me, but it sounded more personal this time. And I can't get a bead on Mikail or Euyn. They're both known killers, but so far I haven't seen any sign that Euyn will be better than Joon. And this is a whole lot of treason to replace one shit king with another.

"Why do I feel like you're not a guardsmith?" Mikail says to me. Sora looks over as well.

"Because he's not. Not really," Aeri says.

Mikail's sharp eyes bounce from me to her. "Then how are you two involved? Romantically?"

I fight the blood that threatens to race to my cheeks. "She's paying me to guard her." I glance over at her legs… Face, I mean. Face. "It's just not what I normally do."

"I see—what do you normally do?"

I walked right into that. Aeri takes this moment to stay quiet. Figures. "I'm a strongman."

That's the nice term for it.

Mikail doesn't react much aside from raising his eyebrows a little. "Muscle for hire and blood work."

"He saved me from pirates already," Aeri says, choosing now to butt in. "You should've seen him. He took down like a dozen."

Six, but I don't mind her exaggerating.

"Pirates?" Prince Euyn says. He looks deep in thought as he strokes his beard. "Where did you come from?"

"Umbria," I say. "They're not real pirates. It's a gang that works the Sol now. Your brother doesn't do nothing about it." Then I remember he's royalty, so I bob my head. "Your Highness."

"You don't have to use titles," Euyn says. "It sounds awkward, and I'm not a prince right now anyhow."

Wow. I didn't think he'd be down to earth none. The Baejkins are worshipped as gods, and I believed that as a boy, but here's Prince Euyn saying I don't need to use titles. Respect takes root in my chest, and I decide to press my luck. I want to know if what I heard about him was true, because I need to know if he's a danger to Aeri.

"Because you were…banished?" I ask.

He casually brushes a piece of lint from his pants. "That's a nice way of putting it. My brother sentenced me to death by exile. I believe being dead strips me of my titles."

"He seems to like killing off people," I say. "Your brother just ordered the execution of thousands of prisoners."

Aeri's mouth falls open, and her stare volleys between the prince and me.

Euyn's brow wrinkles as he looks over at Mikail. "Is that true?"

He nods. "He signed an edict last month to cleanse the prisons."

"Why?" Euyn asks. I've wondered the same thing.

Mikail shrugs. "Cost cutting."

"When he's offering a four-million-gold-mun purse at the Millennial Championship?" I ask.

"Correct. Those are the priorities of Yusan," Mikail says.

There's something off in the way he says it. Like he's not also Yusanian. But he is. Royal spymasters have to be.

"Cleansing." Euyn spits out the word like he didn't enjoy the taste.

Suddenly, a little hope lights up inside me. Just one tiny firefly in a moonless night. Maybe Euyn will be better than his brother. Maybe. No one's denying he's a killer, but the Baejkins ain't known as peaceful.

"All prisoners in Yusan sentenced to longer than ten years are to be executed starting immediately after the celebration," Mikail says.

The timing fits what Savio told me. They're not in a rush to do it, a couple a day, but Salt only has a few hundred men with sentences that long. They'll be through all of them within two months.

Euyn's brown eyes scan from side to side. "But they weren't originally sentenced to death?"

Mikail shakes his head.

Euyn looks troubled, stroking his beard again.

"Would…would you undo it as king?" I ask.

I lean forward, one, because Aeri keeps getting in the way, but also I feel like I'm going out on a ledge asking, because who am I to question him? I promised myself I wouldn't have nothing to do with all this, but I want to know that we're working toward putting someone better on the throne. And I need a man who will save Hwan if I can't get back to Umbria in time.

"I would," Euyn says. "If they were not sentenced to die for their crimes, death is inherently unreasonable."

Mikail's eyes shoot over to him. Not sure why—I can't make out his expression. They're real comfortable together, but I think Euyn's answer just surprised him. Or I dunno, maybe he just surprised me.

I still don't know about Mikail. How can anybody feel good about trusting a spy? And this whole plan is his. I don't know what

Sora has to do with all of it—why kissing the king matters. But I just don't think we can depend on Mikail to kill Joon. And if Euyn doesn't take the throne, Hwan could die. A million things from pirates to bandits to an early monsoon could delay me getting back to Umbria. Not to mention that Savio could just get drunk and forget. Two months ain't much time when it's life or death. But if Euyn is king, he'll reverse the law. Hwan will live. And so will a lot of other folks who weren't supposed to die.

"If…if I have your word you'll undo the law once you have the crown, you have my sword," I say.

Euyn's eyes widen, but he recovers quick and nods. "You have my word."

"Then you have my sword." I take my dagger from my belt and put it on the floor. The carriage is dead silent as I take a knee and bow my head.

It's pledging my loyalty and fealty to Euyn with my life. Aeri stares like she's just seeing me for the first time. And I get it. I wasn't in on her job, I didn't want any part of it, but now I've given Euyn my sword. If I got to run my own blade through Joon to get Euyn the crown, I will.

CHAPTER THIRTY-SEVEN

EUYN

THE EASTERN ROAD, YUSAN

It's a strange grouping of people in this carriage.

When we climbed back into the fleet ship after a quick meal, Mikail sat next to Sora. He's quite taken with her, and I suppose it's hard not to be. I felt it the first time I saw her at dinner with Rune. But Mikail seems more than physically attracted to her. I'd worry about their connection, but in the end she's just a girl.

Aeri sat next to Royo, which is unfortunate, as I would've liked to talk to him more. I am not sure why the execution of prisoners matters to him, but it clearly does. The fact that he's a strongman is interesting. They do their jobs without question. They follow orders and aren't afraid to get their hands dirty. So he is obviously a man I want on our side. Maybe he'd make a good assassin or palace guard one day.

But the silly little thief's attachment to him left me next to Ty. I'm not sure which of us dislikes this more.

Seok was the one who bought Chul's daughters. I'm sure of it, since Athora and Daysum are not exactly common names. They were from a northeastern village, nearly the border of Khitan, and Sora is pale like the people traditionally of the north. Before the Dragon Lord, Yusan was four distinct nations, and some regional differences remain.

When I first learned Sora's full name, I thought Chul had deceived me. He said his daughters were sold to pleasure houses, and I thought it was a lie, but I've realized that's what he believed. Seeing how beautiful Sora is, I would've assumed she was sold for pleasure, too. It's quite possible Chul was never told the truth.

He said the nobleman who took his daughters threatened to slaughter his whole family if he didn't let the girls go, and he had a wife and two young sons to protect. But he swore he never signed the indentures. Someone faked his hand, and the magistrate, who was supposed to witness the signature, filed it. I had trouble believing that part of the story, as magistrates are agents of the king, but if it was Seok, it's possible. The four counts hold more sway than even my brother sometimes.

I haven't told Sora any of this, though. Mainly because I don't know how to say: "Oh, by the by, I was hunting your father for fun and he told me he never stopped looking for you." I don't know what good it will do for her to know, anyway. I do know that if I told her, it wouldn't exactly build camaraderie in this coach. Plus, it would likely alienate the southern count's son.

But he looks more vexed by Mikail than anything else right now.

I study him staring at them. And I know that look—that inability to turn away. The set of his jaw. I've seen it in the mirror when it comes to Mikail. Jealousy. Ty also looked miserable at dinner with the western count. I didn't understand it then, but I get it now.

"You're in love with her," I say, speaking low.

Ty turns to me. He hesitates like he's about to deny it, but then he exhales. "Yes."

I stare at the other divan. Mikail has checked over here a few times. She hasn't turned once.

"And she hates you," I say.

"That's correct."

I raise my eyebrows.

"Yes, I don't recommend it," he says. There's resignation and true heartbreak in his tone.

It's odd that the handsome son of a count would be in love with a girl who can't stand the sight of him. But I suppose I understand better than anyone else how a man of privilege can fall for the most difficult person possible.

Mikail says something, and Sora laughs. Ty's eyes drink in her happiness like a thirsty man in an oasis pool.

"Was Rune correct? Is her body poison now?" I ask.

Ty shrugs. "I don't know."

I suppose he doesn't want to risk death to taste her. I'm not sure I'd feel the same about Mikail. No, actually, I'm certain I would risk it. He's almost as toxic as they come, and I've never been able to help myself.

"It keeps her safe that men believe it, so I'm thankful for that much," he says. Then he clears his throat and looks indifferent again.

I look at Sora. Maybe it was a blessing in disguise that she became a poison maiden.

"Does your father still have his poison school?"

Ty shakes his head. "It was too costly. Twenty children yielded just three assassins. And he didn't recover enough selling their siblings to make the venture profitable. I don't know what he'd expected, but he didn't get it."

"There are three?"

"Three survived the training, but one died on assignment," Ty says. "My father gifted you one of only two poison maidens in the country, sire."

I sit back on the banquette, glad I didn't tell Sora about her father. I would be a fool to alienate a count who gave me a gift this valuable. Sora will be free once we succeed. And once I am king, I will find a way to reunite her with her father. I tell myself that's just as good, despite shifting uncomfortably. For some reason, it doesn't feel right. It feels like I should tell her the truth.

I shake off the uncomfortable feeling and set my shoulders. No. Sora is just a lovely commoner. Just a woman. I can't let sympathy affect my goal.

But the promises are already adding up, and we're not even in the capital yet. And I can't tell anyone, not even Mikail, that I'm not certain I can be king. That I may turn to ash and be exposed as an imposter in front of two hundred and fifty thousand people—the ultimate undignified death.

Maybe it would've been better to have died in that horse stable in Outton.

I silently curse my whore of a mother again. There are doubtlessly good mothers in this world—my mother wasn't one. On her deathbed four years ago, she called me to her side and told me my real father was not the king. It was just like the Lesser Queen to refuse to pass to the hells before she unreasonably burdened me. But I hastened her death. I grabbed her by the shoulders and shook her until her neck snapped. I hadn't meant to do it, but because of that moment, that surge of anger, I have no idea who my father is. By the time I got ahold of myself, she was already dead.

I started hunting prisoners a week later.

The guilt and shame of it all makes me want to tell everyone in the carriage. Yell out: I am not the son of the old king! But I'd rather be turned to ash once I'm crowned than ever admit it to Mikail. He loves me and I'm sure of it, but even love has to have limits—and being a bastard and killing my mother has to surpass it.

CHAPTER THIRTY-EIGHT

MIKAIL
THE EASTERN ROAD, YUSAN

Half of the carriage is asleep, but I'm still talking to Sora. It must be two or three bells in the morning, but I can see her in the moonlight. I'm sitting farther forward than I normally would—my wounds are still aching far too much to lean back or sleep sitting up. But at least the worst of the drug cravings have passed.

We're speaking in hushed voices to not wake the others. Euyn is the only other person still up. He's pretending to be asleep with steady breathing, but I know he's awake and trying to listen in. It's why I'm whispering.

"I'm sorry, I couldn't hear that." Sora tilts her head and then taps her ear. "I don't have much hearing in this one. Erlingnow poison."

She says it casually, as if Erlingnow isn't the most deadly poison in Yusan. Distilled from poison frogs near the Strait of Teeth, it's potent enough that two milligrams can kill a man. I don't know anyone who's survived the nerve collapse caused by the toxin.

Except for her.

"There's so much pain in your face when I mention the poisons," she says.

Her eyes are the color of Gayan violets. I have never seen eyes like hers in my life. And even at night, when I can't really make out the color, they strip me bare.

"I understand what it's like to be turned deadly," I say.

She glances in Euyn's direction. "I know you do. But you also know love. Love is a balm…as well as a blade on your neck."

I swallow hard. That's exactly the feeling of it. Of loving Euyn. But she said it more to herself than to me.

But I laugh, trying to change the subject. "You can't possibly mean Ty."

She chuckles softly. "Not even a little… Although I suppose he's a blade, as he's here to kill me."

"I beg your pardon?"

She said it so casually, and no one would be that unconcerned about someone wanting to murder them. Especially someone with power.

Other than me.

"Rune said that is Tiyung's real mission," Sora says. "It would be just Seok's style, too—to control us both at the very end. But Rune also said that I could never have total freedom. I haven't been able to shake the thought since he uttered it. Do you think there can be freedom for people like us?"

She pauses, her expression hopeful. I can't decide whether to tell her something nice or what I actually believe.

"The truth, if you please," she says.

Stars, she has a read on me. I file away the new piece of information on Seok and sigh. "No. I think we're too deadly for powerful men to leave us alone. The best we can do is seek the vengeance we were yoked with when we were young."

She's silent for a beat. "Your family?"

It's an educated guess. Her family is the leverage over her, so she assumes it's the same for me. But my parents, my nine-year-old sister, and my seven-year-old brother are all already dead. I was supposed to have joined them in the Ten Hells long ago.

I look away. "I don't talk about it."

Euyn often prods me, hates that I won't tell him everything, and claims it puts distance between us. But some secrets need to be kept. And he's not exactly an open book.

Sora sighs. "I understand. There's someone I don't talk about, either. It's just…" Her breath catches, and she swallows. "It's too much to even remember sometimes. But then you feel like you're wronging their memory by not shouting their name to anyone who'll listen."

"And then something happens, and all of it rises to the surface again," I say. "Like no time has passed."

I'm thinking about Kito. About how I killed him—a boy who was just like me, alone and scared, who'd covered his ears to atrocity. A boy I'd wanted to help the way I'd been saved. But he wound up dead anyway, thanks to me.

If I were a different person, I'd tell her about what happened in the mountain pass and what happened in Gaya. Because I think she'd understand, because I want to get rid of this heaviness in my chest. I know this is her role—to build connections and seduce men. I can see how easily it comes to her. Her marks must flock to her like flies to blood. But that's not what she is doing. Or if she is, she's like no one I've ever seen. And then her skill deserves the same amount of respect as if she were honest.

Sora places her hand on mine. "Let it rest."

I exhale, trying to breathe it all out. I couldn't save him. I couldn't save any of them. But I can seek vengeance.

My fingertips find their way to the hilt of my sword. I want to be of service to her. "Do you want me to kill Ty?"

"Tiyung?" She glances over at him sleeping. A war of emotions plays out over her face as she considers it, and then she shakes her head. "No, he's...he's not really the problem."

"Seok, then?"

"He is mine." Suddenly, her light, musical voice is as fierce as any soldier I've known. The kind of warrior who wouldn't flinch staring down an army by herself.

The Baejkins do themselves a disservice by discounting the female sex. Not all girls could make great fighters, but the same can be said of boys. Few people have the steel to be forged into true blades.

"Very well, Sora," I say.

"And who is it you want dead?" she asks.

"You will be taking care of that."

It's nice having coconspirators. For the first time, I can be honest about what I want. Well...*who* I want dead, at least. I can't tell anyone, even Sora, that I want to destroy the crown. No one will understand that part of Yusan's hold over Gaya is the immortality of its kings. The belief led to the slaughter of my family as much as Joon himself did. Without Gayans thinking he's a god, more people would've joined the rebellion and Gaya could've stood a chance at freedom. And even outside of the island, no one, not even Euyn, should be immortal. Mortality makes people careful, makes them care, makes them reasonable. Gods are not reasonable.

Sora draws a deep breath. "Do you think there's peace after vengeance?"

"Probably not," I say. "But I hope to find out."

Her lips turn up. "Me too. Or I hope we'll meet again in the Kingdom of Hells."

"I'd like that, Sora, but I plan on you having a long life," I say.

Her eyes shine, but her smile falls. "But not yourself?"

I shake my head. Lord Yama will collect his due soon, I'm sure. "The success of these plans tends to come down to whether you're willing to make the ultimate sacrifice. And I am."

She glances at Euyn. "I understand."

And I know she does. But it has nothing to do with Euyn.

CHAPTER THIRTY-NINE

ROYO

THE EASTERN ROAD, YUSAN

Fuck, I fell asleep. This plush carriage rides smooth. I'd just meant to close my eyes, but I got rocked to sleep like a baby. I wanted to watch everyone, but that'll have to wait for another night because it's already sunrise.

"Good morning, Royo," Aeri says.

Chipper as ever, up with a smile. I hate it. It's also the only thing I want to see in the morning. I don't know. I don't know about Aeri. Every time I think I have her figured out, I don't. And so I try harder and I get closer, knowing I shouldn't.

Sora and Ty are asleep, but Euyn and Mikail are awake. I'm not sure either slept by the looks of them. Euyn is probably younger than me, but he has dark circles under his eyes. And Mikail just doesn't seem human.

"Is there a rest stop coming up soon?" Aeri asks.

Mikail nods.

"We should be in Capricia in a few minutes," Euyn says, glancing out the window. "We'll have time for a quick meal and a quick washup."

I'm not real familiar with the cities between Rahway and Tamneki, but obviously Euyn is. It's his country and all. The only time I went to Tamneki, I didn't take a fleet carriage like this. I went by regular packed coach with my mother. She'd saved up for years to take me to see the Royal Tuhko Championship—the deadly match that's only once every four years. The game was a month before I turned fifteen, so it was an early present. Like every boy in the country, I was obsessed with tuhko. I knew all the players, coaches, and the teams' chances at winning. I knew how many points the players had made, how many blocks, how many interceptions, how many assists. I knew all the odds, since betting on tuhko is the biggest business in Yusan after laoli. But I'd never expected to see it in person. We lived hand to mouth, and going to the capital cost a month's expenses. But my mother wanted me to see it at least once in my life.

Sometimes I wonder if I'd still have a mother if I hadn't been so into the game. But then I look at what loving Hwan like a father has done, and I think I'm better off with nobody. Loving somebody is needing two hearts to live instead of just the one. You're better off alone.

The carriage stops in a town that's much smaller than Rahway or Umbria. This must be Capricia.

Aeri, Euyn, Mikail, and I get out. The men all grimace as they stretch and then pretend like they didn't. But Aeri bends all the way to the ground, flexible as anything I've seen, like we haven't been cooped up for days. I look away before she catches me, and I focus on trying to crack my back and neck. Both still hurt from falling off the boat, but I don't show it none. I'd rather bleed in front of a pack of wild dogs.

I start toward the center of town. All the buildings have that shimmering quality like they did in Rahway, but there's a green field in the middle. We pass the field, and men are playing tuhko. Unlike in the royal arena, the vertical hoops are on poles instead of attached to the stadium walls. Men are practicing now, passing the hard, round ball, but they're amateurs. Professional tuhko players usually start as boys in special academies, but sometimes players are scouted as adults.

"Tuhko fan?" Mikail asks.

I didn't even notice I'd stopped walking or that he'd snuck up on me. "I was, yeah."

His eyes aren't blue or green. They're teal, and they scan me. He's forming some kind of judgment. I bet it's no good.

"We're going to the travelers' inn," he says after a few seconds.

I nod. I could use it. Pretty sure I smell.

Aeri is currently talking Euyn's ear off a block ahead of us.

"Where are Sora and Ty?" I ask, looking behind us.

"Still asleep."

"I'll go back and wake them. This is our only stop until supper, right?"

"She didn't get to sleep until late, but yeah, that's probably a good idea," Mikail says.

He pats me on the shoulder before following Euyn and Aeri across the street.

I'm still not sure what to make of the guy. He was talking to Sora for a long time yesterday, and he seemed genuine with her. But it could've been an act. He's a spymaster. Can't trust nothing about him.

I watched everyone as we ate last night. Euyn is kinda detached except when it comes to Mikail. Mikail is a peacock—colorful and charismatic. Sora seems honest, but she's a professional seductress, so she can't ever be trusted. And Aeri is weird as ever, but I've gotten used to her. And there's something honest about her quirks.

I get back to the coach and open the door. Ty wakes up.

"Where are we?" he asks, looking around.

"Some town. What's the difference?" I reply.

He looks offended for a second and then shrugs. "Yeah, I guess it's all the same until it's Tamneki."

That catches me off guard. I'd expected him to be pompous and put out, and he's not.

They both get out, and we walk to the travelers' inn. Men on horseback and on the street stop to stare at Sora. They tip their hats or just gawk. Must be weird to have that constantly. I guess it makes sense why she uses it.

We get to the inn and find Euyn and Mikail seated at a back table. But it's just the two of them. With two coffees.

"Where's Aeri?" I ask, looking around.

"Oh, the girl?" Euyn says. "She went to wash up."

"That sounds like a lovely idea," Sora says. "Excuse me."

Mikail points to the left, and both Ty and Sora go down the hall. The way Ty stares at her makes me think something is up there. But it's none of my business. I sit at the table across from Euyn and Mikail.

A barmaid comes and takes the mun off the table. "Breakfast and washroom for six, right?"

"And good service, please," Mikail says, putting down another silver mun.

She nods and leaves six plates. Then she comes right back with four more coffees. We drink ours so quickly she'll have to bring more, but with a silver-mun tip, she'll come around a lot.

Ty is back from the washroom first. I don't get how he looks well rested and clean-shaven. My face has stubble the second I put a razor down, but his is smooth. I grumble about the nobility's good looks into my coffee.

Five minutes later, the girls still aren't in their seats. Man, broads always take forever, and we gotta hit the road soon. Even in a fleet, this'll be tight. But Aeri is probably doing makeup. She insisted on going to a beauty house while we were in Rahway. She likes to paint her eyes until they look like gems and her lips until they look like the juiciest of fruits.

I shift in my seat, pushing away thoughts of her mouth. Where's the food?

But it's not long before breakfast is served. Eggs, rice, pumpkin porridge, mushroom pancakes, fish stew, and banchan.

Sora comes back at just the right time. She takes a seat next to Mikail.

"Aeri is still washing up?" I ask as I help myself to some fish stew. It's a little greasy looking, but I'm starving.

"I thought she was out here," Sora says, looking around. "I didn't see her in there."

"At all?"

She shakes her head.

Shit. I drop the spoon in the stew, and it splashes. Then I push back from the table, nearly breaking the legs of the chair. I'm halfway to the restrooms, my steps pounding on the tile, when I remember I can't just barge into the women's washroom without getting kicked out of here. Instead, I look around the inn. There's no sign of her. I go back to the table, and the four of them look up.

"Sora, do you mind checking the washroom again?" I ask.

She's just taken a bite, but she stands. "Of course, Royo."

She goes into the washroom. A few seconds later, she comes back out, frowning. I know what she's going to say before she even says it.

"There's no one in there."

I push open the door and then search myself. It's empty.

Aeri is gone.

CHAPTER FORTY

SORA
TOWN OF CAPRICIA, YUSAN

Royo is panicked, and it's understandable. Aeri is missing, and it's his job to protect her. I'm not sure that's all there is to their relationship, given the way they look at each other and the state he's in. But I return to the table with Royo.

Euyn, Mikail, and Tiyung are eating breakfast, completely unbothered. Tiyung is the only one eating his food with decorum. The other two are wolfing down their plates. I noticed it at dinner, too—how Euyn doesn't eat like any nobleman I've ever seen. He eats like the food will be stolen from him.

I'm hungry as well, but we have bigger issues at the moment.

"Aeri is gone," Royo says.

That gets Euyn and Mikail to stop eating. They stare up at us.

"What do you mean?" Euyn asks.

"We just checked the washroom," Royo says. "She isn't in there. You saw her go in?"

Euyn shakes his head. "No, she said she was going to wash up and went in that direction."

The vein on the side of Royo's head rises, blue against his pale skin.

"Neither of you saw her go in?" His hands grip the back of a chair.

He's upset, so he's forgetting his tone. Mikail barely reacts, but danger flashes in his eyes. Royo needs to be more careful.

"It's a washroom, Royo," Mikail says. "Calm down. I'm sure she's somewhere."

"It's my job to protect her." Royo's shoulders are so tense, and his hands have a vise grip on the chair. I think he might snap the wood.

Mikail casually sips his coffee. "Then you should probably go look for her."

I don't think Mikail has anything against Royo personally. He just doesn't like more people with us than absolutely necessary, and he views Royo and Tiyung as excess.

Royo storms off. I stand still, not certain if I should go after him and smooth this over or not. And no one else seems concerned that the key piece of our plan is missing. Or that nothing good will come out of a girl lost.

"Sora, sit, please," Mikail says. "I'm sure Aeri just wandered off somewhere. She couldn't have gone far in the daylight."

I sit down. Tiyung is to my left. I'd rather not be seated next to him, but it's only breakfast. He stares at me as I take a seat.

"I could help you look," he says. "If you wanted assistance."

"Why?" I ask.

"Because you seem troubled. I suppose I was wrong." He stares at me for a moment and then resumes casually eating. But it's… an act. He cares. He wants to help.

Tiyung is the son of my enemy, literally here to kill me. But last night, I couldn't shake something Mikail said right after dinner, about how men born of more powerful men have fewer choices than they realize. How we're all trapped in the circumstances of our birth in Yusan, in one way or another. I know he was referring to Euyn, but it also applies to Tiyung.

Rune said he's here to kill me after I've completed my task—and yet, every word and gesture from Ty says the opposite. I try to remind myself that he is the same man who whipped my sister, and yet, I expected a very different man than the one presently sitting next to me. The one who gave money to beggar children and is concerned about a peasant girl right now.

I'm considering taking Ty up on his offer when Aeri waltzes into the room.

"You escaped," Mikail says, jabbing his utensil into another salt potato and lifting it to his upturned mouth.

"I didn't know I was a prisoner." She laughs and takes a seat at the one empty plate across from Tiyung.

"Your guardsmith is furious," Euyn says.

She frowns. "Oh. Oh no. I should go get him."

She leaves the room again. I resume picking at my plate. The food wasn't great when it was warm. It's barely edible cold, but we won't stop again until it's dark.

A few minutes later, Aeri comes back with Royo in tow. He's red-faced, and you can tell they just had a fight. Royo seems to care a lot more about her than an average guardsmith. Or maybe he just needs our mission to succeed. I was surprised when he pledged his loyalty to Euyn. He must love *someone* very much to give his blade to an exiled prince. Maybe it's Aeri; maybe it's someone else entirely.

Royo and Aeri sit, and she happily starts piling food onto her plate. But there's something off about all of it. Like she took the first opportunity to run away from the group, from her guardsmith.

"Where did you go?" I ask.

The table falls silent as all eyes focus on her. She only looks at me. She knows I'm certain she wasn't where she was supposed to be.

"Oh, the town was just so cute," she says, bubbly as ever. "I wanted to see it. I'm sorry I worried you and Royo. I shouldn't have wandered away. It won't happen again."

The men all dismiss it like a silly girl being flighty, but I lived with nineteen other girls. I know what women sound like when they're lying. I know what they say when they've snuck off to do something they weren't supposed to do. When they have a secret they don't want anyone to know. They sound like Aeri right now.

I can't imagine what she'd be up to in a random town off the Eastern Road, and until I figure it out, I smile pleasantly like she fooled me, too. I dig into my room-temperature eggs. But Aeri is playing a game, and with so much at stake, I need to know what it is.

After breakfast, she and I go to the washroom together. We use the toilets, and then I needlessly rearrange my hair in the mirror as she brushes hers.

"Your secret is safe with me," I say, careful to take in her reaction.

She turns and blinks at me, doe-eyed. The picture of innocence. Sun-ye used to have the same look when she'd sneak in.

"What secret?" Aeri asks, pulling a wide brush through her thick hair.

She's a decent liar. But she has a tell.

I simply smile and walk out of the washroom.

There are many ways to bond. Keeping a secret is one of them—but only when the other person knows you can wield it as a weapon.

CHAPTER FORTY-ONE

AERI

TOWN OF CAPRICIA, YUSAN

That was…odd.

Everyone got so bent out of shape about me taking a walk—Royo most of all. But I guess having to tell people what I'm doing all the time is the downside of working as a team.

Royo is still mad about something as we go back to the carriage. His jaw is tight, and his muscles are tense, and he won't really look at me. I hate it. It's awkward. And the worst part is, I don't know what's bothering him. But Royo being upset with me feels different. It makes my stomach twist and settles in my bones. I can't think about anything other than making him happy again.

"What's wrong?" I finally ask. I have to walk fast to keep pace with him. He's trying to outstride me, but we're almost the same height, so I easily keep up.

"You can't just disappear like that," he grumbles, running a hand over his close-cropped head.

Oh, this again. Good gods, you'd think he was my father, not the man I'm paying to guard me.

"I didn't know I had to ask permission," I say.

We're replaying the argument we had earlier, when we yelled at each other on the street like drunk peasants. He charged at me like an ox, red-faced, as I came out of the travelers' inn, demanding to know where I'd been. I was in the messenger house, sending a letter to my father to let him know I'm safe. You'd think I was doing something illegal from Royo's reaction. Sora's too.

"I already told you—it's not permission," he says. "I'm trying to keep you safe. I can't do that if I don't know where you are."

"Then you should've stayed by my side instead of going back for Sora," I snap.

Royo shuts his mouth.

I'm not jealous of Sora. Or maybe I am. I mean, she's *Sora*. She wakes up looking like she spent all day in a beauty house. Her voice sounds like a harp. And she's so deadly, she can kill a man with a kiss. On top of all that, she's a nice person. Who *wouldn't* be jealous of her? But I like her. I like them all. Each one of them is so different than they appear—Royo most of all. And maybe I shouldn't like them as much as I do, since I can't trust any of them.

A thief, a strongman, a spy, an assassin, a nobleman, and an exiled prince add up to a ring of liars. Trust is a surefire way to wind up with a blade in your back.

"Fine," Royo says.

I stop short on the walkway, snagging his arm to make him hold up. "What?"

"I shouldn't have lost eyes on you," he mutters.

It takes a while for his words to sink in. I blink twice. "Are you saying I'm right?"

He side-eyes me, looking murderous. His jaw ticks, and a vein in his neck throbs.

"Are you?" I ask again, cocking my head.

He groans and sighs like I'm draining his life force. "Yes."

I smile. These little victories, when he gives in just a quarter of an inch, thrill me, and maybe they shouldn't. But they do. They make happiness tap across my chest. Then I remember to be serious. "Okay. I promise I'll tell you where I'm going next time."

It's a big concession. I've lived on my own for seven years—the one and only upside being I wasn't beholden to anyone.

Royo takes a breath and then nods. "Okay."

"Friends?" I ask, holding out my hand.

He rolls his honey-colored eyes. "You are not my friend."

"Do you *have* friends?" I say it before I can even think about whether that's a rude question. But he seems like such a solitary creature that I can't picture it.

"No."

"Neither do I," I admit.

He looks at me, appraising, searching. I guess that might come as a surprise to him, but I really don't. My mother used to be my best friend, although I was never hers. She had a million friends. But after she passed, none of them were at her funeral pyre—just my father and me. So it never seemed that important. Father is really all I have, even though he didn't speak to me for years. But I guess if I do want a friend, I should apologize to Royo.

"I'm sorry I worried you," I say. "I really didn't mean to."

He nods and then finally meets my hand with his. This time, I don't wave his arm up and down. It's different now—it has been since the riverboat. My hand slips into his, and I feel his strength, his warmth. He hasn't touched me since we ran from the king's guard. We don't talk about how he almost kissed me or how I was pressed against him. He did not appreciate my comment that *every* part of him is thick and imposing. But this is something new. This is him touching me in the light of day.

His hand squeezes mine, and his thumb runs over my skin. I don't think he's even aware that he's doing it. But the same sensation runs through me as when we met—of following thunder. He feels like home, but not the one I grew up in or have now, the promise of returning home after years away. Somewhere warm and safe and inexplicably familiar. I step closer to him. My heart beats like heavy footsteps; my lips part. He stares at them, but, surprisingly, he doesn't move away.

"I hate to break up this enchanting moment," Mikail says. "But we need to be on our way."

When did he catch up to us?

Royo drops his hand away from mine. Moment gone. Thanks a bunch, Mikail.

Royo straightens his spine and then gestures for me to go first. We get back in the carriage and head east. And all I wonder is what could've been.

CHAPTER FORTY-TWO

ROYO

CITY OF OOSANT, YUSAN

We spend our days riding east and our nights sleeping in the carriage on the road to Tamneki. I can't even think about how much it sucks. I'm so stiff, and even though my bruises healed, I have a near-constant headache. But I don't say nothing. If they all can handle it, so can I.

We're just about to Oosant, and I dunno whose idea it is first, but everyone agrees to stop overnight before we hit the capital. It'll cost us some time, but we're making progress. As long as we leave by sunrise, we'll be fine.

I don't remember feeling this uncomfortable last time I went to Tamneki, but I was a teenager. I also wasn't traveling with Aeri. She's... I don't know. She makes this both the best and worst trip of my life.

She seems no worse for wear, though. She's bobbing her legs up and down, and every so often they brush against mine. I don't know how many times. Okay, it's fourteen. There's a certain feeling when we touch. I keep telling myself she's just a paying client. She's just a woman I need to protect, and I'm getting a fortune to do it. But when her hand brushes mine or our legs graze, it's something. It's the thrill of winning a bet or the toe curl of getting a treat from a sugar house that you saved up all week to buy. It's the first sunny day when monsoon season ends.

Whatever it is, I haven't felt it in years, but I force myself to remember why that is. Why no one, especially a girl as full of life as Aeri, should get close to me.

I move out of the way. She looks a tiny bit disappointed—but maybe I just want to think that.

As the days pass, it's getting harder and harder to remember to put distance between us. It becomes natural to have her at my side. I'm just glad we're finally getting out of the carriage and ready for the space that comes with it.

We check in to the Evenglow Inn, and the six of us go to our rooms. I drag Aeri's new trunk up the stairs.

"Sora and I decided—we're going to try the tavern in town for dinner," Aeri says, bubbly as ever as she unpacks. Why she's unpacking is anyone's guess.

"Where's the tavern?" I ask.

"It's like five blocks away."

"All right," I say.

Travelers' inns never have great food, and that's all we've eaten. I wasn't looking forward to another meal in one of these places, so I let my stomach decide.

"Yay! Let's go." Aeri links her arm in mine.

I ignore it. The swelling in my chest I get when her hand holds my biceps. It's nothing.

We meet Sora and Ty in the lobby and then start walking.

I'm not sure where Euyn and Mikail are—probably up in their room. I think we all don't want to bother them.

Before the carriage stopped, Mikail had said something about making sure we stay at the inn, but he's not the boss of me or any of us.

Oosant isn't as nice as Capricia, but it's a lot larger. The roads are dirt, and dust kicks up off the horse hooves and carriage wheels. Sora frowns at her light-blue dress getting dirty, although she doesn't say nothing. Between the two of them, Aeri cares more about clothes and that kind of stuff. I would've thought the opposite.

Four and a half blocks later, we get to Hearst Tavern. It's a rough joint—a step down from Butcher & Ale. But that never prevents these places from having good eats.

I push open the door, and it's a locals' kind of pub. A dozen tables, same number of stools at the bar, all kind of worn. Sora follows me in, and all eyes are on her. She's in a modest dress for her, which means it's outrageous for Oosant. When she steps inside, conversation stops. Not an exaggeration—the whole place actually gets quiet.

We're not three feet in the door when the hair on the back of my neck stands. I turn, and there's a table of six men in the corner. With one look, I know: it's a gang. A cold chill runs through me. I don't know nothing about gangs in Oosant, but if they're anything like Umbria, we're in a lot of trouble.

I nod, acknowledging them—that this is their place. A couple nod back. They know I'm dangerous and from out of town, but I just promised not to cause any trouble. Hopefully that will be enough to defuse this whole thing.

Then, a second later, Ty saunters in with Aeri at his side. They both look all around but are somehow oblivious to the gang. Half of the men are now watching us like wolves. Great.

"Come on," I say. I find a table on the opposite side of the tavern.

"Well, this is nice," Aeri says, all smiles like normal.

No situational awareness. Zero. But that's what I'm here for.

Just as she's glancing around, another man comes in. He looks right at her and Sora before he goes over to the gang. The men get up and move around for him—he's about my age, but he's their leader. Now, they all stare over at us.

I run my hand down the scar on my face. This won't end well.

"What...what was that?" Aeri whispers. She plays with the hem of her dress when she's nervous. She's nervous now.

"A gang," I say.

Aeri's eyes widen, and Ty stiffens. Sora just looks resigned, closing her eyes for a second longer than blinking.

Anger and a little worry flash through me. Just my luck there's a fucking gang here. We would've been better off staying in the travelers' inn and having another shit meal. But it's too late for that.

A young barmaid walks up to our table. She's maybe eighteen. Her red hair is pretty, but her face ain't, and she's got an air of thinking she's important. Definitely the owner's daughter. "What can I get you?"

"Should we—" Ty begins. He looks to the door.

"We'll take four dinners," I say. "Two to stay and two to take away. And four pints of ale."

The barmaid nods and leaves.

I have a plan. Or at least the start of one.

I wait until the barmaid is out of earshot. The three others lean in.

"Okay, listen, maybe it's nothing, maybe it's something, but that gang could be trouble. We need to come up with a plan for how to get the girls back to the inn. Better to have a plan and not need it than be screwed if we do."

"All right..." Ty says. I doubt he's ever had to face a real threat in his whole life, but he's putting on a brave face.

"What are your thoughts?" Sora asks. She's been quiet since she noticed the gang.

What are my thoughts? Time. We need time, and some backup wouldn't hurt any. But I've never had backup in my life, and wishful thinking won't help.

"When the barmaid gets back with our food, we'll say we changed our minds and need all four dinners to go," I say. "Then we'll leave with the takeaway and hopefully get back to the inn. If the gang attacks any of us, I want the rest of you to run. Make it to the inn, to Mikail—got me?"

Aeri and Sora nod.

"But why did you order if we're in danger?" Ty asks. "Why not just leave now?"

"To buy time. Maybe the gang leaves while we have our beers and wait for the food. Maybe they target other people. Maybe Mikail and Euyn come looking for us. I don't know. Anything can happen if there's time."

"All right," Ty says.

In that moment, I hate him for having had such a plush life that he's never had to worry about gangs. Never seen what they can do. Never had to think about how to make it home. That nose has never been broken. It should've been.

But he's not the problem. And he's staying here when he don't owe me a thing. That earns some respect.

My scar hurts. But I remind myself that it's not real pain—it's a memory. But memories can cut like a blade.

Our beers come, and Ty pays for our food and drinks. He quickly tucks his full coin purse back into his pocket. The thing has to have at least fifty gold mun in it, probably a hundred. There's no doubt in my head that the gang noticed, too.

I raise my beer. "To averting disaster."

I hit my pint glass against the table and drink half of it down. Aeri sips some of hers. Ty and Sora leave theirs untouched.

The beer is cold and tasty. The crisp bite on my tongue reminds me of Butcher & Ale, of taking jobs and planning marks. A beer makes me slow down and think things through. Maybe the gangs here aren't in control the way they are in Umbria. Maybe I'm just overreacting.

But my gut says otherwise. And nothing good has ever come from me ignoring my instincts.

I didn't see much law as we came into Oosant. I'm not even real sure where Oosant is, but it's not too far outside of Rahway, so we're under the protection of the western count.

No. Wait. We're not. We took a fleet carriage, so we're more than a week away by normal horse. That places us in the old borderland between western and eastern Yusan. The farther you get from the four ancient capitals, the less law there is. That's why Mikail didn't want us to leave the inn—Oosant isn't safe.

Son of a bitch. Why didn't he just say that?

"We shouldn't have stopped in Oosant," I say. "And we shouldn't have left with the girls. Can't do nothing about it now."

Aeri and Sora exchange glances.

"If it comes down to it—can you fight?" I ask Ty.

He takes a deep breath, and then he nods. "I served two years in the king's guard."

It's...not really an answer, but it's better than nothing. I finish my beer.

The barmaid comes back with our dinners. She sets the takeaway meals on the table and says, "Bring back the utensils later. You can leave them outside the back door."

Dinner is pork ribs with rice and braised bok choy. It smells real tasty. At least it'll be a good meal if we can get it to the inn.

"Change of plans," I say. "Box them all up. We got to meet people."

She looks confused but nods. A minute later, she brings the other two boxes, and then she goes to flirt with the gang. One of them pulls her onto his lap, and she giggles. I don't get girls who think they'd be safe with a street gang, but Umbria is full of them.

They think they'll be loved and protected. At best, they get used up. But there aren't a lot of options, I guess. Refusing them don't end well, neither.

I hope she tells them we're meeting other people. It's why I said it.

I pull the lids off the takeaway boxes. Inside, there's cutlery.

"Four knives," I say. We each take one discreetly. Except Ty. He turns the knife over in his hand.

"Slip the knife up your sleeve," Aeri says.

Again, she sounds like a cocky little thief. But street sense will only help us now.

He does it, then looks at me. "You were right about brass knuckles, Royo."

He drinks some of his beer, and I realize he's admitting there's no point to a fair fight—the first conversation we had in Rahway.

I glance at the gang. Seven. There are seven armed men. We have two girls, four steak knives, and the two daggers and brass knuckles I always have on me.

It's not fair. But life ain't.

I keep watching the door. Every time it swings open, I snap my head up, hoping it's Mikail. It's not.

Sora passes me her beer, then takes lipstick out of her purse and puts it on. I really don't get girls. Why get made up now? But maybe it's her nervous habit. Like Aeri and her thighs… I mean dress.

The gang gets their food. It's the best chance we've got.

"All right." I leave half of my second beer and stand. "Let's go. Sora, grab the boxes, please."

Aeri takes my arm, and we leave. The table stares at our every step out the door.

Let's hope Ty can actually fight.

We each take a breath once we're outside. Gods be with us.

We start walking in the direction of the inn. Fast but not running. Silent in the still night. The moon is out, and there're no clouds or wind. I'm tense, listening for any sounds around us. My brass knuckles are on my left hand. My right is on my dagger.

Aeri plays with the collar of her dress with one hand. In the other, she has a knife up her sleeve. She's totally quiet, but she looks behind us at Sora and Ty. They're keeping pace with us despite Sora's long dress.

The four of us make it to the end of the block. My muscles feel so strained, it's like they'll snap. I'm breathing shallow, but we make it another street. We have to turn and then go two and a half more blocks to get back to the inn.

We make it halfway down the third block. I start to relax, let my shoulders move an inch away from my ears. Maybe I read the whole thing wrong. Maybe the gang had a dangerous vibe but wasn't after us. Maybe it was just what happened in Umbria making me paranoid. Maybe this gang ain't like those.

Then I see something strange up ahead. A glimmer.

The buildings here don't shimmer. We get closer, and I realize what it is: someone is hiding in the shadows with a dagger. The moon reflected off the blade.

"Aeri. Sora. Run—" I begin.

Then there's a loud crack and an explosion of pain. Next thing I know, I'm falling forward. I see the stars in the night sky, and then all I see is black.

CHAPTER FORTY-THREE

MIKAIL

CITY OF OOSANT, YUSAN

Someone is pounding on the door. Any city in the old borderlands is dangerous, and anytime someone is pounding on the door, the news isn't great—either for you or someone else.

I look at Euyn, and, wordlessly, he grabs his crossbow. I have my hand on my sword's hilt.

"Who is it?" I ask through the door.

"It's Aeri!" she says. "Open up!"

Euyn keeps his bow trained on the door in case it's a trap, but I throw it open. It's just Aeri. But she's frantic.

"You need to come now!" she says. "Sora. Ty. Royo. You need to come."

Her hair is messy, and her eyes are panicked. She's pulling on my arm, trying to get me out the door, but I can't tell what's happened.

"Wait. Slow down," I say.

"You have to come!" she says, stomping her foot.

I exchange glances with Euyn. "All right. I will. But tell me what happened first."

"We went to get dinner at a tavern, and there was a gang. We thought we were fine, but then three guys attacked us out of nowhere. They knocked out Royo first. I don't know if he's alive! Or Sora or Ty! You have to help!"

Stars, I fucking told them not to leave the inn. Why didn't they listen? We can't afford foolish mistakes like this.

"Stay here, both of you," I say.

"No, I'm going with you," Euyn says.

"Me too. I have to show you where Royo is…if he's still there. Please, I need him… We need to help him!"

I don't have time to argue with them. And she's hysterical over her guardsmith. If we lose him, she might abandon our plan, and I need her.

"Fine," I say. "Euyn, grab a cloak and hide that bow. Aeri, grab a weapon from the trunk."

We take off down the stairs and out of the inn. Aeri leads the way, running surprisingly fast. Then again, she's nearly as tall as Euyn, and that's how she steals—by being faster than anything I've seen. But she's sprinting with a battle-axe. What? What kind of girl picks an axe? Which leads other questions to spring to my mind.

"How did you get away if three men attacked?" I ask.

"I ran," she says.

Makes sense.

We're two blocks down, and she stops suddenly. My hand goes to my hilt, but there's no one there. Just a pair of fine shoes and food all over the ground. Ty's unconscious, lying on his back in the alley, but he's breathing. His nose looks broken, but he's not bleeding much. Then I see the other body on the ground. Royo. He's face down.

Stars, how did someone get the jump on him?

I check him. He's breathing, too, but he's knocked out with an impressive egg on the back of his head.

"Breathing," I say.

"Oh, thank the gods!" Aeri says. She's crying and strangling the axe handle. "Good gods!"

I keep looking, but there's no Sora. No trace of her.

"Sora," I say to Euyn.

He starts searching—tracking. Aeri looks worried as she's pacing by Royo. Her eyes keep darting to the end of the alley. But there's nothing there. The attackers must've come from that direction, though.

I kneel down and take salts from my cross-body bag. I wave them under Ty's nose and then Royo's. Ty comes to gradually; Royo springs to his feet. I back up, which is good because he immediately starts slicing the air, blade in his hand.

"Aeri!" he yells. "Aeri, run!" His desperate voice echoes in the alleyway. Then he looks at me and blinks. "What? Mikail? What are you doing here?"

He spots Aeri and exhales a relieved breath. She looks ready to burst into tears again, and his lip quivers. She jumps at him, wrapping an arm around his neck, axe screeching along the ground.

"Sora? Sora! Where is Sora?" Ty begs. He stands, clutching his face, but his eyes are wild.

"Gone," Euyn says. He holds a scrap of fabric. It's light blue—the same color as her dress.

Stars.

We all freeze. Aeri holding Royo. Ty holding his nose. Euyn with the fabric out.

"What happened?" I ask.

"They knocked out Royo," Aeri says. "Then Ty fought as best he could, but they already had ahold of Sora. There were at least three armed men."

Smart move on their part—to go after the best fighter first. But if Aeri saw all of this, I'm suddenly not sure how she made it out. They shouldn't have been so sloppy as to let her run. I've seen her skills as a thief, know how impossibly fast she can be, but something here doesn't track. I shake it off for now, though, and focus on the important thing. One of our group was taken.

"It must have been a large gang—more than three," Euyn says. "There are a number of footprints heading south."

"They really took Sora?" Ty asks.

His head swivels, and he looks like he's thinking about stealing my sword and fighting a gang by himself. Maybe he does love her, like Euyn thinks.

"I need to find her," he says. "I can't… I have to find her."

There's so much genuine panic and distress in his voice that it's hard to believe this is the same man who is supposed to kill her. Rune might've made the whole thing up. I wouldn't put it past him. Euyn gives me a look that says, *I told you so.*

"What should we do?" Aeri asks.

"Get back to the inn," I say. "The three of you. Euyn, come with me."

"I'm coming with you," Aeri says. "Please. I can help."

"I'm positive that isn't true," I say.

"Stay behind," Royo says. His head has to be splitting. He draws a pained breath, and Aeri puts her hand on his chest. "I'll go."

"We'll all go," Euyn says. "There have to be at least seven men. We'll need everyone we have."

I truly don't see how Aeri would be anything but a liability, Royo is hurting, and Ty already lost a fight tonight, but we don't have time to debate this. Every minute Sora is gone, the more likely it is she'll be killed, raped, or sold. Every passing second makes it harder to track her.

I swore she'd have a long life. I meant it.

"We need answers," I say. "Let's go to the tavern where you saw the gang. Someone give Ty a weapon."

Euyn hands him a dagger. He's always more armed than he needs to be. I've never convinced him it slows him down more than it helps.

Aeri gives the axe to Royo, trading it for a throwing knife. Ah, that makes more sense. I doubted that the girl would have the power to swing the axe, but Royo could take down trees.

We get to Hearst Tavern a minute later. It's a rough place, but a strongman like Royo wouldn't have thought twice about it.

"Stay here. Watch the door," I say to Royo and Ty. "Euyn, watch the back—no one in or out. Aeri, come with me."

There's a bald bartender, two girls working, and three old men inside. It's unfortunate they're here. It simply wasn't their night.

"Who was your barmaid?" I ask Aeri.

Aeri points her out. The girl takes her time walking over. And I realize—she knows everything, including why I'm here.

"Who took the girl who was here tonight?" I ask.

The barmaid shrugs, tossing her red hair over her shoulder. "I dunno what you're talking about."

I nod. Then I swing around and grab her jaw. In the same second, I draw my sword. It flames to life in my hands. "I don't have the time to ask again."

She stares at my sword, wide-eyed, too stunned to speak.

"The Bulgae, sire," the bald man says from behind the bar. I look from her to him. It's his daughter—I'm sure of it. They have the same upturned nose. "They're the gang that runs this city."

"Where can I find them?"

He hesitates. I grip the barmaid's face harder, and she whimpers.

"They're usually in the Barrelhouse," he says.

"Where?"

"North end of the city, in the gaming district. But I don't know if that's where they took her."

They didn't go north. Euyn's tracking skills are unmatched. But the barkeep believes what he is saying. He's inaccurate, not lying. I turn my attention back to the barmaid.

"Where did they take her? Before you speak, know that whatever happens to her will be done to you four times over. I swear and I vow it."

I stare into her eyes.

"A place called The Mine in the southern warehouse district," she says. "That's their den—their hideout. They're either there or the Barrelhouse."

I release her.

"You have all colluded to steal a royal courtesan," I say, raising my voice. "An attack on the king's property is an attack on the king himself. I judge you all guilty. Flee now, except you and you." I point to the father and daughter.

The three patrons and other barmaid run out of the back door without even sparing a glance for the doomed father and daughter. They only care about their own hides. But it doesn't matter. They'll be met by Euyn's bolts when they get outside.

"Come with me if you want to see another dawn," I say.

I put my sword back into my scabbard and walk out the front.

CHAPTER FORTY-FOUR

EUYN

CITY OF OOSANT, YUSAN

When we came into Oosant, I truly didn't expect seven of us to be marching south to somewhere called The Mine to retrieve a poison maiden, but that's what is happening.

I stop about four blocks from Hearst Tavern. There's another piece of blue fabric on the side of the road. Another piece of Sora's dress. The fourth so far. She left a trail for us to find. She's very smart for a girl, but then again, she *is* an assassin. Maybe I should give her more credit.

On the fifth piece, we're almost in the warehouse district. All seven of us. Including two people I don't know.

"Who are they?" I whisper to Mikail.

"Bait," he says.

A cold feeling washes over me from his tone. This deserted warehouse district is eerie, and knowing the borderlands are more like Fallow than Yusan doesn't help. Tall buildings flank us, every noise echoing. I don't like it—it's too quiet, and there are too many places to hide.

We stop as we come to the main street.

"It's the third one down," the bald man says. His arm and voice shake as he points to the building with two guards on the roof and lights in the windows.

Mikail stares down the street, eyes taking in all the details of the mark. "You're going to knock on the door. Both of you. Tell them a king's man came to look for them. And then come back and tell me how many are inside. And then I may spare you."

I can't tell if it's a genuine offer or not.

The man stares and wipes his forehead. "They'll kill us if they find out we betrayed them."

Mikail raises his eyebrows. "And you thought, what? That we were just taking a lovely stroll together? You have committed treason. Refuse to cooperate, and at best I'll let you die first and quickly. At worst, you will count the pieces of your daughter. I swear it."

The man looks around wildly for help. Of course, there is none. But Mikail's plan is flawed.

I step to the side and wave him over to me.

"We should lure the gang outside in groups," I whisper. "That's a dog's den. We don't want to fight our way inside when we won't know what we'll be facing in there."

"That's what they're going to tell us," he says, pointing to the man and girl.

"Let them go," Ty says as he approaches.

We both turn to face him. Gods on High—he's serious. There is a difference between bravery and stupidity, and Ty doesn't seem to know it.

"What did you just say?" Mikail asks. Aeri and Royo move closer as well, but Royo keeps half an eye on our bait. It's not necessary. Both are too afraid to run.

Ty, to his credit, doesn't slink away. He takes a step closer, his chest out. Apparently, taking a punch has made him a warrior. It's foolish to think he can last a single round with Mikail, though.

"I said to let them go," he says again. "They're peasants in a gang-controlled city. They're just trying to survive. They weren't involved in taking Sora."

Mikail points to the barmaid, who is visibly shaking as she stares at Royo. "She's a whore for the gang, and he's no better."

"I'm with Ty," Aeri says, keeping her voice down. "There has to be a better way."

"Aeri…" Royo says. She gives him a look, and he sighs but stands by her.

The tension on the street is at a breaking point. Royo getting involved means it is the three of them facing off with the two of us.

"You're with Ty?" Mikail looks Aeri over and then smiles. "Did you know he's here to kill Sora?"

I raise my eyebrows, staring at Mikail. I heard Sora say that, but they'd spoken so casually, I thought perhaps it was a joke. I couldn't ask for clarification because I was pretending to be asleep at the time. But no, Mikail is deadly serious.

Aeri's expression changes. Royo notices.

"You're here to kill Sora?" she asks, turning on Tiyung.

Mikail and Royo both have their hands on their weapons, but Ty doesn't notice. He's a count's son, not used to being in any danger. He shakes his head, but it's a beat late. Those were his orders—Sora was telling the truth.

The father and daughter look completely confused, their stares landing on each of us as we air our dirty laundry.

Mikail shakes his head. "I don't have time for this. Go. Now."

He pushes the father and daughter forward, and they start walking toward The Mine.

"I'll deal with you later," Mikail says to Ty.

Shit. He might kill him. And then we'd lose Seok as an ally. I have to find a way to calm him down.

"Get ready to shoot," he says to me.

"Mikail…" I start.

"Or don't help. I don't need any of you."

I widen my eyes. No. I've seen this Mikail—the demon. The one who tortured the man in the mountain pass. There's no reasoning with him now. He's going to kill every man in that warehouse or die trying.

"I'm with you," Royo says. They nod at each other. And then Mikail looks at me.

"I am always with you." I pick up my crossbow and put it to my shoulder, a little hurt there was any doubt.

Mikail nods, then whispers in my ear. "Kill the father and daughter quietly once we're inside."

My stomach drops, but I should've seen it coming. He says something to Royo, and he also nods.

We start scheming on the best way to attack. To fight our way inside. But there's no doubt in my head at least one of us will die trying to take The Mine.

"Wait—use me," Aeri says.

Everyone turns to her.

"Aeri, don't—" Royo starts.

"No, it'll work, Royo," she interrupts. "When the barkeep and barmaid get back, use me to get inside the warehouse. The gang didn't see you or Euyn. Take me to them and ask for a bounty. They'll bring you in. And then you can see what's inside the building and gauge how you can attack from in there."

Mikail nods. I run the plan through my mind—it'll work. The little thief is cleverer than she looks.

"Actually, I'll bring you both in," Mikail says. He points to her and Ty. "Royo, go around back. Euyn, go to the rooftop across from The Mine and pick off their scouts."

"Aeri, I really don't want you to go in—" Royo tries again.

"It's okay, Royo," she says. "I'll have Mikail to guard me." She reaches out and strokes his arm. Mikail and I both catch it—the real affection there. Royo stiffens but reluctantly nods.

We're all agreed by the time the father and daughter walk back to us. They're both shaking as if there's an earthquake beneath their feet. The bald man looks slightly green and ready to pass out.

"There are ten inside," he says.

Mikail looks at him. I'm certain that whatever the number of men inside is, it's not ten. I hope it's not twenty, but it probably is. I shift the bolts around on my chest.

"I see," Mikail says. "You may go."

"Yes, sire," the man says with a clumsy bow.

I switch swords with Mikail so they won't see his royal blade. Mikail is going to pretend to be a bounty hunter, not a king's guard, and the fancy hilt would give it away. Royo starts down the side street after a lingering look at Aeri.

"Yours—in this life and the next," Mikail says to me. His gaze sears into me as his sword strikes mine.

I nod. "Yours—in this life and the next."

I take off to the building facing the warehouse called The Mine. This one is abandoned, but I'm able to break in and run up the stairs to the roof. I'm in better shape now than I ever was in the palace—faster, stronger—because I had to be in order to survive. It's barely a minute before I'm in place. But when I look, there are no guards on top of The Mine.

No one.

Gods on High—it's a trap.

The gang knows. They must've pulled their lookouts inside, which means the father and daughter gave us up.

I fire two shots, killing them both, and then check my bolts again. I'll need all of them tonight.

CHAPTER FORTY-FIVE

ROYO

CITY OF OOSANT, YUSAN

Ten Hells, my head.

I'm seeing double. I shake it off, blinking hard. I'm going to mutilate the son of a bitch who sucker punched me. And a bunch of other men inside that warehouse. They could've killed Aeri. They may be hurting Sora. I'm gonna make them regret not taking me on like men.

I lumber down the alley, staying in the darkest shadows, but I don't feel right. And it's not just the headache. I pause, wondering what it is. I have my blades and an axe. But then I realize I feel off because I don't like being away from Aeri. It's not that I like her or nothing. It's that I promised I wouldn't lose eyes on her again. I take a breath and remind myself she's okay. Mikail won't let nothing happen to her—he needs her. And she somehow followed my directions earlier and made it back to the inn. I dunno which is more shocking—that she listened or that she got away. The relief I felt when I came to and saw her was massive. Tears pricked my eyes. It took away from the pain for a second.

And Aeri's face when she saw me…

I exhale a shaky breath. The girl means something to me, and it's not right. Nothing good can come from this. I'm her guard.

And I shouldn't be thinking about her right now. I need to focus. I've got blood work to do.

I force Aeri from my thoughts and take in my surroundings. I need to stay alert. Especially because this whole thing feels off. I don't know why Mikail trusted the barmaid and her father, but I bet he's got a plan he told no one about. It don't really matter, though. We know Sora is in there, alone with a gang as bad as anything in Umbria. We have to get her out.

I won't leave another girl alone with a gang. Not ever.

I adjust my handle on the axe. Aeri did a good job choosing a weapon for me. I can kill quietly with this thing.

Ready to murder, I creep around to the back of The Mine. There should be one or two guards standing watch at the back entrance of the warehouse, but they'll be the lowest rank of the gang—the least experienced, the least aware.

I come around to where I can observe the back. The door is gray, but no one is guarding it. No one.

No. That can't be right.

I blink hard and look back down the alley, but there's nothing. Then I look up. There's no one on the roof, neither.

My stomach knots, choking the breath from my lungs.

Ten Hells. We've been set up.

CHAPTER FORTY-SIX

SORA
CITY OF OOSANT, YUSAN

Everyone in the warehouse is on alert as men move all around, whispering to each other and getting in place. The barmaid and her father told the gang that a king's guard and three men are here to take me because I am a royal courtesan. They said the men also have the girl who was at dinner—Aeri.

Mikail and everyone else are walking into a trap, and there's nothing I can do to stop it. Not when I'm tied to this beam in the middle of the room. My stomach turns and my arms tremor, but I can't slip out of these binds. The knots are tied too well. I need to think. There must be something I can do to save them. But what?

There are seventeen men in here. The leader said to tell Mikail there were ten, so ten stand armed in a wide circle around me, but seven are hiding behind various boxes and crates. Another two are outside guarding the back door. And two scouts cover the roof. The three men who attacked us haven't returned yet, but they should be back any minute.

Twenty-four gang members in total. It's too many.

There's no way six of us can kill twenty-four armed men. The lipstick I put on at Hearst Tavern could kill three men, but I've never had to kill multiple men quickly—just discreetly.

I know Mikail and Royo are experienced killers, but there are odds that can't be beaten. I can't imagine Aeri will be much help, and Tiyung has never had to get his hands dirty. The Count has plenty of men to do that for them. And I don't know Euyn at all, but I doubt he can kill *ten* men. He has a slighter build than Ty, and he's a prince.

There's a knock at the door. Everyone gets into place.

I hold my breath. I need to help them. But how?

CHAPTER FORTY-SEVEN

MIKAIL
CITY OF OOSANT, YUSAN

The door opens, and a man nearly as wide as he is tall answers. Royo will be jealous—this guy is even wider than he is. But the gang member has pockmarks on his face and a clueless expression. Royo is better looking.

"Yes?" the man says.

"I'm here to return two things that belong to your boss," I say. I shove Ty and Aeri forward. "I found them in the alley. Thought you might be interested."

The man looks over his shoulder and opens the door. He doesn't check us for weapons, figuring we're so outnumbered.

As I said: clueless.

I stroll in, pushing Ty. I'm not sure if he's acting or what, but I genuinely have to make him walk. Aeri walks in herself, looking all around. There are stacks of boxes and crates, giving plenty of cover for men who want to hide, but I'm not paying much attention to that because in the center of the room there is a beam and Sora's arms are tied to it. Her dress is ripped, but I think she did it to herself, judging by the fabric strips Euyn found. Her cheek looks red, struck by someone here or when she was taken.

Standing next to her has to be the leader of the gang. He's younger than I'd expect from a gang leader, but he looks self-important and there's a ring of men around him.

"You must be the king's guard," he says.

I smile. "You seem to have me confused with someone else."

"Cora was very specific," he says.

I shrug. "About someone else. I'm not a king's guard."

A few of the men look at one another, confused. Not the smartest crew.

"What do you want, then?" he asks.

"A reward," I say.

There's a knock at the door. I turn at the sound. The same huge guy goes to answer it.

"Wait," Sora says.

The leader turns to her and holds up a hand.

She pulls at her binds. "That must be the king's guard here to take me," she says. "Don't let them."

Her violet eyes plead. Her lip quivers. Her distress is palpable. Entranced, the leader steps closer to her.

"You want to stay here?" he asks, skeptical but obviously interested.

She nods eagerly. "My parents sold me for gold. I don't want to go to the old king. I've never wanted it. Please, help me."

"Now you want to cooperate?" he asks.

She looks away, chastened. I can bet that he was the one who struck her.

"I was scared," she says. "You're so young—I didn't realize you ran this city. I thought you were a lowly kidnapper, not a great man. Please. Hide me."

He reaches out and takes her face in his hand. "You want to be mine?"

"Yes," she says, breathless. She looks at him, all desire, parting her lips. Then she looks away demurely like she's fighting her impulse. "Please."

He tilts her face back to him and kisses her.

I am nothing but impressed. I've seen royal actors with less talent.

There's a second knock at the door. Two knocks, actually—Euyn's signal. The first was to get ready, but now it's time.

I draw my sword and run it through the man next to me. He doubles over and collapses on the ground. At the same moment, Euyn kicks in the front door and starts shooting. A second later, Royo flings open the back door. Suddenly, it's shouts and chaos inside The Mine. Blood and guts spill; death screams and rattles through the high-ceilinged space.

I soak it in, but only for a moment until the next man rushes at me. He's very eager to meet Lord Yama, I suppose.

The other gang members back up, looking to the leader, but he's clutching and clawing at his own throat as he collapses to the ground. Another man, probably his second-in-command, races to help him, but it's far too late. Sora does her best to act confused and concerned, still tied to that beam.

We need to get her out of there.

I grab the sword of the first man I killed and toss it to Ty. He has a dagger, but it's not enough for this kind of fight.

"Try not to die," I say. "And watch my back."

"Done," he says, catching the sword effortlessly. Perhaps there is more to him. There will need to be, for him to survive this with his head still attached.

I cut down the man who rushed at me. My blade is not as sharp as my royal sword because it's whatever shit Euyn purchased. It's pissing me off, but it's doing the job. I slit the man from his neck to his navel, but with way more effort than it should take.

The next man who saw my handiwork turns and runs in the other direction. I fling my sword into the fleeing man's back in one fluid motion and then grab the sword from the man I slit open.

Two men attack Royo at the same time, but he's larger and stronger than them. Plus, he has the battle-axe. It's…messy and more thorough than he needs to be. But he's a strongman, used to having to ensure a kill.

I'm about to go help when another man slashes at me. The sword I picked up is even worse than the crap Euyn bought. These bladesmiths should be hanged. I fight with my glorified butter knife, but I might as well bludgeon him to death with the handle.

Movement flashes out of the corner of my eye. Aeri, quick as ever, has used the chaos as a distraction. She runs up and tries to untie Sora's rope. She doesn't see the man behind her or the blade in his hand.

"Aeri!" I yell.

She turns just as a bolt hits the man in the chest. He falls to his knees, pierced in the lung. Nice shot, Euyn.

Aeri's mouth opens in shock just as blood sprays on the center of her yellow dress. Ty has run his blade through the man's back, issuing the killing blow. She stares at the blood splatter and then at Ty. He's breathing hard and looking like he might pass out. And I'm pretty shocked, too, at his lethality.

I didn't think he had it in him.

I kick the man fighting me, and he falls to the ground. Finally, I get the correct angle to cut his throat. I'll try his sword next. Has to be better than this shit.

Aeri scrambles to take the sword from the body of the man Ty killed. With the large blade in hand, Aeri approaches Sora. I'll be honest—Aeri swinging a sword doesn't seem like a great plan. From the look in Sora's eyes, she doesn't think so, either.

Just as Aeri is about to cut the rope, the second-in-command finally gets to his feet and draws his blade to strike her. Aeri's face goes slack, but before the man can swing back, Ty slashes his throat. He uses too much force, though, making blood spray everywhere.

I have to teach him how to kill cleanly.

But Aeri cuts Sora free.

Euyn fells men left and right, bolts raining down like leaves in the fall. Someone stabbed Royo's left shoulder, but it doesn't seem critical. I keep an eye on him, the women, and always Euyn. Always. But another gang member swings at me, eager to take a journey to the Ten Hells.

He's already dying when Aeri screams.

"Royo!"

She throws her knife and hits a man. The one running at Royo's back. She drops him with one shot.

Royo turns and watches the man collapse. Aeri's arm is still out. He's stunned as he looks from one to the other. Finally, he nods in thanks to Aeri, and she smiles, beaming. And then he crushes the windpipe of the man he was fighting.

Where'd his axe go?

Apparently the remaining gang members have realized that coming at me one at a time means death, so three men charge me all at once. Euyn shouts and tosses me my sword. I catch the weapon, thankful to have a real blade back. I could kiss this thing. Unsheathing it, I crank my arm back, then unleash a spinning move. I slice all three men in the chest in one smooth motion, and then I land on one knee. My blade drips blood, my arm extended behind me. All three men look down at their gaping chests at the same time, then crumple to the ground.

With that last kill, no one else comes at us. But the six of us stand ready, weapons drawn for a few moments.

I can't tell how many bodies there are—definitely more than ten. The father and daughter betrayed us, as I knew they would.

I sent them in because I wanted the gang to pull all their men inside; that way, Euyn and Royo would have easier access to the doors. I knew we could kill everyone once we were let in.

I'm not even a little sorry that I whispered "null" to Euyn. And "no survivors" to Royo.

"What happened to the axe?" I ask Royo, curiosity getting the better of me.

He motions his head to the side, and I turn.

"Oh." A smile stretches across my face. His axe is being used to pin a man to a wall map showing all of Oosant.

Royo shrugs. "Axe got stuck in the wall, so I left it."

With no other gang members coming at us, we stand down. I let go of the energy surge I always feel once I lift a sword. There's a peaceful feeling after killing this many men. Like how loud noises make you appreciate the quiet.

Normally, I'd sweep the area, but I want to make sure the women, particularly Sora, are okay.

I'm about to congratulate Aeri on her impressive shot when her eyes go wide. She's staring straight at me. Her mouth opens. Then I realize she's trying to warn me. But from the look on her face, I know it's too late.

I'm about to be killed.

CHAPTER FORTY-EIGHT

SORA

CITY OF OOSANT, YUSAN

Mikail's name shatters the quiet of the warehouse.

I look around, and then I see why. There's a man behind him with his sword drawn.

The coward stayed hidden behind boxes this entire time. He remained in place as his brothers were slaughtered, as they screamed for help, as they cried out to the gods or for their mothers. As they tried to claw their way to safety only to be felled by bolts. Now, he is brave because Mikail's back is turned.

I scream to warn him, but I'm too late. The man is too close, his blade already swung back.

At the same moment, a sword goes flying through the air. Ty has tried to kill the man, but he's too far away. It won't reach him before he can strike.

I close my eyes, not wanting to see Mikail die, but then I realize I'm now being the coward. He came in here to save me. He's killed to free me. I owe it to him to watch, to witness his death. The same way I owed it to the girls in poison school. The same way I failed to witness the death of my lover.

But when I open my eyes, the gang member drops his blade and falls to his knee. He cries out and grips the back of his leg.

Mikail whips around and stabs him right through the chest. The man goes to the ground, howling in pain as he's impaled.

The blade Ty threw lands a few feet in front of the man, skittering to a stop. Mikail glances at it and then looks around.

What just happened? Did the man really just…trip?

We're all staring at one another.

Aeri is next to me, breathing hard. Blood drips from her hand, but we all have blood on us, myself included. Ty is to my left, and Royo was still making his way to us. Euyn is farthest away and reloading his bow. We were all too far from Mikail to help. So I'm not sure what just happened. Maybe it was the gods.

One thing I do know for sure is that the gods rarely shine upon killers without exacting a price.

CHAPTER FORTY-NINE

EUYN
CITY OF OOSANT, YUSAN

We sweep the room to make sure all the Bulgae are dead. The six of us work together until every foot of the warehouse has been cleared. Obviously, Mikail takes the lead, and I'm right over his shoulder with my bow. Ready to protect him, ready to die for or with him. But there's no one else. Everyone is dead or dying.

We then all stand around the body of the man who almost killed Mikail. My heart is still lodged somewhere in my throat. I'm not sure I'm going to shake this feeling until I get him alone and feel his heartbeat against mine. I almost lost him again.

"But I don't understand," Aeri says, shaking her head.

Mikail rubs the back of his neck. "He must've tripped on a weapon, although…I really don't know how."

It's hard to tell what happened because the warehouse is a bloody mess. But they're right to be confused. I was certain Mikail was about to die, and then the gods intervened and saved him.

"Luck," Royo says, although he stares at Aeri.

Or the Gods on High.

I don't say it aloud, though. Mikail laughs at any thought that he's favored by the Heavens—but he is. It could also be that the Kingdom of Hells refuses to have him. It's hard to say.

He shakes off his stupor. "We need to clean this up."

I get his meaning—he's going to torch the place.

"What's even in here?" Ty asks, looking at the crates.

It's a good question. With all that happened, I didn't think to look. None of us did.

I kick one of the fallen, blood-splattered boxes, and velvet pouches fall out. I stare at them, waves of shock and confusion hitting at the same time because I know that kind of pouch. With that snake insignia. But it can't be.

I open one. It is.

It's laoli.

Stunned, I hand it to Mikail, and then I take in the space. This entire warehouse is full of laoli. At least a million gold mun's worth. Laoli is not supposed to be grown, processed, or stored on anything other than royal land. And we are certainly not on royal land.

Gods on High, what is this?

Mikail puts his pinkie in, tastes it, and nods to me. "Laoli."

Rapid emotions wash over the faces of the group as we all realize that we're in the middle of a major drug-smuggling operation. We need to go. Now.

Everyone gets to work.

Royo and I drag the bodies of the barmaid and her father from the street into the warehouse. Royo pulls the man's legs. I take the girl, although she's heavier than expected. We leave matching blood trails in the dirt.

When we get back inside, Ty and Aeri are nearly done making piles of boxes. They look over at the bodies as we bring them in and then turn away and get back to work. Sora waves us, one at a time, to the back washroom to clean blood off us and stitch up our wounds. Royo and Ty are both bleeding. No one asks why she's so good at this. No one has said much at all. Instead, we all work quietly as a team.

Soon, everything is done and everyone is decently cleaned.

Royo pours oil from a jug he found all through the inside of the warehouse. With a single nod from him, Mikail lights his sword and then the first pile of boxes. The oil goes up in flames, and the remaining piles all catch fire.

We walk out the back of the warehouse, leaving the dead and dying behind. We move as a group, at a good pace but not running. Everyone is tense but trying to act normal as we make it to the end of the block. Then another. Then another.

Once we pass Hearst Tavern, I chance a look back. Flames climb high into the dark sky, and the blaze is so large that the nearby buildings must've caught fire, too—it's hard to tell. People are shouting and running toward and away from the warehouse district.

"No one is going to argue that we should stay in Oosant tonight, are they?" Mikail asks.

Everyone is silent.

"Good," he says. "Change and pack up your things as quickly as possible, and we'll be on our merry way."

"But what about…" Aeri begins. Then she purses her lips.

Mikail looks over at her and frowns. "The barmaid and her father are dead. I had to… They could've—"

"No, I saw that. I mean… We didn't get any dinner," she says.

Mikail and I exchange glances. She murdered a man. We all did. But all she can think about is her stomach. This girl is unusual.

He breathes out a laugh. "We'll get some food in the next town."

We reach the inn and take the side staircase to our rooms. Within minutes, we're all in fresh clothes and back on the Eastern Road again.

I hope we don't leave a trail of carnage all the way to Tamneki, but it's not looking good. Death seems to follow me like a hungry dog.

Once we're moving, I sit next to Mikail and stare at him. I still can't figure out how he's alive, but I'm grateful. I put my hand over his. He smiles and weaves his fingers through mine. His skin glistens with sweat, with energy, and he looks content. But I'm still troubled by the warehouse. Why was there a fortune in laoli in this old border town? Who did it belong to? It had the royal insignia, but Joon doesn't have an unmarked warehouse in a border town.

All I know is that the men we killed couldn't have been in control of the drug supply. They didn't have the foresight or the intelligence to smuggle laoli in from Gaya. No, only a high noble—a count—would have enough money and power to get an illegal warehouse full of the drug into Oosant. But which count and why?

Finally, I notice no one is speaking. Everyone is variously staring into space except for Mikail, who is rubbing blood splatter off his heel. I'm confused for a moment about the silence, but then I remember it's a heavy thing—taking the lives of so many men. Almost being killed ourselves. And we did it together. Aeri saved Royo's life. Ty and I saved hers. We all saved Sora.

Sora glances at each of us and then clears her throat. It draws everyone's attention. "I...I don't know how to thank you all."

"You would've done the same for any of us," Mikail says.

I write it off as a nice thing to say, but then I think about it and realize: it's true.

We're all bound by this mission.

They're risking everything to see me on the throne, or at least to make sure my brother is dead. I suppose we all have our own reasons and secrets, but we just killed for one another and hid one another's crimes. That's a kind of bloodship stronger than kin or clan. And I don't think that even a god king can stand against six people who'd kill and die for one another.

CHAPTER FIFTY

TIYUNG

THE EASTERN ROAD, YUSAN

It has to be twelve bells at night, and I think I'm going to be sick. I've put the window down for air, which, surprisingly, no one objected to.

I lean my head where I can best feel the breeze. I finally understand Royo's reaction in the tavern when he asked if I could fight and I said I had two years in the king's guard. It was totally meaningless. I patrolled, trained, and practiced in the king's guard. *Now* I've killed.

I ran my sword through a man and had him die at my feet. I took another human's life. Whatever I was before tonight, I'm not anymore. My soul is no longer clean—assuming it was when I happily took my father's blood money my whole life and when I whipped Daysum, a defenseless girl. Even if it was to save her from the savage lashing she would've gotten from my father, it's still not exactly a spotless soul.

But I didn't know my victim's name tonight. That has to be worse when Lord Yama judges my sins in the Kingdom of Hells. The man was around my age—and now he's ashes. I don't know why he was in that warehouse, who he loved or hated, or what he thought in his last moments. All he became was a blood smear to get off my clothes.

Who am I now?

I shudder. I'd rather not experience any of that again. But I'd do it all a hundred times over to save Sora.

I look at her. She's worth going to the Tenth Hell for.

Aside from the wind, it's quiet in the coach, although we're all still awake. Well, except Mikail. He's asleep. I guess murder is so ordinary to him that it doesn't keep him up.

I couldn't believe what I saw—how a man can kill like a god. But he's the only reason we were able to pull this off. It was his foresight, his planning, and his quick perceptions that kept her alive. I didn't agree with killing the barmaid and her father, but they did betray us in the end.

I remind myself they could've cost Sora her life, so I shouldn't feel anything about seeing them dragged in like pig carcasses, crossbow bolts sprouting from their chests.

But I do. Bile rises in my throat. I want to throw up, but I swallow it down.

There's enough moonlight coming in to make out everyone's faces. For the first time, it seems like the others accept me, so I suppose that's a vast improvement over the rest of the trip.

I catch Aeri's gaze, and she smiles even though she looks exhausted. I like Aeri. I have from the start. Maybe because she wasn't a killer like the rest of them…before tonight. My stomach roils, and my mouth waters.

"You saved my life," she says, sitting forward.

I nod, swallowing hard.

"Thank you," she says. "You…you didn't have to." She sounds like she's confused as to why I would do it.

"I wasn't going to let someone kill you," I say. "And actually, Euyn shot him first."

"Only the first one," she says.

That's right. I killed two men tonight. I've only been thinking of the one—the first. The one I could justify as already dying by someone else's hand. I take a deep breath. Gods, there's a whole other murder to weigh against my soul.

I suck in some more of the breeze. My fingers are still numb, and my chest feels strange. Not to mention the pain of my broken nose, which, frankly, I'd forgotten about in the rush of murder and mayhem. There's also a cut on my thigh, but it's shallow.

"You did well," Royo says.

It takes me a moment to realize he's talking to me. I'm so shocked by the compliment that tears spring to my eyes. But I absolutely cannot cry in front of a man like Royo. The only thing worse would be crying in front of my father. Either one might beat me to death just out of sheer disgust.

I'm not sure how they figured out I was told to kill Sora. I guess I might as well address it. We all just murdered and almost died. Seems pointless to have secrets after tonight.

I clear my throat. "Thank you. I...I would never hurt Sora. I want you to know that."

And most importantly, I want her to believe it.

Her eyes dart in my direction, and then she stares forward again. She's been very quiet. I doubt poisoning the leader bothered her. It's probably whatever happened before we got there. My hands ball into fists when I think about it. I don't ask. I'd never ask what happened in the bedchambers of the nobles she's killed. It's not that I don't want to know. I'd listen for days if it would help unburden her. But I don't want to make her feel worse by asking. And she wouldn't confide in me anyhow.

"It's what my father said to do once the king is dead," I admit. "To burn her indenture and then kill her. But I couldn't. I won't."

"Why?" Euyn asks. "Why is your father giving her to us but then asking you to kill her?"

It's a great question, but I don't know the answer. My father expects unquestioning obedience. All he will tell me is what I stand to lose. In this case, if I don't kill her, he'll cut me off financially until his death—which is no small consequence. Without his money, I can't live my life, let alone secretly pay off indentures. And I've spent years tracking down the siblings of the girls who died in my father's poison schools and arranging to buy out four of their contracts. A fifth was just located when I got to Rahway. And all of that would be for naught if I am cut off.

My father was also kind enough to remind me that I have few useful skills. But he is wrong. I wouldn't be destitute. I'd reenlist in the king's guard, serve Yusan. Even if I had no prospects, though, I wouldn't take her life. Now, more than ever, I know I never could've.

I gesture with my palms up. "I don't know. I assumed it was so she couldn't get revenge on him—on us—but I'll never know."

"You can never ask Seok his reasons," Sora says.

There's a hollowness to her tone and expression.

Ah, so she's also felt my father's backhand. I suspected as much. But I hadn't wanted to believe it.

I exchange looks with Sora. She just defended me, and she didn't need to. Maybe she finally understands that I meant what I said: I'll do anything to help her. We've suffered because of the same man.

Pain radiates through my broken nose right on cue. I grimace and go to touch my face even though I know it'll make it worse. Sora reaches out for me. Not fully—just a slight movement of her hand before she thinks better of it, but even that little motion makes my heart fill and takes my pain away.

I still don't understand why the men who attacked us in the alley, who knocked me out, left me in the street. They took my purse. They had to at least suspect I was a high noble. So why didn't they kill me or take me for ransom?

"I should be dead," I whisper.

"No one here is dying," Royo says. "Not if I can help it."

From his mouth, it sounds like the truth.

Aeri leans her head against Royo's shoulder. He recoils, and she looks wounded, but it was a knee-jerk reaction. Some men think softness is contagious. Royo takes a breath, then slowly rests his arm on the banquette. His fingers reach out tentatively before he finally touches her shoulder. She smiles, beaming, and shuffles right in against him. He...almost smiles back.

I glance at Sora again. If Royo can let Aeri close, maybe people can change. Maybe there's some measure of hope for us.

But something else about tonight doesn't sit well with me. As we left The Mine, I turned around. I was the only one who looked back. And just as I did, I caught a flicker of movement. Someone in black was on the roof of a nearby building. But when I looked up again, the roof was empty. And no one else has mentioned it. Yet I keep thinking about it.

It doesn't make sense. A gang member up there could've killed all of us. We were kettled in the alley behind The Mine and could've been easily picked off. So it couldn't have been a member of the Bulgae. But if not them, then who? I'm about to ask if anyone else saw the man, but Sora speaks.

"Does it hurt very much?" she asks. Her eyes are full of sympathy as she looks at me. My mouth goes dry. She has never once glanced at me this way.

"I'll be all right," I say. I fake being stoic.

She nods but then shivers, goose bumps painting her skin. I remove my jacket and offer it to her. She hesitates but accepts.

I rest my jacket on her shoulders, and joy fills me. Maybe she's realized that I am not my father. Or maybe she's just cold. But she's allowing me to help her, and that's a monumental shift.

Maybe there really is hope for us. I allow myself to dream.

Content, I lean on the banquette and then drift off to sleep. But I'm not out long before the nightmares start.

CHAPTER FIFTY-ONE

SORA

THE EASTERN ROAD, YUSAN

We stopped once it was daylight, and everyone ate as if they'd been fasting for days. But as soon as we wiped our mouths, we got right back in the carriage. We all want to put as much distance between us and Oosant as possible. And there's not that much time before the millennial celebration.

If we make it.

I generally don't think about the men I've killed—nothing good will come of that. But last night was different. I wasn't sent to kill, to be a poison maiden. To them, I was just a girl to take, to devour, and then to discard. Then again, I suppose my noble marks have thought the same of me.

Best to not think about it at all.

But as I sit in the carriage, I can't seem to help it. I'm groggy. I woke a few times in the middle of the night because Ty was whimpering, and then I was just awake. I assume he was having nightmares. Murder is a heavy thing that dirties your soul and infects your dreams. And it's still new to him. It was just as heavy for me after the first noble I killed. It's why I ran without any regard for the consequences. I was lost in the nightmare.

Mikail looks at me appraisingly. He's next to me again, since we switched around after breakfast.

"Are you okay?" he asks.

I nod and fake a smile. He arches an eyebrow.

I smile genuinely. Of course I didn't fool him. "I'm as well as can be expected. Once they knocked Royo out, I only resisted a little. I didn't want them to know I had any combat training because it would've marked me as something different. So I went with them fairly willingly. The leader had taken me to a back bedroom, but we weren't in there long before the barmaid came and told them a king's guard was coming."

"Were we...in time?" His teal eyes scan my face.

"You were." I shudder, my stomach twisting. "Of course, I was prepared should he have gone further."

I don't like to think about it—all of the almost assaults, the number of would-be rapes. The leader had thrown me to my knees after I refused to take my dress off. He hit me so hard that he left marks. Aeri was kind enough to apply makeup to my face this morning to hide the bruises on my cheek and throat.

The leader had his hands on my throat, threatening to let all of his dogs taste me if I didn't want to belong to him. And he probably would've given me to his men even if I'd been docile. There are many men like the western count who only want to inflict pain. For whom women are just another way to feel powerful. I'd come so close to kissing him just to put an end to him, but I didn't have an exit strategy. And I was holding on to hope that the group would find my dress trail.

Right as I was considering kissing him, there was the blessed knock on the door.

"Has the Count ever mentioned Oosant?" Mikail asks.

I raise my eyebrows. It's a strange question. "Seok? No. Not that I can remember."

He nods.

Maybe he's just trying to understand why Ty is alive. I've been wondering it, too—why they didn't kill him in the alley or take him for ransom. But it didn't have anything to do with the Count of Gain. Oosant is under the protection of either the western or the eastern count. Or no one's, as it seemed.

But it's not like the Count confides in me.

"Daysum would know more about Seok's business than I do," I say. "She listens at the walls."

"Your sister." He smiles.

I nod. "She's smarter than me."

"Well then, that's a terrifying girl," he says.

I laugh. "Do you have a sister?"

"I... No." Mikail looks out the window.

He's lying. His mouth takes a certain shape when he's not being fully honest. I'm not sure why he'd lie about a sibling, but he just did.

His eyes meet mine again. I must've given it away—that I realized his tell.

"She died very young," he says quietly.

That makes sense. He said the reason he's doing this is because of his family. King Joon must've had something to do with his sister's death. It could've been any number of things, from the king's guard running her down to the famine nearly twenty years ago to something else entirely. Power is responsibility. It means everyone blames the king when things go wrong.

And a lot of things go wrong in Yusan.

Euyn eyes Mikail. He's next to Royo, but he heard us. Mikail notices, and something in his expression shifts—the set of his brows, his eyes, the line of his mouth. He closes off. He won't talk any more about her. And men like him don't appreciate being probed.

"Well," I say. "Tell me about the restaurants in Tamneki."

He laughs at the sudden change of subject, his eyes kind again. "Sora, they're the best in the country. The food and entertainment districts make up the third ring, and every shop is the best Yusan has to offer."

The Count has told me about it—how Tamneki is a city of concentric rings, with the King's Arena in the very heart of the city and waterways dividing every district. The civic buildings are in the first ring, with the Temple of the God of the East Sea standing as the tallest structure in the capital. Businesses are in the second ring; food and entertainment, the third. The outer rings are lodging and pleasure, residential, and ancillary businesses.

"We can't get there soon enough," I say. "I could use a bed, a good meal, and a hot bath."

"You'll have those things sooner than later," Mikail says. "We'll stop at Count Dal's country estate first. It's between here and Tamneki."

That's a welcome surprise. "How much farther is that?"

"Not far, depending on whether we stop overnight somewhere."

"Without killing dozens of men and setting a building on fire this time?" I ask.

"I mean, we can't do that in every city," Mikail says with a wink. "People will start to talk."

I smile and look to the side. Aeri is chatting with Ty. She is still the only person in this carriage I don't understand. Not fully. I don't understand her motivations for being here or her relationship with Royo. And I still don't know where she went to in Capricia. But she's the one I need. Because as much as everyone here saved me, as thankful as I truly am, and as much as I like them, Daysum is still more important. She's more important than my own life. And I'll get her the crown if I have to double-cross every person here to do it.

CHAPTER FIFTY-TWO

ROYO

THE EASTERN ROAD, YUSAN

Ty ain't so bad. I can admit it—I was wrong about him. He's a lot braver than he looks. He killed to save Aeri, and that makes him tops in my mind. She's sitting next to Sora right now, safe and sound, because Ty and Euyn spilled blood to protect her. I owe them both a debt I can't hope to repay.

I try not to look at Aeri much, and I fail. But she could've died, and as I was trying to kill my way to her, she…saved me. Somehow, this girl I thought would be knocked over by a stiff breeze killed a man to save my life. All because I went overboard and lodged my axe in a wall.

Aeri smiles at me, and my chest squeezes. I look away. It's just money. Just a job. Just gratitude and now owing her a debt. I'm relieved because I need her to survive until Tamneki. I'm grateful because she saved me. That's all I care about.

That's what I tell myself over and over.

But I keep thinking about how I could've lost her in the warehouse. And it makes my stomach drop and my palms damp. There were so many ways that night coulda gone to shit—but it didn't. We're all still here on the Eastern Road. Maybe thanks to the gods, but mostly thanks to Mikail.

I can't get over how he can kill. I thought I was a good strongman, but Mikail is a different breed. He kills like he was born to do it. Like he's slashing through water, not muscle and bone. He murders without hesitation and at a speed I've never seen. Four men were dead before I killed one.

And I had an axe.

Euyn catches me staring at Mikail.

"Question?" Euyn asks.

"Do they teach how to kill like him in the king's guard?" I ask.

I have to serve my two years before I'm thirty, but I've been putting it off. Serving pays ten gold mun a month, which ain't too bad because they give you food and a bed, but I couldn't do it when I was trying to earn Hwan's freedom. Besides, I'm not a real patriotic guy—not with trying to kill the current king. But if they teach skills like that, it could be worth enlisting.

Euyn shakes his head. "That can't be taught, really. Mikail is made of steel, formed and sharpened from when he was a boy. You'd probably be as fast under the same circumstances."

"I dunno. He don't seem human when he's killing."

Euyn nods and then frowns. "Our enemies call him a demon."

"Yeah." I can see that.

Something in his expression says that Euyn can, too. And it's not a bad thing. Being so feared that your enemies make a legend out of you.

The girls laugh, and it draws his attention.

"Hard to believe the two of them can kill grown men, though," he says.

It is.

I asked Sora why the leader died after she kissed him, and she explained that she's a poison maiden. A girl assassin who seduces to murder. She said the lipstick she put on after dinner had enough poison in it to kill three men. Three grown men. It still makes my head spin—that she's immune to poison, what she had to do to become that way, and that the southern count even thought to create her.

Yusan is falling apart at the seams, with everyone taking matters into their own hands. And instead of fixing the country, Joon is holding a tuhko championship. To distract everyone and celebrate himself.

He has to die.

"Will you be a good king?" I ask Euyn.

He draws a breath. "I don't know, Royo. I hope so."

"I need you to do more than hope."

The words come out of my mouth and seem to hang in the air. I never could've imagined talking to royalty like this, but it's been a weird trip.

"Whether a king is good or not usually depends on what he's done for the person asked. But I'll try to be fair…if I become king."

I get what he means. This plan is pretty flimsy, and the closer we get to Tamneki, the more that matters. But we're supposed to meet the eastern count tomorrow at his country estate, and he'll have more information. A lot more. That'll give us time to prepare—and for Sora and Euyn to cozy up to him. All I need to do is protect Aeri. And I will.

But I'd feel better about this whole thing if I weren't certain one of them is keeping a massive secret. The more I think about it, the surer I am that somebody killed the men who were guarding the back of The Mine. I thought it'd been left unguarded intentionally, but right before I kicked in the door, I noticed a little bit of blood on the doorjamb—fresh blood. But I couldn't dwell on it, because Euyn gave the signal and it was time to kill.

All I know is that it couldn't have been anyone in the coach. So someone here has to be working with outside people.

I'm going to figure out who it is and what they really want. And then I'm gonna kill them.

CHAPTER FIFTY-THREE

EUYN

TOWN OF ASEYO, YUSAN

Dal's country villa is the definition of ostentatious. It spans acres and acres of land, as all the counts' estates do, but the Count of Tamneki is the richest of the four. And Dal is always in the mood to remind everyone of that fact.

Everyone but Mikail gapes through the carriage windows as we approach the towering glass dome and dancing fountains, but this Aseyo house is actually less grand than his city villa.

I've been to both plenty of times. After all, Dal used to be Joon's best friend.

It's a long story of love, betrayal, and, since it's my family, murder.

As we pull up to the villa, the head of household sprints out and apologizes profusely for Dal's absence. The second he sees me, he throws himself to the ground to bow to me. Of course, he instantly recognized me, but for the life of me, I can't remember the man's name.

"My most abject apologies, Your Highness," he says. "The count has business keeping him in Tamneki as we prepare for the celebration. I was not told to expect guests until tomorrow at the earliest. And I was not aware Your Highness would be among them."

Meaning: he didn't think I was still alive. It's a less-than-auspicious beginning to our stay.

The head of household leads us to bedroom suites. As we walk down the airy halls, I realize Dal changed the uniforms of his valets. They now all wear green instead of blue. Otherwise, this place is mostly the same as it was five years ago when Dal's father died and he became the count.

While my servant draws a bath, I go into Mikail's room. I certainly won't be left alone with valets who might be willing to kill me for the bounty on my head. There are far too many ways to die in this villa, and most involve drowning.

As I walk in, his servant is also preparing a bath.

"Let it never be said Dal is useless. The green is an improvement," I say, looking at her uniform.

Mikail raises his eyebrows. He's relaxing on the bed, flipping through a book. "Remember you're here to cement an alliance to support your claim. I doubt snark will help, especially when I don't recall Dal as ever having a sense of humor."

I purse my lips.

"Go bathe, Euyn." He points to the room given to me—next to his.

I hesitate. "What…what if they try to kill me?"

Mikail draws a long-suffering breath. "Oh, good. I thought you'd stopped being paranoid for a little while."

It's not paranoia. Twenty thousand gold mun would pay off a small indenture or set up a salaried commoner for life. And even if it's not for the money, any of the nobles are capable of backstabbing. They might kill me to win back favor with Joon. Dal is a little doubtful, considering how hard he fell out with my brother, but it's possible. Anything is.

"Bathe in mine," Mikail says with a sigh. "When you're done, I'll go into yours. Be quick about it, please. I want the water to still be warm."

I hate to admit it, but it feels much better to know he'll be right outside the door while I clean myself.

"Unless you want to scandalize the servants and share." His full lips turn up in an irresistible smirk.

The scandal wouldn't be because we're the same gender. No one would bat an eye about that. No, the issue is that Mikail isn't noble. Class is more important in Yusan than simple differences like skin color or sexual preference. And I am at the top of the hierarchy, and Mikail is a commoner.

Still, it's tempting. I've never cared about rumors or scandal, at least where Mikail is concerned. I pause with my hand on the doorknob. We've been in the coach for so long, and we haven't had time alone since we snuck up to our room in Oosant. Everything that happened afterward makes that pleasure feel like a distant memory. It's been far too long since I've felt him inside me.

"Tonight, Euyn," Mikail says with a wicked smile. "I still feel blood in my pores."

I'd be ashamed of how eager I am for him, how I please him with more enthusiasm than a courtesan, but we're way past that. It's always been this way—unbridled, degrading lust. I'm already hard just thinking about the way he said "tonight."

I shake my head at myself and walk into the bathing room. A large tub is steaming. White rose petals float on top of the fragrant soap bubbles. The servant stands in the corner, holding a towel and a scrub brush. She's just a girl, but I dismiss her. I've seen what harmless-looking girls are capable of on this trip. Particularly Sora.

Aeri is a mystery, though. She's not a professional killer like Sora. She should've been a wreck after the murders in the warehouse. But…she wasn't. Not even that night or the next day when the shock had a chance to wear off. So why wasn't she? Is it perhaps because she's killed before?

I'd point it out to Mikail, but he'd tell me I'm being paranoid… again. Besides, she's just a girl.

I shake it off, disrobe, and sink into the tub. And fool myself that all my worries will vanish into the steam.

CHAPTER FIFTY-FOUR

AERI
TOWN OF ASEYO, YUSAN

This place is amazing. Like totally amazing. The fountains, the waterways, the cute little fish. I love it all. After the murders in Oosant, we were cooped up in the carriage for days, so it's nice to finally have space. Air to breathe. Room to stretch out.

I wander the cool marble halls, then come to a stop and stare into the huge glass dome in the middle of the villa. Inside the orb, colorful birds fly around rare trees.

One man actually owns all this. This is luxury. This is living. This is what I want. This is what I can have if I complete this mission—I can live like a king.

I realize I'm leaving fingerprints on the glass, so I wipe them with my sleeve. I'm so glad I had new dresses made in Rahway. Unfortunately, only three were ready before we had to leave, and the yellow one now has bloodstains that didn't totally wash out. The others I ordered are long behind us, being couriered to the capital. I wonder if I can get more made here. I can't look like a pauper surrounded by the likes of this.

I also need to message Father soon, but since everyone got so bent out of shape about it in Capricia, it may have to wait until we're in Tamneki. But all that suspicion happened before The

Mine, before we killed and bled for one another. Maybe there's more trust now.

There probably isn't.

Mama said I should never trust a man, but I do. I trust Royo. He's made mistakes before, but who hasn't? At least he owns them. Coming to terms with what you've done wrong is better than just being a good person.

He's by my side right now, and every once in a while I catch him looking at me. I pretend I don't. For all of his bravado, for all of his strength and violence, he's shy when it comes to me. And the feeling makes my heart skip and bounce in my chest. Every time he gets an inch closer, he scurries a foot away. So I do my best to hold still and let him come to me on his own terms. He's like a skittish wild animal I want to trap and tame.

That sounds really bad.

Oh well. The truth sounds bad sometimes.

"We have to get ready for dinner soon," Royo says.

"Aren't we securing the premises right now?" I ask.

He rolls his eyes at me. The more I look at them, the prettier they get. Amber, stained glass, crystalized honey. Mine are brown. Plain old brown. But when he looks into them, they feel different, special—like Mikail's or Sora's, like the expensive jewels Ty wears.

I was so worried about Royo in the warehouse. Not just when I threw the blade but when two men attacked him at the same time. It was different, more chaotic than on the riverboat. But he handled them. He put an axe through a man and crushed a throat with just his bare hands. I've never seen anything like that. Well, I guess I did see him snap a man's neck on the Sol.

I pause as my lower stomach clenches. It's so damn hot.

Sora was the one who stitched together Royo's shoulder, but I've babied him with changing his dressing and checking on him since. He's pretended to hate it. But I think I'm wearing him down.

I imitate his broad-shouldered walk.

"Stop it," he says. But then he laughs. Actually laughs. And good gods…that's an incredible sound. It rings so clear off the glass, and the melody makes me feel like I could leave my shoes and fly like the birds in the orb.

"Did you just laugh?" I ask, my hand swinging near his with each stride.

He shakes his head, serious again. "No."

"Hmm, weird…" I scratch by my ear. "I've heard laughter before, and I'm pretty sure it sounded just like that."

He side-eyes me, but the hard veneer cracks. His face softens for just a second. Half a second. If I blinked, I would've missed it. But I'm so glad I saw it. Royo with his guard down, even the tiniest bit, is the best thing I've ever seen.

I can't tease him about it, though. Because if I do, he'll crawl back into his shell and stay there for who knows how long. And we don't have much time until my mission is complete, and then I'm not sure what becomes of us. Of any of us.

Just then, Mikail and Euyn come down the hall. Mikail has his usual saunter, and Euyn looks regal. They're in dress clothes, ready for dinner.

"Did I just hear Royo laugh?" Mikail asks.

"Certainly not," I say. "That sound isn't possible."

Royo rolls his eyes again, but his lips threaten to smile.

"We're almost to the capital now. Anything is possible," Mikail says. He glances over at Euyn.

I try to imagine it—Euyn as king. The crown of the Dragon Lord on his head. But I just can't.

"Why are you looking at me like that?" Euyn asks.

"Oh, sorry." I shake my head. "I was just picturing you in the crown."

"The thousandth-year king," Royo says, standing straighter. "Are you ready to be immortal?"

Euyn breathes out a laugh and looks to the side. Mikail eyes him closely—very closely. Euyn watches the birds in the orb and then faces us again. I'm surprised he didn't automatically answer yes.

"I suppose we'll find out in three days," he says.

Gods. Three days. Three days until Dal brings Sora close enough to the king to kill him. I knew that, of course, and yet I wasn't thinking about it. It's so little time. A disquieting feeling rocks me—I don't want this to all come to an end. But I shake it off. I resolve to make the most of our time together. The truth is that none of us can ever be guaranteed tomorrow, so there's no sense in worrying about something days down the road.

"We were on our way to the armory before dinner," Mikail says. "Euyn needs more bolts. Royo, should we pick you up another axe?"

"I wouldn't say no," Royo says, rubbing his hands together.

"I'll take one, too," I say.

All three men give me various looks of disbelief.

"I'm kidding, but a dagger would be nice."

Euyn nods.

"Done," Mikail says.

They leave, and we head back toward our suite. They gave Royo a separate room, but he stays in mine.

I made Royo laugh. That's all I will care about today. I'll worry about tomorrow tomorrow.

I dance down the hall.

"You're the weirdest person I've ever met," he grumbles.

I raise my palms. "I don't know what you want me to do about that, Royo."

"Nothing," he says, then adds, "I like it."

I miss a step and stop. Heat flushes from my toes up to my face and takes a really long detour to pool in my hips. I stand, blinking at him.

He looks away, pretending like he didn't say it.

But I know he did.

CHAPTER FIFTY-FIVE

SORA

TOWN OF ASEYO, YUSAN

The six of us just had an outrageously good dinner in a splendid dining room. The nobility has few virtues, but fine hospitality is one of them. And because there was a prince at the table, everything was twice as extravagant as usual—which is saying something. It was the finest meal I've ever had. Wasteful, as they always are, but unbelievably delicious.

After so long on the road, the hot bath and fantastic dinner could not have been more welcome. I think once I have a good night's sleep, my tremors will stop. Or at least I hope.

Our group laughed and joked at dinner like we didn't slay a warehouse full of men and now plan to kill a god king. We were able to put it all aside and just relax and enjoy one another's company. Even Royo smiled as Mikail told a ridiculous story about a sea serpent taking his dagger.

I was confused for a minute, both by Royo's face being capable of a smile and by what I was feeling. I couldn't place the tightness in my chest, and then I did—it felt like family. But this time, a bond that isn't blood. It's forged by circumstances, but it can provide the same comfort. Then I needed to excuse myself from the table because it soured the night for me. I know better than anyone that families don't last—they always end in betrayal or heartbreak.

But this time I will be the one betraying all of them. I have to get that crown, and it's not like I can ask Euyn to hand me the key to immortality. The life of one peasant girl won't matter in this scheme. But even if I can steal the crown, how in the Kingdom of Hells will I make it all the way to Gain? If Seok finds out, he will murder me just for taking it. Maybe kill Daysum before I could even reach her.

It's impossible.

I pace in my room, clutching at my head and shaking out my hands. The truth is, I like everyone here. Through time and blood, I feel connected to them. And I haven't liked anyone since the girls in poison school. The ones I watched die, one by one, unable to save them or help in any way—as I said, that family ended in heartbreak. I don't want to hurt any of these people, but I also can't just give up on my sister. I'm all she has. I've defied the odds by staying alive. I can complete an impossible mission.

But how?

How?

I'm not smart enough to figure this out on my own. I wish I could talk to Daysum. I wish I could play with her long hair and feel the comfort of her familiar smell. I wish I had her mind.

There's a light knock. I freeze, surprised. I want, more than anything, for it to be her at the door. Even though I know it can't be.

"Yes?" I ask.

"Sora, it's me," Ty says.

It's not Daysum. Of course it's not. I sigh and unlock the door.

"I just came to see if you were all right." His blue eyes scan me.

"I…" I try to say I'm fine, but suddenly, I start crying.

I don't understand it. I haven't cried in years. But hot tears stream down my face, and my breathing hitches.

Once the first few tears escape, it's like a dam breaks inside me. Everything from the fear that's settled into my bones since I was sold by my parents to guilt over the lives I've taken comes spilling out in the form of tears. Layered in is racking my brain with how to save Daysum. How to survive. How to keep any bit of my humanity I have left. How nothing good ever lasts because I was doomed by my face and my family long ago. Why, in the end, they didn't love me, and, unforgivably, why they didn't love Daysum.

Ty rushes in and wraps me in his arms. I hold still, shocked by his touch. I pause, waiting to see what he wants from me, from my body, but it's…nothing. He's just holding me.

My whole body is tense, but slowly, gradually, I lean on his shoulder.

He doesn't ask me what's wrong or pester me to talk. He just holds tight as I cry. And no one's held me like this in years. I hold Daysum. It's a different feeling to *be* held. But Ty shouldn't be holding me. It's all wrong.

I catch my breath, wipe my face, and move to take a step back. Ty lets go. His arms slowly drift to his sides.

"I'm sorry." I brush my remaining tears away. My face feels hot, so I fan it with my hands.

His forehead knits. "Why are you sorry?"

I sniffle. "For crying."

He shakes his head. "That's not something to apologize for."

I blink and stare at him. We've had a truce of sorts since Capricia, and certainly since he fought twice to try to save me in Oosant. He's killed, and I cleaned the blood off him, defended him, and stitched his wounds. But this is something different than being allies. This is kindness and caring.

"You are Seok's son," I say. "How can you be kind?"

"I've told you before—I am not Seok. And it's not difficult to be kind to people you love." His voice is a murmur. Then he clears his throat and straightens his posture and moves a step away.

It takes me a second to catch on, and then I blink hard. "People you love?"

He blanches and looks at the shiny tile floor, shifting his weight. I would think I misheard him, but he was on my right. And from his reaction, I know I didn't. Tiyung, the future Count of Gain, just admitted to loving me.

Ty nods to himself a single time and sighs. He pushes back his shoulders. "I've loved you since I first saw you, Sora. When you were only nine but you faced armed men with your chin up and tried to hide Daysum behind you. I fell for your beauty, of course—I'm human—but it was your spirit that did me in. Your capacity to love is deeper than the West Sea. You're honest. You're true. You are everything."

I shake my head, refusing to process it. "But…you don't. You don't love me. You hated me. You hunted me. You…you…"

But no other words come out because there was that look on his face when we were only kids and then again at Lord Shan's estate. That was the look I couldn't place. Tiyung thinks he loves me.

But that's not possible. His father owns me. He was miserable to me at the poison school. He dragged me back through the Xingchi forest.

Ty wanders toward the half-open window with his hands behind his back. "When you ran, my father told me, 'If you love her, bring her back to me alive.' But it tore me apart to take your freedom from you. And then to whip Daysum was even worse. I knew you'd never forgive me, but I volunteered because I knew I was the lesser of two evils. I was certain that if my father whipped her, he would've done real damage."

I shake my head. Tiyung did do damage. Daysum bears the scars. But I think back… The healer had been surprised she didn't need internal sutures. She'd raised her brows when she looked Daysum over, and I asked about her expression as I sat, clutching Daysum's hand.

I'm just surprised, that's all. And I'd let it go because I'd been so devastated and guilty.

The truth hits so hard, it shatters me—everything I knew, everything I *thought* I knew was wrong. And I don't know what to do with the pieces of me. So I just watch Ty lean against the window frame, the muscles in his back shifting as he stares into the night.

"I enlisted in the king's guard just to get away from Gain, from everything I've done," Ty continues, speaking to his reflection in the glass. "I tried to forget you while I was gone. It would've been better for both of us, I'm sure. But it's not possible. It's never going to be possible."

I take a few steps closer to him. "Why is that?"

He turns and faces me. "Because I'd know you in this life and the next hundred."

He states it plainly—not the romantic declarations of acting troupes but a resigned fact. And something about that is more moving.

I don't know what to say. And given two more lifetimes, I don't know that I'd know.

I'm about to speak when his eyes suddenly dart past me. I turn just in time to see someone run from the window. Someone has been watching us.

Kingdom of Hells, what was that? Who was that?

CHAPTER FIFTY-SIX

ROYO

TOWN OF ASEYO, YUSAN

Aeri sprawls out on the canopied bed, smiling.

"That was such a good meal," she says, patting her stomach.

She turns her head and looks over at me with those eyes, and I want her. I can't even lie to myself and say that ain't what this is. The stirring I feel isn't the job. It isn't gratitude for her saving my hide. I want to have her long legs wrapped around me. I want to taste her lips. I want to peel that green dress off her. I want to hear her moan my name.

I need to get the fuck out of here.

"I'm going to do a round," I say.

My hand shakes a little as I tuck two throwing knives into my suit. Out of here. Seriously, I need to get out of this room.

She sits up in the bed. "Should I come?"

"No," I say, too harsh. Her eyes go wide. I change my tone. "It's just a quick patrol before we settle in for the night."

"Oh, um…okay." She's confused, and she's right to be. I'm now the one acting strange.

"Lock the door after me and don't answer it for anybody. I'll knock three times in a row so you know it's me."

I don't wait for her to respond. Instead, I race out of the bedroom and close the door behind me. Then I lean against it and take a breath. I can't want her. Well…apparently, I *can*, but I can't *have* her, so what the fuck am I doing? Losing my mind is what I'm doing.

A deep sigh escapes my chest. Ten Hells.

I need to focus on something other than the softness of Aeri's touch. Something other than her unblemished skin and the curves of her hips and breasts. Those long legs. Something that isn't going back in that room and putting that bed to good use.

Patrolling. Patrolling is what I need to do. There are private guards throughout this villa, but they don't matter. Who knows if they're any good. Besides, even if the dozen or so guardsmiths were all top-notch, they'd still be pretty meaningless in a house full of killers.

I glance down at my scarred hand still on the doorknob—and walk away.

I start down the hall and focus on the villa. The ceiling goes way over my head like it's a temple, not just a guy's house. The floors are white marble with blue veins that remind me of water—real water, though, not the shitty Sol. There's an enormous glass globe in the middle of the building with a garden. Who even thinks to put that in the middle of their place? It looks nice, but since all the rooms are around it, the globe prevents any clean lines of sight.

The bright lights of the orb start giving me a headache. Although I've really never lost it since I was sucker punched. Stupid fucking goons. Sora had to sew up my shoulder. It aches, but I pretend like I don't feel it.

I pass the dining room where we had the best food I've ever eaten. On one of the nicest nights I've ever had. Sora and Ty left early, and then Aeri went to our room and I followed her. But I could've eaten more. I wonder if there's any food left. I need to do something with my mouth. Something other than what I want to do.

Mikail and Euyn are still at the table. A plate of fruit, a hundred little cakes, chocolates, candies, and sparkling wine are still out. A sugar house would charge a fortune for what's casually strewn around the dining room right now.

"Something wrong, Royo?" Mikail asks. He's a ways from me at the other end of the table.

"No, everything is fine," I say.

"Where is Aeri?" Euyn raises one brow before sipping from his fluted wineglass. He seems a little flushed. Too much wine, I guess.

"She's getting ready for bed."

"It's been a long journey." Mikail relaxes in his chair, looking more like a king than Euyn. But he stares at me, and I feel a need to explain myself. I don't know why.

"I'm going to do a patrol round," I say.

He nods.

Ever since the warehouse, I trust him more. But not entirely. I can't trust anyone entirely—not even Aeri.

I just have to keep reminding myself of that.

I grab a torte and walk the perimeter. It's warmer outside of the villa than inside, and it's cloudy tonight. There's something in the air, something that makes the hair on my arm stand. It can't be rain. The monsoon moon is coming, and with it, downpour rains, but that shouldn't be until after the millennial celebration. And who knows what Yusan will look like at that point.

And who knows what will happen with Aeri. No. I know what will happen: we go our separate ways in three days.

I shove the torte into my mouth.

We only have three days until the celebration. Three more days, and then I'll get the payment to free Hwan. I'll go back to Umbria, and then…I don't know what I'll do after that. I haven't really thought past buying his way out of Salt because even that was so hard.

Hwan won't want anything to do with me—I sure as hells wouldn't want anything to do with the man who let my daughter be murdered. The guy who caused it. But so long as I get the bonus from Aeri, I'll give him half the money. That should allow him to restart his life somewhere. And twenty-five thousand is enough to make a new start for me, too. But…

I find myself wondering where Aeri will go. What she'll do.

What fucking difference does it make?

Why am I trying to imagine a future with her when there ain't no future? I won't go through this again. No way am I gonna let a girl, especially one like Aeri, get close to me. Strange as she is, she's as pure as fresh snowfall. I could only muddy her. The truth is, I'm not worth her.

I stop and take a breath as the realization hits me. I'm not worth any good woman.

And that's always been true.

I was too young and hopeful to admit it with Lora, still thinking that I could change, make something of myself. But all I am is muscle for hire. All I do is make guys bleed. That's no man for a girl like Aeri. And she'd realize it sooner or later. Maybe if we pull this off and free Hwan, I'll have enough left to—

Nah, it's better for her if I can put her out of my mind. I can do that much for her.

So I do.

With the clouds rolling over the bright moon, I focus on my steps. And that's enough to keep my brain busy—it's hard to avoid falling into all the damn water features on this posh estate. I plod along slower than I'm used to. The roar of the fountains makes it difficult to hear. There are some oil lamps, but they're tough to see with the water spray. It's like the whole place was built for assassins and spies to go unnoticed. Maybe this count doesn't think anyone can get to him. Who knows. But I wouldn't want to live in a place like this.

I'm halfway through my patrol of the villa when I notice there's something off. A movement. I pause in a fighting stance, my hand near my dagger. It could just be one of the guards out patrolling. Hopefully one of these dummies doesn't kill me by mistake.

I'm listening for someone coming, but it's impossible to hear over these fucking fountains. I'm about to move forward when footsteps rush toward me. I can't see who it is because of the water spray. I grab my throwing dagger, ready, but I stop my hand.

It's Sora.

What the fuck.

We freeze and stare at each other. Then a bloodcurdling scream rises over the roar of the fountains.

Somebody has just been killed.

CHAPTER FIFTY-SEVEN

MIKAIL
TOWN OF ASEYO, YUSAN

This place is a little bit much. It was originally modeled after the capital—meaning an excessive amount of water—but Dal went a step further and added a bunch of new fountains and waterfalls out back after his father's passing. I've been here once before to spy on him, but never as a guest. And never with Euyn underneath me.

"Please, Mikail." His fingers grip the silk sheets, and his desire throbs. "Please."

I've been teasing him relentlessly, really since the others left the dining room. He'd just gotten off his knees when Royo came around patrolling. But since we got into my bedroom, I've been truly merciless. My back is healed, so there's nothing that dulls the pleasure of him writhing under me. I know the wait is excruciating for a prince used to getting everything at the snap of his fingers—and that's why I do it. To see him lower himself even more. To be nothing more than desire— not a prince, not a royal, just someone swept up in the moment.

We're both rock hard, and I'm about to give him what he wants. I've been teasing his thighs, playing with him.

"Beg," I say in his ear.

Euyn opens his mouth—and a scream erupts from somewhere outside the villa.

We jump apart and reach for our weapons. I hastily throw my clothes back on, and so does Euyn.

Well, that ruined the moment.

Dressed in seconds, we sprint outside, me with my sword and Euyn with his bow. We search, having each other's backs, trying to find the source of the noise. But we're too late. Everyone is already gathered. Sora, Ty, Aeri, and Royo stand in a half circle. Two villa guards stand opposite them with their swords drawn but hanging down. Everyone is silent and stock-still. I stare over at Euyn.

This can't be good.

The clouds part, and the moon gives a clear view of what everyone is staring at. A man is face down, dead on the ground, a throwing knife in the side of his half-slit neck. And then I realize what he's wearing—stylized all blacks.

It was a palace assassin.

CHAPTER FIFTY-EIGHT

EUYN

TOWN OF ASEYO, YUSAN

A violent chill runs through me, and I shiver in the warm night air. What was a palace assassin doing here? Who was he looking for? I assume me, but the palace is not supposed to know I'm alive. Moreover, it lacks logic—an assassin would not have missed this badly.

Gaslights suddenly illuminate the exterior like it's midday. There are so many fountains back here—Dal must've put more in. The villa guards sweep the area, but they're far too late. And I don't know why they bother. They're searching for the murderer when whoever did this is likely standing right here.

Mikail kneels next to the body, examining the wound. He yanks the knife out of the man's neck and turns it over.

"Royo, isn't this one of yours?" He rinses the blood in a nearby pool and then spins around the blade to show the handle.

That makes sense—he was out patrolling and must've seen him. I'm not sure how he got the drop on a palace assassin in all blacks, though. All blacks are earned by the best killers in Yusan—we also call them shadows. And the shadows who can lie and manipulate, on top of murder, become spies. And the head of those is the man I love.

Mikail waits as Royo looks at the handle.

Royo's brow furrows. "I mean, all knives look the same, I think, but it wasn't me."

"Come again?" I say.

"I didn't kill nobody." The furrow becomes a deep crease. He keeps looking from the body to the group, suspicion in his eyes. He means it—it wasn't him. "Sora came running my way, and then we heard a scream."

All eyes turn to Sora. She blinks. "I was with Ty, and we saw someone moving outside my window. I went to see who it was but only found Royo before there was the scream from over here."

"You saw someone outside and went alone to look?" Aeri asks.

"She ran out, and I followed her," Tiyung says.

"Where were the two of you?" Royo asks.

It takes me a moment to realize he means Mikail and me. That they now think it could've been one of us. I glance at Mikail, but he's unfazed.

"You saw us in the dining room, and then we went into my bedroom," Mikail says. He turns slightly to focus on Aeri. "Where were you?"

"She was locked in our room," Royo says, suddenly defensive. He's taken half a step forward, physically shielding her before she can answer. She simply nods.

We all exchange glances. Mikail rubs his forehead.

"Okay, just to recap: We have a dead palace assassin here, and no one killed him? That's what we're all saying?" Mikail says.

Everyone is silent.

He turns to the villa guards. They're both simple-looking fellows. The high nobles have personal guards but also property guardsmiths. The less capable watch their houses. I don't expect miracles out of these two.

"What did you see?" Mikail asks, his hand still on the hilt of his sword.

"Nothing. We came out after the scream."

Predictable.

"Of course," Mikail says with a sigh.

"Wait. Who screamed?" Ty asks.

Ty has a talent for asking good questions. We all wait for the guard to answer.

"I think him," the guard says, pointing at the dead man. "It was a man's voice."

I shake my head. The only reason the assassin would scream would be if he saw the knife coming. If someone struck him as he was looking at them. Which is possible, given his wound, but there are six killers here and no one did or saw a thing. No one has blood on them. Which can only mean that someone is lying and covering it up.

"Was he after you?" Sora asks me.

I draw a breath. "I have to assume he was."

Mikail shakes his head. "No, I doubt it."

Everyone turns to him.

"Why not?" Royo asks.

Mikail scans around. "A palace assassin wouldn't have missed. He was here for someone else."

"To kill one of us?" Sora points to her chest, looking pale.

"No," Mikail says, glancing at each person before adding: "to talk to one of you."

The accusation is heavy and settles on the group like a fog. He's saying that someone is trying to hide their connection to a palace assassin. Someone is trying to betray everyone here, and for some reason they killed the man they were working with.

"And not you? A royal spymaster?" Royo tips his chin at Mikail.

"I suppose it could be any of us. Bring him inside. We'll search him," Mikail says to the guards.

We start walking back toward the house.

"We won't find anything," I whisper to him.

He shrugs. "Assuredly not, but it's better than arguing by these damn fountains."

He's so casual that for a second, just a split second, I wonder if he did it. He *is* the royal spymaster. He is supposed to be loyal to my brother. And he knows all the palace assassins. Maybe Mikail is actually working for Joon. Maybe he's double-crossing me.

But no, Mikail was in bed with me. That's not possible.

Unless he had someone else do it. Unless two of them—like, say, him and Sora—are in on it together. But to what end? No. I'm just being paranoid. He's risked his life for me again and again. He can't want me dead.

I pass yet another fountain, and cold spray hits me along with a thought: maybe the plan is to bring me in alive.

CHAPTER FIFTY-NINE

SORA

TOWN OF ASEYO, YUSAN

The six of us gather around a table again, but this time there's a dead body on it. We're in the game house, not the sumptuous dining hall. Meaning we're currently surrounded by death. Creatures, skinned and intact, hang from the rafters. There are blades everywhere. The air is heavy with last breaths and scented with blood.

But I suppose I'm looking around to avoid what's in front of me.

The assassin was about our age—early twenties—and now he's dead with a very ugly neck wound. The valets put sheets under him, and Mikail has stripped him down.

It's been very tense since Mikail accused someone, or really everyone, of colluding with a palace assassin. But watching the man being stripped naked is unbearable. Everyone has winced in turn, but it's worse for me. I don't know who this man was or why he was spying on us, but I do know this is how I would've been treated if I'd been caught and killed during any of my jobs. I would've been dragged in, undressed, and displayed for people to inspect. No dignity, even in death. And we are supposed to respect the dead.

We search him, but there's nothing to find. It's not surprising—there'd be nothing to find on me, either.

"But I don't understand. How do you know he was a palace assassin and not one of the eastern count's men or someone else entirely?" I ask.

"Because palace assassins wear all blacks when they're on a mission," Euyn says.

That seems odd—a dress code for murder. Then again, I have one, too—a dress, perfume, and poisoned lipstick.

"Couldn't anyone have put on a black shirt and black pants?" Royo asks.

"Of course, but that's not the case here," Mikail says, pointing to the man's clothing. It lies next to the corpse. "The cut of the pants and the diagonal piping of the shirt are unique. Plus, his shirt and pants are partially reinforced with steel mesh. It's not exactly common."

"But why was a palace assassin outside my window?" I ask. "And why did he run?"

"Those are the questions we need to answer." Mikail crosses his arms, holding my gaze for a second.

We all look at one another. No one says a word.

"I...I thought I saw someone in Oosant," Ty says. "In black clothes."

Everyone whips around at him. I sigh, and it's all I can do not to grab at my own hair. He hasn't said a word about this, and he picks now, when suspicions are at their highest. It's like he *wants* the people here to kill him.

"Why didn't you mention it then?" Aeri asks.

But he turns to me and answers, "I don't know. I thought perhaps I was seeing things. No one else said anything, and it happened so quickly, and there was so much going on that I thought maybe I just saw a shadow."

"What did you see?" Mikail asks, eyes intense. "Exactly."

Ty runs a hand through his hair. "I thought there was someone on the roof of the building next to The Mine."

"When?" Mikail asks.

"When we left. After we set the fire, I looked back, and I saw a movement out of the corner of my eye. But then I looked again and there was no one."

The group is stunned silent. How could there have been an assassin watching all of us in Oosant?

"Gods on High," Euyn says.

"In Oosant," Mikail mutters.

"I could've just been seeing things," Ty argues. Everyone's gaze is narrowed on him. He tries to walk it back, but with a dead assassin in front of us, it's unlikely he was simply imagining a shadow.

"Maybe your father sent him," Aeri says.

She throws out the accusation so casually. But it's a bolt. Suddenly, I want to defend Ty, but I can't. I can't rule it out, knowing Seok.

Ty flushes. "Why would he?"

"Maybe he's working with the king," she says. "Or maybe to watch and protect you. I don't know. I'm just trying to figure it out. What could have happened."

Ty is the Count's only heir, and Seok would want to ensure he survives, though a palace assassin reports to the throne. But then again, so does Mikail. Kingdom of Hells. It could've been any of them except for Royo. We were staring at each other when the scream happened.

"Where are you from, Aeri?" Ty asks, his tone harsh.

She looks wounded as she blinks. "Saylee."

It's a city in the northeast—not far from Inigo, where I was born. It makes sense. She's pale like Royo and me.

Royo's eyes narrow at her. "Why were you in Umbria, then?"

"I'm *from* Saylee. I've been living in Pyong for the last seven years."

Pyong is southwest of Umbria. Nearly at the foothills of the Khakatan Mountains. I, of course, have all the cites at the border of Khitan memorized.

"Home of the largest gem district in Yusan," Mikail says. "That is where I saw her lift a diamond worth fifty thousand, which is how I knew she could do this job."

"If you caught her so easily, why do you think she can do this?" Ty asks.

"Because she couldn't have known I was watching. I was there to spy on someone else and happened to see her."

It strikes me as a little too convenient. Aeri was the one who disappeared in Capricia. She said she was sending her father a letter, but maybe she was meeting with the assassin. What if we've been followed this entire time?

But why kill this man if he was protecting her? It doesn't make sense.

"So, we all suspect one another at this point, right?" Aeri raises one brow. "Good feelings gone?"

The room is silent.

"I don't think we're talking nearly enough about this guy"—Royo waves a scarred hand in Mikail's general direction—"who's a spy for the very throne we're trying to take and the one who organized all of this."

The group looks at Mikail, but he just shrugs. "We can if you want, but I was with Euyn when we heard the scream. Not to mention that I wouldn't be clumsy enough to kill loudly."

We all nod at that, and my heart sinks.

So we're back to it being none of us. And maybe that is the point.

"What if it was a setup by the eastern count?" I suggest.

"By Dal?" Euyn asks.

"He's the only one who knows we're here," I say, thinking aloud. "And conveniently, he couldn't make it tonight."

"Why would he do this?" Royo asks.

"To cause this," I say, gesturing to all of us. "To sow doubt so we're more eager to turn on one another. Or to just see what our allegiances are. I'm positive the valets are listening outside. They must have been reporting on us since we got here."

Everyone looks around. Aeri is wide-eyed. Ty takes a deep breath, likely knowing that counts are capable of anything. Royo is still glaring at Mikail, who looks nonchalant. Euyn and I seem to be the only ones actively trying to figure out who this man was and why someone killed him.

"I suppose we'll know more tomorrow based upon how Dal behaves," Euyn says.

Mikail nods. "I'll tell the servants to burn the body and bury the ashes."

Euyn side-eyes him. It's what needs to be done, but burning his body also prevents anyone else from looking at the assassin. And burying the ashes is exactly what Seok used to do.

Suddenly, I wonder if there's more of a connection between them than just this plot.

CHAPTER SIXTY

MIKAIL
TOWN OF ASEYO, YUSAN

It's been a rather tense day. Everyone has kept to their own pairings—Sora and Tiyung, Aeri and Royo, and myself and Euyn. But we all meet in the dining room for dinner with the count.

Royo looks genuinely uncomfortable in a new suit. Aeri is in a blue dress that shimmers like water—I can bet she had it made today. Sora is in another stunner, this one yellow. Her long hair is twisted over one shoulder and studded with gems. Ty is in his noble jacket but without his stupid hat, and Euyn looks immaculate in his imperial red jacket. Imperial red can only be made for and worn by royalty. I had to sneak some of his things out of Qali Palace after he was banished in case the moment ever came when he could return. I brought them with me.

We all take our seats, with Euyn at the head of the table. Despite it being Dal's house, Euyn outranks him as a prince. Even if he is technically dead. The seat to the right of Euyn sits empty, waiting for the count. I am on Euyn's left. A variety of small plates is already laid out, but the kitchen is holding the entrées for the arrival of their master. The head of household said to start on the banchan because the count may be delayed, but no one is eating much.

Unlike yesterday, we're all quiet as the servants tend to us. There's no laughter, no good stories. Just suspicion.

Ten minutes go by, then twenty, setting everyone on edge. We've gone past Dal being fashionably late, meaning something is wrong.

After thirty minutes, a messenger comes flying in. All eyes are on him as he bows on the floor to Euyn. Then he kneels with a small silver tray extended. On it is a single calling card. No doubt a message from Dal.

Euyn picks up the paper. His face drops, and he flings the card onto the table.

Stars, what now? I grab the hilt of my sword.

We're all silent, waiting. Euyn has his hand to his mouth, his face pale. He pulls on his beard in a way that looks painful. I reach over and read the card. It's not from Dal. It's from his Tamneki head of household.

I read the note, and suddenly it feels like falling into that cave in Fallow again. Not knowing how we'll survive, what happens now, or what lies ahead. But this time I have a group waiting on me to act.

I clear my throat. "The eastern count is dead."

Gasps and breaths echo in the room. Royo accidentally snaps the stem of his wineglass.

"How?" Euyn asks the messenger.

"A heart attack at the villa, Your Highness," he says. "His body was just found. The message was sent by eagle post."

So...definitely not a heart attack. So many strangulations can look like heart attacks as long as no one checks closely. I'd suspect Sora, but it's a sixteen-bell round trip between here and Tamneki. She simply didn't have the time, since I saw her this morning. But Dal's death is less than ideal. I will figure out who killed him, but I already know who gave the order. Joon has had a long-standing hit out on him. It's not exactly a surprise—but the timing is. I need to go back to Qali and tell them something or we'll all be doomed.

Euyn waves the messenger away and dismisses all the servants in the dining room. I'm sure there are spies hiding, but they don't matter. The count was in on our plans.

"What do we do now?" Sora asks in a low voice.

"Do we call it off?" Aeri asks at almost the same time.

Silence takes over the room as one by one, they each consider their options. I look around the table.

"I don't see how we go forward now…" Ty says.

Euyn strokes his beard. "I don't, either."

"Maybe another time…" Sora says, twisting her hair over and over. She doesn't normally play with her hair, but I think it's to hide her arm tremors. She hasn't said a word about them, but I've noticed. Same as I've noticed Aeri looking tired instead of bubbly.

"Maybe a different plan…" Aeri says. "We need to stop. We can't go forward with this one."

No. They all want to abandon ship now, and we've come too far to go back. Euyn will die staying in Yusan, and it's not like I can just deposit him back in Fallow. It was no easy feat to keep tabs on him the last three years—not easy to live each day not knowing if I would hear that he'd died. I've worked too hard and have too much riding on this for the plan to fall apart due to the death of one man.

"The plan stays the same," I say, my voice louder than theirs. "We will just have to find another way to introduce Sora to the king. The northern count will be at the celebration. We can use him."

Euyn wrinkles his nose. "Bay Chin is seventy."

"And since when has age prevented men from having young courtesans?" I ask.

Euyn shrugs, glancing to the side. He sees my point.

"Bay Chin is with us?" Royo asks.

"He's not committed," I lie. "But he won't mind being introduced to a beautiful woman. We can use him without his knowing."

Bay Chin was adamant that no one know he orchestrated this plan, so I told no one. Even Rune thinks he's unaffiliated. Given what happened eleven years ago, I don't blame Bay Chin. But we're now out of options.

Again, silence fills the room. They all are thinking about getting out of this. But now is our time to strike, and I can't do it without them. Well, without some of them. There's deadweight in here.

"Mikail, I don't know..." Aeri says. "Maybe we should just—"

I hit my hand on the table. They all startle like children—except Sora. "I know what this mission means to me. I know what it means to Euyn. I don't know about the rest of you. Perhaps consider what brought you here."

The five of them are silent. People often are in the face of impossible choices. But going through is the only way out of this.

Sora stares at her empty plate. "If the king dies, my sister is free. I am with you, Mikail."

"I go with Sora," Ty says. They exchange meaningful glances.

"I'm here to protect Aeri," Royo says. "But Euyn has my blade. If he's in, I'm with you."

Euyn looks me in the eye and nods.

Aeri is the last one. She looks at Royo, then shakes her head. "I..."

"We'll find another way to kill the king without you," I say with a shrug I don't mean. It's important I remain calm, or the rest will run like rats from a sinking ship. "You aren't the only thief in Yusan. But we cannot change course now. It has to be the Millennial Championship. There is no telling when Joon will leave the safety of the palace after the celebrations are done. It could be years. And there has never been a successful assassination in Qali Palace."

"Never?" Sora asks.

"One suspected but never proven," I say.

Euyn looks over at me, confused. That's right—I've never told him that I suspect Joon killed his father. It wasn't mission critical, especially since it was an inside job. I'd tell him now, but it would just be distracting. And really, what's another secret between us?

"Aeri, I gave you the choice in Pyong. Cooperate with us and make a fortune, or you're free to go," I remind her.

But I hope that she's with us, because I don't know how we'd do this without her. All of us are capable of killing a man, but only one of us has the speed and sleight of hand to remove Joon's crown and make him mortal. She has the most essential role.

She glances around the table and then slowly nods. "I'm with you."

CHAPTER SIXTY-ONE

AERI

TOWN OF ASEYO, YUSAN

I have to go along with this plan, but I don't want to. I've tried again and again to get them to reconsider, but everyone is barreling ahead. I'd tell them no, but I don't really have a choice. Without me, they'll fail, and failure would mean they all die. At least with me, they have a chance of walking away with their lives. Not to mention the fact that I need this job.

Still, I wish I could convince them to abandon this mission. Things are changing too quickly, and the wisest thing would be to delay until we can regroup. I don't believe for a second that the eastern count happened to have a heart attack today. And he was supposed to be the way we got close to the king. Our avenues are being cut off, but Mikail won't change course. He wants Euyn on the throne, and his wants are stronger than reason.

Royo and I walk back toward the suites after we finish dinner. It's a silent march to our room. We're staying the night, and then we'll leave in the morning for Tamneki. If we're all still alive by sunrise.

Two days left. In less than two days, this will all be over.

I didn't expect to feel so conflicted. I didn't think that these killers, this ring of liars, would be willing to risk their lives to protect me or that I'd feel the same. They like me simply for being me. And I've never had that before.

But this bond is temporary. Completing this job means we'll all go our own ways. And the most important thing is that I'll win back my father's approval. I'll never have to steal again, never be alone. I'll have a home—a real one. And yes, I'll have to be what my father wants, but why not change for someone you love?

So, I guess my wants are stronger than reason, too. Because I also want Royo, and I know, deep down, that my father will never approve of him. Not once he learns that Royo is a strongman. I will have to leave him in my past in two days.

But that just doesn't seem possible. The thought makes me sick, honestly. The thought of never seeing him again makes ice run through my veins and numbness spread across my chest. It shouldn't be a choice. My father is my blood. But Royo has saved me, and I've saved him. There's something deep here.

I let out a sigh.

"What's wrong?" Royo asks.

"I just… Nothing."

He raises his eyebrows. "Yeah, it's really like you to not want to talk."

I smile in spite of myself. He's been the biggest surprise of this mission.

"I like you," I say.

Emotions from boyish glee to regret flash across his features at a rapid pace, and then he looks away.

"You shouldn't," he says.

He's the most haunted, interesting man I've ever met. But he is right—I shouldn't like him. Yet that doesn't matter when I do.

"I wish we could stay here forever," I say.

He looks everywhere but into my eyes. His lips part. They're nice lips. How have I never noticed how nice they are?

"Would you spend forever with me?" I ask.

His whole body stills, so I playfully grab his hand, smile, and bat my lashes at him. And I ignore the band tightening around my chest.

"There are too many fountains," he says—and then his gaze meets mine.

My heart feels like it's going to explode out of my chest, because something in his expression said yes.

CHAPTER SIXTY-TWO

ROYO
CITY OF TAMNEKI, YUSAN

The six of us make it to the capital. We're staying at the Fountain Inn—another swank joint—all marble and waterfalls and shit. This area is obsessed with water. And it's fancier than the rich-merchant houses in Umbria, which is saying something.

With the millennial celebration tomorrow, all the lodging had been booked solid for a year, but Dal got us four suites. There are benefits to owning a whole damn city, I guess. Although it didn't stop him from being killed. The timing don't make sense for a heart attack. But I guess we're the only people who realize it.

All the flags in Tamneki are at half-mast, and everyone wears black armbands to mourn the passing of the count. But, really, everybody goes on with their days. I wonder if it'll be the same when there's a new king. I would think so. Don't really matter who's in charge when you're a servant or commoner. That's for fancy nobility and swells to worry about. It only matters to me because of Hwan. And now Aeri. And Euyn.

She does matter to me. I can't deny that anymore.

We all went over the plan in detail on the ride to Tamneki. The game is at five bells tomorrow night. It will end by eight, with the losing team and hopefully one king dead. By the end of tomorrow, this will all be over. Euyn will be on the throne, or we'll all be dead or in Idle Prison.

I'm not comfortable with any of this, but I'm the muscle, not the brains. With the death of Dal, everyone has been focused on how we'll be able to get Sora to meet the king. Everybody just shrugged off the death of the palace assassin and has moved past it. Everyone but me.

"Royo, it doesn't make sense for it to have been Mikail," Aeri says with a sigh. She's on the couch with her legs tucked under her, reading a book she stole from the Aseyo villa. She said Dal wouldn't miss it, which was equal parts cold and funny.

"Well, someone killed him, didn't they? And Mikail's a spy for the throne," I say.

Aeri is bored of this topic. I've talked to her about the dead palace assassin and my theories probably four times now. She wasn't interested the first time.

"I'm hungry," she says. "Let's find the others for dinner."

She gets up and walks out of the room.

So I guess that's fucking that.

But it's eight bells, and my stomach growls. She's right. It's time for dinner.

We go down the hall to the corner room. I knock on the door to Mikail and Euyn's suite.

"Who is it?" Euyn asks from inside.

"It's us," I say.

Thirty seconds go by. Things move around behind the door. Aeri and I exchange glances. Finally, Euyn cracks open the door, and a crossbow sticks out. Whoa. What the fuck is this? I back up a step. We both put our hands in the air as I step in front of Aeri, shielding her.

But Euyn doesn't shoot. Instead, he peers suspiciously into the hall—left, right, and back again. Then he quickly waves us in. We go inside even though I'm seriously weirded out. I look around the huge suite, wondering if he's protecting something or someone in here, but he's alone.

"Where's Mikail?" I ask.

"He had some business. He should be back soon."

I can feel the wrinkle in my forehead. What business does Mikail have at eight bells at night? Then it dawns on me: Euyn doesn't know. Maybe that's why he's so paranoid.

"Where are Sora and Ty?" I ask.

"In their rooms, I think," he says. "I'd check, but…" He trails off, pacing with his bow loaded.

"It's fine," I say. "I'll look later."

"Are we going to dinner?" Aeri asks.

"I can't," Euyn says. "You all can go."

I think we learned our lesson about splitting up for food in Oosant.

He catches my expression.

"Or we can just send a valet out for anything we want," he says. "The third ring has any number of great restaurants."

We're in the fourth ring, which is lodging on one side and pleasure on the other. I don't get why so many people go for pleasure houses. I tried one once because a girl outside resembled Lora and I missed her to the point that I didn't know what to do with myself. But it wasn't Lora. She didn't smell, feel, or sound the same. And I left feeling even worse about myself than when I went in. Most of the workers are drugged out on laoli so they can get through their nights. Maybe it's different here in the capital, but probably not. They're almost all indentures no matter where they are.

"Okay, we'll see what Sora and Ty want," Aeri says.

I move to go with her.

"It wouldn't be a bad thing to have a last meal together. But here," he adds. "In this room."

Aeri's eyes meet mine. There was something off about him calling it a last meal. Not to mention that his overall paranoia is weird as fuck. But I dunno. I'm not a prince with a bounty on my head. And I guess after tomorrow, we all do go out on our own. I'm just not sure that's what he meant.

We go to the other side of the hall and knock on Sora's door. Ty answers. He looks flustered, his hair a mess. With the exception of getting his nose broken, I haven't seen a hair out of place on his head. For a second, I think we got the wrong room, but no, there's Sora standing by the window.

I think we just interrupted them. Great timing.

"We're going to order dinner and then eat with Euyn and Mikail," I say.

"Oh, okay," Sora says. "In their room?"

"Yeah, in about a bell."

She nods.

I close Sora's door.

"Well…that was awkward," Aeri says.

I laugh and then pretend like it was a cough. It doesn't fool her.

We're about to go down the stairs when Mikail wanders up. He smiles casually.

"Were you looking for me?" he asks.

It's a smart question. He wants to know if we've already been to Euyn's room. If we know that he went out and didn't tell anyone where or why.

I nod. "We're all going to order dinner in."

"That's a good idea," he says. "Tell them to add the bill to our rooms, but tip the boy well and it'll arrive hot. Or I can go get the valet. Whichever."

He's so casual. He's casual about everything—slaughtering the men in the warehouse, finding the assassin dead, hearing about the death of the eastern count. And there's no way he just doesn't care. So what is it, then?

"Where were you?" I ask.

"Securing the final arrangements for tomorrow." He pauses and pointedly glances around. His meaning is clear: we're in a public inn. "You can ask me about it more when we're all together."

He saunters down the hall and knocks twice before Euyn opens the door. He looks over his shoulder at us. "Use Salt and Shore and tell them to send the entire menu."

With that, he disappears into the room.

I just do not trust this guy. Especially not with Aeri's life.

CHAPTER SIXTY-THREE

SORA

CITY OF TAMNEKI, YUSAN

That was very poor timing. Or maybe it was great timing, since I'd run my hands through Ty's hair and I was about to kiss him and I can't be sure if a kiss from me is toxic—even without my poisoned lipsticks.

Seok has said it—that I've been exposed to so many varietals so many times that my bodily fluids are likely poison. But if it's true, it means I can never be intimate with anyone. That Seok has taken love and passion from me, too, along with everything else.

Fury fills me, hot as molten metal. I swear I'll take everything from that man. I almost unwittingly took his son from him just now.

The closer we get to tomorrow, the further I am moving from logic or reason. After all, what's the difference in doing something reckless, like wanting my enemy's son, when we'll probably all die? I just wanted to feel. I wanted to feel something other than dread and fear and sorrow. Something that wasn't worry or pain or guilt or hopelessness. I wanted to feel loved, and Ty said he loves me. I wanted to believe it. And then I wanted to feel it. With no regard for the consequences. Apparently, lust, like grief, can make you disregard the future.

Then Royo and Aeri knocked, and we jumped apart and tried to be normal. I think we failed.

I still need to steal the crown, but I'm no closer to figuring it out than I was in Rahway. And there's only a day left. I'm out of time. But I can't just give up.

"Sora, what are you thinking about?" Ty asks.

I refocus on him. I forgot he was still in the room. He's staring at me, eyes piercing. I'm about to do the most reckless thing I can think of: trust Tiyung.

He said he would do anything to help me. I'm about to put that to the test.

I step closer to him. "I need your help."

"All right," he says.

I draw a deep breath, because this may spectacularly backfire and then I'll only have myself to blame. But I don't see any other option. I can't do this alone. I can't even figure it out on my own.

"I have to find a way to get the crown from Aeri before it's on Euyn's head."

Ty blinks, opening his mouth and then closing it. "I'm going to need you to explain this. The crown? As in the crown of Yusan?"

I nod.

He squints, shaking his head slightly. "I don't understand, though… The crown won't give you the throne. We aren't Baejkins, and the country can only be ruled by them. That's the Edict of the Dragon Lord."

"I know. I don't want the country or the throne. But you heard what they said in Rahway—the crown makes the wearer immortal. I need to get it back to Gain and give it to Daysum."

Ty blinks. "What? Why does your sister need to be immortal?"

"Because she's dying."

He draws a sharp breath. Then he frowns and rubs his forehead. "Are you sure?"

I sigh. "I don't know. She seemed a little flushed and out of breath when I last saw her, but I couldn't ask about it because she's so sensitive about her health. I didn't want to upset her, so I didn't say anything the whole visit. But right before our bell was up, she whispered that she thinks she's dying. I...I wasn't supposed to hear it."

"My father didn't mention anything about it."

I shrug. "Why would he? She is how he controls me. Well, her and my indenture. But we both know I'd risk running if it weren't for Daysum."

Ty shakes his head, looking grave. "Sora, I already burned your indenture."

"What?" I gasp. Now it's my turn to stand still and blink at him.

"I burned your indenture before we left Gain."

"Why? Why would you do that?" I ask.

"I told you—I've loved you all my life. It was the first time I had your indenture in my hand. You know my father keeps yours and Daysum's hidden. If I had found Daysum's, I would've burned it, too. But I couldn't locate it."

I shake my head, and I can't stop. It doesn't seem possible that I'm free. He wasn't supposed to burn the indenture until the king was dead. I shudder thinking about what the count would do to me if I disobeyed him like this. Probably send me a piece of Daysum's body.

"I should've found both indentures and destroyed them long ago, Sora," he says. "But I wasn't brave or cunning enough. I'm sorry for that. I've never done enough to stop my father. I've been trying to make up for it."

I can't even process his apology.

"Why didn't you tell me?" I ask.

"I thought..." He stops and exhales. "At first I thought you might use it against me in some way because of how you hated me. I'm sorry. I didn't trust you. And then I tried to tell you but you were crying. Then I came in here to tell you, but then…" He gestures over to the window.

Right. The almost kiss.

I stumble back and sit on the edge of the bed as the realization hits my chest.

"I'm free."

Legally. There's a paper filed with the magistrate, but that's not enough to enforce an indenture in a court. You need the indenture certificate signed by both parties and the magistrate. So right now, Seok no longer owns me. But with Daysum still under the Count's thumb, I'm no freer than I was a second ago. And if she dies, I will be free, but what good would freedom do then?

I grip the quilt in my hands.

"I don't know how to save her, Ty." My shoulders slump under the weight of it. Despair tugs at me, constantly threatening to pull me asunder. And I'm so tired of fighting it.

He steps closer. "I know, Sora. But if you take the crown, they *will* kill you. Maybe it will be Mikail, maybe palace assassins. I don't know, but you won't survive."

"I don't care."

He sighs, his expression heavy. "I know you don't, but you're not thinking about what kind of life that would be for Daysum. Her sister would be dead, and while they can't kill her with the crown on, they can easily remove it. She'd still be just a girl. She wouldn't be a king with a palace guard to protect her. She'd be dead moments after you."

I put my face in my hands. He's right. I wasn't thinking it through. I wasn't thinking at all. But what do I do now?

I really wanted to believe that if I just had the crown, it would solve all my problems. The same way I made myself believe that I could poison enough men to one day free us.

Suddenly, I feel Ty's hand on my back. I tense under his palm, but then I realize I like the feeling of his hand on me—the way he's rubbing my back in gentle circles.

"What do I do? I can't just give up."

He puts his thumb under my chin and raises my face. "We put Euyn on the throne as planned, and then you bring Daysum to the palace. They have the best healers in the country in Qali."

"It might not be enough," I say.

"We have to try."

I look to the side. I know he's right, but I still don't want to give up. Not when there's something I *know* can save her life.

"One step at a time," he says. "Kill the king and get her freedom, and then we'll worry about what comes next. It's too much to consider the weight of everything right now."

I close my eyes for a long blink. "It still feels like I'm failing her."

He leans down to be eye level with me. I realize I like it. I like being able to talk to him. I like *him*.

"Give yourself grace," he says. "I don't know anyone who has as much love for their sister as you. I don't know anyone who's done more."

I purse my lips. "You mean killed more."

"I mean you sacrificed yourself time after time for her."

I shake my head. "I'm nothing but a blade."

"You are made of steel." His voice reverberates through the room. "But you are so much more."

My breath catches.

His eyes dart away. He's not used to being able to compliment me any more than I'm used to confiding in him. "Every day you didn't run to Khitan was a day you gave for her."

I smile slowly. Of course he knew I wanted to try to make it to Khitan, where indentures are outlawed. There's not much to our neighbor to the north, but there's promised freedom for Yusanians who can make it across the Khakatan Mountains. The border marks the difference between a free life in the frozen north and imprisonment or death in Yusan. It is against the king's edict for indentures to leave the country without their masters. We can be executed on sight until we clear the safety of the mountains.

"What will happen to you if the king lives?" I ask.

Ty grimaces but then stands straight. "He won't live, Sora. You'll succeed, and you and Daysum will be free."

He says it with so much conviction that I have no choice but to believe him.

And then there's another knock on our door. Royo and Aeri must be back with dinner.

Ty extends his hand to help me off the bed, and this time, I take it.

CHAPTER SIXTY-FOUR

EUYN

CITY OF TAMNEKI, YUSAN

"You've got to calm down," Mikail says from the couch. "I love your paranoia, but this is a bit much, even for you."

I stop pacing and stare at him. Handsome and casual as ever. Mikail sits with his arm slung over the couch cushion, not a worry on his brow.

"Where were you?" I ask.

"I already told you—I was making the final arrangements for tomorrow."

"What does that mean?"

I want to know if I'm walking into a noose. If we all are. But it's not like he'll tell me that. He's been evasive since we got to the capital—even more than usual.

"Do you have something else to ask me?" Mikail's teal eyes scan me, his expression unreadable. "You're rarely concerned with the details of how dirty work gets done."

I draw a breath. I might as well just say it. "Are you setting us all up?"

"No," he says.

I stare at him, searching for the truth, trying to look into his eyes, his mouth, to find a lie. Then I give up. I don't know why I asked. It's not like I can tell when he's lying. As much as I've grown to like the others, I don't trust them, either. Someone must be deceiving us. At least one person. Or maybe they're all in on it except for me.

"What happened with the palace assassin?" I ask.

"Haven't we been over this? Neither of us knows. It had to be one of them, but obviously no one has come forward."

He's right, of course. Everyone claimed they didn't know or didn't do it. The one with the weakest alibi is Ty. If he had an assassin keeping him safe, it explains how he made it out of Oosant. But he was also the one who told us he saw someone on the roof in the warehouse district. That doesn't make logical sense—to draw our attention to the fact that he saw someone. Unless it was to throw us off his scent. But then why would he kill the assassin? Why risk being unprotected as we enter Tamneki?

"Why aren't you more concerned?" My annoyed voice bounces off the walls. It comes out shriller than I meant it to.

Mikail raises his eyebrows. "Because in the end, they double-crossed the assassin, not us. We don't know if the man was a traitor to the throne, and it's not like I can ask around the palace."

"Shouldn't we get the truth out of them?" I slap my hands against my thighs, frustration coursing through me.

Mikail sighs. "What would you have me do, Euyn? Torture the four of them to get to the truth? I doubt that will build team morale."

I mean, put that way, our options aren't fantastic.

He shakes his head. "I can only keep my eyes on them, and I have. The bigger concern should be that Joon killed Dal."

I stop pacing. "How do you know it was Joon?"

He looks at me like I'm a foolish child. Right—obviously his death was especially well-timed with the celebration tomorrow. Everyone is too busy to look into it closely, and so Dal will be burned without further inquiry. The eastern count had a son and

heir, but the child is eight years old—far too young to be count—
and that means Joon can appoint a regent. And regents have a
funny way of taking over. Just ask my sister.

"Quilimar is still with us?" I ask in a low voice.

"There's no change," he says.

A knock on the door makes me jump. Mikail calmly rises to
answer it, giving me a look. The others will join us for dinner
now. I have to act normal, but I can't shake the feeling that Mikail
isn't being honest. Probably because he never is. He'll tell me
what he thinks I need to know without regard for the whole
truth.

Like, for example, I still don't understand why he is betraying
the king. The man raised him to be equal to the general of the
palace guards. There is no higher station a commoner could have.
Why murder him? I cannot believe he would do it all out of love
for me. I'm not naive enough to believe in unconditional love.

As the others come in, I know I won't figure it out in the next
few bells. But I will get to the bottom of it tonight.

For now, we sit around the dining table of the suite. This
won't be as fine of a meal as we had at Dal's villa, but if we pull
this off, I'll be dining in Qali Palace for the rest of my days. I'll
never have to eat lousy food at travelers' inns or sleep in a carriage
again.

A twinge of something hits me as I sit at the head of the
table. Sadness? It feels like that, but sadness doesn't make sense.
I'm surrounded by murderers and thieves. Tomorrow night, I'll
be back where I belong—dining with courtesans and nobility.
Servants will rush to do my bidding, and a country will bow to
me. I mean…assuming I'm not a pile of ashes.

I don't want to die tomorrow. I don't want my shame to be
exposed for all to see. But we've risked too much to change course
now. And without telling them why, without admitting that I'm

a fraud, I'll only seem like a traitor. I have no choice but to go forward with the plan and hope the legend is a myth. But the closer we get, the more I'm worried about it. About all of it.

"To our future king," Royo says, raising his glass. The others all raise their glasses, too.

I bow my head and then sip my wine.

"To the death of the tyrant," Sora says.

We all drink to that and start passing around dishes. It looks like they ordered the entire menu from one of the great eateries here. It won't be as good as the palace, but it will be close.

"Sora and her sister get their freedom. Euyn gets the crown. Mikail, what happens to you after tomorrow?" Royo asks.

"King consort has a nice ring to it." He laughs. He smiles at me from across the table.

I raise my eyebrows. It's not like I haven't thought about it—giving him an official title—but I hadn't considered that Mikail might want something in exchange for putting me on the throne. Now I feel intensely foolish for not considering it. Didn't I just wonder why he'd betray Joon? Of course it's to be elevated to nobility. It's the least I could do. But they all might want things from me, to control me—including my sister.

It's moments like this when I don't feel wise enough to rule.

"I'm kidding," Mikail says. "Of course, I'll continue to spy for the throne and keep Euyn safe. As I always have."

"You could be both. The first-ever consort and spymaster." Sora smiles.

Mikail smirks and runs his finger over his wineglass. He glances at me. "Anything is possible."

"Ty, what happens to you?" Royo asks.

He pauses, his chopsticks in the air. "I suppose not much changes. My father frees Sora and Daysum and, I'm sure, continues his political moves and countermoves. I…figure out what I want."

He stares directly at Sora as he says this. He wants her—anyone can see that. And she looks like she's at least considering it. It's far closer than where they were at the start of this trip, when I thought she might murder him.

"Aeri, what will you do once the king is dead?" Sora asks.

"I…I don't know." She blinks like she didn't expect anyone to ask.

Sora tilts her head. "Surely you've planned something with the half million Mikail offered you."

I wasn't aware that was the cost of her skills. Something in me balks at the high price, but Mikail would tell me this really isn't the time to bargain shop.

"No plans," Aeri says. "I'll give Royo his cut of a hundred thousand, and then I'll have to figure it out. What I wanted most was a family, and I'll have that. I haven't thought past my one goal. But I guess my father and I can live the rest of our lives very well on four hundred thousand."

Sora smiles pleasantly. "You're last up, Royo. What do you plan to do with the hundred thousand?"

He swallows his huge bite. "I'm going to right some wrongs. There's an innocent man in prison, and I'm going to pay someone off to get him out. So long as Euyn makes good and reverses Joon's edict."

"Can't Euyn also pardon him once he's king?" Aeri asks. "Then you can keep all the money, Royo. Be as rich as a lord."

The table turns to me.

I take a sip of water. "Of course."

That satisfies everyone. And I do mean it. I just hope I can actually pull it off.

CHAPTER SIXTY-FIVE

ROYO
CITY OF TAMNEKI, YUSAN

"You seem...tense," Aeri says.

I've been prowling around the room for a while, but I stop for a second and look at her. She tilts her head, her short hair skimming the high neckline of her dress. She's so beautiful. And I've been so lost in my head, I've barely noticed her tonight.

I don't like this city. Too many memories. But I can't focus on the past. What I got is tomorrow. Everything changes tomorrow. But I just don't trust it. I don't trust this plan or any of them.

The food sits heavy in my stomach, and my gut is never wrong.

The plan is now for Ty to introduce Sora to the northern count at tea tomorrow, and then everyone just assumes Bay Chin will bring them both to the Millennial Championship. Aeri will pretend to be an arena servant. And I'll be there as Sora and Ty's guardsmith.

Euyn will be hidden under the arena and surface at the two-minute warning. The last two minutes of each half are the best because the points double, so all eyes will be on the field. That is when Aeri will steal the crown, Sora will kiss Joon, and Mikail will crown Euyn.

Yeah, nothing can go wrong with any of this. In front of two hundred and fifty thousand people and who knows how many palace guards. Twenty? A hundred? And we won't even know if Sora can make it into the game until after noon tomorrow.

I rub my face. My scar hurts.

And to make things worse, Aeri's not even a little bit stressed. It's eleven bells at night. A day before we commit treason—and she's reading a book by candlelight.

"Why *aren't* you tense?" I ask.

She shrugs, turning a page. "I dunno. I guess it doesn't seem like worrying will help. Whatever happens tomorrow is what's meant to be, you know?"

"I don't."

"No, I guess maybe you don't."

She places the book to the side and goes over to her velvet bag. For the first time ever, she opens it where I can see in. A second of digging later, she gets frustrated and dumps it all out on a table. Expensive jewels, a portrait of a woman—maybe her mother—a bunch of mun, and a hairbrush all fall out. That's it. That's all that was in there. Oh, and the stuffed dragon I won for her. She...she put that in there with her treasure.

Aeri picks up the diamond she promised me. It's the biggest and has a special cut. That's what the gem guy said—a million cut. That's why it's so valuable.

"As promised." She drops the stone in my hand. "So, you have one less worry."

The weight of it hits my palm, and she smiles, her fingers grazing my calluses and scars.

"You could just steal it back," I say. I'm half joking but also I ain't.

"I could, but I won't. You kept me safe, and I want to make sure you get paid in case anything happens at the game."

Having the diamond in my hand feels different. It *is* actually one less worry, like she said. This is it. The rest of the money I need to buy Hwan's freedom, even if everything goes to shit and Euyn isn't able to pardon him. Once Hwan is out of Salt, I've made it right.

"Don't run off with it," Aeri says with a wink.

I stare her in the eyes. "You have my word and my vow."

"Good." She smiles before settling back onto the couch and picking up her book again.

I should be happy. This is everything I've wanted. Everything I worked and bled for for years. I just made it—one hundred thousand gold mun. But…I don't feel good. And it's because I won't see her after tomorrow.

I've never met anyone like Aeri. She's weird and way too happy, but she really cares. I saw it when she apologized in Capricia. When she realized I was alive in Oosant, and then when she murdered to keep me that way. I've never had nobody feel this way about me. Lora loved me when we were kids, but it wasn't the same as this. And then it hits me: this is our last night together. Whatever I want to say, I gotta say it now.

I clear my throat, and she looks up. "Aeri… I…"

"Yes?"

"I…" I don't have the words. I swallow hard and try again. "I want to apologize."

She knits her eyebrows. "For what?"

"For not being the nicest to you. You…you saved my life. You care about me. And I…I am…"

I try to tell her I'm sorry—for my temper, for not trusting her, for all our fights. But I can't remember the last time I said sorry to somebody's face. It's almost like if I start, I'll never be able to stop.

I try again, but the word doesn't come out.

She closes her book. "Royo, this apology looks more painful than your stab wound. It's fine. I get it. You're cagey and crabby and you have your past, but you're a good person. I like you. I've liked you from the start."

I crash down on the couch. It's like she just hit me with a bolt to the chest. Warmth spreads through me, and I don't know what to do with myself. I hold my head in my hands.

"What's wrong?" she asks. "Does your head hurt again?"

I take a breath. "Nobody calls me a good person."

She shrugs, scooting closer. "I don't know. I see it. That's why I wanted you to guard me."

"I don't like this plan, Aeri." I look right into her eyes.

She frowns. "I don't, either. I wish we could just abandon it—I do. But we all have too much riding on this. We're past having a choice now. Just make sure you remember that you're supposed to protect me, no matter what happens tomorrow."

"I could never forget that."

"I really do like you, Royo. More than I ever thought." Her voice is low and warm.

Aeri takes my hand in hers. She's never been afraid to touch me, even from the very beginning when nobody else came near me. I turn my wrist and hold her hand. She draws a breath and looks down, surprised.

"I don't want to leave you," I say.

She tilts her head. "Then don't. Keep me warm tonight?"

Aeri lets go of my hand and gets into bed. It's not cold in here, but she wants to sleep like we did on the isle. When we had to. When I first felt her up against me. If I'm honest, I haven't been able to stop thinking about that feeling.

"Royo." She grins and pats the bed next to her.

There's gotta be a million reasons why I shouldn't, but I can't remember any of them.

I blow out the candle and get into the soft bed next to her. The second I'm down, she wraps her arms around me and nuzzles her face in my neck. I hold her the same way I did in the sand. I breathe in her scent—still smells like flowers.

And it feels so fucking good.

I think about telling her how I feel. But telling her what? That I like her, too? It doesn't sum up this feeling at all. I could tell her that she's the first good thing to happen to me in so long that I didn't believe anything good would happen to a guy like me again. Tell her that I want to stay no matter what. And for what? I don't deserve her. I'll only ruin any woman who gets close to me.

No. If I really am falling for her, I have to say nothing. I gotta let my own heart break to save hers.

But I can't shut my trap.

"Aeri…" I say.

She moves her head. "Yeah?"

"I don't want this to be the end," I say. "I want to stay."

I can feel her smiling into my neck. "So then stay."

"I meant tomorrow and tomorrow and tomorrow."

"I did, too."

My chest feels weird, and the muscles in my face hurt, and I realize I'm happy. There's nothing left to say, so I stroke her arms. Her skin is so soft beneath my rough hands. I wonder how my touch even feels good to her.

It must, though, because within a few minutes, she's asleep. I can't imagine being that secure, but I don't hate her for it. I hope one day I can feel that way, too. I start dreaming about a life past tomorrow even though I'm awake.

Just a little more blood to shed—the king's and the traitor's—and then we could have a future.

CHAPTER SIXTY-SIX

SORA

CITY OF TAMNEKI, YUSAN

Royo and Aeri left first after dinner. Ty and I stayed to go over what to say to the northern count tomorrow. But now we're in front of the door to my room.

I unlock it and then turn.

"Do you… Can I…" Ty begins. He trails off and rubs the back of his neck. "Good night, Sora."

I realize I want him to come in. I want to spend this last night together. I take his hand, and he follows me into the suite. We stop feet inside the door, our hands entwined.

"Do you think that after tomorrow…" He sighs. "Will I see you again?"

"I'll come back to Gain with you," I say.

His eyes widen, round like saucers. "You will?"

"Yes. Daysum will be free, and I need to get her and bring her to Qali."

"Oh, right. Of course."

He's so disappointed, he drops his hands away. It hurts my heart. I'm confused for a moment, but then I realize he was asking if I would consider staying with him.

"I can't stay in Gain," I say gently. Like my tone can soften the blow.

"Where will you go once Daysum is healed?" He tries to suppress the pain in his voice, but it rings out.

I hadn't even considered it. "I don't know. I suppose back to Inigo, where we were born."

"What will you do there?"

I don't know. To have made a plan, a dream, would've been setting myself up for disappointment. Especially as there was no way it could happen. But now it could actually be possible.

"Maybe be a seamstress," I say. "I'm not sure."

He laughs and then looks guilty. "I'm sorry. Really. I think you should have anything you want. But I just can't picture you as a seamstress."

"I know. My sewing is average." I smile. "Maybe I'll be a headmistress. I love kids."

"I know you do. I hope one day…" He swallows the rest of the sentence because we both know that's not possible. Even if my body itself isn't poison, the toxins made it impossible for me to physically bear children. That's what the healers have said. But there is adoption. If there's a future for me, one day I can consider it.

"I hope you find happiness," he says.

"You're so serious. This isn't goodbye. Not yet," I say.

"It is, Sora. You…" He takes a breath and then swallows hard. "You won't ever feel the way I do about you. And I understand why. But tomorrow, we'll go our separate ways. It's for the best."

Something inside me twists, and I want to yell out in pain. But I don't know the reason, and my hands start tremoring again. I suppose I assumed he'd always be in my life. And I hate that I might lose him, too. But instead, I focus on him needing to be in Gain.

I fold my arms. "Are you that eager to return to your spot under your father's thumb?"

"Sora, I am nothing without my title."

I shake my head. "That's not true. You're...you."

His eyes search mine. "What does that mean?"

"I don't know," I say. "I just..."

I gesture, but my feelings are so diffuse it's hard to put them into words.

He takes a small step closer. His muscles tense, his eyes bright. "Sora, if there's any chance you could one day love me, say it now."

I don't know. There's so much that has happened and will happen. It's hard to know anything for certain. But he's not asking me for certainty.

"Anything is possible," I say.

I find myself repeating what Mikail said at dinner. Because suddenly it does feel like anything could happen once Joon is dead. I don't dare dream it, but I know there's the possibility of a new realm on the horizon. A new life—for me, for Daysum, for Ty.

He smiles broadly.

"Then I'll wait for that anything."

Ty leans down and then slowly presses his lips to my forehead as he wraps his arms around me. His touch is so warm and strong. But he gently leans his head against mine. Our noses touch, and our breath mingles. I close my eyes and shiver.

I keep my eyes closed as he kisses my cheek, then makes a trail of kisses and little bites down my neck. My skin prickles with goose bumps, and I run my fingers through his short hair. It feels amazing—his soft lips, the rising anticipation of waiting to see where his mouth will land next. Each inch of skin he kisses feels aflame; each part begs to be next.

I was wrong about not being able to be intimate with someone. This is far closer, more passionate, than nobles sticking their tongues in my mouth.

He gets to my collarbone, and then, instead of going farther, he kisses up the other side of my neck. I'm a little disappointed, but then he presses his mouth to mine. It's all I can do not to part my lips. But I don't know if my kiss will kill him.

My chest rises rapidly. He's breathing hard, too.

"I've wanted you all my life," he says.

I feel it, too—desire. The throbbing at my core. Xitcia poison causes something similar before it kills you. And I don't know if my body would be the death of him.

"I don't know if we can…" I begin.

Ty shakes his head. "I don't know, either, but it doesn't matter. We can please you. It's all I want."

"I…" I want this, but I don't know what to say. My entire body aches. I want him to touch me everywhere. I want him to continue his kisses. I want to forget about our mission, and poison, and murder, if only for tonight.

I wrap my arms around his neck. He picks me up and carries me over to the bed. Instead of tossing me down, he lays me gently on the sheets and lies next to me. I pull at his shirt, and he undoes the buttons. It's a sight. His chest is smooth but roped with muscle. I run my fingers along the cuts and valleys. Then he reaches behind me and unbuttons my dress. He decorates my neck with kisses and little bites in between the torturously slow movement of his hands. I want him. Badly.

I kiss his arm, his cheek, trying to get him to move faster. I push at his trousers.

He smiles. "Sora, I'm going to take my time."

I purse my lips, but I can't help smiling. "Then I'll wait for anything."

"I love you, Sora," he says. Then he continues kissing down my body.

I arch my back and start to believe anything really is possible— even a future for us—if we can only survive tomorrow.

CHAPTER SIXTY-SEVEN

EUYN

CITY OF TAMNEKI, YUSAN

Mikail pulls his trousers up. We're both silent and tense as he sits on the bed, his back facing me. He lights the oil lamp. His brown skin is crossed with the deep scars from the samroc. They cover up the older injuries—the ones he won't talk about.

"Do you want to discuss it?" he asks over his shoulder.

He's not referring to his scars. He's asking about the fact that I haven't been aroused at all tonight, despite his attempts, and that's never happened. Not with Mikail. He, on the other hand, had no problem getting hard or getting off.

I twist the sheets in my hand. "No. There's no point when you'll just lie."

He sighs deeply and turns around. "What do you want to know, Euyn? I already told you that tomorrow is not a trap."

"Why are you doing this?"

"Doing what?"

"All of it! Why are you going to kill Joon? What's in it for you?"

His eyes dart away. He doesn't want to answer me—as usual. But I can't let it go. Not tonight.

"You told Sora that you had a sister who died young, and that's literally the most I've ever heard you talk about your past." I fling my arm up and slap the bed. Perhaps I should've gotten dressed before I started this argument, but it's too late for that.

Mikail stares at me. "And you've never considered whether there's a reason for that?"

I shake my head. "You've never said."

"And you think that's just because I prefer to be secretive? Because I work in secrets and murder and torture? A demon without a conscience?"

His expression closes off, and my stomach turns. I know how much he hates to be thought of as something other than human. And normally I'd let it go, but I don't know *why* it bothers him. I don't ever know the why with Mikail because he never tells me anything. I'd trade the throne, an entire kingdom, for just one of his secrets.

"No, I think you refuse to belong to me," I say. "Or anyone. And if you share something real, then you might. You might let someone be close to you."

He raises his eyebrows. "I'm sorry that I am the one person you can't possess the way you want, Euyn."

"Is that what this is?" My knuckles go white, strangling the sheet in my frustration. "I am fully yours, Mikail. I have been since we were boys. I don't want to own you any more than you already own me. Than the way you've always had me, body and soul."

"I keep secrets to keep you safe," he snaps. Every naked muscle of his is tense. "Under torture, I wouldn't have revealed where you were in Fallow or even that I saved you. Can you say the same?"

I want to say yes. I open my mouth. But I don't know if it's the truth, so I close my lips.

He points to my face. "That hesitation is the answer."

I swallow the truth of that.

"Fine, but I don't understand what the harm is in telling me about your family," I say. "In telling me something real."

He closes his eyes for a long blink. He's equal parts frustrated and exhausted by me. "Why does the past matter?"

"If it doesn't matter, then why not tell me?"

"You weren't exactly forthcoming about hunting people in Westward." He pauses and lets the shot land. And it does. It tears into me—what I did to those men, to Sora's father. "Let the past stay buried, Euyn. What matters is the future."

"But you know everything about me," I say. It's a lie, but it's more an exaggeration than a falsehood. The point is the disparity. He knows nearly everything about my family and my past. I don't even know his father's name. He's from somewhere near here, but I don't know where. I've never even seen where he grew up.

"It should be enough that I saved you," he says. "That I've risked my life for you and I've been willing to die for you since we were young."

I shake my head. "That's loyalty. That's not love."

Palace guards risk their lives, and they're willing to die for the king. For the throne. To protect the crown of Yusan and thereby the rule of law. Because lawlessness is worse. Or maybe the reason for risking their lives is their own money and status, since palace guards are the best soldiers in the country and are well paid and well respected. But regardless of the motivation, none of them love the king. They're loyal. It's not the same.

"Because loyalty is cheap to you," Mikail says.

I have nothing to say in return. I don't know if that's true. I was raised to expect loyalty. For the country to bow to me and honor my will under penalty of death. But I don't discount Mikail's loyalty. In fact, I need it. I always have. And I love that he is loyal. But that's not the same as love.

He gives me a cold stare. "Euyn, I'm giving you the throne of Yusan. If that's not enough, I really don't know what is."

With that, he tosses on a shirt, grabs his sword, and leaves the room.

He didn't answer a single question.

CHAPTER SIXTY-EIGHT

MIKAIL

CITY OF TAMNEKI, YUSAN

For the life of me, I don't know what Euyn wants sometimes. Frustration makes me walk quickly through the Fountain Inn. I didn't leave because he was asking uncomfortable questions. All right, I did, but I also need to make sure the building is secure and, importantly, that none of the other four try to sneak out and rendezvous with anyone. But perhaps that's hypocritical.

In this inn, all the staircases flow down to the lobby. It's possible to escape off the balconies, but it's doubtful any of them would attempt it from the third floor.

I reach an armchair that has a view of the staircases and the front door, and I sit. A family passes me—a mother, father, and three children. Two boys and a girl. The same as my family—my birth family. The youngest is lagging behind like I used to. That habit was the thing that saved my life. I was last out of our house that day. And by the time I got outside, they were all dead.

Our Gayan village was on a hill so close to the Strait of Teeth that you could smell the salt in the air. But it smelled different when I stepped out that day. Not like the charm plants and sea but fire and blood. I sniffed the foul air, then looked at my sandals. It was only then that I saw my family staring up at me from the ground. A fly landed right on my sister's open eye. She didn't blink.

I froze seeing that—the fly on her iris. Then I noticed my mother, brother, and sister were all lying on their backs, covered in blood. It took me so long to realize that they were dead and people were screaming. That everything around me was chaos. People were trying to flee as the charm fields blazed. In the distance were the standards of the empire, of Yusan. The black snake on the red flag. I was only five, but I knew to fear the image. My mother and father used to whisper about Yusan while the house was filled with men. I hid in the rafters and listened to them, a spy even then, desperate to know what other people wanted to keep secret. And the word they kept whispering was "revolt." I didn't know what that meant at the time. Nor did I understand "independence," the other word they kept saying. It didn't matter, though—what we got was a slaughter.

Later, I learned that the northern villagers had banded together and killed the Yusanian king's guard stationed in north Gaya. And then they began working south, hoping to get more Gayans to join them. But many islanders refused because they thought of the king as a god.

And once Joon crossed the strait, he brought the hells onto earth. He arrived with his army and palace guard to crush the colony's revolt. Rebel Gayans saw the ships and set fire to the charm fields, triggering the fury of the crown.

That began the day known as the Festival of Blood. Everywhere I looked, people were dead, dying, or being carried off by soldiers to be raped and killed. Joon ordered "null"—no survivors. No women, children, or elderly were spared. No one. Not the ones who joined the rebels or the ones who refused. All. Even the dogs, cats, and donkeys were slain. Nothing with a heartbeat was safe. The slaughter extended from the shore until the Yusanian Army met the rebels and massacred them. In total, thirty thousand men, women, and children were murdered. Most unarmed like my village.

My stomach twists as I swallow back the bile creeping up my throat. I was just a helpless child. But my age and innocence didn't mean anything during the Festival of Blood. I was running away when a soldier came at me with a morning star.

Even as a boy, my reflexes were unnaturally fast. I rolled out of the way, but the weapon still ripped apart my back. I was smart enough to fall on the ground, lie still, and pretend to be dead.

I wish I'd died.

Euyn thinks he knows suffering. He doesn't know the first thing about it. He has no idea what it's like to hear your people being slaughtered like pigs, raped and mutilated for fun. All because soldiers believe you are less than them. To lie there and wonder if you'll be found. If the same will happen to you. Being powerless to stop any of it. Feeling like a coward for not trying to help. Closing your eyes and wanting everyone to die just so the horror might come to an end. But then it doesn't. And having to live with that feeling of wishing death on the people being tortured.

The Festival of Blood brought out the worst atrocities I have ever heard of. Babies torn apart, pregnant mothers bayoneted, children beheaded. Body parts fed to war dogs. All permitted by Joon to teach the island a lesson. The cries echo in my head on still nights nearly twenty years later. And worse is remembering the laughter and lust of the soldiers.

It went on through the entire night. Survivors kept being found, and then the horrors would start again.

My hands grip the armrests of the chair as I remember Ailor finding me the next morning—dehydrated, injured, and having soiled myself through the night. I didn't dare move to relieve myself. I didn't move a muscle.

Ailor was supposed to make sure there were no survivors, to kill or burn the wounded alive on the pyres. But instead, he smuggled me out of the village and into my new home of Cetil, the city across the strait from Gaya. I don't remember much from the time he found me until we silently watched the enormous funeral pyres from across the water. When the flames died down, he asked me to choose a new name—and from that day on, I was Mikail. The name of my favorite storybook hero.

I get up and leave the inn, my chest feeling tight. I need fresh air more than I need to watch the others. If they betray me, I'll end them. I'll end them all.

I walk until I'm alone and then lean against the cool marble exterior and breathe in gulps. Sora was right—it feels wrong to forget, but remembering is too much. I wonder who she misses, and I hope that after tomorrow she can find them, but I think, like me, the ones she loved are already in the Ten Hells. And in that case, I hope it's a long time before we meet them. But I doubt it.

By the time I've shaken off the memories, I'm made of stone again. I grit my jaw, the will to watch Joon suffer settling across me like darkness over daylight. My family has waited long enough for their revenge. I will get it. Even if it means I have to sacrifice Euyn in the end.

CHAPTER SIXTY-NINE

SORA
CITY OF TAMNEKI, YUSAN

I wake up in Ty's arms. The sun pours in from the drapes we forgot to close last night, and the sheets are tangled around us.

I lie still and think about his touch sending shivers across me. The way I dug my nails into his shoulders. How he admired me and said I was magnificent. How my desire built layer upon layer until I was desperate for him. The expert way he moved his fingers. How I saw stars and how the sensation felt like burning and freezing at the same time, but in the best way. How I felt like I came alive for the first time. The look on his face and how he was satisfied even though I didn't please him.

I smile thinking of the mad way he risked death to give me the smallest kiss. I held my breath and was so relieved when he survived.

"Why did you do that?" I asked. "You just risked death to kiss me."

"Sora, I'd die a hundred times to kiss your lips."

He's still asleep next to me. Ty is lovely in slumber, his eyelashes long, his face peaceful. When he's asleep, he doesn't have the weight of being Seok's heir or a high noble. Right now, he's just mine. For a moment, I lie in bed and think about abandoning the mission. I'd like to just stay here with him and know peace and pleasure like other young couples.

But that isn't my life. That is a fantasy.

I shake my head at my whimsy and slip out from under his muscular arm. In the future, maybe anything is possible. But the future is not the present. Right now, I have a job to do. We both do.

Today is the day.

I rise. It's already ten bells. I walk to the washroom, run a bath, and start to prepare. We have to meet the northern count for tea at noon. I lay out my second-best dress. My nicest will be worn to the tuhko game later this evening.

"Sora!" Ty yells. His desperate voice turns my blood to ice. I turn, looking for a weapon, a threat, only to find him still lying down. Another nightmare. He's had many since Oosant.

He startles awake and feels around the bed. "Sora? Sora!"

"I'm here," I say, stepping back into the bedroom. "You were dreaming. It's morning now, though. It's time to get ready."

He runs his hands over his face, his forehead glistening with sweat. Then he offers a shaky smile. I give him a kind one back.

"It'll all be over soon," I soothe.

He nods, but his eyes look haunted. Something terrible must have happened to me in his dream, and his mind isn't completely present.

"Was it about Oosant?" I ask.

Ty shakes his head. "No, it was today. Someone betrayed us, and you…you were killed."

I shiver, my shoulders shaking. I wish he hadn't spoken it. Nightmares spoken aloud have a funny way of coming to pass. Or at least that's what my mother used to say.

Funny. I haven't thought about her so vividly in a decade. It's very strange for my mother to come to mind now. I'd think it was the danger of this mission, but all my jobs have been life-and-death. Maybe it's the prospect of actually being free that's making me think about her. After all, twelve years ago, she and my father sold my happiness for gold. And I could actually reclaim it today.

Ty reaches out and takes my hand, his expression grave. "Sora, if it goes wrong…I want you to run. They won't suspect a beautiful courtesan fleeing the arena. Just get out of Tamneki. Don't worry about anyone else. Not even me."

We've talked about this as a group—the way for each of us to make it out of the arena if our plan fails. Mikail showed us a drawing of the layout so we could all silently choose our own exits. But it feels strange for Ty to say it now.

"It won't go wrong. We'll kill him, and Daysum will go free," I say.

"Just promise me." His blue eyes are intense, scanning mine again and again.

"All right. I promise."

He nods, then gets dressed. A minute later, he plants a kiss on my forehead.

"I'll wait for anything," he says, holding me.

I smile. I want to tell him that I want to see where the future leads us. But I don't. Because even though I trust him, I don't know if I can trust these feelings. He understands me and what I've been through on a level that no one else ever has. Maybe Sun-ye, but we don't speak. All of this is too new, too early for me to have the certainty that he does. But maybe after today, I'll figure it out.

Instead, I say, "Anything…after today."

CHAPTER SEVENTY

TIYUNG
CITY OF TAMNEKI, YUSAN

A few minutes before twelve bells, Sora and I take a carriage to meet the northern count. I've never seen her look more beautiful, and that's saying something. Her hair is up, piled high in braids and curls. Having her hair back showcases her spectacular face. I drink her in like a man dying of thirst, savoring every drop.

I have no doubt she'll charm and seduce Bay Chin the same way she does everyone. Myself included. But after my nightmare, I fear that we're doomed. The cold, hard truth is that my father doesn't want Sora to survive. He certainly doesn't want her to be free. I don't know what he's done—if he was involved in Dal's death or if he had anything to do with the palace assassin following us—but I know that Seok always gets his way.

We arrive at the Palm Teahouse in the city's third ring. It's the finest in Tamneki, and the perimeter is lined with springs and palm trees. The back garden is empty except for one man and his guards—the northern count.

"Bay Chin," I say, bowing slightly to the old man. He outranks me because he is the count and I am simply an heir, but he is also seventy years old. Even my father would have to incline his head to Bay Chin; age commands respect.

"Tiyung," he says. He keeps his seat but shakes my hand. His hands are strong from the muscular man he used to be, and he makes certain it's known. At seventy, his hair is white and he's apple-shaped, but it would be a mistake to underestimate him. He's just as dangerous as when he was young.

"This is Sora, my father's courtesan," I say. Bay Chin does not know about my father's poison school, and it is better that way. "Sora, I'd like you to meet the northern count, Bay Chin of Umbria."

"It is a pleasure, Your Grace," she says, curtsying low and holding it until Bay Chin responds.

"The pleasure is all mine," he says, and she lifts her head.

He eyes her more discreetly than Rune, but Bay Chin shows the same hunger. They all want to devour her. Possessiveness rises up in me, but she also doesn't belong to me.

Bay Chin gestures to the seats across from him. "Please, join me."

It's a bright, sunny day. We sit under the shade of the table's umbrella. Bay Chin is in a white suit, sweating in the humid air.

"I cannot get used to this heat." He fans himself with his hat, and two servants run over with palm fronds to cool him. "Sora, my dear, is it warm where you're from?"

She smiles. "Yes, Gain is roughly the same. A little more humid than here."

He nods, but his eyes narrow slightly. "But you're not from Gain originally, are you?"

"No, I'm from a northeastern village called Inigo."

"Under the eastern count? Gods recognize his soul."

He doesn't seem shaken by Dal's death, even though they were allies. Then again, the counts would climb over one another's dead bodies to get an inch closer to the throne.

Sora finds us confusing at best, disgusting at worst. But she can't understand because all she wants is to be left alone. Men who have freedom and power want more than that. At this level of nobility, they want the country. They want to be gods.

"Yes, I believe so," she says. "But the village fell into the old borderlands."

Bay Chin frowns. "The old borders have been difficult lately."

Judging from Oosant, it's an understatement, but Sora nods sympathetically.

"Tiyung, how is your father?" Bay Chin turns to me but keeps his eyes on Sora until the very last second.

"He is well," I say. "He sends his regards."

"Yes, well, I know what those are worth. Send Seok mine."

"I will."

"So you will attend the ceremonial Council of the Lords in your father's stead today?"

I nod.

Sora looks over at me. I forgot to mention the ceremony because it doesn't affect our plans. All the counts and high nobles from the major cities will meet for a Council of the Lords at three bells. The western count, northern count, and, I suppose, Dal's young son, and I will be there. My father originally declined to attend because of his hatred for Dal, and it's far too late for him to travel to the capital now. The ceremony will be held here in Tamneki instead of in Qali Palace because of the game, but it'll just be a lot of glad-handing and flattery—nothing I can't handle.

"And you, my dear—how will you occupy your time here?" he asks Sora.

"I have heard the shops are second to none," she replies with a soft smile.

Sora despises shopping, but the northern count is a traditionalist. She knows what he wants to hear. It doesn't matter what the truth is, because she's playing a part right now.

"That is true, but they will all be closing soon," Bay Chin says.

"Why is that?" Sora looks from the count to me.

Bay Chin raises his gray eyebrows. "For the celebration parade and the Millennial Championship."

"The champ— Oh, tuhko?" she asks.

The waiters silently bring out cakes and buns to go with the tea. All of them wear black armbands, mourning the eastern count out of obligation, not out of any real sorrow. They discreetly flee as soon as the plates are placed on the table. None of them dare interrupt a conversation between high nobles.

"You will be attending, won't you?" the count asks, one brow raised. "Don't tell me you don't enjoy the blood sport. I won't believe it."

Bay Chin is a known tuhko enthusiast. Umbria has its own team, and he lavishes mun on their training academy and field. My father believes that Bay Chin fixes games, but he would be killed by the royal game minister if that were true.

"Oh, no, I do like it, although it's quite intense," Sora says demurely.

Bay Chin leans forward. "That's what makes it enjoyable."

I clear my throat. "We won't be attending."

He pauses with his chopsticks nearly to his mouth. They're ivory and jade. He must travel with them—smart, when there are poisoners like Sora.

Bay Chin furrows his brow at me. "Why not?"

I wipe my mouth with a napkin, keeping him waiting. "My father wants to keep this trip business. She doesn't have arrangements for a seat, and I'm not to leave her side."

High nobility would never just buy tickets to the game. We're not commoners. We sit in the luxury boxes or not at all. Of course, I could occupy my father's seat, but the point is to get Bay Chin to invite Sora. To make him believe it is his idea.

Bay Chin waves his spotted hand. "Nonsense. This will be a once-in-a-millennium event. Sora, you will be my personal guest this evening."

"Oh, I…" Sora seems excited, then looks at me and quiets. She speaks to her untouched plate. "Thank you for the kind offer, but I have to decline."

The count looks surprised. And I imagine he is. It can't be every day that someone says no to him—especially not a common woman. Not even one as stunning as Sora. "Decline?"

She just looks from me to him and back again.

This is exactly how Mikail said to do it. But she's so genuine, it catches me off guard.

"I… I really…" I stammer.

"I insist. You both will be there tonight."

His tone is final. I stop arguing. But Sora shakes her head.

"You are so kind," she says. "I appreciate your generosity ever so much, and I would love to attend the game. But the Count is my lord and master. I cannot betray his orders."

"No, my dear. You have one master." He raises a finger. Sora stares at him. I look, too, wondering what he's about to say. "King Joon. I will introduce you to him tonight."

Sora looks to me, and I nod slowly, ignoring the racing of my pulse. This is exactly what we needed to happen—and yet it all feels too easy.

"Thank you, Your Grace," she says and offers him another soft smile. She picks up her tea, so she misses the satisfied gleam that flashes in his black eyes. But I don't.

CHAPTER SEVENTY-ONE

EUYN
CITY OF TAMNEKI, YUSAN

It's two bells, and I'm going mad in this room. I pace by the windows, trying to absorb all the daylight I can—in case I find myself in the darkness of Idle Prison again. But nothing can prepare you for that place. The damp. The dark. The moaning song of the iku and the wails of the other prisoners. Then again, I doubt my brother will send me there a second time.

No, if we fail, I will either be ashes or beheaded as a traitor.

I chuckle softly. Maybe they'll behead me with the losing tuhko team. Drain my blood into the fountain of the God of War.

A prince of Yusan bled alongside a sporting team. A fitting end to a bastard.

I look around as a hysterical laugh rings through the suite. Then I realize it's mine.

I stop pacing. I have to get it together. I don't need to prepare for death. I need to prepare for success. I could be king by sunset. What kind of ruler will I be? I know what kind of prince I was. I know Joon marked his rule with the Festival of Blood. But what will mark my reign, aside from the murder of my own brother?

It's not an auspicious beginning, but global history is flexible. The country of Wei is known as dignified despite their atrocities because they're rich, powerful, and haven't done anything lately.

Memory is short; the past can be rewritten—well, if you can get to the Temple of Knowledge and change the records of the Yoksa. But it's been done before.

Despite being the Butcher of Westward Forest, I can be a benevolent king—I've lived among commoners. I've now traveled with them—trusted them and killed for them. I could help the people. Care in a way Joon never has. I could be the type of king prayed to in the Divine Temple. Not all the kings are. Some, we've chosen to forget.

I wonder if Joon will be forgotten when I'm king. We don't even speak about Omin. I don't remember him well, since he left Qali Palace in quiet disgrace when I was thirteen and then died a couple of years later.

But...do I murder my own brother? What would my father think?

And then I remember once again that he is not my actual brother and my father was not mine, either. I'm not Baejkin. I may not even be of noble blood. And the closer we get to the game, the more I think about that. The more I swear I can feel the eyes of my mother on me. And then I see something...*someone*...in the corner.

Absolutely not. I shut my eyes and will her away.

When I look again, the corner is empty. I take a breath. That's good. The last thing I need today is to see the ghost of my whore of a mother.

Maybe I wouldn't be losing my mind if I weren't alone right now. Mikail isn't here. He came back to the room last night, but he didn't speak to me. And then he was gone at dawn. And once again I don't know where he went. I trust him, but should I? Or am I the greatest fool in history, to trust a spymaster?

I listen constantly for the sound of footsteps approaching the door. For soldiers to take me to Idle Prison. Or for Mikail to come back. But there's nothing.

I ordered food, but it sits uneaten on the table. I should eat. I should have a last meal. But for the first time since I woke up in Fallow, I'm not ravenous.

The bells are both my friend and enemy. Aeri and I are leaving for the arena at four bells. It's close and yet a lifetime away. I will wear an imperial red jacket under a cloak. It's too warm for both, but the cloak will help hide my identity until it's time to reveal to the arena that I am the king. I hope.

The air is humid. The whole country is bracing for the rain of the monsoons. For the lifesaving and life-taking floods. It's coming. The storms. The lightning, thunder, and ceaseless rains. The pace of Yusan slows for a month—it's a holiday of sorts for the people. And a month is a perfect amount of time to switch rulers. To have the official coronation after the rains end.

I stare at myself in the mirror and imagine the crown on my head. The rubies, onyx, and diamonds of the golden crown of the Dragon Lord. And then I see her again, this time in the mirror—my mother. I don't know why the evil woman picked today to haunt me.

With a yelp, I move away and back to the window. Maybe I'm alive simply because I'm too afraid of what awaits, of who waits for me, in the Ten Hells.

After a few minutes, I run a bath and pray I don't find out today.

CHAPTER SEVENTY-TWO

MIKAIL

QALI PALACE, YUSAN

General Salosa is a short, puffy little man with far too much shit in his office. The space is grand, with the high ceilings and ornate carvings Qali is known for, but it's hard to tell with all of this clutter.

I stand in front of his massive desk, just shy of being at attention. My back is straight, but my weight is on my left hip. The general has an oversize mustache that very nearly matches his ego. He frowns, sitting behind his desk, busy with paperwork. Qali loves nothing more than leaving a paper trail for everything. But he doesn't need to fill anything out right now. It's a power move, designed to make me feel his importance.

I glance out of the enormous windows at the sun reflecting off the water. The palace sits on a rocky island in the middle of a deep lake, accessible by one narrow bridge.

Most times I wish the earth would swallow the whole thing.

I turn back to the general and play with a paperweight on his desk. His brow furrows every time I touch it, so I spin it like a top on the varnished wood. He immediately snatches it back and sets it far away from me. Then he finishes his overly elaborate signature. The general of the palace guards is a lot of fun.

"What news of the planned assassination?" he asks, finally done.

"There's no change," I say.

He grabs another sheet to sign. "Still after the tuhko game?"

"That's what 'no change' means, yes," I say.

Generals and spies don't typically get along, and we're no exception. They want to be in control of us; we are answerable to no one except the king. Hence, the conflict.

He looks up, annoyed. I smile my most winning grin.

Salosa reddens and opens his mouth, but then he remembers that, according to the king, we have the same rank.

"Very well," he says.

"Is the king to stay behind the walls of Qali, then?" I ask.

"No change."

"I suppose I deserve that."

"You certainly do." He stares at me with his beady little eyes. "Bring the traitors in alive, Mikail. You'll be rewarded."

I nod and waltz out of his office, although I don't feel like dancing. This is a very dangerous game, but I have to play it out now.

I proceed down the vaulted marble corridor to the Hall of Spies. My office is on the other side of Qali, past the massive, beautifully painted interior dome. I remember being astonished the first time I came to the palace. My father, Ailor, was receiving a medal for his service, and I stared with my mouth agape. All this gilded luxury and splendor can almost make you forget it's built off the deaths and suffering of so many.

Servants bow and guards salute me as I pass. They're not used to seeing me roam the western halls. Spies have our own eastern entrance and exit. I don't normally come this route unless I'm needed in the throne room or spying on Salosa or one of his lieutenants.

No one is above suspicion in Qali.

I get to the eastern hall, and it takes me a moment to remember which key to use for my door. I've had this office for two and a half years, but I'm not here unless I have to be. My space is the same size as the general's, but unlike Salosa's, my office isn't full of shit. Spies don't write everything down, and for good reason. We'd be pretty lousy at our jobs if we left secrets lying about.

Despite the pre-monsoon heat and humidity, the palace is always cool. My office has an enormous fireplace. It's so wide, I could roast Salosa on a spit in there. This is where I burn all correspondence. I open the flue and start a fire. Warm or cold, I always have a smoky fire going when I'm in the hall in case someone is hiding in the massive chimney or trying to listen from above.

I'm leaning on the mantel, watching the flames, when there's a light knock on my door. I know who it is without looking.

"Enter," I say.

"Welcome back," Zahara says.

I'm positive that is not her real name. She's beautiful—not quite how Sora is, but in her own unique way. Her hair is brown, nearly the same shade as her thick-lashed eyes. She has my coloring, and she's around my age. Spies are all young. It's not a profession where you worry about wrinkles and grandchildren.

As spymaster, I normally choose the spies, but she came to me through Joon. She rose quickly and is my number two, although I don't trust her. No offense to her; I don't trust anyone.

Zahara comes in and shuts the door behind her.

"Was it you?" I ask.

One corner of her lips turns up. That's answer enough. She killed Count Dal. I don't bother asking how—it's not important.

"He's making moves," she whispers. She can only mean Joon. He is the only one we can't properly track. We are not allowed to follow or spy on him. We'd be fed to the iku if we disobeyed that order. While no man is above suspicion, Joon isn't a man. He's a god king. For now.

"Who sent Thorn?" I ask.

Thorn was the assassin killed in Aseyo. Assassins aren't technically in the Hall of Spies, but they can kill at our direction. They can also operate under the direction of General Salosa.

"Not us," she says.

"The target?" I ask.

"Unknown. Salosa claims the assassin was operating outside of Qali."

Rogue. Salosa is saying that Thorn went rogue.

Assassins are more likely to go rogue than spies. They have the ability to kill but not the intelligence or reliability for espionage. They're respected less, so they're more susceptible to bribery or just saying "fuck it" and changing allegiance.

Still, that answer seems too easy. But I know better than to show my skepticism.

"What news out of Khitan?" I ask.

"Unchanged. Queen Quilimar wears the ring and is receiving dignitaries from the throne. The boy is alive...for now."

The Prince of Khitan will be four years old next month. Quilimar is his mother, and one would think she wouldn't kill her own son, but I wouldn't put it past her. Family ties have never stopped a murder for the Baejkins. And Quilimar is the most ruthless in decades.

"Gaya?" I ask.

"We are looking into the missing laoli you found in Oosant. No answers yet. The suspicion is falling on the eastern count."

"How convenient," I say.

She smirks. "Isn't it, though?"

A million gold mun worth of drugs in a warehouse in the middle of nowhere, and a dead man is taking the fall. Someone is making major moves, and we need to figure it out quickly as it's a threat to Euyn's throne. Of course, the fact that we killed everyone in The Mine and set the evidence on fire doesn't help. But I didn't have time to torture men for answers, and if I'd left the drugs with the bodies, the laoli would've disappeared the next day. Guaranteed.

"Continue pursuit," I order.

"Of course," she says.

"Wei?" I ask.

"The priest king retains his iron rule, despite our best efforts. Two disappearances."

Two spies killed or as good as dead in Wei. That brings the total up to fourteen since I became spymaster. We can't keep losing good people to that country. We also can't stop sending them. Not when we have to give Wei millions of gold mun in seasonal tribute.

"The northern and western counts are in Tamneki?" I ask.

She nods. "No sign of the southern count."

"That is all for now," I say. Normally, Zahara would immediately be out the door, but she lingers. It's odd. We aren't the type for long goodbyes. "Yes?"

"You'll bring in the traitors tonight?" she asks.

I smile. Of course she already heard. General Salosa is a fucking sieve. But there was a reason I told him—it wasn't supposed to remain a secret. After we found the assassin, I rode out here without sleeping, burst into Salosa's office, and loudly complained about him nearly compromising my month-long mission to bring in the traitors to the crown.

"That's the rumor," I say.

"Safety in death," she says. I nod, and she leaves.

"Safety in death" is something of a goodbye to each other—and also advice. For spies, taking one's own life is preferable to being captured. We all carry Erlingnow pills for practical reasons. Under torture, you have the risk of breaking. There's no risk of your corpse talking.

But in this case, Zahara is saying to bring in the traitors' bodies instead of taking them alive.

Interesting.

I'm still thinking about it when the tower strikes three bells. I have to get back to Tamneki by four.

With a final look around, I leave out of the eastern side of the palace. We have a rowboat to discreetly come and go under the watchful eye of a hundred palace archers. It is the only boat permitted to cross Idle Lake, and they observe our faces and every oar stroke with spyglasses. But instead of taking the boat, I decide to walk the bridge.

Idle Lake looks like glass because the water is so still. But the pleasant surface hides the monsters beneath.

What a perfect metaphor for Qali.

If I happened to slip off the stone bridge, I'd wish and pray for death. Iku have the jaws of barracudas, but with four humanoid arms on human-shaped torsos. At the ends of those arms are five-inch talons. The lower halves look like enormous fish. The legend is that the iku were once human—servants of the Dragon Lord turned monstrous and sentenced to live in the water after trying to steal the Dragon Lord's treasure hoard.

They're cunning, moving without even causing a ripple at the surface. The iku also hunt in packs, communicating in their own language. You can hear their song in Idle Prison. It adds atmosphere to the dank cells.

The palace offers the iku sacrifices of deer and makes sure large fish are stocked in the lake. But the worst aspect of these creatures is how they torment their prey. They are known to let their victims swim until they're almost at the shore and then grab them and drag them under. It can go on for bells. And sometimes, humans are thrown in. Because the bodies are eaten and therefore can't be properly burned, it's a punishment saved for only the worst criminals—murderers and traitors.

People like me.

I make it safely to the other side once more. I look back, meeting the steady gaze of hundreds of soldiers stationed along the palace walls. Briefly, I wonder if I'll be fed to the iku today. Will I be pushed off the bridge by the guards while the nobility looks on with interest and horror?

No. I'll bring in the traitors. One way or another.

CHAPTER SEVENTY-THREE

AERI
CITY OF TAMNEKI, YUSAN

Euyn's eyes look so tired. They search so often that I start
looking around, too. Who knew paranoia was catching? But
there's nothing to see. Or everything, since we're in a crowd of
people.

"Are you all right?" I ask, my voice just above a whisper.

He nods. He's been real quiet since I knocked on his door
at the Fountain Inn. Maybe he's sick to his stomach like
I am.

But we are almost there.

A few steps more and we're in the shadow of the enormous
King's Arena. I've never seen anything so large. I didn't think
people could build something like this, and according to stories,
they didn't. The myth goes that it was put here by the God of
the East Sea. I'm not sure I buy that, because why would a god
build an arena? Regardless of who built it, though, it's used for
the violent, super-popular game of tuhko.

A sea of people streams in alongside us. Most ticket holders
seem to be forgoing the celebration parade in order to find their
seats on time. The arena has dozens of exits and entrances, but
with two hundred and fifty thousand people attending today,
there will still be lines to get in.

Euyn has his hood pulled up and his head down as we walk the ramp into the northern servant entrance. No one stops us as we enter—everyone is too busy to care.

I feel vulnerable and kind of naked, walking without Royo by my side, but Mikail is waiting for us where he said he would be. He's leaning against the wall with his fancy sword against his hip. Weapons aren't allowed in the arena, but he's a spymaster, so the rules don't apply. Most rules don't seem to apply to Mikail.

He smiles small instead of his normal cocky grin. I guess today is getting to all of us. I was fine yesterday, but I've felt like I want to scream or throw up ever since Royo left with Sora earlier. As he went out the door, I wanted to grab his arm and beg him to stay with me, but I couldn't. We all have our jobs to do today. I just have to find the courage to do mine. But I've never been this conflicted in my entire life.

"Are you ready?" Mikail asks, looking at me.

I take a breath. This is it. No turning back. But I want to turn back. I want to run away. I want to tell them to forget this whole plot. But I can't now any more than I could in Aseyo. I'm in it, and I have to see it through. Nothing's changed.

When Mikail offered me this job, he asked if I really wanted to steal for the rest of my life. I said no, but he doesn't know why. The truth is, I *can't* keep stealing. And I can stop once I help my father. He matters most. Repairing the relationship, making him proud, finally having him be my family and the safety that comes with it—that's all I've ever wanted. Somehow, I keep forgetting that. But my father is blood. The bond with these people is made of water, and it will evaporate after today.

So, I nod, and Mikail hands me a bag with a valet uniform in it.

My mouth goes dry. I want to say something to them, something meaningful, but I don't know what. Instead, I take a step away.

"Aeri," Mikail says.

I freeze, my chest tightening. I swallow hard and then turn around. "Yeah?"

"If it goes wrong…run. Save yourself and forget you know us."

I inhale sharply because that's what Royo said. Because he cares. Which means Mikail cares, too.

I didn't think he did. I didn't think any of them cared, aside from Royo. But my stomach twists as I think back. Ty and Euyn saved my life in Oosant. Sora scrubbed blood off my dress, and I hid her bruises with makeup. And Mikail brought me a dagger from the armory in Aseyo.

Is this what having family really feels like? I've never had this. Even before, when I was a kid, it was just me alone. My mother was a good mother, I think. But she was more concerned with having a son and securing a future than she was with me. And my father didn't want to have anything to do with me until recently.

I take a step and I stumble, my knees weak. What am I doing? Mikail reaches out to help me, raising his eyebrows in question. I mumble something about nerves and being all right, but I feel anything but fine. In fact, I think I'm going to be sick.

These killers are the only people who have truly ever cared whether I lived or died. And maybe it was all the mission. But it didn't feel that way.

I was wrong when I thought nothing's changed.

Everything's changed.

But I don't say anything. I just nod and walk away.

CHAPTER SEVENTY-FOUR

ROYO
THE KING'S ARENA, YUSAN

Everybody's got tuhko fever. Around the arena, banners flap for Silla and Rouran—the blue octopus and the yellow mountain lion. Silla is the team from the southern region. Rouran is from the west. The rich guys who fund the professional tuhko teams like to name them after themselves. The current northern and eastern champions already lost in the rounds before today, making these two the best in the nation. It also makes one of them doomed. While all of the other eighteen teams will live to train again, half of the players on the field today will die.

And we will watch the game from right by the goals.

I'm in a suit, pretending to be a guardsmith for Sora and Ty. The royal box is above the goal wall. Unlike the shit night-carnival game I played in Rahway, these hoops are iron and are bolted into the stadium wall.

There are two luxury boxes to either side of the royal box. Twelve high nobles to the right. Twelve priests to the left. The priests are the ones who'll kill the losing team. Their white robes will be drenched in blood and guts, their daggers dripping as the crowd cheers.

But even championship tuhko is not enough to distract me from looking for Aeri. I hate that I don't have eyes on her—that I had to leave her.

I take a breath. I gotta trust she's all right and where she's supposed to be—and I *do* trust her.

I just don't know about everyone else.

Palace guards line the royal box next to us. Black-and-gray armor glitters in the late-afternoon sun. Crimson feathers stick out of their helmets. You couldn't pay me to wear one of those flashy helmets, but I wish I had their steel protecting my chest right about now.

Looks like maybe twenty guards. Hard to tell because the box has a shade over half of it. In the center, though, there's a single gold throne. It's empty now, but soon a hundred horns will shout the king's arrival, and the entire arena will bow. Two hundred and fifty thousand dead silent for the king.

I'm unarmed and I hate it, but everybody is searched on the way in, and they confiscate any weapons. Obviously, the palace guards are armed to the teeth, the priests have their ceremonial gutting knives, and the arena guards have bully sticks. But nobody else.

Weapons are the last thing needed when there's a quarter of a million violently passionate people packed into here.

When the arena gets unruly, the palace guards close in around the king, and the stadium guards club the shit out of the crowd to get everybody back in line. Sometimes the arena guards die if they get mobbed. Sometimes people get beat to death.

Emotions are always high when there's so much at stake.

I know the feeling.

The northern count greets Sora and Ty. I'm just a guard, so I'm not introduced, but I swear his eyes land on me. We've never met, but, obviously, I know who he is. He's run Umbria my whole life. He's the one responsible for letting gangs get their way. For letting the Sol go to shit. For causing Joon's sanctions to strangle the city. He's the one who wouldn't even agree to see me when I tried to go to him after Hwan's arrest to tell him they got the wrong guy. I clench my jaw and keep my eyes on the field as he passes.

"I'm so glad you two decided to join me," Bay Chin says. "This will be a match like no other." Then he pauses and ogles Sora. "And you, my dear, are a woman like no other."

She's in a rose-colored dress that shimmers gold as she moves. I've never seen nothing like that before—it's like she glows.

Bay Chin takes Sora's hand.

There are two rows of cushioned chairs in the high-noble box, and all the seats are filled except for three. Bay Chin takes his chair in the center of the front row and gestures for Sora to sit on his right and Ty to his left. There's a child in the corner seat who's probably the dead eastern count's son.

I stand to the side with the other guardsmiths, watching the crowd fill in. I hold myself like the real guards, with my hands clasped behind my back. It's a stupid way to stand, but whatever.

Still no sign of Aeri in the royal box. I keep checking.

All of a sudden, drums beat in rhythm and the two teams take the field. The roar of the stadium is overwhelming as the crowd cheers. The teams walk around the perimeter and then come to a stop facing the royal box. They stand in one long line with their shoulders back, waiting for the king.

I recognize most of the players. Like every boy in Yusan, I wanted to play professional tuhko. Yeah, you can wind up dead if you're second-best, but the average day for a strongman is more dangerous. Plus, professionals get treated like nobles. Everybody knows them, and they can be richer than merchants if they're good. It would be a pretty sweet life.

Still no Aeri.

All at once, one hundred trumpets go off and everybody stands. The king is here. The whole crowd turns to face the royal box.

Joon comes out in an imperial red suit with a cape over his shoulders. It's hot for a cape, but I guess he has servants to fan him. He looks the same as when he visited Umbria over a decade ago. A little gray at the temples and more wrinkles, but otherwise the same. He and Euyn both have black hair and brown eyes, but they don't look alike. Joon is maybe Sora's height with a slight build, while Euyn is taller than me. Joon's features are sharp, and Euyn's aren't. But it makes sense. Euyn is about twenty years younger, and they had different mothers.

The entire stadium is silent as we all bow to the king. Then Joon waves, and a giant cheer erupts. The two teams shake hands and go to their ends of the arena.

Mikail saunters into the royal box, and, a moment later, finally, I see Aeri, dressed in a brown valet uniform. I breathe out a sigh of relief, and my chest feels lighter. She's all right. She's made it this far. And now she's in place.

The only one I can't see is Euyn. But he's supposed to be somewhere underneath us, near—but not too near—the royal stairs, until it's time.

We're ready.

The first half of the game is played in two thirty-minute periods. The last portion is the two minutes when points double.

And that's when we'll strike. But first, the game's gotta start.

Joon steps to the edge of the royal box, and the crowd settles down. He holds a red flag with a solid gold snake wrapped around it. The winning coach will keep the serpent as a prize. The most winning coach in history had three. The Silla coach has two.

The king looks around the arena and smiles. Every eye here is on his hand. Everybody leans forward, waiting. When the flag hits the field, the match begins. The two teams will sprint to the ball sitting in the center.

Even I'm standing on my toes. Waiting. Expecting.

The goal of tuhko is real simple: score more points. But that's easier said than done. Teams have to decide who'll be on offense or defense and how many players on each. Defenders wait beneath the hoops to block attempts. Like in that carnival game, a shot from far away has gotta be perfect to go through. Violence is fine, but cheap hits, like dick shots, draw penalties. Judges in black stand on the field, ready to toss gold penalty flags. If a player gets one, he's gotta sit on the sideline, and his team's at a disadvantage for however long the penalty takes. Between penalties and rest breaks, that first half takes way over a bell. More like a bell and a half.

But first Joon needs to drop the flag.

It's like I can feel the steady breathing of the teams. The eyes of all the fans. The excitement. I'm not here to watch tuhko, but it's still hard not to get swept up. A quarter of a million people all want the same thing.

Joon opens his hand, and I release my breath as the flag drops, red splattering on the green grass. The crowd roars so loud that it shakes the stone arena, and then a bunch of people burst into song. The musicians beat the drums in a frenzy.

The game begins.

CHAPTER SEVENTY-FIVE

SORA

THE KING'S ARENA, YUSAN

Tuhko is so very violent. I've seen it before, but not at this level—not when it's life-and-death.

The two teams hit each other with such force, I shudder in my seat. There's no padding, no protection for the players. And we're seated so close, I can already see blood staining their uniforms.

Bay Chin cheers, his lips wet from excitement. He doesn't speak much to me. He eyed me when I came in, but otherwise his attention has been solely on the game. I stare at all the light-blue banners, and I wonder if Silla is the same as Maricelus Silla—the man Seok had me kill. It probably was. Was his murder related to this game? I doubt I'll ever know.

"Whom do you favor?" I ask, leaning toward Bay Chin. I have to tip my head so I can hear him, since he is on my left and there's so much crowd noise.

"I placed a substantial wager on the Rourans," he says without looking at me. Then he stands and screams about a pass. It is one-nil Rourans, but you wouldn't know it from his anger or the reaction of many in this arena.

Aeri is in the royal box. She stands holding grapes on a silver tray. Four servants fan the king with enormous black feathers— samroc feathers, I think. We can feel the breeze over here. The king is all alone except for servants, guards, and Mikail. It is strange, the isolation these men seek and then become saddled with.

Bay Chin catches me looking at the throne. I smile and face forward.

"I haven't forgotten, my dear," he says. "I'll introduce you after the first half ends."

I don't react, but my stomach drops and I resist digging my nails into the armrests. That timing won't work. I have to figure out a way to meet the king sooner. Aeri said the last two minutes of the half were the best time to strike because everyone will be focused on the game.

Halftime will be too late.

"That would be lovely." I smile.

I now have just under forty minutes of gameplay to come up with something. Some way of getting next to the king.

I can't look past Bay Chin to Ty, no matter how much I want to. I need his brain, his input, his comfort. Which is an odd thought. I haven't had much comfort in my life, and now I'm not sure how I got by without it.

But we have to pretend.

I quickly realize that there's no way for me to meet the king without Bay Chin because Ty doesn't have the rank to approach the throne. It's why we needed Dal. I think about going to the washroom and then pretending to walk into the wrong box, but the palace guards would stop me. Mikail can't introduce me, or he'd risk exposing that we know each other. So how will I get next to Joon? How will I do this? I didn't come this far to fail.

"My dear, you missed a great play," Bay Chin says.

I was lost in my thoughts and staring off, but, of course, he expects me to watch every moment. And then I see my opportunity.

A few minutes later, after a penalty flag is thrown, I yawn. I pretend like I'm trying to hide my boredom, but Bay Chin notices.

And men like this can't stand not to be the center of a woman's attention.

"Come, my dear," he says. "While they discuss this penalty, let me introduce you to the king."

I act like I can't contain my excitement. And it's real, because I can't believe that feigning a yawn worked. "Really?"

He stands and offers his hand. At the same moment, Ty rises as well.

"You've already met the king," Bay Chin says to him. He puts a hand on Ty's shoulder, seemingly pushing him back down in the seat.

"And I always relish the chance," Ty says.

Bay Chin puts on a jovial mask. "Ah, of course."

But I don't miss the look in his eye. Something is wrong, but I don't have time to sort it out. It's almost the two-minute warning.

CHAPTER SEVENTY-SIX

MIKAIL
THE KING'S ARENA, YUSAN

I casually watch the game and the king, but I get a creeping sensation. It feels like the air before a lightning storm, when wise men and beasts take cover.

Sora should have met the king by now. It's the second period, but she's still seated next to Bay Chin in the high-noble box.

I'm glad Euyn can't see this. He'd be beside himself insisting he was right. Euyn, in all of his paranoid glory, had gone on and on demanding we do a test run. But there was no way to get access to the arena without hundreds of workers seeing us. Plus, there was nothing to practice. Aeri can steal, Sora can kiss. There was nothing left to chance but Bay Chin introducing her. And he is the holdup.

I don't like trusting the count with the final phase of this plan. Yes, the entire plot was his, but he was adamant that he didn't want to be involved or even mentioned. Now, because Zahara killed Dal, he's literally in the center of all of this.

But I suppose it doesn't matter. The most important piece is Aeri, and she's in place. If needed, I'll stab Joon myself. I'll die, of course, torn apart by twenty palace guards. But General Salosa will be happy—he might be able to give the killing blow. No matter what happens, though, I'll send Joon to Lord Yama with me.

However, if I'm being honest, I'd really prefer for Sora to find her way over here. Joon's murder was supposed to look like a heart attack. It's cleaner that way. I remind myself to wait. That if anyone can accomplish this, it's her. Today, she glimmers like candlelight. And we still have time.

I've become uncharacteristically impatient lately, but I think that comes from being so close to revenge. I've waited for so long, it feels cruel to have to wait longer. But that is reality—impatience only makes for sloppy regret.

Once Joon is dead, I'll take a knee to Euyn as our king. With the chaos, some of the guards will kneel with me, and so will the counts and Ty. With the palace guards and the nobility behind us, it should be enough to make Euyn king—even without a crown. And it won't matter what I told Salosa, which was the point of telling him anything. We either all succeed—or they'll die traitors anyway.

Besides, Euyn will hate me for destroying the crown. Honestly, he might kill me himself, but the price of one man's life is nothing to free an entire nation. What I'm about to do, I'm doing out of love.

Just not my love for Euyn.

CHAPTER SEVENTY-SEVEN

EUYN
THE KING'S ARENA, YUSAN

The horns. I'm just waiting for the horns to blow. The sound will signify the two-minute warning. Joon will be dead, and I'll take the stairs up into the royal box. And it'll all be over. I'll be crowned by Mikail and become the new king of Yusan.

The arena shakes with the stomping of thousands of feet as fans root for their favorites. The crowd roars and screams, sighs with disappointment, cheers on good plays. The people love tuhko. Especially the deadly championships. Yusan has an unquenchable bloodlust. And I will be Yusan.

Or I'll be a pile of ashes.

I grab at my head and then shake my arms out. No. I'll be king. The rumors about the crown are just that. Yes, there are skulls on pikes in Idle Prison, but who knows why they're in there or where they came from. If the general really turned to ashes, his head would've burned, too. So it's just a story.

Maybe.

The crown is etherum. Who knows how any of it works. It could've been true.

No, it's a myth. A rumor spread to discourage people from stealing the crown. I think.

But then, why has no one taken it? Why have we had a thousand unbroken years of Baejkin rule? The people haven't loved them all. They don't particularly care for Joon.

I pace in the torchlit corridor, my cloak brushing against the stone floor. Still waiting. Still sweating even though it's cold down here. It has to be soon. I can't hear bells, but it seems like it's been too long. I think about going up to the arena to check, but I can't. I have to stay in place.

No. The crowd is still cheering. It hasn't been too long. I just have no sense of time. Like when I guarded Mikail overnight in that cave in Fallow, every second seems longer. Every noise more meaningful.

Unless something went wrong. Unless everything went wrong.

A chill suddenly careens down my spine. Something is off. I get that same sense I did in the Tangun Mountain pass—that I should run. Get out of this arena. Out of Tamneki. Save myself.

I start toward the exit, then turn on my heels. No. No, I'm being paranoid. It's all in my head. It's no more real than my mother's spirit in my mirror. I shudder, but I have to stay put or Mikail will have no one to crown, and then the capital will descend into chaos and innocent people will die. Mikail might even die if people think he's stolen the crown for himself.

But where are the horns?

I'm looking toward the stairs when I feel the sharp metal of a sword at my back. And there's only one kind of person who can sneak up on me: a palace assassin.

"Don't move, Your Highness," a voice says. I can't tell who it is because the voice is muffled. Sometimes the all blacks wear masks.

I take a breath and look up at the stairs. Surely, Mikail will fly down with his sword aflame. Or Royo will stomp down with his fists. Or even Ty will race to me, kill this assassin, and protect me.

No one comes.

Because I've been betrayed.

Cold acceptance washes over me. I knew we had a traitor. I've known it since no one came forward about the dead assassin, but I still went through with all of this. Because I had no other options. Because I'm a fool.

I don't have my crossbow. Mikail said it would be too conspicuous to bring my bow, so I left it at the inn. But I do have my ceremonial sword. It's encrusted with rubies, gold, and onyx. I consider grabbing the hilt and trying to fight my way out. It's just the one assassin…I think. But there's no telling if another shadow is lurking somewhere. And as I saw multiple times on this trip, I'm no match for experienced swordsmen.

The metal presses harder against my back. It doesn't cut my skin, but it's far from pleasant.

"Hands up, please, Prince Euyn. My orders are to bring you in alive…if possible. And I'd rather not kill you, since your lover would like a word."

I close my eyes as my stomach churns.

Without any other option, I raise my hands.

Mikail betrayed me. He was the traitor all along.

CHAPTER SEVENTY-EIGHT

AERI
THE KING'S ARENA, YUSAN

I'm waiting in the royal box. A penalty flag has the judges talking for a really long time. It should already be the two-minute warning, but they stopped gameplay to argue.

My nerves are getting worse and worse with every passing second. I stand here, holding this fruit tray like I'm a statue, but I'm too hot and too cold at the same time. My fingers are frozen, but I'm sweating. My heart is racing, and my head feels light.

What do I do? What do I do?

The king is just six feet away, watching the game. The golden crown glints on his head. Mikail is in the box, but Sora still isn't in here yet.

She's next to Bay Chin, just…talking.

I keep glancing over, and then finally, finally! Bay Chin, Sora, and Ty head toward the royal box. Royo moves to follow them, but Bay Chin orders him to say behind. I can't make out his words, but his gestures are clear.

No.

No, no, no. Royo can't protect me if he's not in here. And I can't protect him, either.

But I can't say anything. I can't signal to him or even really look in his direction. Maybe it's better, though, that he's safe in the other box. There are so many palace guards in here, so many blades. So many ways this can all go wrong.

Bay Chin huffs along. I hold my breath as he passes right by me. He pretends we don't know each other. Then I exhale.

He bows low to the king. "Your Majesty, I'd like to introduce you to Sora of Gain, the southern count's courtesan."

"Your Majesty," Sora says, dropping into an elegant curtsy. "I am so honored to meet you."

"I wasn't aware Seok had a mistress, let alone such a splendid one," the king says. He speaks to Bay Chin instead of to Sora.

"A rare bird indeed," the count says.

They talk about Sora like she's an animal or a piece of art. But Sora stands and smiles as if it's pleasant. It's the game we have to play. The game I would've played for the rest of my life. But no longer. This ends today.

I don't want to pretend for the rest of my life. I don't want to be noble or recognized by my father anymore. I want to be with the people who value me for me, not what I can be if I change. I want tomorrow and tomorrow and tomorrow with Royo.

And I know what I have to do.

As I firm my resolve, my stomach stops trying to tie itself in knots. Suddenly, for the first time today, I'm calm. And then I know: it's the right decision. These liars and killers are mine.

I have to betray my father.

The game resumes, and then horns blow. The sound reverberates through me. It's the two-minute warning. That's the signal. This is it.

I glance at Royo, but Bay Chin waves me over. Naturally, his timing is perfect. Sora is next to King Joon, and Mikail stands off to the side. This is exactly what we wanted, precisely how we designed it.

Maybe it's too easy, but everything is pretty straightforward—when you're a thief of time.

I reach into the neck of my uniform and grab the amulet. It's a bell glass so small, it looks like a yellow gem. I wear it on my necklace, always hidden under high-necked dresses. And I never take it off. I haven't since the night I stole it from Prince Omin's dead body.

With the yellow gem in my palm, time stands still. Banners halt mid-wave; people pause mid-stride; players stop mid-strike. But I can move. For a terrible price. Each second I freeze ages me, and it seems to only be getting worse. It's why I'm nineteen but look twenty-four.

But I freeze time when I have to. I did it to take a million-cut diamond, to plant the card on Royo, to get us away in the lifeboat when pirates attacked, to remove the hat from Euyn, to save Mikail in the warehouse, and now to complete this mission. And after this, I'll never have to do it again.

In seconds, I grab the crown off Joon's head, and then I run and place it in Mikail's hand. Then I move aside and unfreeze time by dropping the necklace back into place.

I sigh. It was easy. It is done.

Time resumes, and no one knows I stopped it. Exhaustion hits me hard, over a month of aging crashing into me at once, but etherum is never suspected because people think there is no more magic in Yusan. So they believe it's sleight of hand. Because no one knows I have the Amulet of the Dragon Lord.

CHAPTER SEVENTY-NINE

SORA

THE KING'S ARENA, YUSAN

In the length of a blink, the crown went from on King Joon's head to sitting in Mikail's hand.

I don't know how she did it, but it doesn't matter. Joon is now mortal.

Without a moment's hesitation, I lean forward and lock my poisoned lips with the king. He gasps, surprised, but kisses me back.

I'd thought of using Erlingnow because it's the deadliest poison, or tabernacle, the second most toxic, but they are also the most common. Instead, my lipstick is full of Heroti, a poison derived from a plant in the Outer Lands. Heroti killed five girls in poison school, and even the smallest dose leveled me for two months. It leaves no trace and should look like a heart attack. This poison causes immediate, intense chest pain as you bleed inside of your chest. There is no known antidote.

I put on enough to kill five men. The hum of success flows through me. Joon will be dead within several heartbeats.

But when I pull back and open my eyes, King Joon is…fine.

"That was delightful, my dear," he says.

Stunned, I take a step back. Joon's head is bare. He should be clutching his chest, falling out of his throne in copious amounts of pain.

But he is not.

I turn toward Mikail just in time to see him slice the crown in half with his flaming sword. The pieces fall to the ground as one of the palace guards knocks him unconscious.

Kingdom of Hells, what is happening?

Why did Mikail just destroy the crown? Where is Euyn? And why is Joon still breathing? Why is he *smiling*?

I look to Ty, but he's just as wild-eyed as I feel.

"Sometimes, I wonder…" The king pauses and utters a weary sigh. "How many times will people try to kill a god? Seize them."

The palace guards close in around us. Hands grab at me. Bay Chin is pulled out of the royal box.

"Run, Sora!" Ty says. He punches the guard who put his hand on my arm, but before he can strike again, two guards have him. A third knees him in the stomach.

"Stop! Please," I plead.

Ty doubles over and is dragged out. I'm lifted past the ruins of the crown of the Dragon Lord and carried out of the arena.

Everyone lied to me—King Joon really is a god. And Mikail betrayed us. And now we're all going to die.

CHAPTER EIGHTY

ROYO
THE KING'S ARENA, YUSAN

How the fuck is Joon still alive?

It all happened so quick that I couldn't do nothing about it. And now it's chaos—not just in the royal box but all around the arena. People know something happened but can't see what. *I'm* not even sure what. Aeri stole the crown and Sora kissed the king, but somehow the fucker is still breathing.

We did everything we were supposed to do—except Mikail, who I think destroyed the crown. Well, that, and Euyn never showed up...

Then it hits me: this was a setup.

Euyn fucking set us up. He's the only one not here as everyone gets rounded up.

The Butcher of Westward Forest.

How could I not have seen this coming? Euyn pretended like he'd be a better king, like he was a reformed man. He was full of shit. And I'll get even.

But first I gotta get to Aeri. I need to get her to safety. I swore I'd protect her, and she's in the middle of everything.

I sucker punch a guardsmith in my way. He falls to the ground, and I leap over him. I run out of the high-noble box. I'm going to reach her if I have to kill the whole palace guard to do it.

But I'm too late.

Guards already have her. They lift her up and out of the royal box. I throw people out of the way. I'm going to save her. She locks eyes with me and shakes her head. And it's so weird that I freeze.

"No, Royo," she mouths. I think. I can't hear her over all the fucking shouting.

And then she's gone.

The most intense pain I've ever felt rushes through me. It feels like every broken bone, bruise, cut, or concussion I ever got—added together. And then multiplied. I've lost her. I failed again.

I release a guttural scream, but I can't hear the sound over the alarm drums, signaling an attack on the king. People start shouting, confused. Some have decided to flee. Others are using this chance to fight each other. The players are being swept off the field.

Hands grab my arms. I shove the men off before even realizing they're palace guards. I don't care. I don't care if it means death— I'll break their necks. I have to. I have to get Aeri.

The guards draw their swords. I don't got nothing but my fists.

"Don't fight. Don't make it worse," a guy says in a low tone.

I turn, my fists still up. The man who spoke is posh, and he has a hand raised for the guards to wait. I dunno who he is, but his snake eyes look around. And the palace guards are listening to him, so he's gotta be a count.

"Surrender now," he says.

"Why the fuck should I?"

"To fight again."

His tone leaves no question—he knows I was part of a plot. He knows it went south. Dal is dead, Seok ain't here, and Bay Chin just got hauled out, so he's gotta be the western count.

The guy takes off, surrounded by his guards. I stop struggling and put my hands up. I let myself be dragged out—not because the count told me to but because the only way I'll get answers or have a shot at protecting Aeri now is to let them take me. I have to hope they bring me wherever she's going. And then once I'm there, I'll kill *everyone* to free her.

I just hope that includes murdering Euyn with my bare hands.

CHAPTER EIGHTY-ONE

MIKAIL

QALI PALACE, YUSAN

When I come to, my head is splitting, and my body doesn't feel all that great, either. The guards probably dragged me out by my arms—assholes. I'll be writing a very strongly worded complaint to General Salosa about his men.

But where am I? I doubt I'm in the King's Arena. It's silent in here.

I open my eyes, and my stomach drops. I know this floor mosaic. Without even looking up, I know I'm in the throne room of Qali Palace.

I close my eyes again and use my senses. It's always better to pretend to be asleep, to observe undetected. I'm in chains with my arms behind my back. Hands have me, so I'm being held upright by two guards—one left, one right. But as I listen, I learn there are more people in the room.

How did this happen?

I know I destroyed the crown of Yusan after Sora kissed Joon. But when I last saw him, Joon was somehow still breathing, and that shouldn't have happened.

Unless Sora betrayed us.

Maybe there wasn't any poison on her mouth. It would've been impossible for me to tell.

I hadn't suspected her because I thought she'd been genuine with me. I breathe out a laugh. What a fool to believe that I was special. That we had a unique connection. I got fooled by a professional seductress.

Maybe she turned on all of us for Daysum's freedom. She loves her more than anything, and she's been honest about that the whole time.

But my main question is: If Joon survived, why am I in the throne room and not Idle Prison? And where are all the others? Where is Euyn?

With some effort, I raise my splitting head. When I look around, I'm genuinely shocked.

Everyone else is in here, and we are all chained together. Including Euyn and Sora. So that means she didn't betray us. But now what do I do?

After we found Thorn, I knew I had to tell the palace something, so I claimed this was my plan the whole time. That I was playing along to bring all of them in after the tuhko game—no mention of when the actual assassination was planned to occur. But now what? How can I save them? And who betrayed us?

Royo is next to me, then there's Sora, and next to her is Ty. Aeri is shaking and crying in her valet uniform. Then there's the northern count, staring at the ground. Last is Euyn.

Stars, I'm grateful that he's alive. But he's staring daggers at me. He must know I destroyed the crown. It's another betrayal, but at least the relic is gone, and Gaya now stands a chance at being free. At least I did that much.

The doors open, and Joon walks in from the royal chambers. The guards force us all to our knees. I roll my eyes. It's excessive. But I look up, and there, on the top of Joon's head, sits the crown of the Dragon Lord.

What the fuck?

I destroyed it. I know I did. I saw it fall to pieces. Does the fucking thing stitch itself back together?

I stare at his crown as he stops in front of me. I cut it right down the middle. I know it. But there is no scar, no cut mark at all near the center ruby.

"You'll find, Mikail," Joon begins, "that the real crown of the Dragon Lord is no less brittle than the throne of Yusan."

Lord Yama. It was a decoy.

All of the blood drains from my face. We've been outplayed. But by whom?

"Hello, brother," Joon says, walking over to Euyn. He's kinder to Euyn than I expected. And that worries me.

Was it him? Was it Euyn this whole time? I hold my breath.

Euyn holds his chin high, his expression neutral, regal like he's not in chains. "Brother."

I exhale. Not him.

Joon then stops in front of the northern count. "Bay Chin."

"Your Most Gracious Majesty," he says with his head low.

Joon rests his hand on Bay Chin's shoulder. "Admirable performance. As promised, the sanctions on Umbria are now lifted. You may return north."

The king gestures, and the guards help Bay Chin to his feet. The old man moves his arms for balance—because he was never really chained. Not because of his age but because he was working with Joon this whole time. He's the traitor. He's the one who orchestrated this whole thing, who approached me from the beginning, and he gave us up in order to make amends for his previous assassination attempt. So that Umbria wouldn't have to pay a quarter of its earnings in sanctions to Joon.

My heart pounds against my ribs, but it makes sense. Money, love, and revenge are the most common reasons for betrayal. And money is always first. I should have seen this coming, but the old man is a convincing actor. I believed he wanted Joon dead because he had tried before. And he likely still does. His loyalty is only temporary.

Once he gets to his feet, Bay Chin bows low to the ground in front of the king.

"You are most generous and forgiving, Your Majesty," he says. "But may I ask—"

"Leave us." The king's face and tone harden. Forgiveness doesn't mean favor, and Bay Chin should've realized that.

The count shudders and scurries out of the throne room. He spares me a glance. I stare back. I will hunt him down like a stag. I swear and I vow it.

"I want to congratulate you all on a job well done," the king says. "My assassination was as great a success as I'd hoped."

All of us look around in various states of disbelief. But I bet I'm most shocked of all. What is he talking about? Why hope for a successful attempt?

The realization dawns on me slowly at first and then knocks the breath out of my chest.

No. No, it can't be.

Joon meets my stare and slowly smiles.

It is.

The *king* orchestrated the whole assassination plot, all of this, himself.

And now there is no chance to save any of us.

CHAPTER EIGHTY-TWO

ROYO
QALI PALACE, YUSAN

What in the Ten fucking Hells is going on right now?

That fucking coward Bay Chin gave us up—that much is clear. My hands ball into fists. It's not right to attack an old guy, but I can make an exception.

But why did King Joon just congratulate us on assassinating him? One, he's still alive. And two, what kind of man is happy about people trying to kill him?

Joon's eyes land on Aeri. He steps closer to her, and I struggle in my chains, the metal biting into my wrists. Two more guards rush over to help the other two contain me. Good fucking luck if Joon touches a hair on her head. I'll end him, god or not.

I'm making a racket with my chains, and the king glances over at me before he turns back to Aeri.

"Daughter, you both delighted and disappointed me," he says.

"Father," she says, bowing her head. But she doesn't take her eyes off him.

What. The. Fuck.

I stop struggling and look around at the group. Everyone is in various states of shock—because what is happening right now?

My brain feels like it's being pulled through the mud. Maybe I took one too many hits to the head, because I swear I imagined Aeri calling Joon her father. She couldn't have. It's not possible. Aeri's not royal. She's a street thief, a pickpocket, a girl who runs from the king's guard with me. Maybe "father" is her weird way of addressing royalty. I dunno.

"Oh, that's right," Joon says, looking around. "I haven't had a moment to properly introduce my daughter." He gestures to Aeri. "This is Naerium Lin Baejkin. The daughter of Soo Lin."

A numb horror washes over me. And my brain works again. That name. That's the name Aeri gave me when we first met—Soo. Aeri Soo.

She's the king's daughter.

And she fucking played me from the start.

A wave of emotions hits my guts. My face and my torso go numb. I killed for her. I was ready to die for her. For a fucking *princess*.

This whole time. This whole fucking time, from when she was looking for me in Butcher & Ale, I knew there was something up. I knew I never shoulda gone to the Black Shoe Inn. I got a bad feeling from the second Yuri said a pretty girl was asking 'bout me. But I ignored it. I kept ignoring all the shit that didn't add up. All her lies, all her slips. Then I got close to her, and I stopped seeing them. I fell for her. And I even *trusted* her. I was king of the fucking chumps.

It all makes sense now—why she disappeared the first chance she got in Capricia. Why that gang in Oosant didn't take her when they took Sora. When she disappeared in that town, she really *was* sending a message to her father, but her father was the fucking king.

Every time she talked about her father, how she was doing this for him, she was talking about Joon. And I just never got it.

She's why the palace assassin was following us. The assassin must've been protecting her. And it was Aeri meeting with him in Aseyo, but she put a knife in his throat after he was seen by Sora—just to cover up her connection to the throne. It *was* my fucking throwing knife, just like Mikail thought, because she'd taken it from our room.

But I *believed* her. I defended her. I kept giving her the benefit of the doubt because of the money, the job, because she pretended to like me, pretended to want me, pretended to fall for me.

It was all an act.

My breathing is shallow. My heart actually hurts. I wonder if I'm gonna die right now. It feels like it.

Why? Why did she do this to us? What was the point? And why is she in chains if she was working for him?

The room is dead silent.

"What the fuck is going on, Aeri?" I ask. My voice echoes through the whole room.

A guard punches me right between the shoulder blades. Cheap fucking shot when I'm handcuffed. I square my torso toward the guard. "Try that weak shit when I'm not chained."

"Guards, take that one to Idle Prison," King Joon says.

I brace myself. I'm not going to fucking cower. I sure as shit won't beg. Idle Prison is supposed to be hells on earth, but I'm ready to go. I'd rather be in a dark dungeon under the lake than spend another second with Aeri.

Aeri struggles to her feet and opens her mouth, horrified. "No! No! He had nothing to do with any of this."

"I know that, my dear. I never asked you to bring this one in," King Joon says.

The guards pull up Ty, not me.

He's sending Tiyung to prison.

"No!" Sora cries. "No! Please! Please. He is Seok's only son."

415

"And he committed high treason," King Joon says. "Take him."

Sora and Ty exchange glances so full of despair that it's hard to even look at them.

"It's all right," Ty says. "It'll be all right, Sora. I'll wait for anything."

Ty puts on a brave face, but his hands are trembling. Somehow, though, he manages to leave the throne room, walking with his head held high. Tears stream down Sora's face, and she crumples as the doors close.

But King Joon isn't looking at Mikail or Sora. He's focused on Naerium. Something about his expression makes my stomach pitch. Pride mixed with…fury?

"You really are Baejkin after all, double-crossing your own father," he says.

Aeri says nothing. She simply stares back at him, her eyes as cold as anything I've seen. This is the creature I got flashes of beneath the joyful, carefree girl. The one made of flint and teeth. I just didn't realize she got it all from Joon.

"When you stopped sending updates, I assumed you threw your lot in with them," he says, sniffing in disgust. "If I hadn't been prepared for your treachery, you would have killed your own father. What a pity to have a daughter so typical of a weak-minded teen girl. Our deal is off."

What? What deal? And Aeri is twenty-four, not a teenager. But maybe that was just another lie. My pulse pounds, my head feels like caving in, and it would be really nice if everyone could just say what they fucking mean for once.

"You asked me to bring in Sora, Mikail, and Euyn, and I did my part," she says. The shock waves of that ripple through the group in turn, and I feel like I'm chewing on ash. I sputter and choke on her next words. "Let Royo and Tiyung go."

The other three all look like they might kill her where she stands. My fists curl, and I still feel that urge to protect her, to defend her, because I haven't learned how to be cold yet. I will.

But I think she's trying to…save Ty and me?

"*You* don't make demands," Joon says. "I have a score to settle with Seok. And you and the guard Bay Chin told you to hire can go to the Ten Hells with your friends." Joon levels a stare at the *princess*. But he's got no need to worry.

I'm going to kill her myself.

CHAPTER EIGHTY-THREE

EUYN
QALI PALACE, YUSAN

I really don't understand what is going on right now. I *do* know that Mikail didn't betray me. He didn't betray anyone. It was all Bay Chin…and Aeri.

Joon claimed Aeri is his daughter, but that's impossible. I haven't seen her since she was a baby, but his daughter died years ago. Joon has no living children. It's what made me next in line.

"Naerium died in a fire seven years ago—when she was twelve," I say when I finally find my voice. "Aeri can't be your real daughter."

"Yes, I thought our dear brother Omin had killed her, too," Joon says with a shrug. "But then I found Aeri at her mother's funeral pyre this past year. Alive and well."

I grimace. That would make Aeri nineteen, not twenty-four, but who can really tell the difference? Not to mention that she hid the truth so we'd never suspect her identity. I'd heard rumors Omin was murdering young girls. That he was banished from the palace because he was caught dumping one into Idle Lake to dispose of her body. But I'd thought it was a story that had spun out of control, the same way I was called a butcher.

But no.

I sigh inwardly. What a family.

But the larger question is: Why on earth did Joon plot his own murder? And what did he mean when he said Aeri could go to the hells with us? Because my brother is many things, but prone to dramatics is not one of them.

"This is elaborate," I say, raising one brow. I'm done being paranoid. Because being paranoid means you fear death, and I am staring it in the face. "If you wanted to bring me in, why not just up the bounty and demand I be brought in alive? It was always rather cheap."

"I never put a bounty on you," Joon says. "That was from the Council of the Lords. And I don't want you dead. In fact, it's the opposite. I want to forgive your crimes and reinstate you as prince."

I'm struck silent. Out of all the things I expected my brother to do—kill me, torture me, make me watch while he tortured Mikail—offering reinstatement is one I didn't see coming. What is he up to?

"The five of you are all guilty of high treason and can be sentenced to lingchi or beheading or life in Idle Prison," he says. "But…I am a merciful lord. I am inclined to forgive you. Reward you, even. On one condition."

Of course he wants something. He had to have a good reason for going through all of this, for bringing all of us here alive.

I hold my breath, my heart racing, waiting to find out what it is.

CHAPTER EIGHTY-FOUR

MIKAIL
QALI PALACE, YUSAN

O h, good. Excited to hear what Joon wants.

But I'm distracted. I can't believe that I didn't realize Aeri was his daughter. That I invited a traitor into our midst. I truly believed Aeri was a common thief, and I thought I happened to catch her stealing a million-cut diamond. I thought I was so good of a spy that I found a girl who could lift the crown—the last piece Bay Chin said we needed. I thought I was clever enough to convince Aeri.

Hubris. My downfall was nothing more than hubris.

How unoriginal.

Joon knew me well enough to know I'd need to think this plan was all my idea. And I was so distracted by my desire for revenge, by the fact that I'd waited so long, that I continued despite all of my reservations. Despite finding Thorn dead and the rather suspicious death of Dal. Because I didn't want to stop. All I saw was an opportunity for revenge. And now a plan nearly twenty years in the making has fallen apart due to my impatience. Now I'm at Joon's mercy—not a trait he's known for.

"What is the condition?" Euyn asks.

Joon smiles. "You know our sister sits on the throne of Khitan."

Euyn slowly nods. "So I've heard."

"She wears the ring." Joon waves a hand as though discussing a trifle. "Bring it to me."

That gets Euyn to blink. "Bring you...the Ring of Khitan?"

I laugh. The Golden Ring. The relic of the Dragon Lord that turns anything to solid gold at the whim of the wearer. Of course he wants that. Of course that would be the goal of all of this. He already has the Immortal Crown, and he stole the real Flaming Sword of the Dragon Lord from Gaya during the Festival of Blood. Now, he wants the third relic. He may be trying to get all of them, but the amulet was lost long ago somewhere in Fallow, and the priests of Wei keep killing the spies we send to try to steal the Water Scepter.

But Quilimar would burn this whole country to the ground before she gave anything to Joon. Which, as it stands now, might be fun to watch.

"It would be so much faster to kill us," I say.

"Why would I want to?" Joon asks. "The five of you were able to take my crown and survive. Had I not had the real relic on my arm instead, I would be dead, thanks to my daughter." He stops and glares at her. There is legitimate pain in his expression, but then he blinks and it's gone. "Therefore, the five of you could also get the ring and make it out of Khitan."

"Why not just tell me you wanted the ring to begin with?" I ask. "Why the elaborate charade?"

Joon stares at me, slight color building in his cheeks. He's annoyed by my question. "In what realm would you have given up where Euyn was hiding? And nothing would've made Seok disclose having a poison school. By setting up this plot, the best killers in Yusan came right to me, bound with a purpose." He shrugs. "And with Quilimar, I can't risk failure. Call today an audition, if you will."

I glance over at Euyn. I hate how much I follow Joon's logic. What better way to bring us all in? From Euyn's unamused stare, he follows it, too. And we both know of Quilimar's legendary brutality and that gold buys impressive defenses. I can't blame Joon for not wanting to risk failure. Well, I can...

Joon continues. "Bring me the ring, and you'll all be rewarded handsomely. Euyn, you'll be crown prince of Yusan again." He walks in front of Sora. She hasn't done more than stare straight ahead since Joon sent Ty to Idle Prison. "Sora, how would you like your and your sister's freedom? The count's house in Aseyo, where you can be left in peace? Maybe the chance to kill Seok yourself once he is captured?"

Sora blinks several times. Whoever his source is has excellent information. That's exactly what she wants.

"My sister and me living in the house that belongs to the eastern count?" she asks.

"He's unfortunately deceased, and his son is too young to rule," Joon says. "That leaves his properties under my control. And I am a generous lord. Bring me the ring, and I will parcel out the villa to you."

She's stunned. Land is no small concession in Yusan. Nobles or the crown own all of the land, and commoners must rent and be at their whim.

"And Tiyung?" she presses.

Joon is actually surprised by her request, but he recovers rapidly. "Yes. Bring me the ring, and I'll release him—you have my word."

She goes quiet again.

"Speaking of the recently deceased eastern count," the king says. "Mikail, you could be regent for the boy."

He...would make me the eastern count for the next ten years? The king can make or take nobility from anyone—it's just not common. The nobles like to imagine their position is secure in this realm. But as the Count of Tamneki, I could do great things for Gaya. Funding, support for laoli addiction, decreasing the military presence or even aiding in a coup, finally getting the independence for the island that even my parents only whispered about.

My pulse speeds up as I start to dream, but then I realize that's exactly what it is: a fool's dream.

"You'd give me Tamneki?" I ask with a laugh. "After I just tried to kill you?"

Joon shrugs. "Who hasn't tried? If I were to hold grudges for my attempted murders, I wouldn't have any nobles."

He has a point.

"You all just saw me allow Bay Chin to walk out of here alive and prospering. Do not doubt my mercy."

All right, that's fair, and Joon has always been a remarkably practical ruler. Still, stealing the Ring of Khitan is about as easy as stealing Joon's crown. There's a reason it's never been done. The legend is that you must be royal to wield the ring. But we'd have Euyn with us, and I suppose Aeri, so it would be at least possible.

We're all silent, no doubt thinking about the spoils if we succeed and the likelihood of this actually working out. In many ways, his condition is better than I expected, and in many ways it's far worse.

"Speaking of Umbria, I hear you're a strongman," Joon says to Royo.

Aeri's head snaps up.

Royo doesn't answer. He stares at Joon.

"Bay Chin tells me a man went to prison for a crime you committed long ago," the king says. Royo suddenly goes rigid. Sweat dots his brow, and his breathing picks up. "I have to say, I don't like the idea of my daughter being guarded by a man who killed a girl. But I suppose people can change."

Royo looks gutted, and Aeri's mouth falls open.

This is all new information to me. But Royo *did* want Euyn to pardon a criminal. And he gave his sword because Euyn swore he'd reverse the edict. And from the look on Royo's face… No. It wasn't him. This is some manipulation by the northern count.

Stars. Royo may kill Bay Chin before I get a chance to.

Royo faces Joon dead-on. "Bay Chin knows exactly who killed Allora, I'm sure."

Joon shrugs. "Regardless, do this job, and the man will be pardoned," Joon says. "And you will get the hundred thousand my daughter promised you."

He stops in front of Aeri last. She looks shattered as she stares at Royo. Which is pretty hypocritical, if you ask me. But then again, I suppose we all are liars and hypocrites, outraged to be betrayed as we planned to double-cross one another from the start. Liars and killers don't make the best lovers. She and Royo are just newer to it than Euyn and me.

"And you will be acknowledged, just as I promised before you betrayed me," Joon says. "You will be a princess of Yusan. And your mother will be posthumously acknowledged as my first queen."

You could hear a sewing needle drop, it's so silent in here.

Then Aeri's head falls as she agrees.

CHAPTER EIGHTY-FIVE

EUYN
QALI PALACE, YUSAN

"One more thing," Joon says.

Wonderful—there's more. I thought that going to do the impossible by taking the ring off our vicious sister was enough. Apparently not.

"Come back before monsoon season is over," Joon says.

What?

Monsoon season starts soon and will last a month.

"You expect us to go to Khitan, steal the ring, and make it back here, all within a month?" I ask.

Joon nods. "Technically, five weeks, give or take, but otherwise, that is correct."

"Why the rush? That eager to have me back in the palace?"

Joon gestures with his arms apart. "I never wanted you gone. If you return with the ring before the season ends, you will all be heavily rewarded. Fail, and you all will wish for death. If Quilimar finds out I sent you, I'll roast your loved ones alive before you watch me feed them to the iku. I swear and I vow it."

The threat settles on each of us in turn. For Sora, that's obviously Daysum; for Royo, it's the man in prison; for Aeri, I don't know, but it could be Royo.

I only love Mikail, so, of course, that's who he means. I'm not sure who Mikail loves. Me, allegedly. But I don't know for sure because Mikail never fucking tells me anything. And what was all of that about Mikail destroying the crown?

Then I realize: if this plan came from Joon through Bay Chin, that means Mikail never spoke to Quilimar. And if he didn't get the idea from her…

My stomach bottoms out, and my blood runs cold. He lied to me from the very beginning.

"Now, if you'll excuse me, I have other matters to which I must attend," my brother says. "And you need to meet a fleet ship."

The guards pull all of us to our feet.

Joon pauses. "Take what you need from the armory. Oh, and Mikail…"

Mikail meets his eye.

"I will take good care of Ailor until you return."

With that, my brother walks out of the room. And I have a new question: Who the hell is Ailor?

Whoever he is, Mikail blanches paler than I've ever seen him before. Including when he nearly died of blood loss. The realization cuts through me and sticks like a broken blade: I don't know a thing about him.

CHAPTER EIGHTY-SIX

SORA
QALI PALACE, YUSAN

N one of this feels real. Not that we failed to kill the king even though we did everything we were supposed to do. Not that we were captured. Not that Bay Chin betrayed us. Not that Tiyung is in a horrible dungeon under a lake. Not that Aeri is the king's daughter and double-crossed him and brought us all in or anything else I just learned within this last bell.

It's all too much, so I shut down. I focus solely on putting one foot in front of the other on the marble floors. But I don't want to walk. I don't want to do anything but lay down and die.

Within a breath, I come to my senses. I can't give up. The king alive and me missing and presumed dead means Daysum may get sold to the pleasure houses. If I fail, Ty stays in Idle Prison. Panic runs through me, and I snap out of it.

No.

No, I can't lose her. Or him. I have to keep going. But how?

Kingdom of Hells, why me? It truly is a liability—to care the way I do.

Palace guards bring us to the armory, and it's a tense walk. The five of us are all still chained to the people we hate, the ones who lied and betrayed us. But Mikail directs the guards to grab weaponry as if this is normal.

I hate him. And Aeri. And Bay Chin. And Joon. And Seok.

I want to break down. But I won't. I draw a breath. My sister and I *will* live together in that big, fancy villa. And I will get Ty out, too. He burned my indenture. He defied his father. He let me forget my misery for a night. I'll figure out a way to do this—for them.

One foot in front of the other. I keep walking.

When the guards bring us out of the entrance to the palace, there's a carriage waiting, and my trunk is already on the back. The king knew where we were the entire time because of Aeri and Bay Chin. Through plotting his own assassination, the king was able to bring in the deadliest killers in Yusan and prove that we could take a relic. And now we have five weeks to steal a ring from Khitan.

I'm not sure what the ring does, but everyone called it a relic of the Dragon Lord, which means it's like the crown. Which means it'll be nearly impossible for us to steal. But something sticks in my brain about all of this. I'm just not sure what, because I'm not built for these games.

The five of us are unchained at the last second before we're tossed into the carriage. We're sent off immediately, rolling over the narrow bridge.

There's suspicion and hurt in everyone's eyes. We all sit as far apart as we can, but this isn't a large fleet carriage—just two benches—so we have to face one another. And we're on our way to a ship that will take us to another realm. Khitan—the place I'd once wanted to flee to but is now the last place I want to be, since I have to go with all of them.

I rub my wrists, wondering why I'm thrown into the fire again and again.

You are made of steel, Ty said.

Yet steel becomes stronger in the forge. I'm not a blade. I'm just a pawn.

Royo is across from me. His wrists are bleeding. I rip off a piece of the lining of my dress and then wrap them. He looks at me with his brow furrowed but nods his thanks.

I don't know why I helped him, why I'd help any of them now, except this is who I am. This is what Seok never took from me with all of his poison and torture. I still love. I still care. And that's why this all hurts. I trusted all of them. But people like Seok and Joon love no one. All they will ever be is hate, isolation, and fear.

And I'd rather live a life caring and getting hurt than a life in fear.

"Wait," I whisper.

The four of them look at me.

"Wait," I say, louder. "He fears her." They all blink at me. "Joon fears Quilimar."

Euyn nods. "He sold her—in marriage."

The pieces fall into place rapidly. "He went through all of this trouble. All of these lies and moves and countermoves just to make us audition. Why?"

Aeri, who truly looks miserable, speaks to her knees. "Because he can't risk failure."

"Exactly," I say, sounding like the headmistress I want to be.

"So what?" Royo grumbles. "Just means we're fucked more than we were the first time."

But Mikail's gaze narrows on mine. "Where are you going with this, Sora?"

I lean forward. "He showed his hand. His weakness *is* his fear—and we can use it."

"And how would you suggest that?" Euyn asks, skepticism making his voice thin. "We have to take a ring from my sister's hand, which is going to be impossible."

"No, we actually don't," I say, lifting my chin. "Because if she's *his* enemy...she's *our* new best friend. Joon can think all this was an audition, but...he's overlooking the fact that we did accomplish something—the most important thing."

"We accomplished nothing," Royo says, turning his wrists over.

"We did the unimaginable—we didn't just meet at the arena from four parts of Yusan; we worked together. We killed and bled for one another. We were able to gain one another's trust, while lying and deceiving the whole time. If we can do that, we can find a way to make the queen our ally. And then we will use her to get everything we want. Including revenge."

I leave my chin raised and wait for their reactions. Either this is the most foolish thing I've ever said—or it could work. Slowly, they all nod in turn.

"I'm listening," Mikail says with a small grin.

Maybe Ty is right. Maybe I *am* steel.

And I swear I will break his chains and Daysum's before King Joon feels my blade.

The End For Now

ACKNOWLEDGMENTS

Not one of the Five Blades would have been possible without my brilliant editor and publisher, Liz Pelletier. Thank you for your brainstorming, your unwavering support, and spending late nights and early mornings working on this together. Thank you for bringing this gem of a book to life and then helping me polish it. To say this process has been extraordinary would be a gross understatement. Thank you for changing my life! Thank you also to Jen Bouvier, whose constant championing has uplifted me in every stage of what is supposedly a solitary career. Thank you for always being a true friend. None of this would have happened without you.

Thank you to everyone at Red Tower for your tireless efforts shaping this story into a book. Thank you to the amazing edit team including: Rae Swain, Hannah Lindsey, Stacy Abrams, Molly Majumder, Nancy Cantor, and Jessica Meigs. (Hannah, I'm still sorry about the double edit!) Thank you to the incredible art and design team including: Bree Archer, Elizabeth Turner Stokes, Juho Choi, Jennifer Valero, and Britt Marczak. Thank you to Curtis Svehlak and Viveca Shearin in production. And thank you to the fantastic publicity and marketing team including: Ashley Doliber, Meredith Johnson, Heather Riccio, Brittany Zimmerman, and Lizzy Mason. Special thank-yous to Aaron Aceves and Nicholas Macoretta for your valuable input and feedback, and thank you to Nicole Resciniti for bringing this book worldwide.

A special thank you to the entire team at Bonnier Books UK. I am delighted that *Five Broken Blades* found at home at their Zaffre imprint. Thank you to Kelly Smith for your kind words and belief in this story. Thank you as well to Eleanor Stammeijer in publicity, Ellie Pilcher in marketing, and Kate Griffiths and Robyn Haque in sales for facilitating a gorgeous special edition.

Many thanks to my agent, Lauren Spieller, for your tireless advocacy, for seeing my potential, and for talking me out of my worst ideas. Thank you so much to Hannah Morgan Teachout for your ridiculously fast and yet incredibly thorough notes. This book is better because of you.

Thank you to my four children, who inspire and delight me. Thank you for being my family. For understanding, even when you don't quite know why I'm in my office or why my mind is some place called Yusan. Thank you to my mother for being there for me every step of the way. With every page, I hope to make you and Dad proud. Thank you to my sister for helping me with the very early draft and for shouldering the brunt of being the eldest.

Thank you to my friends and family who've been there for me through the highs and lows of this wild author ride, especially Karen McManus, Alexa Martin, June Tan, Caroline Richmond, Jennifer Dugan, Matt Weintraub, Jessica Norgrove, Susan Thibault, Kiana Nguyen, Sarah Howell, and Jenn Kominsky.

Thank you to the influencers, booksellers, reviewers, and most of all readers for spending time in my violent but hopeful world.

Lastly, but most importantly, thank you to John Coryea for giving me my name and a heart to call home. Like iron and flame, we make each other stronger. Thank you for being my man of steel and my inspiration today and tomorrow and tomorrow and tomorrow.

The adventure continues in

FOUR RUINED REALMS

Coming soon